Angel Isle

Also by Peter Dickinson

The Ropemaker
The Gift Boat
The Tears of the Salamander
The Kin
The Weathermonger
Heartsease
The Devil's Children
Emma Tupper's Diary
The Dancing Bear
The Gift
Chance, Luck and Destiny
The Blue Hawk
Annerton Pit
Hepzibah
Tulku
City of Gold
The Seventh Raven
Healer
Giant Cold
A Box of Nothing
Merlin Dreams
Eva
AK
A Bone from a Dry Sea
Time and the Clock Mice, Etcetera
Shadow of a Hero
Chuck and Danielle
Touch and Go
The Lion Tamer's Daughter

PETER DICKINSON

Angel Isle

Illustrated by Ian Andrew

MACMILLAN CHILDREN'S BOOKS

First published 2006 by Macmillan Children's Books
a division of Macmillan Publishers Limited
20 New Wharf Road, London N1 9RR
Basingstoke and Oxford
www.panmacmillan.com

Associated companies throughout the world

ISBN-13: 978-1-4050-4995-5
ISBN-10: 1-4050-4995-2

Text copyright © Peter Dickinson 2006
Illustrations copyright © Ian Andrew 2006

The right of Peter Dickinson and Ian Andrew to be identified as the
author and illustrator of this work has been asserted by them in
accordance with the Copyright, Designs and Patents Act 1988.

1 3 5 7 9 8 6 4 2

A CIP catalogue record for this book is available from
the British Library.

Typeset by Intype Libra Ltd
Printed and bound in Great Britain
by Mackays of Chatham plc, Kent

For Hugh
(and Jean, who doesn't have to read it)

Contents

Prologue

A woman led a lame horse across an unpeopled land-scape. For much of the way all seemed peaceful, but then she would come to an area where buildings were shattered or gutted with fire, young crops trampled flat, and bodies, both human and animal, sprawling in their blood and now rotting unburied. Ahead of her lay the heavy line of the forest, and close beneath it the remains of one last farm. So Saranja came home to Woodbourne.

Six years ago she had left, swearing to herself she would never return. For five of those years she had been the house-slave of one of the war-lords beyond the East Desert, until he and the two children she had borne him had died when his keep was stormed by his brother's army. In the chaos she had escaped, and continued to stagger on through the darkness. When dawn had broken she had found herself already in the desert.

Six years ago she had almost died, crossing it, though then she had carried food and water. Now she had nothing. But she did not turn back. Death would be better than the life she had been living. This time, though, the desert seemed to let her through as if it had chosen to do so. It provided her with two freak thunderstorms and a waterhole large enough to support a colony of birds which, having no predators, laid their eggs on the ground. With those, and things that she had learnt from her first crossing to recognize as food, she had come through.

And then, seeing what had happened in the Valley, she had known that she must go and find out if anything was left of Woodbourne.

Not much. When a thatched and timbered building goes up in flames, very little remains but the central chimney stack, standing amid a pile of ashes and a few rafter ends.

No voice answered her call. She hadn't expected one. Her brothers would be fighting the raiders, or dead, her mother and aunt hiding in the forest with the animals.

She scuffed with her feet among the fringes of the heap. It was a way of preventing herself from weeping, because she felt she had no right to. Of her own will she had cut every connection with Woodbourne, even grief. All that was over.

Something glinted in the ashes. She stooped and eased out a golden feather, perfect, looking as if it had been shed that very morning. She pulled it free, and another came with it, attached at the quill by a twist of golden hair. She laid them together and ran her fingertips along them. The idiot story flooded back into her mind, the story that she had never believed, thinking it just a mechanism by which her mother could bind her for all her life to Woodbourne, as she herself had been bound, because Saranja had once made the mistake of admitting that she sometimes imagined she could hear the cedars talking.

With a sigh she turned to the horse, a useless old gelding she had found yesterday – or rather he had found her, wandering out of nowhere and nosing vaguely up to her, and had then simply followed her. She hadn't driven him off, because he was company of a kind, and also fresh meat that she didn't have to carry. She had imagined till now that he followed her so persistently only because he didn't want to be the only living creature in the landscape.

If it's you, you'll need a horse as well as the feathers.

'Waiting for me, weren't you?' she said. 'Now all we want is some fellow from Northbeck.'

She looked back along the way they had come. A man was limping up the road towards her, leaning heavily on his staff. Without thought her fingers caressed the golden feathers as she waited for him, until she realized that her hands were full of a peculiar glowing warmth. She looked down. Feathers and hair seemed to shine with their own light. There was no need to go up into the forest. If she could do it at all, she could do it here.

The man came into the yard. He was about forty, slight, dark, with a look of arrogant energy beneath his obvious weariness and pain. There was a bloodstained bandage round his left calf.

'Ribek Ortahlson,' he said.

'Well, I'm Saranja Urlasdaughter. Hold his head, will you?'

She moved round to the horse's flank.

'I've no idea if this will work,' she said.

She whispered the name.

'Ramdatta.'

Her hands knew what to do.

PART ONE

Tarshu

Chapter

Chapter 1

COLD, HUNGRY, terrified, Maja watched the two strangers from her secret den beside the mounting-block, beneath the burnt barn. That was where she'd run when she'd seen a troop of the savage horsemen from the north come screaming up the lane all those days ago, and lain there cowering. Her uncle and the boys were away fighting the main army of the horsemen, but they must have caught her mother and her aunt. Maja couldn't see what they did to them because of the smoke, but she'd heard their screaming. Then the smoke of the burning buildings had got into the den and overcome her. After that she didn't remember anything for a while, and when she woke the savages were gone and the farm was ashes around her.

She had felt to ill to move, and too terrified of the savages, and her throat had been horribly sore, but at last she'd crept out and climbed up to the spring and drunk, and then stolen round the farm like a shadow and found her mother's body and her aunt's lying face down in the dung-pit, and a lot of dead animals scattered around. Her aunt used to make her help with the butchering, so she cut open a dead pig with her knife and roasted bits of its liver on the embers of her home, and despite the soreness of her throat had managed to swallow it morsel by morsel. By the time she'd finished it was beginning to get dark so she'd crawled back into her den and curled up in her straw nest and slept there all night without any dreams at all.

She'd spent next day collecting dry brushwood and straw and the burnt ends of rafters and beams and piling it all into the dung-pit on top of the two bodies. As dusk thickened she'd used a still smouldering bit of timber to set the pile alight.

'Goodbye, goodbye, goodbye,' she'd whispered as the flames roared up, then turned away dry-eyed. She didn't seem to feel anything. She was vaguely sorry about her mother, and vaguely guilty that she'd never learnt how to love her. There hadn't been anything there to love. She'd dreaded and hated her aunt, but her aunt had shaped her world and she felt a far greater sense of loss at her going. Now that shape was shattered and all she had was emptiness, until her uncle came back from the fighting, if he ever did.

The dead animals had soon begun to rot, but some of the chickens were still alive and hanging around because they didn't know anywhere else to go. There was good barley out in the little barn in Dirna's field, which her aunt grew there every year to feed to the unicorns, so the chickens learnt to come to her again when she called to them, and she managed to coax some of them into lay. She ate the cockerels one by one and found a few things still usable in the vegetable patch and the orchard, and survived, afraid and lonely.

She had found her den long before. Ever since she could remember she had needed somewhere to hide. Hide from her uncle's sudden, inexplicable rages, from her aunt's equally savage tongue, from her boy cousins' thoughtless roughness. Only occasionally did anyone hurt her on purpose. Indeed, once or twice when she was small and at the end of one of his outbursts her uncle had slammed out to the barn, her aunt had deliberately sent her out to call him in, despite her terror of him. It was one of her aunt's ways of punishing her, though she'd never been told what for. So she'd crept through the barn door, tensed for his anger, but instead he'd called to her and put her on his lap and stroked her like a kitten for a while, and spoken gently to her, though she could feel his rage still roiling inside him – and it was the rage itself that had terrified her, not the fear that she herself might suffer from it. Usually it had been her big cousin Saranja who'd suffered, or the two boys – and they had been always angry too. Even her own mother had been too vague and feeble to notice her much, let alone stand up for her when she needed help. She must have had a father, of course, but she'd never known him, and had no idea who or where he was. She didn't dare ask. Saranja had been the only person besides her uncle who had sometimes smiled at her as though she had meant it.

But then there had come the day she had taught herself never to think of, and at the end of it Saranja had gone away and the rage had been ten times worse than before and her uncle had never spoken to her kindly again.

And it was all Maja's fault. It always had been, even before that. Since she was born.

There was a bit of the heap of ashes that had been Woodbourne, which she fed with fresh wood to keep the embers going, and then hid under layers of ash when she'd finished her cooking. She'd just done that when she'd spotted the woman trudging along the lane with an old horse trailing behind her, and a solitary figure limping along further back. They hadn't looked dangerous, but all the same she'd clucked to the chickens, who'd come hustling over, imagining it was the start of the evening drill that kept them safe from foxes. She'd laid a trail of barley to lure them into the den and lain in the entrance to watch, letting the scorched branch of fig that screened it fall back into place.

Now the woman came into the yard and stared around. She was grimy with long travel, but despite that was beautiful in her own fierce way, with a mass of glossy dark hair hanging well below her shoulders. Maja had a vague feeling she'd seen her before – or perhaps it had been in a dream, or perhaps she'd just imagined her in one of the stories she told herself. She had the look of a queen, angry, proud and sad – a defeated queen who refuses to accept her defeat. Maja used to tell herself a lot of stories like that during her lonely and miserable years, stories of adventures she would never have and courage that would never be hers.

The horse shambled in behind the woman and stopped, as if it didn't know what else to do.

The woman called in a strong voice.

'Anyone there?'

No one answered, so she started to wander around, scuffing here and there with her feet at the edges of the pile of ash that a month ago had been Woodbourne. She stooped and pulled what looked like a golden feather from the ashes. Another followed, dangling below it.

Maja stared. The roc feathers! Why hadn't they burned with everything else? She knew them well. Once a year, after supper on the eve of Sunreturn, the whole family would sit and listen to her mother telling them the old story of Tilja and the Ropemaker, and her aunt would fetch the feathers out of the box where she kept them – she never let anyone else touch them – to show them it was all true, and then put them back when it was over.

The woman smoothed them between her fingers and turned and said something to the horse, then looked back along the way she had come. After a while the man limped into the yard. He too was stained with travel, but unlike the woman looked sick and exhausted. There was a bloodstained bandage round his left leg. All the same, he also looked like someone out of one of Maja's stories, the last loyal soldier in the queen's defeated army, perhaps, a laughing warrior, an officer used to giving orders. Despite everything, his neat triangular beard gave him a jaunty look. Maja decided she liked him. She wasn't afraid of him.

'Ribek Ortahlson,' he said.

That was obviously his name. Ortahlson! That was in the story too. He must come from Northbeck and a man in his family sang winter after winter to the snows to make them fall and block the passes, so that the savage horsemen of the northern plains couldn't come raiding, the way they had now – just as a woman from Woodbourne sang winter after winter to the unicorns in the forest so that the sickness stayed in the forest and the armies of the great empire to the south couldn't get through to tax the Valley of everything it owned.

The woman answered but she was facing away from Maja, who couldn't hear what she said. They both turned to the horse, which had wandered up to the mounting-block, letting Maja hear and see everything. The woman laid the feathers on the horse's back, behind the shoulders, and began to stroke them. She whispered something, and the whole Valley seemed to shake and shimmer. The shock wave thundered through Maja's body, and she passed out.

When she came to – it could only have been a few seconds – the quills of the feathers were sinking into the hide. The horse shrugged, raised its head, and gave a long sigh as if of sudden, huge contentment.

The woman stood back beside Ribek, watching the feathers twitch as they embedded themselves into the muscles that had grown to receive them. At once they started to thicken and extend themselves. The quills became bone. The individual barbs lengthened into

12

vanes. A joint appeared below them, dragging with it a fold of hide along the undersides of the quill. All along this fresh plumes erupted, as golden as the original pair. The horse itself started to grow to accommodate the major muscles that its wings were going to need and still remain in the true proportions of a horse. At the same time its original indeterminate dunnish hue lightened and brightened to a glowing chestnut. It raised its head, stamped a hoof and snorted like a charger. The movement allowed Maja to see that it was no longer a gelding, but a stallion, entire. The whole landscape seemed to pulse and quiver as the woman continued to stroke the now enormous wings.

Vaguely for some time Maja had been noticing a dull drumming that had been coming from the south-west. Abruptly it changed its note. Absorbed in the wonder of the event, neither of the other two seemed to have noticed it.

The woman sighed.

'I never believed it,' she said. 'I was still hoping it wouldn't happen.'

'I've always believed,' said Ribek. 'To see it is something different. What now? To judge by the story we're expected to ride it. I've never ridden a horse – we're boat people and millers.'

'We can't go on calling it "it". What do you call a horse that's partly a roc?'

'A rocking horse? I've ridden a rocking horse at the Gathering when I was a kid.'

'A *name*,' said the woman. The tone of her voice, Maja thought, meant she didn't really get it that anyone could be light-hearted at a moment like this. She seemed to change her mind.

'Well, I suppose Rocky's not a bad name for a horse,' she said, and repeated it, trying it out on her tongue.

'Rocky?'

The horse tapped a forehoof gently on the ground as if it approved.

'Rocky it is then,' said the woman. 'Bareback's possible, but it'd be tiring any distance. Suppose . . . it can't do any harm . . .'

She moved forward and laid her spread hands on Rocky's back. With apparent confidence – but diffidence seemed not to be in her nature – she spoke the single word, 'Harness'.

Again that shock wave. This time Maja stayed conscious, though if she'd been standing she'd have staggered and fallen. Then the tremor and glitter of the landscape and a series of piercing thrills, as one by one a double saddle appeared, stirrups, saddlebags and scallop-fringed reins and bridle, the leather all glossy scarlet, the buckles and studs gold, and the plume on the bridle a fountain of golden feathers. The woman looked up, frowning. The movement broke the spell of the wonderful and beautiful event, and Maja looked up too, and gasped. Something almost as astonishing, but this time terrible and strange, was happening in the sky.

Hidden till now by the treetops of the forest edge beyond the farm, an immense, dark bag-thing had appeared, floating towards it, shaped like a fat sausage pointed at both ends, held up by nothing, but carrying below it a sort of long, thin basket, as big as the largest

14

boat on the river. Even more dangerous and terrifying because they were so much nearer, five enormous birds were flying steadily ahead of it. Each of them towed a bag like the first one, nothing like as huge but still as big as a haystack, below which dangled a harness carrying a man in a bulging dark helmet and jet-black uniform. They seemed to Maja to be flying directly towards her. This had happened to her before, many, many times in dreams – the monsters who knew where she was hiding, and were coming for her, now. Always in dreams, she had woken before she saw them. This time she was awake, and they were real. Her limbs locked rigid with terror.

The two humans had their backs towards them and hadn't seen them. But now the horse had. He didn't like it at all. He started to fidget, to stretch his great wings for flight, to try to rear. The woman shouted to the man to load the kit into the saddlebags and come and hold the bridle. And as soon as she could she darted round to the mounting-block and slid into the front saddle. The man hurried to follow. The horse was almost on his hind legs. Maja broke out of the terror-trance. She scrambled from her den and up the block.

'Take me too!' she shouted. 'Don't leave me behind! Please! Please!'

The horse was rearing, his hind legs tensed to spring, his wings spread for the first mighty buffet that would carry them into the air. Maja felt herself caught by the collar and flung forward and upward. She grasped desperately for something to hold on to. Another hand caught her out of the air and sent her crashing against

15

the horse's neck. Rocky squealed and bolted north. Maja clutched, found a handful of mane, and then another, and then just clung there, while the great wings smote the air in panic.

She felt some sort of a struggle going on behind her and managed to crane round. By now they were well clear of the ground. Ribek's legs and waist were dangling down by the horse's flank, with him grasping the after-saddle and wrestling to hoist himself further, while the woman, with one hand twisted into Rocky's mane, was reaching round with the other to help him. At last he made it and settled down, gasping, into the saddle.

'Sheep-faces, and an airboat,' shouted the woman, as soon as she'd got her breath back.

'More magic?' asked Ribek, like her, shouting to be heard above the wing-thunder.

'Sheep-faces don't do magic. We'll be all right. A horse at a canter is faster than bird-kites, and the birds get tired. The airboat is even slower but it's driven by engines and can go on forever.'

'Any idea where we're going after that?'

'Just getting clear of the Sheep-faces, for the moment. After that . . . Maybe Rocky knows. He isn't just bolting. He's bolting somewhere. I've got to get him slowed down. He'll kill himself, this speed.'

Maja crouched out of the way to let her lean past her and over Rocky's neck, murmuring in his ear, nudging gently on his bit, letting him feel her legs against his flanks. Ribek watched their rear, calling the news. The bird-kites, far outpaced, turned back to the airboat

16

almost at once, but it continued to follow doggedly until it was a dwindling dot, almost out of sight.

Sometimes in her dreams Maja could fly, and when the monsters came she could soar away from them. Then, at this exact moment, when the danger seemed gone, the gift deserted her, and she was plodding through heavy ploughland with the pursuers only a field or two behind. Rocky gave a long shuddering sigh. Now. She tensed herself for the onslaught of terror as the frantic wing-beats slowed.

It didn't happen. Instead, she felt the tension of the great body ease as he started to glide. They came lower and lower. Looking down, Maja saw fields and a farm beneath them. A boy was driving cows in to be milked. He gazed up, and his mouth fell open. She heard his faint shout, saw him point, and Rocky shuddered again, deliberately this time, shaking away the final shreds of both nightmares, his and hers, and flew purposefully on. Somewhere.

'If the story's any guide—' Ribek said.

'Don't tell me!' snapped the woman. 'I've changed my mind. I don't want to know. That stupid story's ruined my life. I've never believed it. I never wanted to believe it. I don't now. If you're trying to tell me that Rocky's taking us to look for the stupid Ropemaker, I'm getting off right away, soon as we're clear. You can keep Rocky, and welcome.'

'I don't know how to ride a horse,' said Ribek, obviously teasing. He seemed to be like that.

'Then Rocky can tell you that too,' snarled the woman.

'Maybe our new friend knows how to ride a horse,' said Ribek, still teasing. 'Who are you anyway? We can't just call you Um.'

'Me?' said Maja, astonished to be asked, to be even noticed. 'I'm . . . I'm Maja Urlasdaughter.'

'Maja!' said the woman in a totally different voice. 'You're still alive! Oh, thank the stars! I've thought of you so often. It was the worst thing of all, leaving you behind there in that hell. I was sure she'd have . . .'

She didn't finish the sentence. It didn't matter. It wasn't important, swept away like a leaf in a stream on the flood of hope that welled up in Maja, unstoppable. Normally she would have pushed it away, having decided long ago that hope was only the insubstantial shadow that solid, real disappointment cast in front of it wherever it came. Not now.

'You're . . . you're Saranja?' she whispered, and then had to say it aloud because her whisper was drowned by the wing-thunder.

'Oh, Maja!' said Saranja, laying the reins down on Rocky's neck and hugging Maja to her like a doll. 'That's wonderful! That's absolutely wonderful! Ribek, this is my cousin Maja, whom I never thought I would see again. I think this is the best thing that's ever happened to me.'

'Hello, Maja,' said Ribek. 'Glad to have you with us. Perhaps you can persuade Saranja to stop talking nonsense about not coming to help look for the Ropemaker.'

Saranja snorted, let go of Maja and picked up the reins.

'What happened to them?' she said after a while. 'My parents, your mother, the boys?'

Maja told her about finding the bodies, and the bonfire she'd made on them. She didn't say anything about the screams.

'Your father and the boys went off to fight the horse-men,' she said. 'I don't know anything about them.'

'If they were in the same fight I was,' said Ribek, 'it wasn't good. We held the horsemen for a while and it looked like we were winning, but then some of them came round and caught us from the side, and after that it was a massacre. I got out by the skin of my teeth, but a lot of people didn't.'

Again Saranja was silent for a while.

'Well, that's all over,' she said at last. 'I suppose I can stop hating her now.'

The Valley flowed backward beneath them. Maja had never been so far from Woodbourne and had no idea of the names of any of the farms and villages she could see, but Ribek knew the Valley well and told them old scandals and new gossip about the people who lived there, though Maja had to strain to hear through the wind-whistle and wing-thunder. After a while he got hard biscuity bread out of his satchel and passed it forward.

'How come you showed up so pat at Woodbourne, Ribek?' said Saranja. 'Or were you just running away?'

'At first I was. Slinking back to Northbeck and hop-ing for the best – it's pretty out of the way up there – but, well, I'd known we were for it when the ice dragon didn't show up last winter. My grandfather saw him

19

once, but mostly you don't. You just know he's there. I came down to Woodbourne and tried to talk to your mother. She didn't answer. Her mouth was a slit. She just shook her head and shut the door in my face. So that was that. Nothing for it but to stand and fight and hope for a miracle. It didn't happen.

'I headed for the river with a bunch of others who'd been in the fight, but the horsemen caught up with us just as we got there. Some of us tried to hold them off while the rest got on to a couple of rafts. That's when I got hurt, but someone hauled me onto a raft and off we floated. Downriver, of course. South. That's how I finished up less than half a day from Woodbourne. I thought after all I'd better come and see if your mother had changed her mind – I'd never have thought well of myself again if I hadn't. Pretty sure nothing would come of it, but, well, it didn't turn out like that and here we are.

'Know what we're talking about, Maja?'

'Me?' said Maja, startled to be asked. 'Er . . . er . . . Yes, of course. It's in the story. There's always one boy born at Northbeck who can hear what the stream is saying, and when he's old enough he has to climb up into the mountains and sing to the snows every year so that the ice dragon comes and blocks the passes with fresh snow and the horsemen can't get through; and there's always a girl born at Woodbourne who can hear what the cedars are saying, and when she's old enough she has to go into the forest to sing to the cedars and feed the unicorns so that they bring the sickness that stops the Emperor's armies coming through because they're supposed to be defending us but they're just as bad as the horsemen.'

'And that's what I ran away from,' muttered Saranja.

Maja's words, when they'd come, had come with a rush and now she was gasping for breath. She'd had to crane round Saranja's body so that Ribek could hear her through the wing-thunder. He laughed.

'So you know the story,' he said.

'Do you want me to go on? It's rather complicated.'

'Let's get ourselves somewhere a bit more comfortable, so we can talk without having to shout. Your ancestor Tilja and my ancestor Tahl will have seen things differently, and there's twenty generations of story telling since then, so the stories themselves may be pretty different by now.'

'All right.'

Time passed, and more time. Gradually Maja became aware of a strange, throbbing sensation running through her – through all of her, body, mind and soul. She had no words for it. She had never felt anything like it before . . . Yes, she had! Those sudden, fierce thrills when Saranja was conjuring Rocky's harness up out of nowhere – this was the same kind of thing, but very different, as different as a howling tempest from a breeze so faint that you can't feel it, and can only tell it's there by the drift of thistledown it's carrying along. It came from Rocky.

This was the feel of magic, she realized. When it was strong magic, suddenly happening, when Saranja had whispered the Ropemaker's real name – Maja knew

21

from the story that must be what she had said – it was like a thunderclap straight overhead, stunning the senses. Things like giving Rocky his wings and harness were thunder not far off, startling in its suddenness, thrilling in its power. But what came from Rocky now was like continuous thunder rolling along distant hills, almost beyond hearing, vaguely menacing but at the same time comforting.

Rocky was magical all the time because the two gold feathers Saranja had found in the ashes of Woodbourne were roc's feathers, and a roc is a magical animal. Twenty generations ago the magic that protected the Valley started to fail, and four people, Tilja and her grandmother Meena from Woodbourne, and Tahl and his grandfather Alnor from Northbeck, had set out into the Empire to look for the man who had put the magic there in the first place, a magician called Faheel. He had been very old and tired, and had sent them on to look for a magician who called himself the Ropemaker. But while they were on Faheel's island Tilja had picked up a couple of roc feathers. Then, when they'd found the Ropemaker and he'd done what they asked him, he'd used the feathers to give Meena's bad-tempered old mare a pair of wings so that Tahl and Alnor could fly safely over the forest, without being killed by the magical forest sickness that was only fatal to men and was now back in place to protect the Valley from the Emperor's armies.

The story, as Maja had said, was a lot more complicated than that, so she started sorting the rest of it out in her mind for when the time came to tell Ribek the Woodbourne version.

By the time she'd done that they were flying up a prodigious valley carved into the northern mountains. Soon Rocky curved to the right and, still flying strongly, climbed steadily to cross a snow-covered ridge and glide smoothly down into the next valley.

'By all the waters!' said Ribek. 'I know where we are! Our mill's in the next valley! Think we're far enough in front to spend the night? If we haven't lost them completely.'

'We're going to have to stop somewhere,' said Saranja. 'Anything to eat at your mill? For him, I mean. He'll need more than grass after that effort. Assuming we can get him over that.'

She pointed towards the mountain spur now facing them, almost half as high again as the one they'd crossed.

'There's a good pass a dozen miles south,' said Ribek. 'And it's a mill, you know. Been a rotten year for custom, with all the fighting, so the barn's full of last year's grain. We do a line in crimped grain for horse-feed.'

It was drawing towards evening by the time Rocky had beaten his way up through the thinner air to the top of the pass and started the long glide down.

'He's getting tired,' said Saranja. 'No wonder – any ordinary horse would be dead, what he's done. What are they going to make of him at your mill?'

'If it's there. If they're there. Depends whether the horse people came raiding up this far. But if they're there they'll be all right. We're Ortahlsons, remember – my grandad saw the ice dragon. But listen. I've been think-ing. Those fellows who're after us – they knew we were there. There was a noise, but it stopped, and I decided it didn't matter. They must've been trying to sneak up on us.'

'Yes. My fault. I didn't notice it till almost too late, and I know what engines sound like. You're right. They'd turned them off and started to drift towards us. And when they were close enough they got the bird-kites out to try and sneak up on us. They've got a magician on board. Anything magical the way Rocky is sends out a bit of a signal, and if he's good enough the magician can pick it up until we can land somewhere and I can take his wings off him, supposing I can. I don't know any-thing about flying horses.'

'I thought you said the Sheep-faces didn't do magic.'

Saranja started to explain. Maja tried to listen, sleepy still, and only half hearing.

'They don't. But they want it. That's what they're like. Anything they haven't got. You've got an opal mine, they want it. All the war-lords keep a magician in their household. They're not mighty magicians, not like the ones in the story, and when their war-lords start fighting mostly they cancel each other out, but they can usually tell when someone else is brewing up magic anywhere near. The Sheep-faces have got hold of a few – they pay them the earth. I couldn't help picking up a lot of this sort of thing because my owner liked to have a woman sitting at his feet when he was in Council or anything – pet dogs, we were. Added to his status.

'First off the Sheep-faces ran up against the Empire.

24

Wanted to trade, they said. Empire took a look at them, worked out what they were at, wouldn't let them in. So they tried to force their way in. They've got some amazing weapons, but they hadn't met dragons before, or directed lightning, or some of the other stuff they ran up against. Those airboats burn – get a flame against one of those bags and it goes up like gunpowder . . .'

'Gunpowder?'

'Too long to explain now. So the Sheep-faces started trying to encircle the Empire and ran up against the war-lords. The only thing that stops war-lords fighting each other is somebody else to fight. Magic doesn't work as well the other side of the desert, but some of the war-lords' magicians could fling fire – not as good as dragons or lightning, but enough to stop an airboat getting in close, and the war-lords fought hit-and-run on the ground, which they're good at and the Sheep-faces weren't, so it was a really bloody business down south until the Sheep-faces backed off. Now they're working to set the war-lords fighting each other – doesn't take much doing – and meanwhile mopping up all the magicians they can. I reckon that airboat was a patrol coming up through the desert, looking for magic stuff over on their left, and all of a sudden they found out there was more on their right than they expected now the Valley's open. Six years ago, when I crossed the desert, nobody that side had any idea it was there. The Sheep-faces must have been coming to take a look when I happened to be giving Rocky his wings – that'd send out a signal you could pick up a hundred miles off.'

'So they can follow us wherever we go?'

'Until they run out of fuel for the engines. It's a patrol. They'll be carrying plenty. Could last for days.'

'Not good,' said Ribek.

'Ung?' said Maja, hesitantly breaking the silence.

'Yes, Maja?' said Saranja.

'Are . . . are they *human*? The Sheep-faces?'

'Far as I know. They just don't think the way we do. How far to your mill, Ribek?'

'Five miles from the bottom of the pass. That's it, ahead. You can see the river. Better get him down while we're still over the forest, I suppose.'

'Umph. Not something they teach you in riding school.'

Maja saw her do something with the reins and felt the slight shift of her body. Rocky steepened his glide, landed with barely a jolt and folded his wings. Ribek and the woman dismounted. Saranja lifted Maja down and helped Ribek unbuckle the saddlebags and harness, then moved to Rocky's flank. Her hands seemed to know what to do. She laid one on the root of each wing. She was a tall woman, but even on tiptoe she could barely reach across to the further one. At her touch the horse half spread both wings. Her lips moved, sound-lessly. Again that shock wave, the fierce, glittering tremor in the golden evening light sweeping along the opposite mountainside, that pang of excitement deep in Maja's soul, so intense this time that she cried aloud.

Saranja looked at her with raised eyebrows.

'I . . . I'm all right,' she said. 'It's just when you do that . . .'

'Your Sheep-faces' magician will have felt it too, surely,' said Ribek. 'I felt it a bit myself.'

'Uh-huh. Probably still feel it when they get here,' muttered Saranja.

Gently she stroked each hand up the two massive bones that carried the wings. And again. And again. Each time she repeated the simple movement the wings became smaller, and the horse itself dwindled in proportion, until only an ordinary chestnut stallion stood there, in a harness of plain brown leather, with a couple of golden feathers lying on each shoulder. Even so, it was a handsome beast, tired after a long day, but well-muscled, its coat glossy with health, and with an odd, humorous look in its eye, as if it knew some secret no other horse was aware of.

Saranja unwound a golden hair from her wrist and bound it round the quills. As she did so Maja felt the strange Rocky-sensation die away. Saranja slipped the feathers into her wallet, and the world was ordinary again.

They walked the hundred paces to the edge of the woods. Maja gazed around as they went on. Small interlocking fields, not a square foot of good earth wasted, lay in two narrow strips either side of the river. She could see a dozen farms from where she stood. All had a winter-hardy look. There was no sign of the ravages of the horse people. The slopes above were clothed with dense woods all the way to the treeline.

'Five miles to your mill?' said Saranja. 'They'll be sending patrols out the moment they land.'

'Should be enough for tonight,' said Ribek. 'They

27

won't see much. It's a waning moon, doesn't clear the ridge till well after midnight.'

'Suppose they're here before morning, is there another way out of the valley?' said Saranja. 'We'll need to start well before dawn. They'll have bird-kites up watching for us soon as it's light. We could fly, but I'm not sure he'd make it over the next ridge.'

'I can take us up through the woods and along to the next pass. It's a bit more exposed after that. Won't their magician be able to pick up your feathers soon as he gets near them?'

'I don't think so, not with the hair round them. Can't be sure, but I can feel them sort of come into their power when I unwind it.'

'So can I!' said Maja. 'It was there, like a kind of background buzz, but it stopped as soon as you put the hair round.'

'Funny,' said Ribek. 'I can't tell, but that sounds all right.'

'Let's move,' said Saranja. 'I want to take a look at that leg of yours. You'd better ride – you look dead beat. I ought to be too, but I'm not. Still, I wouldn't mind sleeping in a bed, even if it's just three or four hours. Maja too, I expect.'

Bed! Maja thought, as Ribek climbed wearily into the saddle and Saranja lifted her up behind him. She settled side saddle, leaned her head against his back, reached her arms as far as they would go round his waist and fell asleep.

*

28

It seemed to Maja that she woke in the same place that she'd fallen asleep, sitting side saddle on Rocky, leaning against Ribek's back, with the whole side of her face numb and creased with the imprint of his jacket. Only it was now daylight, daylight sweet with the dewy airs of early morning. Saranja was on foot, leading the way up a steep hill path through dense old woodland. From far down the slope to her right she could hear a drowsy throbbing sound.

'Ahng . . .' she yawned. 'Are . . . are we nearly there?'

'Nearly where?' said Ribek.

'We were going to your mill. We were going to sleep in a bed.'

'Been and gone. You slept four hours in Saranja's bed.'

'Oh! I thought that was only a dream. There was a blue clock on the wall.'

'That's right. In the kitchen. My grandfather made clocks for a hobby. That's where I belong. Best place in the world.'

'I don't belong anywhere.'

'Not Woodbourne?'

'Not now. It's gone. Anyway, it wasn't like your mill. It wasn't a good place. Saranja ran away.'

'She was telling me. That sort of thing shouldn't . . . I wonder if I should have left you at the mill. They'd have looked after you there.'

'No. I'm going with you. Wherever it is. Do you know yet? What's happening?'

'At the moment we're trying to get way from the Sheep-faces. Anything else can wait. That's them you

can hear buzzing away down in the valley. We aren't trying for the main pass, because that's pretty exposed over
the top, and we think they'll have those kite-men up, but
there's another little one they mightn't spot.'

Nightmare flooded back. The throbbing from the
valley was no longer drowsy. It was the purr of the monsters who would find her in the end.

Ribek's voice, ordinary, calm, faintly teasing, dis-
solved them.

'Hungry? There's raisin cake.'

'Umm . . . don't know.'

'That means you need raisin cake.'

He was right.

'Why aren't we flying?' she mumbled between the
delectable mouthfuls.

'Because their magician will be on to us the minute
Saranja puts Rocky's wings on and they'll start following us all over again. We're hoping that if we can get a
bit of the mountain between us and them before she
does it that might damp the effect and perhaps we'll
shake them off here. You agree?'

'Uh . . . uh . . .' mumbled Maja, startled out of the
returning nightmare, simply by being asked, and then
deciding he was probably joking.

'I hope your leg's better,' she said.

'A bit,' said Ribek, sounding surprised in his turn.
'Saranja cleaned it out at the mill and put a new bandage on. She knows a lot about wounds. Rough lot of
thugs she's been living among, she says.'

Maja was bewildered. She wasn't used to being talked
to like this – wasn't used to being talked to at all, in fact,

apart from when her mother took it into her head to tell her one of her stories. Otherwise at Woodbourne she'd been talked *at* – told what to do, or not do, or how furious the speaker was with somebody else. If she hadn't been there, they'd have told the cat. She liked this new experience, but she didn't know how to cope with it so she didn't say anything. The path twisted and began to climb back the other way, and then twisted again. And again. After a bit she settled into a light doze, in and out of sleep, reliving bits of her dream that hadn't been a dream.

'Was there a big yellow cat?' she mumbled.

'Monster,' said Ribek. 'His mother was killed by a fox and our old bitch finished suckling him, so he's got it into his head he's a dog. He won't let another dog through the gate. He'll see foxes off too.'

'And an owl on a shelf?'

'Woolly. My pet owl when I was a kid. My grandfather stuffed him for me when he died.'

And green plates and bowls on the dresser, she thought, *and the steady, peaceful rumble of the millstream over the weir. A place to belong.* She fell into a pleasant daydream of living at the mill, deliberately replacing the purr of the monster with the sound of the weir.

The path zigzagged to and fro, steeper now, and the trees on either side almost all pines, gloomy and mysterious. Even gallant Rocky had begun to plod, but Saranja still strode ahead, apparently tireless. There wasn't much to do or look at, so she settled back into her daydream, less satisfactorily because she didn't

31

know enough about the real mill to make the dream one solid. She'd have to ask Ribek. At last the steady rhythm of Rocky's stride fell still. They had reached the end of the trees. The dazzling light from beyond, bright sun glittering back off a vast white sweep of snowfield, made her screw up her eyes. Through a haze of tears she could just make out somebody – Saranja – out in the middle of the dazzle, shading her eyes as she gazed back over the treetops. She waved to them to come on out into the open.

'All clear, far as I can see,' she said. 'I want to give Rocky a bit of a rest and a feed. You go on ahead with Maja and we'll catch you up.'

It was only when Saranja lifted her down that Maja realized she was wearing someone else's coat, a bit too big for her, but very warm and comfortable.

'One of my nieces lent it to you,' said Ribek. 'You'll need it over the top. We've got other stuff in the saddle-bags. Ready, kid? Off we go. One child and one cripple set out to conquer the mountain.'

He led the way out of the woods and along the edge of the forest to the right. After a little while he turned up across the snowfield. It was last winter's snow, almost as hard and slippery as ice with daily thawing and freezing. Maja couldn't see any sign of a path, but before long the snowdrifts began to rise on either side of them and they were walking along a little valley that soon became almost a canyon with ice-sheeted black crags poking through the snow on either side. The footing was rough and treacherous and Ribek was limping heavily, some-times just taking a single step, and pausing, and leaning on his stick and leading off again with his hurt leg. Maja worked her way up beside him and put her arm round his waist and did her best to help him along.

'Thanks, kid,' he muttered and plodded grimly on. Saranja and Rocky caught up with them just as they reached the top of the pass.

'You don't look too good,' she said.

'Cold's got into it a bit,' Ribek answered. 'Maja had to carry me most of the way.'

He was such a lovely man, Maja decided. He was only joking, of course, but still, when his leg was really hurting him, he'd found a way of saying thank you to her.

'Good for her,' said Saranja. 'We'll get you back on Rocky soon as we're off the ice, and we'll get his wings back on him first good place we come to.'

The slope down wasn't so steep, but still horribly slippery in places. Maja stayed with Ribek, helping him as best she could. Saranja hurried ahead with Rocky, tethered him at the edge of the trees, and came back and took Ribek's other side. Together they heaved him into the saddle, where he pretty well collapsed.

The downward path was much like the one they'd climbed, twisting through pines, and then ancient deciduous trees, which reminded Maja of the forest behind Woodbourne. The air grew warmer. They came to a large, open glade, with a stream tumbling through, and halted.

'Put me by the water,' said Ribek. 'It'll tell me soon as the Sheep-faces cross the ridge. And I might be able to tickle a fish or two for lunch, if you get a fire going.'

'I'll want one anyway,' said Saranja. 'Much better

deal with your leg using warm water. Maja, dear, see if you can find us some dry stuff for firewood.'

'Maja, dear?' Amazing. Unbelievable.

Half an hour later Rocky was grazing contentedly at sweet mountain turf, Maja was nursing a good steady blaze with a small iron pot balanced over its heart, Saranja was carefully cutting a mat of blood-soaked bandages away from Ribek's leg, while he lay face down at the edge of the stream with his left arm trailing in the water. Even as Maja watched he swung it up out of the water, something silvery arced through the air, and there was a plump fish flopping to and fro on the grass. Saranja reached out and grabbed it, reversed her knife in her hand and whacked the fish firmly, just behind the head, with the heavy hilt. She dropped it back on the turf, where it jerked a couple of times and lay still. She went back to Ribek's bandages as if she hadn't done anything clever at all.

Maja realized she was still a bit afraid of her cousin, though Saranja used to look after her and try to protect her when she got the chance, in a way Maja's mother had always been too feeble to do, and her aunt too bitter. Saranja was so strong and certain, so tireless and brave. But deep down inside her, banked and controlled and hidden, Maja now sensed something else. She knew it from twelve years of hiding from it at Woodbourne, raging like a bushfire on the surface of everyone's life there, her uncle's day-long, week-long, year-long fury, and the midwinter bitterness of her aunt's response. It had never crossed Maja's mind to wonder why Woodbourne was like that. It just was, and always had been, ever since she could remember. And somehow it was all her fault.

No wonder Saranja had run away. But it had been too late. That rage was already there, inside her, like a family illness. She'd taken it into exile with her, and brought it back fiercer than before.

And there was something else about her, strange, different. A sort of inaudible hum, rather like the odd, buzzing sensation that Maja picked up from Rocky when he was wearing his wings but not when he wasn't. Except that that had been part of Rocky, coming from inside him. This was much fainter, and it wasn't part of Saranja. It came from something she was wearing or carrying. And it was doing something to her, something magical . . .

How did Maja know all this anyway? She had no idea, but she did.

Ribek shifted a little way up the bank and caught another fish, and then another. Maja knew what to do from tagging along on her boy-cousins' fishing expeditions, and had them gutted and spitted by the time the fire was hot enough to roast them. Saranja disappeared into the wood to look for healing herbs and didn't find any, but came back with a wallet-full of sweet wild yellow raspberries instead.

Ribek unpacked one of the saddlebags and produced fresh brown bread from the mill, and butter churned from the rich milk of mountain pasturage. Maja ate, purring inwardly, like the old farm cat over its bowl of scraps. She'd never in her life felt so happy. Perhaps she never would again. She'd like to have stayed here for ever. But of course she couldn't. The other two weren't just escaping. They were going to look for the Ropemaker. They wouldn't want her with them for that; she'd only be in the way, no help at all. They'd find someone to leave her with on the way. And then it would all be over, probably.

'How far is it still?' she said.

'Where to this time?' said Ribek.

'To find the Ropemaker. You were getting ready to go and do that when the Sheep-faces came and we had to run away, weren't you?'

'Not really,' said Saranja. 'We were being got ready for this, I suppose you could say. All my life I was being got ready, I'm beginning to think. All my life I've been fighting against it, without realizing, and in the end I ran away from it, but it brought me back when the time came, or that's how it feels. I still don't like it. I still don't want to believe it. Why me? It makes me mad. But I've got to start believing it now. I'm stuck with it.

'The snows failed last winter so the glaciers melted and that let the horsemen through from the northern plains. I don't love the Valley the way everyone else seems to, but I'm not going to stand for their being raped and murdered year after year by those savages. Somebody's got to go and look for a magician to renew the magic, so that Ribek can sing to the snows and bring the ice dragon back to block the passes, and someone from Woodbourne can listen to the cedars and feed the unicorns in the forest, so they'll keep the sickness there and stop the Emperor's armies coming through and taxing everyone of all they've got. The Ropemaker's the obvious person. He put it there in the first place, so I suppose we're starting with him.'

'That reminds me,' said Ribek. 'What about the forest? Did your aunt say anything, Maja?'

'Who to? She didn't tell anyone anything, except when they'd done wrong. Um, I suppose she's been in a bad temper all the time, not just some of the time, like she used to be.'

'You can't know everything,' said Ribek. We'll just have to assume it's happening. And I'm no keener than Saranja is on the idea. I've got work to do.'

'You should have seen him last night,' said Saranja. 'He's wonderfully proud of that mill of his, aren't you?'

'Well, I've never asked for anything better,' said Ribek. 'It's a good life. If a farmer wants to send his prettiest daughter up with his grain, because he thinks I'll give him a better deal, why should I discourage him?'

'Only you always knew it might happen, because you believed the stupid story,' said Saranja. 'I didn't. And you didn't either, Maja, because there's no one like you in the story.'

'Me?' said Maja.

'Well, you're here, aren't you?' said Saranja. 'I don't believe you would be if you weren't wanted. Same with Rocky. He looked like a completely useless old nag when he started tagging along after me. Nobody could possibly have wanted him for anything. But there had to be a horse for me to put the wings onto, so there he was, and here we are, the four of us, setting out together at the start of another stupid story. We're going to find the Ropemaker, wherever he is, so that he can seal the

37

Valley off for another twenty generations, and I expect there'll be all sorts of adventures on the way for you to enjoy.'

'I . . . I don't think I'll be very good at that sort of thing.'

Ribek laughed aloud

'Do you imagine I do? Or Rocky? I don't know about Saranja – she's obviously made for it. You know the story, don't you? Do you imagine Tilja thought she'd be good at that sort of thing when she set out with the others to find Faheel? But in the end they couldn't have done it without her. No, kid, you'd better face it. You're going to have to dare and adventure with the rest of us, and Rocky's going to take us wherever we're supposed to be, and that's all any of us knows, and Rocky doesn't even know that. He'll just find himself doing it.'

'Oh.'

Chapter 2

A T THE TOP of a long mountain meadow, with the morning sun full in their faces, sat a man and a boy. Between them on a boulder crouched a squat blue-and-yellow lizard about the size of the man's shoe. A huge old cedar rose close behind them, and below, scattered across the bright upland turf, a small flock of sheep grazed, watched by a neat black-and-white sheepdog.

The man was talking to the lizard.

'I think we may have made a breakthrough – or rather Benayu may have.'

'I didn't do it on purpose,' said the boy. 'I just thought I'd give it a go, running my spell backwards through the screen – not exactly backwards, more inside out, if you see what I mean.'

'What he did, in effect, was to set up an exact counter-resonance to the active resonances of the spell so that on reaching the screen they cancelled each other out. He was lucky, of course, in that the spell was ideally suited to the treatment, but all the same it was a whole level more powerful than anything we've managed to screen before.'

The lizard's voice answered in both their minds. If granite could speak it would do so in such a voice.

'Yes, it will not always be so easy. Each screen must be custom-made to what it screens. But the principle . . . Wait. A thing of power is coming. You may have brought it here. Hide yourselves.'

Man and boy rose and stood for a moment, staring north, and saw a dark fleck in the pale blue sky above a massive snow-streaked ridge. Tension swept up the hillside. It was as if the placid turf had been the nape of a giant neck, every grass-blade prickling with sudden apprehension. Quietly they walked towards the cedar, laid a hand on its bark and disappeared.

By now the stone where the lizard had been was mottled with blue-and-yellow lichen, and the place was empty apart from the sheep and the dog, and the small creatures that clicked and chirruped in the sun-warmed turf. The tension remained, electric.

Rocky circled down towards the mountain meadow, apparently empty apart from a flock of sheep and a sheepdog.

'I think this may be where we're going,' called Saranja over her shoulder. 'To start with, anyway. I didn't ask him to land, and he can't be hungry yet. There's got to be a shepherd somewhere around. Perhaps he'll tell us what happens next.'

The dog below yapped a warning. The sheep started to scatter and the dog raced to round them up as Rocky swung in a full circle and glided in towards the slope, closer and closer, and with a sudden bell-like booming of wings landed some twenty paces below the cedar.

All three riders climbed stiffly down. Rocky folded his wings and started to nose discontentedly at the sheep-nibbled turf, too short to be much use to him. The dog streaked towards them, snarling, only to halt almost as suddenly, but with hackles still bristling.

Maja stared around. Something was wrong. Apart from the spectacular view she couldn't see anything different from any of the half-dozen lonely and peaceful places where they'd stopped to rest, but the feel of this place was like the twanging stillness before the thunder breaks.

'If there's a shepherd he's probably hiding in the wood,' said Ribek, apparently untroubled. 'That's where I'd be, seeing something like us show up. Unless that dog's magical.'

'No,' said Maja. 'But the place . . .'

'What about the place?'

'It's . . . *worried*.'

They looked at her. Saranja shrugged.

'Rocky chose it,' she said. 'We may as well stay here for a bit, anyway. There *must* be some better herbs in this lot of woods. I didn't like the look of that leg of yours at all this morning. How's it feeling?'

'Not too good,' said Ribek. 'It's been throbbing a while. But it'll do a bit longer. I'll just see if that stream's got anything to say.'

Maja helped him limp across the slope. He paused at an odd little pool, an exact circle of still clear water cut into the grass.

'Nothing there for me,' he said. 'Somebody made that.'

'By magic,' she whispered, afraid of her own voice.

'I'll take your word for it,' he said, and limped on.

For a while he stood by the stream with his head cocked, apparently listening to the ripple of the water over the boulders. Maja had a strange notion while she waited for him that she could actually *feel* whatever he was listening to – not hear it, the way he seemed to, but feel it as a sort of soft rippling tickle somewhere at the back of her mind. Momentarily it soothed the throb of tension.

'Well?' muttered Saranja sarcastically, when Maja had helped him back. 'What's the news from nowhere?'

'That tree's watching us,' said Maja.

Ribek turned and looked.

'Isn't that a cedar, Saranja?' he asked gently.

Saranja too turned.

'Oh, Gods!' she yelled as she strode towards the tree and thumped her clenched fists against the bark. 'I never asked for any of this! I tell you I don't want any of this!'

A breeze woke in the stillness of the afternoon and whispered among the needles of the tree. Just as with the stream, Maja imagined she could somehow feel its mutterings in her mind. Saranja listened to them, frowning and biting her lip, and strode back unappeased.

'All right,' she said. 'So this is the place, and we've got

to wait. Same from the stream, I suppose. And I'm starving, and there's almost nothing in the saddlebags.'

'There's mutton,' said Ribek with a jerk of his head towards the flock. 'Only I don't like the look of that dog.'

Maja jumped with sudden shock. A moment later, with a faint sound of air abruptly displaced, a basket landed on the turf beside them. The smell of fresh bread added itself to the mountain odours.

'And you don't want any of that either?' said Ribek. 'What do you think, Maja? You're jumpy about something?'

'I think it's all right,' muttered Maja. 'It was just the way it came. And this place.'

'Still worried? Any idea what about?'

Maja concentrated. The worry-feeling was like an itchy patch of skin round an insect bite that causes it, sometimes almost too small to see, but . . . yes . . . there.

'Rocky,' she said.

'What are you two talking about?' said Saranja, still sounding inwardly furious.

'Maja seems to be extra sensitive to magic,' said Ribek. 'That's why things like putting Rocky's wings on shake her so badly. That must be really big magic. I bet that cedar is watching us too. You're not going to trust her about the food?'

'I'm not that pig-headed,' said Saranja.

They settled either side of the basket and checked through the contents. Ribek took out a mutton chop, shrugged, bit and chewed.

43

'Tastes fine,' he said. 'But I suppose it would. Help yourself, Maja.'

She took one too. No thrill of magic came from it, though it tasted still warm from the grill.

'Well, you haven't grown donkey's ears,' said Saranja sourly, and started to eat. She continued to brood as she munched.

'What now?' she said. 'Just sit here and wait for the Ropemaker? Is there any reason, by the way, why we can't just call him Ramdatta?'

The whole landscape answered her.

The three syllables throbbed through Maja as if she'd been a hard-struck bell. Rocky lifted his head and neighed, a sound that seemed to shake the hillside. Birds exploded from the wood and wheeled clamouring above it. Something thumped on to the turf behind them. They turned and saw two figures sprawled on the ground beneath the downsweeping branches of the cedar. These now rose groggily to their feet, shaking their heads as if to clear them.

All three travellers stood to face them. They saw a man in early middle age, stocky, muscular, with close-cut curly brown hair, a smooth, unreadable face, clean-shaven but with remarkably hairy legs revealed by the odd leather kilt he was wearing. His skin was golden-brown tinged with olive. Next to him stood a gawky boy with a strong family likeness despite the difference in build.

'One moment,' said the man and strode past them with the boy beside him, then stood staring out southward across the immense landscape. They could feel the

44

tension too. Maja could see it in their poses, and feel it humming from them. They relaxed at last, and the man shrugged his shoulders and sighed as they turned to face the newcomers.

'That name,' he said. 'Don't say it again, please. Your horse is more than signal enough of your presence here. Can anything be done to mitigate that?'

Maja could hear the strain in the quiet, slow-spoken words.

'I can take his wings off,' said Saranja. 'Maja says he doesn't feel at all magical without them.'

The man glanced at Maja, frowning.

'Maja seems able to feel magic,' said Ribek. 'She knew you were in the cedar.'

'Later,' said the man. 'The horse is urgent.'

Saranja picked an apple out of the basket, cut it in quarters with the knife from her belt, walked down to Rocky and offered him a piece of it, which he took neatly from her open palm. She waited while he munched, gave him another piece, teased at his mane and moved to his shoulder, and gave him the rest of the apple. She reached for the wing-roots and stroked her hands gently up the massive bones.

'Hold me,' said Maja, and braced herself against Ribek's side.

This time she was ready and could pay attention to the actual event. For a few moments the fierce electric tingle seemed to vibrate through the whole mountain on which they stood, and through her too, as if she'd been a boulder on that mountain. She watched the wings shrink into themselves, dwindling to a pair of golden plumes which Saranja could ease free, and Rocky became his other self, no more than an unremarkably handsome golden chestnut. He followed Saranja up the slope, clearly hoping for another apple, and not thinking anything at all strange had happened to him, but was distracted by a pile of fresh clover that had appeared on the turf beside him. When it was over Maja realized that the mountain pasture was almost at ease, though deep beneath the turf something remained. Something extremely strange.

'I hope that's better,' said Saranja, turning towards where the man had been. But by now he was crouching beside a large blue-and-yellow lizard that had appeared on the rock close to where they had been sitting. It seemed to be having some kind of fit. Spasms of shuddering overcame it and its eyes kept closing to vertical slits and opening again.

'Much better,' he said over his shoulder. 'Thank you, and let us hope it is not too late.'

'We would have known by now, wouldn't we?' said the boy, obviously as anxious as the man.

'Probably,' said the man with a sigh, and rose to his feet.

'I must apologize for the informality of your reception,' he said, pulling himself together. 'I am Fodaro, and this is my nephew Benayu. That's his dog, Sponge. And this on the rock here is Jex. The name you spoke must have affected him even more powerfully than it did us, but he seems to have done his best to protect us before that happened. Evidently he has not yet recovered from the effort. The food is to your taste?'

46

Maja stared at the lizard, bewildered. She'd assumed it must be some kind of pet, but it didn't sound like that. She couldn't feel anything like the magical vibrations coming from it that she'd felt from Rocky when he had his wings on, though there was a sort of silent humming from both the man and the boy. They were still really scared of something too – something, she guessed, that might have noticed the explosion of magic when Saranja had spoken the Ropemaker's name, and Jex had been trying to protect them from that happening. Yes, and they'd have known by now if it had done so . . .

Ribek glanced down at her. His face seemed unusually drawn. She realized that his leg must be hurting more than he let on, but he caught her expression, laughed, shrugged and spread his hands. He was as bewildered as she was.

'The food?' he said, turning back to Fodaro. 'Just what we needed. Thank you very much. I'm Ribek Ortahlson, and my friends are Saranja and Maja Urlasdaughter. They're cousins, but I'm not related to them. In fact we barely know each other.'

'Those are your true names?'

'What on earth is the point of a false name?' said Saranja. 'That's who I am.'

'Hm. And you appear not to be yourselves magicians?'

'Not as far as we know,' said Ribek. 'There's very little magic where we come from.'

'But the horse . . . ?'

'Rocky's different,' said Saranja. 'He doesn't belong there. At least his wings don't. I put them on for him,

47

but I'm not a magician. The feathers told me what to do. It's a long story. Thank you for the fodder, by the way.'

'My pleasure,' said the boy.

She turned and stared at him.

'You too?' she said, as if this was the last straw.

'The talent runs in the family,' said Fodaro, 'though his is in some ways different from mine. He takes more after his father, my brother-in-law.'

'And, um, Jex?' said Ribek.

'Jex is something else,' said Fodaro.

Ribek waited for him to explain, but he changed the subject.

'May we please look at your feathers?'

Without hesitation Saranja drew them out of her wallet and offered them to him, but he held up both hands in a gesture of refusal and simply studied them as she held them, his nephew coming to his side to do so too. Their breathing slowed as they stared, while Saranja twisted them to and fro to let them see every aspect.

'Astonishing,' whispered Fodaro. 'Can you tell us what they are?'

'Ask Ribek. I'm still trying not to believe it.'

'I'm not,' said Ribek. 'After all, I believe in the ice dragon. They are roc feathers, according to the story we tell in the Valley, which so far has proved a pretty good guide, judging by what's happened to us in the last few days.'

'Roc feathers. I have never seen one. But yes, of course. And the hair that binds them? That is something of another order.'

'It belonged to . . . to the Ropemaker – the fellow whose name I said just now, but mostly he's called the Ropemaker in the story we tell in the Valley.'

Fodaro didn't respond, didn't even move. It seemed as if he had stopped breathing. Benayu stared at him, frowning.

'You know the Ropemaker's true name?' he whispered at last, speaking the words even more slowly than before. 'You carry a hair of his head? But you know nothing of magic? What brought you to this place? How do you come by a horse with the wings of a roc? Are you, at last, who I think you are?'

'Rocky brought us here,' said Saranja. 'We were just running away from the Sheep-faces, but he seemed to know where to go. Until I found the roc feathers he was just an old nag who insisted on following me, but then everything changed. Ribek showed up and I knew what to do because of the story, but then the Sheep-faces came looking for us. Rocky was faster than they were so we got away, and after that we just came where he took us.'

'Come to that,' said Ribek, 'I think we're entitled to ask who you are and what you're doing here.'

Fodaro relaxed enough to manage a smile.

'We are in much the same boat,' he said. 'We too are running away, or rather hiding. Until you came we believed we were here to take advantage of certain magical aspects of this place to conceal ourselves from our enemy, and to develop Benayu's powers with the help of Jex. I cannot tell you more about him because we have promised not to, but I'm extremely worried

49

about him, both for his sake and ours. We need him well.'

He turned to Saranja.

'Will you try something for me?' he said. 'I've never seen him like this before. He should have started pulling himself together by now, but if anything he's getting worse. This may not work, but it's the best I can think of. Kneel beside him, and when you are settled untie the quills, lay them close in front of him on the boulder, without the hair – don't let that touch him. Leave them there only an instant. Don't even whisper the name – just think it, and then pick them up and retie them at once. I'm sorry to have to ask you. I wouldn't if I thought it was safe for anyone else to do this.'

Saranja actually grinned at him, if a bit sourly.

'If it works, it works,' she said. 'I just don't have to pretend to like it.'

With deft, careful movements she did as he'd told her. The feathers rested on the rock for little more than a heartbeat, but for that splinter of time the hillside again seemed to twang with tension. The lizard gave a convulsion that almost toppled it from its boulder. And then Saranja was rewinding the long gold hair round the quills, and the hillside was at peace, and the lizard was no longer shuddering but crouched in the sunlight with its eyes closed and the slow come-and-go of its breath gently stirring the ruffles of its neck.

Saranja slid the feathers into her pouch and rose. Fodaro held his spread hands above the lizard, as if warming them over a fire.

'Well, he's here, at least,' he said. 'But not yet as fully here as we need him to be.'

'Would that work on Ribek's leg?' asked Saranja, obviously impatient with such abstractions. 'It's pretty bad, isn't it, Ribek, by the look of you?'

'Not too good, but it can wait. Depends how urgent everything else is.'

'Not that urgent, I hope,' said Fodaro. 'But Jex and the roc from which your feathers came are of a different order of being than ourselves,' he said. 'A human hurt requires human healing, whether physical or magical. Benayu will see to it . . . No, better not for the moment. I'm sorry.'

'I'd rather let Saranja take a look at it first, in any case,' said Ribek wearily. 'I'm sorry, Benayu. I don't distrust what you do the way she does, but I'm not used to it, and I prefer to stick with what I know. And there's always a price, if you'll excuse my saying so. Where Saranja's been these last few years the men did precious little besides fighting each other, so she knows about wounds. Mine wasn't too good when she dealt with it this morning, but your mountain water is clear and clean. I'll ask it to help. They've all got a bit of deep-earth healing in them, water sources, until we start poisoning them lower down.'

He turned and limped over to the stream. The other four followed him. The two magicians watched for a while in silence as Saranja unwound the ragged bandage as far as she could, cutting off a bit of the loose end and using that to sponge and soften the clotted blood until she could pick the next winding free with

51

her knifepoint. It was clear from her movements that, as he'd said, she knew what she was doing.

'Yes, you are right,' said Fodaro suddenly. 'Any use of magic demands a price from the user. Out there, in the Empire, a serious magician would have demanded silver for healing a wound like yours – gold, even, if the wound was badly infected. Up here, though . . .'

'"Would have demanded . . ."?' interrupted Saranja without looking up, but Fodaro waited as she eased the last winding away and began on the blood-drenched pad that covered the torn flesh. The blood was still oozing, and the scabbing for the most part soft enough for her to peel the pad gently away. Ribek's breath hissed between teeth and lip, but he didn't flinch. The wound was a tear rather than a slice, not deep but angry-looking, running slantwise across the upper part of the calf. Saranja sniffed at it and frowned.

'Do you know what you need?' asked Benayu.

'Should do. Ribek told you. Mothermoss would be nice, but I'll be lucky to find it here. There should be harmsain in the wood, though. Here, Maja – clean it up as best you can, while I look. When you've finished, put a pad over it – here – and wrap it up to keep warm.'

She damped one of the cleaner bits of bandage, folded another into a wad, and gave them to Maja.

'Don't go too far,' said Fodaro. 'It's still possible that you may need to leave in a hurry.'

She nodded and walked off towards the trees. Benayu glanced enquiringly at his uncle, who shook his head.

Ribek had caught the look.

'Let her find what's there, if that's what she wants,' he

said. 'I'll do. We aren't used to this sort of thing. There was almost no magic in the Valley. Saranja's family can hear what the cedars are saying, and mine can listen to moving water, and that was about it. There was a chop or too left in the basket, wasn't there?'

Benayu fetched the basket and then joined Fodaro, and crouched with him beside the lizard. They talked in low and worried voices. Ribek ate slowly while Maja worked away at his wound, which had clearly been troubling him more than he had let on. Then he hunkered away from the stream, stretched out in the sunlight and closed his eyes. By the time Saranja returned with a sheaf of twigs and leaves he was fast asleep, and Benayu had a small fire going beside the little circular pool, with a metal pot suspended over it.

Saranja eyed this, frowning.

'How did you know?' she said, instantly suspicious.

'Maja told me you'd need it, and Fodaro says we'd better lay off magic – even silly little things like lighting a fire – for the moment. So I did everything else your way, fetched the pot and the flint with my own hands, I mean. There's good clean water in the pool. What have you got?'

'Nothing I was looking for. Most of this is only a bit better than nothing, but the bitter-bark's fine, only it's got to be an infusion.'

She picked out a bunch of twigs bound with a rag, and used this to handle them as she peeled the bronzy bark from the white wood. Maja reached to help.

'Watch it,' she said. 'The raw sap is poisonous. You can use a couple of other sticks to put the bark in the pot. Keep it stirred and just simmering if you can. Are we actually in a hurry, do you know?'

'There's remarkably little we do know, these days,' said Fodaro, looking up. 'Less than ever now, until Jex comes to himself. He exists simultaneously in two . . . places. That's all it's safe to tell you. But normally he can communicate through his other self with creatures of his kind elsewhere in the Empire and tell us what's going on out there. In the meanwhile perhaps you could tell us this story you've mentioned from time to time. It could very well be useful.'

Saranja sighed.

'I suppose I'll have to,' she said. 'Better get it over. We'll let this cool now. Put me right, Maja, if I get it wrong. It's been a long time.'

She lifted the pot from the fire with a stick and wedged it behind a boulder, then moved with the other three into the shade of the cedar, and they settled down close above the lizard.

'You'll have to check with Ribek,' she said. 'Everyone in the Valley tells it a bit differently, but his family and mine are the only ones it really matters to.'

'The Valley?' asked Fodaro.

'It's over there,' she said, pointing west. 'I don't know how far. We came a bit round about, because first off we were escaping from some Sheep-faces in an airboat . . . forget about that – I'll draw you a picture and explain later.'

She picked up a twig and started to scratch an outline in a patch of bare earth.

'Rocky flies incredibly fast,' she went on, 'and that

second day he kept going till it was too dark to see. Then we slept on a sort of ledge in the mountains and flew on all next day, with one short break by a river. We slept again halfway up a mountain and got here, when? A bit after midday, about?

'Anyway the Valley's completely cut off from everywhere else, and has been for – oh, I suppose it's got to be twenty generations, however long that is. But it wasn't always. According to the story, we used to keep getting invaded by wild horsemen from the north and – just as bad, if not worse – the Emperor's armies coming up from the south to drive them back. In the end things got so bad that we decided to send a sort of delegation to look for a powerful magician to stop this happening. She was called Asarta . . .'

Asarta.

Maja heard the stone whisper in her mind, coming, it seemed, from unbelievable distances away. Saranja must have heard it too. She shuddered.

'I don't know if I can take much more of this,' she said. 'I don't mind giving Rocky his wings and taking them off again, for some reason, but otherwise . . . And I really hate it when it happens inside my head. In the story there's an ancestor of ours – mine and Maja's – called Tilja, who could undo magic. That was the only part I used to like.'

'Many people in the Empire feel the same,' said Fodaro. 'There've been waves of lynchings of magicians over the years. Go on with the story. Your people went to this magician – I know her name, of course, but not much else. What did she do?'

'She didn't. She'd finished her work and was just getting ready to leave, to "undo her days", according to the story, so she sent our people on to a magician called . . . Can I say his name?'

Fodaro shrugged.

'It will not have been his true name,' he said. 'But it will still have resonance for Jex, as Asarta's did. Try mouthing it only. You can tell us later.'

Maja watched the lizard as Saranja's lips moved. It did not stir, but again she heard the whisper in her mind, no louder than before, but nearer, somehow, more resonant.

Faheel.

Then silence. Saranja hesitated a moment, sighed resignedly and went on.

'She gave them a ring to take to him, and in exchange he sealed the Valley off for twenty generations. He summoned an ice dragon to block the northern passes with massive snowfalls, and – I've always thought this bit sounded particularly stupid – some unicorns into the southern forest who brought a kind of disease with them that made any men who tried to go in among the trees fall sick and die. Women were all right, though. See what I mean? Stupid. There was always one woman in my family who could hear what the cedars were saying, and she had to go into the forest each year when the first snows fell and sing to the unicorns and then feed them through the winter. And there was always one man in Ribek's family who could hear what the streams were saying, and each year he had to climb up to the snow-line and sing to the snows to bring the ice dragon back for another winter.

'Well, that lasted twenty generations, and then it broke down, so four of us – Tilja and her gran from our family and a boy called Tahl and his grandpa from Ribek's – went off to look for this Faheel person . . . bother. No, it seems to be all right to call him that . . . and after a lot of tiresome magical adventures . . . I think I'm leaving out something important, Maja . . .'

'The Watchers?'

'Oh, yes. Everything in the Empire was very tightly controlled. You couldn't travel anywhere without having a way-leave. You couldn't even die without a licence from the Emperor. And magic – oh, Gods! I suppose I've got to start believing in all this stuff – that was controlled by a bunch of super-magicians in the city of Talakh called the Watchers, only they were all at daggers drawn with each other, but that didn't stop them cracking down hard on anyone using magic without permission. Faheel had set the Watchers up to stop people doing that, but it went on in secret, and the system got out of hand, so everyone was scared stiff of the Watchers, who were meant to be there to look after them, and meanwhile Faheel had disappeared.

'But Tilja's gran had – wait for it – a wooden spoon, of all things, carved from the wood of a peach tree that had grown from the stone of a peach out of Faheel's garden, and the darned thing knew where he was and if you said his name over it would swivel round and point that way. The trouble was that that sent out a magical signal which put the Watchers on to them whenever they tried.

But they just managed to get away each time and in the end they found Faheel on an island out in the southern ocean, but of course he was incredibly old and tired and longing to give up, but he couldn't until he'd found someone to pass the famous ring on to.'

'In what way famous?' said Fodaro.

'He could control time with it. I'll come to that in a minute. Anyway, Tilja told him about a magician called the Ropemaker they'd met on their journey. Faheel decided he was the one he'd been waiting for, but they looked at a sort of magic table he'd got and saw that the Ropemaker was in the palace at Talakh and just about to be made into a Watcher. So to stop that Faheel used the ring to hold time still for the whole Empire while he and Tilja were carried up to Talakh by this roc and he destroyed the Watchers. But before—'

'One moment,' said Fodaro. '"He destroyed the Watchers." Does your story say anything about how he did that?'

'Yes, but it makes even less sense than anything else. Everything got bent out of shape. There were a lot of towers. They were all straight, if you looked at just one of them, but they weren't straight with each other. Something far off looked bigger than something nearer. Shapes didn't fit together with themselves. In the end the sky came forward until it was inside out and swallowed the Watchers up. And if you know what any of that means you're welcome to it.'

Fodaro was staring at her, oblivious to her obvious outrage. Benayu in turn was staring at him with his mouth half open in astonishment.

'As it happens, I do know what it means,' said Fodaro slowly. 'It is unbelievable, though not in the way you think. Anything else you can tell me about it . . . ?'

'I don't think so. Maja? No, we both know the same version, but Ribek's is a bit different in places. You'll have to ask him when he wakes up. Shall I go on?'

'Please. So, having destroyed the Watchers, Faheel gave the Ropemaker the ring?'

'No, because before he could do that another magician who wanted the ring – he was one of the secret ones – Tilja called him Moonfist – he took Faheel by surprise and nearly killed him, but Tilja managed to use the ring to stop time again and get him back to his island. Then before he died he gave Tilja the ring to take to the Ropemaker.

'They had a lot more stu— . . . I've got to stop saying that – they had a lot more adventures before they found him, of course, and he gave them the power to seal the Valley off again and sent them home. Tahl and Alnor couldn't go through the forest because the sickness was back, but they had a tiresome old mare with them called Calico, and the Ropemaker put a couple of roc feathers – the ones I just showed you – onto her shoulders and turned them into wings, so that she could fly them home. And I think he actually managed to hide the Valley completely this time. I spent several years out on the other side of the desert among the war-lords, and nobody had any idea it was there . . .'

'One moment,' said Fodaro. 'There were magicians there, among these war-lords? And magical objects?'

'Yes. Why? Magic didn't work so well out there, but—'

He interrupted her with a gesture and glanced at Benayu, who nodded.

'Only a minor puzzle,' he said. 'Later, perhaps. Please go on. Nobody among these war-lords knew of the existence of the Valley . . .'

'That's right. I don't think anyone in the Empire does, either. In the old days, before the Ropemaker, the Emperors kept trying to send armies through the forest to recapture what they called their lost province – that's in the story – so they must have known about it then, but I've never heard they've tried anything like that since.

'But the magic must have stopped working now because it was only supposed to last for twenty generations and they're up. My family kept count, and my mother always told me I might be the one who had to go and look for the Ropemaker and ask him to renew the magic. I couldn't stand it. Why me, for pity's sake? I never wanted anything to do with any of it in the first place. I thought it had ruined my life. So I ran away, and that turned out even worse, so as soon as I got the chance I ran back. So there I was, looking at the ruins of my old home, when I found the feathers among the ashes, and I realized that all this had been planned somehow, long ago. I'd even picked up an old horse to put the wings on, and there was Ribek limping up the road. And at that point Sheep-faces turned up in their airboat looking for us. Ribek says that no one had ever seen anything like that in the Valley before. Which shows that the Sheep-faces had only just found out the Valley was there, and . . .'

'Sheep-faces?' said Benayu. 'They've got to be the same as the Pirates, haven't they?'

'It sounds like it,' said Fodaro. 'I want to know more about this ring, as well as anything you can tell me about the destruction of the Watchers. I've heard rumours about that, as a matter of fact, but I've never heard about anything like the ring, not even a rumour. But you tell us about your Sheep-faces first. This may be more immediately important. What do these airboats look like?'

'I've drawn you one,' said Saranja.

She'd been scratching away at her picture all the time she'd been talking. They studied it while she told them about the Sheep-faces.

'Yes, they're the Pirates all right,' said Benayu. 'That explains a lot. I wonder if even the Watchers know all that.'

'Watchers!' said Maja. 'But Faheel—'

'Destroyed the ones he had originally set up, just as Saranja has told us? Indeed he did. But magic is wild, dangerous stuff. All sorts of evils follow its uncontrolled use. The Ropemaker was forced to set up some kind of a system to replace the Watchers. He built in safeguards and for a while it worked well enough, but then he vanished, no one knows where, and over the centuries his system became perverted, just as Faheel's had done, though in a different manner, and then people started to call them the Watchers again . . .'

'That's what you were worried about,' said Saranja, 'that they might have seen us arrive on Rocky?'

'Yes, but if they had they would have been here by

61

now, I think. It depends how much of the magical impulse Jex managed to absorb. That's one of the things he does.

'Where were we? The Pirates. Well, some of our coastal cities have been subjected to raids by a swarm of Pirates using airborne craft, Saranja. That's all anyone has been officially told. We haven't been told, for instance, how widespread these attacks have been, nor that as well as the usual destruction and looting that Pirates have historically gone in for, these ones seem also interested in suborning or kidnapping magicians for some purpose of their own. I needed Jex to tell me that. It's been going on for thirty-odd years now, and emergency measures are in place. These include the central licensing and conscription of first- and second-level magicians, who have hitherto only required local licensing, in order to defend the Empire – in fact a complete crackdown on all unauthorized magic, which is something the Watchers have long been waiting to put in place, and will now have widespread popular backing in a national emergency. That's why Benayu and I are here – not just to escape the conscription, but to find a means to resist it, and in the end, perhaps to overturn the whole system of Watchers.

'Furthermore the Ropemaker has disappeared, just as Faheel did, and now here you come like your ancestor Tilja to find him, and help him to destroy the Watchers and find his successor and restore the world to its natural order for another twenty generations.'

He seemed to have relaxed enough to be amused by the notion, and Saranja's uncooperative glare.

'Where do the Pirates fit in with all that?' said Benayu.

'I have no idea. Perhaps Jex will tell us when he wakes and is fully back here.'

'Your friend's just coming round, Saranja,' said Benayu. 'I'll get you some clean bandages. There's something nasty in that cut still, under a sort of flap near the top on the left.'

Maja looked across to where Ribek lay by the stream. As far as she could see he hadn't moved but now he yawned and stretched contentedly and sat up.

'I'll look,' said Saranja as she rose.

By the time Benayu returned with the bandages Ribek was on his back again, his eyes closed, his face grey-white and covered with sweat. Saranja was on her knees beside him gently using her thumbs to press the wound closed. Blood dribbled down his calf.

'Thanks,' she said, without looking up. 'Cut me a few small squares for swabs, will you, Maja, then a soft pad, and then the longest strip you can make, about a hand's breadth wide, and slit the end a foot or so down the middle. That was hell for Ribek, but worth it. I think I got all of the muck out, but the bitter-bark will take care of anything I've missed. He'd be in a fever without. Now, tip a bit of it on to the squares and squeeze them out and hand them to me one at a time. The same with the pad, and then while you're waiting roll up the bandage, starting with the slit end.'

She settled to work. Benayu went back to Fodaro and they started talking earnestly together. Maja was holding the pad ready for Saranja to take when everything changed. She cried aloud and was almost knocked sideways as the familiar quiver trembled across the mountainside. Rocky neighed as if facing an enemy, the sheep scattered again, bleating, and the dog raced to bring them back. By the time she recovered, Benayu and Fodaro were standing, their faces tense as they stared out towards the south-east. Almost at once they fell into what looked like a furious argument, all the fury on Benayu's part, Fodaro grim and anxious.

'Any idea what this is about?' said Ribek. 'Did they tell you anything while I was asleep, Saranja?'

'Lots, but not about this. But whatever it is, it's urgent. These Watcher people are coming, or something. Let's get this done with. Bend your knee, if you can. Now put your hands where mine are. Right. Now . . .'

They had finished, and Ribek was standing shakily, leaning on Saranja's shoulder, when Benayu came hurrying back. His face was working, and at first he could barely speak for grief and anger.

'You've . . . you've got to go,' he said. 'Can't explain. No time. Straight down. See that tall pine at the bottom? Bit to the right of that, there's a track. Down there till you come to the drove road. Right there. Three miles on, there's a bridge with a village on the other side. Wait in the trees till you're sure there's no one about and then hide under the bridge. I'm bringing the sheep. When you hear the sheep-bell coming, one of you come out and wait in the trees with Maja. I'll tell you what to do next. If I don't come, wait till it's almost dark, then Maja must hold Jex in her hand, and Saranja hold her feathers just in front of him and breathe gently across them into his face. With luck he'll wake up. If he does, do whatever

64

he says. If he doesn't, don't try to help by saying the name. Just do whatever you think best. Here, Maja. Hang him round your neck, and sleep with him under your pillow. He may be able to shield you a bit.'

Before Maja had time to look at what he'd given her, he had turned and was whistling to the dog.

It was a small amulet of some pale mottled stone, remarkably heavy for its size, carved to the shape of a squat lizard. There was a ring on its spine with a chain through it, allowing her to hang it round her neck.

'I'll help Saranja saddle Rocky,' said Ribek. 'See what you can find by way of food, Maja.'

She hurried back towards the cedar, where she found Fodaro stooped over Saranja's drawing of the airboat with a twig in his hand, apparently scratching what looked like magical symbols above it.

'Is it all right if I take the basket?' she said. 'Aren't you coming with us?'

'No. Join you when I can. Tell your friends to look after the boy. He matters, not only to me. Don't let them hang around. I want you well along the drove road before anything happens.'

'We're just going. Thanks for the food, and good luck.'

Fodaro grunted, but didn't look up.

Saranja was helping Ribek up into the saddle by the time she reached them.

'Well done,' she said. 'Pack it into that saddlebag . . . Right. Up you go too.'

Maja grabbed hold of Rocky's mane as Saranja took the bridle and started down the slope at a steady jogtrot.

65

Halfway to the trees they passed Benayu and the dog, herding their flock in front of them. The clank of the bellwether's bell seemed extraordinarily loud in the oppressive silence. Benayu's face was expressionless. He gave no sign that he'd seen them go by.

Chapter 3

I T WAS COOL beneath the bridge. Reflections from
the late afternoon sunlight rippled across the
masonry of the arch above them. The river was low
after a long summer. Rocky stood midstream, swishing
his tail at flies. The three humans rested on boulders that
winter floods had piled against the buttress, Saranja
brooding, Ribek listlessly trailing his fingers in the current, and Maja quietly watching them. There was magic
coming from both of them, she realized. Ribek was just
listening to the water again, but Saranja was different. It
was the same thing she'd noticed earlier on – not something she was doing, something that was being done to
her. Perhaps it was the same thing Fodaro had started to
ask about, a bit of magic she'd found among the war-
lords. But she hadn't told them anything about it. That
wasn't like her.

'There's a strange hawk over the woods,' said Ribek
suddenly. 'It wasn't there this morning.'

'Nor were we,' said Saranja. 'How . . . ? Oh, the river told . . .'

Maja didn't hear the rest of it. Something was happening to her, a sudden intense unease of the spirit, like nausea in the body, not slowly infecting her but suddenly there, a distortion of her place and balance in the world. She had to clutch at the stonework of the bridge or she'd have toppled sideways.

Saranja's voice.

'Maja! What's up? That was the sheep-bell. Come along. Are you all right?'

'I think the Watchers have come. Back at the pasture. I didn't feel them coming. They were just there.'

'Right. Let's get on with it.'

Maja mastered herself and rose.

The small flock streamed by, bewildered by the speed they were being forced to go, with the dog urging the bellwether along in front and Benayu following at the rear, occasionally whacking a rump with his staff. Saranja stepped out of the trees just as the last rank reached her. Maja followed. Benayu whistled and the dog brought the flock to a halt. He looked no less grim than before, but more in control of himself.

'Maja thinks the Watchers have reached the pasture,' she said.

'I know,' said Benayu tonelessly. 'Two of them. If he gets it wrong we've got about ten minutes – maybe a bit more.'

'Ribek says there's a strange hawk over the hillside. The river told him.'

68

'Wasn't there before I got under the trees, but from now on . . . One of them will be looking through its eyes. So you can't take the horse through the village – stand out like a sore thumb. I should look all right, with the sheep, this time of year. You're going to have to work your way round under the trees. Up the river till you get to the old ford. Not far. Then . . .'

His face worked. He waited, eyes closed, until he had mastered himself, and turned to Maja.

'You know when Saranja took the wings off your horse, what you felt then? There'll be something like that. Stronger, probably. It'll mean Fodaro's trying to tackle the Watchers back at our pasturage. The hawk will be looking at that. You should be able to slip across the river then. After that, there's a track down from the ford to the top of the drove pasture. I'll know you're there and come to find you.'

'All right. And good luck, Benayu.'

'Not me who needs it.'

He turned away and whistled to the dog to move on.

The moment came in two waves, the first like a silent thunderclap, electric with horror and power, flinging Maja to the ground. She heard Rocky's squeal of panic, but it had hardly begun before the second wave drowned it, an immense booming bellow, far louder than any thunder, a shuddering of the physical earth . . . And then the wind. She was already flat on her face but that was no shelter at all. It tore at her clothing, yanked at her hair, was about to pick her up and blast her away like a blown leaf when Ribek tumbled across her and pinned her down.

And then it was gone. Silence. No, not silence, because even in silence your ears are awake, listening for sound. There was a blankness, a deadness, where that sense of listening should have been.

She hadn't heard the wind.

By the time she understood what had happened to her Ribek had rolled himself off her and was helping her up. His lips moved. Nothing.

'I've gone deaf,' she said, and pointed to her ears. He nodded and tapped his chest.

Me too.

Saranja was gone, and Rocky, but Saranja's shoulder pack was lying on the ground. Maya pointed at it.

'Where is she?' she mouthed.

Ribek pointed across the stream.

'Roc-ky bol-ted,' he said, mouthing it the same way, so that she could read his lips.

He lifted up the pack but she took it from him and in that awful non-sound helped him across the ford. Beyond that they followed a well-marked track, picking their way past fallen trees. He was leaning heavily on her shoulder by the time Saranja met them, leading Rocky, foam-flecked and heaving, though she herself was barely panting.

She pointed to her ears and Maja and Ribek made the me-too gesture. She nodded and said something, pointing at Rocky, then at a gash in a foreleg, then showing them a ring on his harness, slipping it over her thumb and pointing at the wreckage of branches past which

70

they'd just been scrambling. Rocky had snagged the ring on a broken branch and got stuck till she'd come up. She spoke again, finishing with a nod and a shrug. *Could be worse. He'll be all right.* Grimly they moved on together.

Benayu came up the track to meet them with Sponge at his heels. His face was as grey and haggard as an old man's. He had clearly been weeping. Ribek moved to put an arm round his shoulders, but he shrugged himself free and started to say something.

'We can't hear you,' said Maja, automatically.

No doubt they'd all spoken together, but Benayu held up a hand, *wait*, then moved along the line, pausing briefly in front of each of them to reach forward, touch both ears and murmur something with scarcely moving lips. Saranja. Rocky. Ribek. Maja. Swiftly but gently, hearing returned, the crash of a falling tree, shouts and screams from the village below. Acrid smoke reeked in the wind – something down there must have caught fire.

'Won't the Watchers have felt that?' said Saranja.

'They're gone,' said Benayu in a choking voice. 'Give me your right hands.'

He placed their three hands together and closed his own round them, above and below. His voice steadied, becoming harsh and slow.

'I will help you to find the Ropemaker,' he said. 'I promise you this, because I promised Fodaro, but not for his reasons, not for yours. I will do it so that I can take vengeance on the Watchers. I will destroy them, every man and woman of them, because they destroyed him. That is the only thing that matters. If I have to destroy the whole Empire, or give it over to the Pirates, if magic vanishes from the world, let it happen, so long as the Watchers are destroyed and vanish too.'

'I understand,' said Ribek, not simply humouring or comforting, but instantly accepting the impossible vow as sane and serious. Saranja only grunted sympathetically. She knew what it was like to hate. Maja felt differently again. Until now Benayu had been for her and the other two little more than a chance-met stranger, friendly and helpful, whom she expected to thank and say goodbye to soon, and never to see again. Now she and Ribek and Saranja and Benayu were linked together, and were going to have to learn to live and endure with each other in friendship and trust for as long as their task demanded.

'We'll help you if we can,' said Saranja.

They stood together for a while in silence, with the smashed woods all around them, as if allowing their oath to root itself steadfastly into the soil of their purpose, until Ribek seemed to grow restless and began to limp to and fro, studying the sky between the remaining branches.

'I think the hawk's pushed off,' he said. 'Or been done for along with the Watchers.'

Benayu hauled himself out of the dream of vengeance.

'That makes things easier,' he said, in a quiet, toneless voice. 'Well, we've got a choice. The obvious thing is to get as far away from here as we can before the Watchers . . . No, forget it. They won't send more Watchers, not at once, in case the same thing happens to them. They'll try and find out from a distance. Or they'll send someone they can afford to lose. So we've got a bit of time . . .'

'Ribek's got to rest his leg,' said Saranja. 'He isn't up to anything more today.'

'All right,' said Benayu. 'I left the sheep with Sponge down at the drove pasture. They'll give us a reason for being there. We'd be more conspicuous sleeping out in the open, anyway, and some of the huts haven't been smashed up. No one else is using it.

'And we've got to have something to eat. The village was pretty smashed up too when I came through, but there's a farmer just below it who's a bit further from the blast, so he should be all right. I'll go straight down and see him and get him to come up and look at the sheep in the morning. If I let him have a couple for himself he'll look after the rest while I'm away. With luck he'll sell me something for supper.'

'Any chance of some decent fodder for Rocky?' said Saranja. 'He'll want more than hay. I'll bring him with you so that he can carry it back.'

'I'll ask the farmer. I don't want to do any more magic than I have to. It's a nuisance screening things and then getting rid of the traces.'

Two of the five drove huts had been blasted flat. The pasture sloped away below them, with the village on their left and its fields spreading on down the hill. Some of the houses had lost roofs and chimneys. Beyond the fields more woods, much less shattered, reached into the distance, and further off still the snow-topped peaks through which Rocky had carried his riders that morning now glistened untroubled under the setting sun. He nosed and snuffled contentedly into the feed that Benayu had bought from the farmer, while the humans sat, or in Ribek's case lay, round the small fire Saranja had built. She and Maja were roasting gobbets of liver on pointed sticks and Ribek, flat on his back but looking a bit better now, chewed happily on his, but Benayu remained silent and hunched, gazing into the fire while he nibbled abstractedly at a morsel Saranja had bullied him into accepting.

At last he shook himself into the here and now, stuffed what was left of the liver into his mouth, chewed purposefully at it until he could swallow it, drank a mouthful of water and spoke in a low, anxious voice.

'I don't understand it,' he said. 'There's a colossal explosion of magic, two of the Watchers get wiped out, and they still haven't sent anyone to find out what happened.'

'Would we know?' said Saranja.

'I would if it was more Watchers,' said Maja. 'I didn't feel them coming. They were suddenly there, just before the explosion. They were horrible.'

'I didn't feel them either,' said Benayu. 'We had a system – it worked back up on the hillside, when we first realized they were coming. They must have picked that up and cancelled it somehow. Perhaps that's what took them so long . . . Anyway, it's going to be dark soon. We'd better get the fire out.'

'I'll do that,' said Maja, and began carefully to rake it apart.

74

'What did happen?' said Saranja, but Benayu shook his head.

'I'm afraid I can't tell you,' he said wearily. 'I'm not trying to be all mysterious about it because I'm a magician, but a lot of it's stuff that's dangerous to know. Really dangerous. Not just dangerous to you, dangerous to everybody – everybody in the Empire, anyway. If the Watchers get hold of you they won't just kill you. They'll take you apart, find out everything about you, all you've ever done, all you know. And if they find out some of the stuff Fodaro discovered they'll become even more powerful than they are now – far more – and there'd be nothing they can't do, and nothing to stop them doing it.

'That's why Fodaro died. He didn't do it for our sake. He took two of the Watchers with him for our sake, to help us get away. But he died for the whole world's sake so that they couldn't find out what he knew.

'But I'll tell you as much as I can because . . . well, I suppose because I've got to talk to you about Fodaro. He was a very good man – too good to be a good magician, really. He was only an ordinary third-level magician, but he was a pretty good scholar. He knew a lot more than he could do, he used to say. And on top of that he was a genius.

'Mathematics was his thing. And astronomy, I suppose. I built that pool back there for him. He told me what he wanted but he couldn't do it himself, so I did it. It was his way of looking at the stars.

'But for him the astronomy was only part of the mathematics. He said that if you want to find the how

75

and why of anything you have to measure everything you can about it so that you can put it into numbers, and then you work out how the numbers fit and put that into an equation, and then you use the equation to understand the real world and do things in it. You can get an equation that's almost right, and it'll work well enough until you run into something that doesn't fit. Then you either have to change your equation or start all over again.

'Magic is stuff that oughtn't to fit in the real world . . .'

'I've always said it was nonsense,' said Saranja.

'Yes, but somehow it works,' said Benayu. 'Fodaro wanted to find the equations that would tell him why. I've gone to bed leaving him sitting by the fire, thinking stuff out, and woken up and seen him still there, with his eyes open and the firelight glinting off them, and he's still been there in the morning, wide awake but almost too stiff to move.

'In the end he came up with three equations for the how and why of magic. I know them by heart and I can use them, but I don't really understand them. I can't make a picture in my head of what they're doing when they're working. And I certainly don't understand how he came up with them. I don't think anyone else could have done it, not even by magic. That's why it's safe to tell you about him.

'But I can't tell you much more about Jex. If the Watchers ever found out that he and his kind exist it'd be a disaster for them, but you already know that he's there so it can't be helped. I suppose you'd better know that he feeds on magic. That's why he was useful to us. He could help mop up the overflow of whatever we were doing and stop it getting out to the Watchers. And he can protect Maja a bit now by mopping up some of the heavy stuff before it reaches her. But a sudden overdose of magic knocks him sideways, so he's developed a sort of warning mechanism that can tell him when something like that is coming his way so that he can be ready for it. That's useful too.'

'You were scared when we came,' said Maja. 'Not just you. The whole hillside. Everything.'

'A winged horse is big magic, far bigger than anything we'd been doing. That's scary in itself. But Jex had sensed you coming and was ready for it and managed to absorb it somehow. What he wasn't ready for was Saranja suddenly saying the Ropemaker's name. That took him completely by surprise and knocked him out. I think he might have died if Fodaro hadn't thought of getting Saranja to do that stuff with the feathers.'

'Now he's in a sort of coma. He's still absorbing a little of whatever magic is going on around him. He can't help it, any more than you can help breathing, so he's giving Maja a bit of protection, but he can't do anything extra to shield us or warn us.

'That's why we were worried sick. Fodaro and me. Jex might have absorbed some of the signal before he passed out, but he couldn't possibly have coped with all of it. And Rocky was still there, completely unshielded, far more than I could possibly screen, let alone in a hurry. But when Saranja took Rocky's wings off, the signal from him dropped almost to zero, and nothing happened and nothing happened, and we thought we'd got away with it.

'And then, suddenly, the Watchers were coming after all. We'd always known it might happen, so we'd set up a system, nothing to do with Jex, a sort of maze with a separate warning system to slow them down and give us a bit of time. It wasn't so we could run or hide – that doesn't work with them. They'll find you in the end. The only hope was to use the equations to take them by surprise with something that they hadn't got any defences against. And that fitted in with something else that mattered even more than we did, something about that particular bit of hillside – can't tell you what – it was all to do with Fodaro's equations too – and it would be a disaster if the Watchers found out about it. So the only thing to do was to destroy it. Of course we didn't want to, not if we could possibly help it, but it wasn't something you could arrange at the last minute, so we'd already got it ready to go, just in case.

'Fodaro worked out how to do it and I set it up. It was an extremely delicate balance. Two . . .'

He stopped and stared at his hands. In an unconscious gesture he'd raised them in front of his chest and was holding them, stretched flat and almost touching, palm to palm. Deliberately he folded them together and laid them in his lap.

'No, that's telling you too much,' he said in the same listless, weary voice. 'Anyway, if whoever did it got it dead right, there'd be an explosion, and in the instant before it happened he'd get out. A scrap too little, and it wouldn't happen at all. A scrap too much, and . . . well, you felt what happened. But if he got it right, the Watchers, or whoever had come for us, wouldn't be ready for it. It wouldn't be any sort of magic they'd ever run up against, and that would be two fewer Watchers in the world, and our traces completely covered.

'I think I could have done it. I was pretty sure he couldn't. That's what we were rowing about. Oh, blood, I wish I hadn't had to leave him like that. He didn't try to pretend what he was going to do was a certainty, but he said if I stayed to help him they'd get us both, and that would be his whole life wasted, but if I got away in time it wouldn't. He said that now you'd come it didn't really matter what happened to him, but I had to get away because this was what I had been born for. This was the moment they should all have waited for.'

'Who's *they*?' said Ribek.

'The Andarit. The Free Great Magicians. When the Watchers decided to take complete control they began by picking off the other fifth-level magicians one by one, sucking them in or just destroying them, until the ones who were left realized what was happening and decided to band together and try to fight them. They called themselves the Andarit.

'My parents were two of them. I never knew them. They didn't love each other or anything – magicians don't do that – but they wanted a child to carry on the fight if the Watchers got them. If I was any good, of course. They couldn't even use magic to make sure. It had to be a clean break so the Watchers couldn't trace me. They just had to take the chance.'

'That makes two of us,' muttered Saranja.

Benayu frowned at her, not understanding.

'Not born to be loved,' explained Ribek. 'Her mother wanted a daughter who could hear what the cedars were saying.'

'Oh, I don't blame them for not loving me, you know. It wasn't that they didn't want to. They *couldn't* have. We all have our own – anima, the books call it. It means soul, spiritual essence, inner self, something like that. It's the place where we keep our really important feelings, all the stuff that really matters to us. Even hedge magic is bad for it, if you do it all the time, and a lot of serious, powerful magic eats it away until you stop being human.

'There are just a very few, like the ones in your story – Asarta and Faheel and the Ropemaker – whose anima is strong enough to stand it. But almost all serious magicians have to find a safe place to keep their anima, utterly separate from themselves, out of their reach until the time comes for them to put their magic aside and become human again.

'That's why my father and my mother couldn't love me. Magicians can have feelings – spite, anger, envy, pity even – but they're different, cold, so that the magician can control the feeling and use its power. But there's no such thing as cold love. It doesn't make sense.

'My parents weren't bad people. They knew what was right, and tried to do it, and died for it in the end. But all in a cold way. They died because they knew what the Watchers would do to them if they were caught alive. They booby-trapped every step of the way as they went, in case anyone tried to follow them and bring them back. Yes, they were very powerful magicians, but all the magic in the world couldn't make them love me.

'Fodaro didn't want me to be like that. At first he told them he wouldn't help them unless they could think of a way round it. They said it couldn't be done, it was a sort of all-or-nothing thing. How can your anima be a living part of you, right at your centre, and at the same time utterly separate? But there are things in mathematics a bit like that – impossible numbers that actually work – so Fodaro decided he'd look after me until I was old enough to choose for myself. And then he found a place in the sheep pasture, and there the answer was, waiting for him in the equations.

'There's a lot more to the equations than that, and the one great thing we've got going for us is that the Watchers don't know any of it, and it's going to be too late for them when they find out. Yes, by all the Powers and Levels, they'll find out!'

'What a load to carry at your age!' said Saranja. 'It makes my kicking and screaming about having to take on Woodbourne and the stupid unicorns look pretty petty. Was Fodaro really your uncle? Why wasn't he in with the others?'

'He wasn't good enough. He was my father's brother, but he was just an ordinary third-level magician because he couldn't make the shift. Partly couldn't, partly didn't want to.'

'These levels,' said Ribek, 'they're real? I mean, we do a thing called kick-boxing in the Valley and we have

81

grades for that, but that depends on how many bouts you've won and who you've beaten and so on.'

'They're only sort-of real. That's one of the big things Fodaro found out. It's in his equations. But even he couldn't actually imagine what the real thing is like, the way you can imagine, well, levels, for instance – something like storeys in a building you can go up and downstairs between. He said his mind wasn't the right shape. Nobody's is.

'So magicians have always talked about levels, because that's what it feels like. You know at once when you make a shift, because you have to change yourself to do it. It's like learning to breathe a different kind of air. Third to fourth is the hardest. That's like learning to breathe water, Fodaro said. He never made it, though he knew what made it so difficult. I haven't tried – too much of a risk – I don't know enough – but I don't think it will be a problem for me.

'That whole old theory of magic is one of those almost-fit things. It's worked well enough for centuries and everyone thought it was right. But then Fodaro found the place in the pasture, and looked at some very faraway stars in the pool I built him, and found things that didn't fit. So he went back to the beginning and started again.

'That's all I'm going to tell you about that. I want to talk about Fodaro himself.

'Mostly I don't even think about my parents. Fodaro was the only person I've ever had to love. Him and Sponge –' he nodded towards the dog, half drowsing as he guarded the sheep '– and Jex, I suppose, but you can't really love him – he's too different.

'No, Fodaro was the only one, really. He was my father and my mother and everyone else. My parents gave me to him almost as soon as I was born – as soon as they were sure I had the gifts in me. They chose him because the Watchers were only interested in fourth- and fifth-level magicians, those days, and he took me away and they never saw me again. They wanted as clean a break as they could make.

'He wanted that too, but not for the same reason. Or at least not mainly. He was as keen as they were to stop the Watchers controlling everything, and as far as he could he wanted to help me do it. But until then he wanted me to grow up with someone who really loved me, someone I could love back. And that's what he gave me.

'He hired a wet nurse to feed me when I was tiny, but he did everything else, fed me and dressed me, played with me and carried me around in a pouch on his chest and sang me to sleep and nursed me when I was ill. He never used magic to make me better, only sometimes to find out what medicines to give me, but he never let magic touch me until I began to do it for myself.

'Before I could walk or talk I started making things come to me if they looked interesting. One day, when I'd just learnt to crawl, he left me with a neighbour while he went to market. Her bitch had a new litter. He came back to find that my cot was empty, and the neighbour was having hysterics, and there was an extra puppy sucking at the bitch's teats.

'All that low-level stuff – stuff on the surface of things – it's never been any problem for me. Some ways it's been too easy. If you find everything easy – if you never have to puzzle anything out – then you never have to think how anything connects, because it doesn't, up in the easy levels. That happens way down, at deeper and deeper levels, as the connections on the level above connect with each other. If you wanted to change the whole world you'd have to go right down to the single root of everything, below the fifth and below the sixth to where the Tree of the World grows all alone, that carries the stars on the tips of its branches, and the clouds, and the singing birds, and the tears of humankind.

'It isn't really like that of course, it's just how it feels, like the layers of rock in the cliff or breathing a different kind of air. The last bit, about the World Tree, comes from a poem Fodaro gave me to learn . . .'

He paused and looked up, tense and watchful.

'There's someone at the cottage,' he said. 'He's trying to open the locks. So he's not a Watcher – they'd have no problem. There – he's done it, he thinks. So he's a magician – third level at a guess. There's no one that good round here . . . Wait. Ah, now get out of that, you bastard . . .'

'You don't think he just happened along?' said Ribek.

'Didn't feel like it. He'd come in a hurry. I think the Watchers didn't want to lose two more of themselves, so they sent somebody they could spare. We should be all right for tonight – I'll keep an eye on him. I'll take the sheep down to the farmer first thing, and then we'd better be on our way.'

84

'Do you know where we're going?' said Maja.

'Away from here, for a start,' said Benayu. 'As far and as fast as possible without using magic. That means south. After that we're going to start looking for this Ropemaker of yours, though I've no idea how or where. Jex might know, but he can't tell us.'

'He'll be somewhere in the Empire, won't he?' said Saranja. 'That must mean south too.'

'Are we going to have enough money?' said Ribek. 'We haven't got any. We don't use Empire money in the Valley, and in the story there were endless bribes to pay wherever you went. Or have things changed?'

'No, of course not. It's always been like that. Fodaro says – used to say – the Watchers are all for it, because it means people's lives are one long struggle against corrupt officials and they don't have time to worry about what the Watchers are up to. I've brought all the money we had in the cottage. I hope that'll get us to one of the safe places Fodaro told me about, and there'll be people there who'll give us money. If not I'll have to use magic. It's too dangerous to make or fetch money, because any good magician can smell that at once, and it's a nasty death if you're found with any you got that way, but I should be able to fetch one or two things we can sell.'

'I may have something,' said Saranja, beginning to fish under the coarse, high-necked blouse a farmer's wife had given her on her way to Woodbourne. 'My war-lord was in Council when his brother attacked. He liked to have me there, sitting on a stool by his knee, wearing a lot of his jewellery and precious little else, because I was

85

the mother of his sons. It was a way of showing how rich and powerful he was. This was one of his prize possessions. It's a sort of all-purpose amulet. It's famous. It's even got a name, Zald-im-Zald. It didn't really belong to him, or anyone else. He'd looted it from another war-lord, who'd looted it from somewhere else, and so on.

'Anyway, there I was, sitting on that stupid stool and smiling away till my face ached, when all of a sudden the castle was full of his brother's soldiers. There hadn't been any warning. Somebody must have betrayed him and opened the gates. Everyone was rushing around screaming. Five years I'd been longing for something like this to happen and worked out exactly what I was going to do if it did. I ran down to one of the laundry rooms and put some clothes on over what I was wearing and ran on to the kitchens. Nobody bothered me – they were all eating and drinking themselves stupid, but I grabbed a sack of scraps and I was out through an unused sewer pipe I'd found and well into the desert before I remembered I was still wearing Zald-im-Zald. We'll have to take it apart and sell it stone by stone, of course. We'd never find anyone who could pay for the whole thing. It isn't as if I'd stolen it, at least no more than my war-lord had, and I reckoned he owed me. Three times over he owed me, three times over. Once for myself and once for each of my sons. I was never even allowed to nurse them, you know. They were brought up by eunuchs in another part of the palace. They weren't even told I was their mother. Oh, it's mine all right.'

While she was speaking she'd carefully eased out from under her blouse, and laid across it, a prodigious ornament, far more than a necklace or pendant, a kind of chest-piece the size of a child's face. At its centre was an oval of brown-gold amber, clear as a drop of liquid but filled with inward fire from the refracted and reflected sunset. This was circled by faceted red gems, each the size of a man's thumbnail, and out from these fanned sprays of smaller jewels, dark gold and then paler and then almost colourless, all set into a lacework of gold, stiff enough to hold its shape but flexing to follow the contours of the flesh beneath.

'Perhaps you'd better have a look at it, Benayu,' she said. 'It's supposed to be full of powers, but everyone's forgotten what they are.'

He leaned forward, held his hand for a moment above the ornament, then carefully withdrew it and sat staring at it, breathing deeply. To Maja he seemed suddenly more involved, more alive, than at any time since he'd sworn his oath in the woods above the sheep pastures.

'Well,' he said, 'it's pretty well dormant at the moment, apart from one little stone. Just as well. If it was all activated it would send out a signal strong as a beacon. And there's a curse on anyone who tries to question it or take it apart. I think I can deal with that, but you'd better not be wearing it while I'm at it.'

Saranja slipped the gold chain over her head and handed the ornament to him, but as she let go of the chain the strange vague magical feeling that Maja had all along sensed coming from her suddenly ceased. In the same instant Saranja collapsed forward, almost into the embers of the fire. Maja jumped to her feet and helped Benayu haul her clear and turn her over. She seemed to be fast asleep, her face calm, her breathing slow and heavy. Benayu felt her pulse and nodded.

'Nothing we can do,' he said and returned to the jewel. 'It'll be that active stone. This one. It makes the wearer tireless. Only you pay for it after. It must have been made to switch itself on when the wearer starts to get exhausted. How long ago was that?'

'Five days in the desert, she said,' replied Ribek, reaching for her wrist from where he lay. 'And at least four since. She may have taken it off at night. I didn't see.'

'And she's still breathing? It ought to have killed her. How's her pulse?'

'Not bad. Very slow, but fairly strong.'

'All right. Just leave her there for the moment while I close it down,' said Benayu.

He knelt beside Saranja's body and laid the jewel across her chest. Maja sensed a blip of power suddenly woken, and Saranja began to stir. Supporting her left hand with his right, with his other hand Benayu moved the tip of its middle finger in gentle circles over one of the jewels, three times one way and then three times the other. Maja could feel a second blip as the power subsided and Saranja returned to sleep.

'That's the best we can do,' he said, rising. 'Nothing's going to wake her till she's ready, and that won't be for a day or two yet, at a guess.'

He took Saranja's shoulders and Maja her feet and between them they dragged her into the nearest hut, laid her on sheepskins on one of the rough bunks and covered her with a blanket. When they came out Benayu picked up the jewel, walked a couple of paces down the slope and laid it at his feet. Maja watched him stretch out and turn slowly, taut with concentration, pointing in succession at three boulders spread across the slope, then at the forest edge around and behind the huts, and back to the first hut. A barely visible flicker of light followed his movement and she could feel the rich, humming vibrations of magic as it leaped from mark to mark. Satisfied, he settled down and crouched over Zald-im-Zald, but then glanced up at her.

'That's enough of a screen, I hope,' he said. 'Anyway, it's as much as I can manage. The Watchers have got a Seeing Tower in Talakh. They're bound to be looking this way. There's too much hedge magic going on for them to have noticed what I was doing to Zald just now, but dealing with the whole thing's going to be bigger stuff. Why don't you go out beyond the screen, Maja, and give me a shout if any of it gets through? Sponge can go with you in case of trouble. Just call him. That's all right, boy. Go and keep an eye on her.'

Maja couldn't feel the screen at all until she reached it. Then there was a slight extra tingle as she passed through it. She could feel it stretching from point to point like dew-beaded spiderwebs slung between bushes on an autumn morning. Beyond it nothing.

Without Sponge beside her it would have been scary out there on the edge of the strange, deep-shadowed woods. She tangled her fingers into his fur and waved to Benayu that she was ready. He crouched over the jewel again. Ribek had raised himself on to his elbow to watch him.

For some while he didn't seem to be doing anything except stare at the jewel. At one point his body tensed, but then he relaxed and continued his inspection. After about five minutes he raised his right hand, extended his forefinger, and with the fingertip held slightly above them started to trace the pattern of the jewels, working from the outer edges inwards. In the gathering dusk each stone glimmered or twinkled with its natural light as the finger passed above it, and even at this distance she could see the glow of it flicker off Ribek's face, as though a fiery spark was running from jewel to jewel. Faintly she could feel the web of Benayu's screen flex and quiver as it responded to the passing shocks of magic. At last he rose and waved to her to return. When she reached him, he was trembling slightly, and there were beads of sweat on his upper lip.

'I think it was all right,' she said. 'I could feel something happening, but only just. I wouldn't have if I'd been further away.'

'Trickier than I thought,' he said. 'There was one nasty moment. I knew it was probably booby-trapped, because Fodaro had warned me about that. When we took the sheep to market in Mord he used to look the stalls over for amulets and charms, and buy anything he thought might be useful. Sometimes the dealers had no idea what they were for, and when we got home we'd find out and sell them on or give them to the other shepherds. Anyway, I was just starting to disarm the trap when I realized it was a bit simple for a thing like Zald-im-Zald, and I found the trap itself was booby-trapped. That was a tricky one.

'You know, it's a really amazing object. I don't think we should break it up completely – I don't know if we could, safely. Most of the little stones round the outside are just ornaments, and we could take a few of those, perhaps, and get somebody to replace them later. But look. This is the one that kept Saranja going. These two are healers, for burns and wounds. We can try the wound one on your leg in a moment, Ribek. This is something very strange, very old. I don't dare meddle with it in case it's something I can't screen. These two are finders – you give one to the person you want to keep track of, or hide it on them if you don't want them to know, and you can always find them. This one will stop you getting fever. And so on. I don't think this one's got any powers of its own, but kings and heroes have been killed for it again and again, and that cranks up the power of all the others. And these are locks. They're to guard the amber in the middle and keep the power in it sleeping. I don't dare touch that either, but it must be something really big, fifth level, at least – sixth, even. You can do all sorts of things with amber. It comes from the far north, from the top of the world. They do a different kind of magic there.

'Now let's see what we can do about Ribek's wound. You want to try, Maja? This one here. Middle finger of your left hand, three turns to the left and three to the right to activate it, and the same to put it to rest. They all open pretty much the same way, these basic charms.'

'You don't need Saranja's own hand?' said Ribek.

'You would for most of them. She's been wearing Zald long enough for it to have attached itself specifically to her, but that wouldn't make sense with a woundsain. It draws its healing power from the person who's holding it, so you can't use it on yourself. Trouble, Maja?'

Maja had reached unsuspecting towards Zald-im-Zald. The stone he'd shown her seemed not much different from any of the others, a clear, pinkish gold about the size of her fingernail. She could sense the sleeping power of the whole great object, but it didn't trouble her. Then, just before her finger touched the surface, something had seemed to leap across the gap, and instinctively she'd snatched her hand away.

'It's all right,' she said. 'It was just a surprise. It didn't hurt.'

This time she managed not to flinch, though the buzzy sensation continued as she circled her fingertip over the surface of the jewel, and ceased only when she picked it out of its setting and cradled it in her palm. Now all she could feel was the quiet flow of something passing from her to it.

She waited while Ribek unwound the bloodstained cloths from his leg, carefully cutting them free with his knifepoint where they had stuck to the flesh. The wound, when he reached it, looked perhaps marginally better than it had when Saranja had dressed it a few hours back, but was still oozing blood and pus.

'Do I just touch the place with it, and it's well again?' said Maja. 'It feels . . . oh . . . gentler than that.'

Benayu didn't answer, so she looked up and saw that

he was no longer watching, but leaning back against the wall of the hut and gazing out over the darkened distances.

'Start with an easy bit and see what happens,' suggested Ribek.

She experimented, and saw the edges of a minor laceration gradually close together as she stroked the stone along it until the exposed flesh was covered with soft, pinkish, new-healed skin.

Behind her Benayu gave a deep and lonely sigh and shuddered himself back into the world.

'We'll have to go through Mord,' he said. 'It's the only road south. And there's a woman in the market there who mostly deals in charms and stuff, but she does jewels as a sideline. We can sell something out of Zald to her. I really don't want to sell any more of the flock than I have to. It depends how long I'm away, and whether I've got any money when I come back. If I haven't, and I'm gone for months and months, he'll have to keep the lot, and I'll start again the way Fodaro did, curing the shepherds' flocks and making amulets and charms that actually work.

'I really love shepherding. They're a separate tribe, you know, the shepherds all along these mountains, with their own language and their own customs. They won't let anyone else join them or use their pastures. They're very proud and fierce, the women as well as the men. When Fodaro first brought me here – I was only two then – they had an infectious gum-rot spreading through their flocks along the whole range, and he cured it for them and spent all one summer cleaning the snails that carried it out of their pastures, so they let him stay and gave him some sheep to get started with. They don't live in one place. They move to and fro in a pattern that allows the grass to recover, so we did that too, some of the time, as a way of not drawing attention to what Fodaro found back at our pasture. The great thing about them is that they know who they are and where they belong and what their purpose is. I really love that. I love the life. It hasn't been at all like what Saranja was saying. I've never felt I was carrying a terrible burden. I don't now. I know who I am, and what I'm for. I'm going to destroy the Watchers, and then I'm going to go back to shepherding.'

He rambled peacefully on about his far-off, impossible-seeming future until the flesh had closed completely over Ribek's wound and the skin had grown smooth and clean. Maja rose and stretched. She could feel that something had gone out of her, leaving a sort of satisfied tiredness, as if after enjoyable exercise.

Chapter 4

THREE MORNINGS LATER they halted and looked down on Mord. So far the road had wound its way south across rolling upland, mostly wooded but mottled with blotches of sheep pasture and here and there a village ringed with small-holdings beside a roaring stream. Now it plummeted, zigzagging down an escarpment at the foot of which lay a neat walled town, a wide and level farmland plain beyond with a river winding across. Far south, at the limit of vision, rose another range of hills.

All that time Saranja had slept as though she would never wake again, by night wherever the rest of them were sleeping – drover's hut or farmer's barn – by day in a cunning horse-litter Ribek had adapted from a broken cot in one of the ruined huts. There was just room for Maja to perch sideways in front of it, but it couldn't have been very comfortable for Rocky so she'd walked as much as she could. She'd been doing that when they'd reached the crest of the slope.

'Mord,' said Benayu dully, and then stood gazing down it. He had scarcely spoken an unnecessary word in the last two days, and had marched as though he hated every footstep of the way. They had left him alone, knowing there was no comfort they could offer. Season after season he must have made this journey with Fodaro, cheerful and confident, to sell and buy sheep at the market, and finished standing where they now stood, looking down at their journey's end. This must have been the bitterest moment of all. At last he gave a deep sigh, squared his shoulders and spoke in a level, toneless voice.

'All right. If the Watchers are going to put an Eye on the road, this is where they'll be doing it. You three should be all right. I've put Zald-im-Zald completely to sleep, and Maja isn't picking anything up from Jex or the roc feathers. There's an old ward on the gate, anyway, because the City Fathers like to know what kind of trouble they're letting in. You should be able to spot that as we go through, Maja. It's built into the stonework. Then there'll be all sorts of petty hedge magic going on inside the walls. The Watchers' Eye will be different. I'll know as soon as it picks me out, but that will be too late. If you can tell me before . . .'

There had been a woman in the Valley who had been blind since birth, until one day she tripped on the stairs and hit her head against a newel post and passed out. When she came round she found that she could now see.

At first she could just tell light from dark, then colours, then vague shapes which only gradually became clearer. But even then she couldn't always tell what they were. She had needed to pick up a cup and handle it, as she had done all her life, in order to be sure of what it was.

Maja was just beginning to do this with her new-found ability to sense the presence of magic. First only the awareness of that presence and its strength, then a vague sense of the nature of the magical impulse and its direction, and now, for the first time, its rough form. As they approached the walls of Mord she picked out a heavy, dark vibration, straight ahead. It felt very old, was vaguely arch-shaped, and there was death in it somewhere. She told Benayu.

'That will be the gate-ward,' he said. 'They'll have sacrificed a criminal and mixed his blood into the mortar when they built the gate. Strong magic. Nothing else?'

'A lot of little twitterings – I expect that's the hedge magic.'

'Mord's full of it.'

That was true. As they made their way through the narrow, jostling streets to the inn where Benayu and Fodaro had usually stayed, it seemed to be beaming out at Maja from all around. She tried to pick out separate pieces of it, but it was like trying to listen to one particular song in a cage full of songbirds. Only once, when they were passing a strange little house, so squashed between its larger neighbours that it was barely wider than its own front door, she felt something different, not a twittering, but a slow, quiet stirring, that seemed to be coming from much further away than the house itself – no, it was reaching her *through* something – a screen, perhaps, like the one Benayu had put round the drove huts when he was working on Zald-im-Zald. The magic itself was much stronger than it felt this side of the screen.

She told Benayu. He stopped for a moment and looked at the house. There was a faint liveliness in his tone when he answered.

'That's a ward, not a screen. A pretty good one. It wouldn't bother the Watchers, mind you, but I'd really need to work at it if I wanted to look at anything beyond it. Nothing to do with us, anyway. There are still a few Free Magicians around. I'm tempted to try and get in touch, but we'd better not risk it.'

'Screens. Wards. What's the difference?' said Ribek.

'Wards are permanent and all-purpose. They stop anyone seeing what the magician's up to, and keep out other people's magic. A good one takes a lot of work to build. But they've been around a long time, and the Watchers have got a Seeing-Tower in Talakh that can look straight through them as if they weren't there. Screens are something Jex and Fodaro thought up. I mean they saw that it was theoretically possible, but they needed me to find out how to do it. You have to build into the screen a reverse mirror image of whatever magic you're trying to hide, so that they cancel each other out when they meet. They won't keep magic out unless you know roughly what's coming, but Jex used to be able to do that for us. And they do have the great advantage that you can put a small one around you, so that it stays with you wherever you go. We didn't think the Watchers had found out about them because they'd need Fodaro's equations. In fact I'm probably the only person in the Empire who knows how to do them.'

It was strange to hear that astonishing boast in a voice so dull and hopeless.

The inn was in a quiet street near the western gate. Maja stayed with Saranja and Rocky in the inn-yard while Ribek and Benayu hired a room for them, and then went with a friendly old ostler to see that Rocky was comfortably stabled while the other two carried Saranja up the narrow, dark stair. It was mid-afternoon by the time they'd eaten and settled in, and Ribek and Benayu were ready to set out and try to sell some of their jewels.

'You come too, Maja,' said Benayu. 'You'll be useful. We'll leave Sponge to look after Saranja. He won't let in anyone he doesn't know till I come back.'

The trinket-sellers occupied only a small section of a busy country market that filled a fair-sized square and spilled into the neighbouring streets. For some reason it was not as crowded as the other sections of the market, less rowdy but with subtler and stranger reeks and odours, and lacking the otherwise ubiquitous petty magicians busking their wonders for coppers. But to Maja the area made up for that by the ceaseless murmuration from charms and amulets on many of the stalls.

'The trouble is, I don't know anything about jewels,' said Ribek. 'I can haggle over a bag of grain with the best of them, so I was thinking I could play it by ear, picking up from their tone and gesture and so on how much roughly they were trying to do me for, but now that I'm faced with it . . .'

'Don't worry,' said Benayu. 'You'll know all right, because . . . Stop. Don't let her see you looking, but that woman at the stall we've just passed. She's trying to sell the stallholder something. Right?'

Maja felt a quick, soft pulse of magic come from him, and then repeat itself like an echo.

'Looks like it,' said Ribek, 'but . . . oh, she thinks it's a love charm, only it doesn't work. She's asking three imps for it, but she'll be pleased if she gets one and a quarter. He knows that it's actually a spiteful little curs-ing-piece – multiply any curse by seven, worth about eight imps in the trade, but he'd expect to get fifteen off a sucker, so he's prepared to let her have two for it. So they're both going to be happy with the bargain. You put all that into my head?'

For a moment Maja concentrated on the charm, and realized she could sense its nastiness.

'Uh-huh,' said Benayu, more animated again – it was the chance to use his magic that did that, Maja guessed. 'Fodaro used to bring me down here to practise, after we'd traded our sheep. He wouldn't let me do it at home, or among the shepherds. He said that was dis-honourable. But if somebody's trying to cheat you . . . You can see how useful it is, especially with me picking the stuff out of the dealer's head and passing it on. Mind-reading isn't that easy – anyone else's mind is a wildly complicated place, and some are a lot more hid-den than others – and all the dealers carry amulets

100

against it, which you have to get past, and they'll lynch you if they catch you trying, so they reckon they're safe. Even so Fodaro used to keep an eye open while I was doing it, just in case anyone was noticing what we were up to. They'd need their own magic to do that. That's where you come in, Maja.

'The woman we're going to talk to knows her stuff about jewels, though they're only a sideline for her. She's a crook with the customers, but straight with the other dealers. And the great thing about her is that she's got a very open mind, very close to the surface. We haven't traded with her much, in case we ever needed to sell something serious. All right?'

'I think I may enjoy this,' said Ribek, as Benayu led the way.

They followed him to a stall whose holder was having some kind of friendly argument with her neighbour, but as soon as a customer showed up she left him and came over smiling. She was a soft-skinned, bosomy woman, her face heavily made-up to enhance her dark and liquid gaze. She lavished this on Ribek with obvious approval. He responded with a touch of manly swagger.

'And what can I do for you, my dear?'

'I've a few small gems I'd like a price on, if you'd be so kind. I was told to come to you because you knew about this sort of thing.'

'A pleasure.'

She cleared a patch on her counter and he laid a folded cloth on it and opened it out to display three stones from Zald-im-Zald's decorative curlicues. She picked them up one by one and studied them through a

101

lens. Maja could sense a softly cooing vibration starting to come from her – no, not from her, from something she was wearing.

'Thank you for choosing me,' she said. 'It's not often I get shown anything as nice as that little garnet. Very rich, unusual colour. The small topaz isn't bad either, but the larger topaz – it'd be a very nice one if it weren't for the flaw – this white streak running across it here, but as it is . . .'

'You haven't seen a snow-stone before?' said Ribek, not mockingly but with kindly concern. He moved closer to her as if that was his main interest, took the stone and turned it to a precise angle.

'See how nicely it's cut to show the structure of the snowflake,' he said. 'I don't know when I've seen a better one. As for the other "garnet", that's a perfectly good ruby, first water, interestingly dark in colour, four and a sixth tams, and you're right that you won't often be offered as good a one in an out-of-the-way place like this. The same with the yellow diamond, four tams or near enough, not my taste as a matter of fact . . .'

The stallholder looked up, still smiling, but differently.

'That wasn't fair,' she said.

'My apologies,' he said, with a gallant turn of his hand. 'I've found it a quick way to establish a relationship in a strange town. I need to make a sale, because there's something else I want to buy, but not at any price. I gather you're the only dealer in Mord who knows enough to be sure you're getting a fair bargain, so if we can agree figures I'll give you ten per cent off for a quick sale.'

'Fifteen,' she said.

'Twelve and a half.'

'Done. Have you any idea where they come from? They were obviously set into some larger piece.'

'That's right. I was told it was looted from the hoard of some war-lord way out beyond the eastern desert.'

'Mind if I just run my crystal over them? There'll have been power-stones in something like that, like as not. They could have picked up a bit of magic, in which case I'd need to think again.'

'Go ahead,' said Ribek easily, Benayu having already dealt with the problem. 'And then perhaps you'd care to join me for a glass of wine while we settle a price . . .'

'Thought so,' whispered Benayu. 'She's not going to let pleasure interfere with business. She'll take him to an eating house and point him out to a couple of thugs she knows. They're going to waylay him on his way back to the inn and take the money off him. I'll let him know, but the way things are going they may be doing a bit more than having a glass of wine together tonight, and we're going to need to leave early. Idiot! Who can you trust?'

'She's wearing a love-charm, isn't she?' said Maja defensively. She had no idea how she knew that was what it was. It just had to be.

'He's still an idiot. I'd better hang around here for a bit and keep an eye on him. I'll tell him what's up and hope he comes to his senses.'

'He isn't going to.'

'In that case I'll find a quiet place where we can meet in the morning and tell him where it is in case he doesn't get back to the inn tonight. You'd better go back yourself now and have a bit of a rest. Even with Jex's help you're going to find picking up all this stray magic all the time pretty tiring at first. Do you want me to show you the way?'

'I think I can find it.'

He was right about both things. Already half dazed by the ceaseless petty bombardment from every corner of Mord, she got lost almost at once. In the end by pure luck she came to the inn from the wrong direction.

Sponge welcomed her back to their room with a thump of his tail on the floorboards. Saranja still slept unstirring, so she curled up in one of the other beds and almost immediately herself fell into deep and dreamless sleep. At some unknown nowhere in that peaceful oblivion, a voice of stone spoke faintly in her head.

'*Maja.*'

'Jex! Are you all right? I can only just hear you. How can we get you back? Can we help? Do you know what's been happening?'

'*No, you must tell me. Normally I exist simultaneously in two separate worlds. When your companion spoke a certain name, the shock of her utterance was such that I was forced to withdraw from your world, leaving behind only an extension of myself, which is now in the shape of the stone pendant you carry. Being stone, it can neither see nor hear, and exists only to absorb some of the magic around you, without which I cannot live.*

'*Communication between my separate worlds is difficult when I do not exist fully in one of them. We are now in the nowhere between the worlds. I am speaking to you and not to Benayu because the pendant is under your pillow, and yours is the younger and more flexible mind. Even so, it is accessible to me only with considerable effort and only when you are asleep. So tell me now all that has happened since your companion spoke that name on the mountainside.*'

It took some time, only there seemed to be no such thing as time in this dream between the worlds.

'*You have done well,*' said Jex when she had finished. '*I grieve for Fodaro, a good man, and brave, and wise. Yes, you can help me, and, since you cannot succeed in your quest without me, you will need to do so.*

'*First we must restore me to my true balance. Saranja could do this anywhere and at any time, simply by holding the roc feathers in one hand, bound by the strand of the Ropemaker's hair, and the pendant that you have under your pillow in the other, and then speaking his name. This will set off a major magical spasm similar in kind to the one that originally created the imbalance, and provided that I am ready for the event I will be able to exploit this to restore myself to my natural condition. But the process would send out an extremely powerful signal, more than Benayu can ward or screen, and I will not be there to absorb any part of it. It is certain to attract the attention of the Watchers. They will already be on the alert after the spasms back at the pasture and the destruction of two of their number who came to investigate the first of them.*'

'Our best chance is to attempt to conceal the event among a complex of other equally powerful events, if we can. There are some of my kind who exist in the same mode as me. I cannot communicate with them in my present imbalance, but I can listen to what they tell each other. They have some knowledge of the Watchers' doings. They say that something of the sort that we are looking for appears likely to happen near the eastern port of Tarshu. The Watchers have somehow learnt that the Pirates are preparing for a major raid and are gathering to repel it. I suggest that you take me to Tarshu and we will make the attempt. It is some distance, and you dare not travel by magical means, so you must leave Mord as soon as you can.

'Farewell, Maja. I shall not be able to speak to you for a while, other than in an emergency.'

'Goodbye, Jex. And good luck. And thanks. I'll tell them.'

She was not surprised by his last sentence. Even in her sleep she had been straining to hear. No, it had not been a dream. That was real.

She was woken by the triple thwack of Sponge's tail at the sound of his master's returning footsteps. Saranja must have woken to the sound too, and was starting to sit up as Benayu came into the room, slamming the door brutally behind him.

'Where is this?' she said, dazed with her long sleep. 'Why's it so dark? What's up? You look—'

'We're in an inn at Mord,' he said harshly. 'You've been asleep for three days. You ought to be dead, if you

106

want to know. There's a stone in Zald-im-Zald that was making you tireless, but you pay for it after. Two days ought to have killed you, and you'd been wearing it for ten. I suppose the roc feathers must have kept you alive somehow.'

'Where's Ribek?'

'Ribek?' he snarled, and told her.

'He swears he can handle these two thugs,' he added. 'The woman told them she'd be keeping him with her till dawn, but I took the money off him to be on the safe side.'

'Men!' growled Saranja. 'They've got just one idea in their heads!'

'It wasn't his fault really,' said Maja. 'She was wearing a love-charm.'

'I still hate men. And what if he isn't as good as he thinks he is and these fellows are too much for him? Where does that leave us? Is there anywhere I can watch from and not be seen, just in case?'

'There's an archway a little way down across the street. Room for all three of us, as well as Rocky. Then if we've got everything packed up we can be on our way as soon as the gates open.'

'That'll have to do. Where are the latrines? I'm bursting.'

'I'll show you – I've got to take Sponge out,' said Benayu.

'I've got a message for us from Jex,' said Maja. 'He talked to me in a dream, only it wasn't a dream. He says we can't find the Ropemaker without him, and he told me how we can get him unstuck in a way the Watchers won't notice. It's rather complicated. And it's really scary.'

'Tell us when I get back,' said Benayu more calmly. 'We won't be more than a couple of minutes. I'll order some food on the way up. Come on, boy.'

Usually when Maja tried to tell someone about what had seemed a vivid dream, all its sharp certainties seemed to go vague and unreal as she spoke. This wasn't like that. The single stony voice seemed to be still in her mind, putting the exact words into her mouth as she needed them, though in places she wasn't sure she really understood them. It didn't take long. Saranja and Benayu listened without interruption. Their meal arrived as she was finishing. By the time they settled down to it, the night outside was fully dark.

Saranja ate with a wolf's hunger after three days and three nights without food, her whole body wasted by the magic-driven energy-use of the ten days before. Benayu ate in silence, but more steadily now that he had magical matters to brood about.

'Yes,' he said at last. 'That's the best we can do. I'll settle up tonight and we'll start before dawn.'

Chapter 5

THE STARS WERE barely beginning to fade as they followed Benayu through the warren of darkened streets. Saranja had padded Rocky's hooves so that even he made barely a sound. Somewhere near the market they turned into the pitch darkness under an archway and waited. Maja took Rocky's bridle, leaving the other two free to act, if they needed to.

A little later they saw two men come silently along the street and stop near an ornate porch, further along on the opposite side of the street, and in their turn start to watch as if for something to happen beyond them. Time passed. At last a door opened, sending a glow of soft light out into the night. The two men disappeared into the shadows of the porch. Ribek came out of the lit door and turned. A woman followed him on to the doorstep and bent to kiss him, then retreated. The door closed, and Ribek strolled towards the five watchers, whistling softly.

He was just past the porch when the two men rushed him, their bare feet almost noiseless on the paving. He seemed unaware of their attack until, at the last instant, he skipped to his right, swivelling as he landed, with his left leg swinging out to hook the first man's feet from under him. His momentum carried him smoothly into a single dance-like step and counter-swivel, with his right foot punching neatly into the hollow at the back of the second man's knee. The man yelled as he fell. The first man was halfway to his feet when Ribek kicked him in the abdomen and he tumbled forward, his curses replaced by retching gasps.

'It's called kick-boxing,' said Ribek, informatively. 'Your friend warned me you'd be waiting for me.'

He left them, walking fast and no longer whistling. As he passed the archway the others came out and fell in beside him.

Approaching the south gate of Mord, Maja became aware of its gate-ward, very like the first one, but less old and without the underlying presence of blood. At the same time, almost concealed by it, she sensed an intense, steady, focused beam of magic. Yet another Eye. Faint, as if coming from far away, but at the same time powerful – the same effect she'd felt emanating from the strange little house they'd passed soon after entering Mord. There was something else about it. Unlike the other Eye and the one at the northern gate, it wasn't built into the masonry of the gate, but added later. Much later.

She tugged Benayu by the sleeve.

'I think there are two Eyes on this gate,' she whispered. 'One of them's warded, though. And I think it's new.'

He stopped and concentrated. The others waited.

'I can't feel anything except the old gate-ward,' he said. 'But if you're sure there's something there, that must mean it's got a powerful ward, so you're right. Bother. You three are probably safe to go on, but you'd better split up. Ribek can take Sponge, and Saranja and Maja can wait a few minutes and then ride Rocky through. I'll come my own way and meet you further down the road. Don't wait for me. I can travel faster than you, and we want to get on.'

The dawn mists had melted away into a clear still morning when they came to a small stand of lime trees growing close beside the road. As they passed it a pigeon came gliding down on to the roadside turf, strutted for a moment and became Benayu.

'Know I was there, Maja?' he asked.

'I didn't feel a thing – not even when you changed.'

'Great. Shape-shifting's small stuff, mind you. You didn't notice my screen, either? Then we're getting somewhere. I'll need to find out a lot more about screens if I'm to operate at all out in the Empire.'

They headed south all morning, stopping for their midday meal at the bridge over the river that they had seen from the escarpment. This meant both river-traffic and road-traffic, so there was a small market, with stalls selling food for man and beast. There was also a horse-dealer, buying from travellers who'd come this far by road and were now journeying on by water, and selling to those going the opposite way. Saranja looked the horses over and Ribek made a show of doing so, while Maja and Benayu watched from the side. Using the same technique that they had with the jewel-dealer in Mord, they bought a couple of nags, and saddles and harness from one of the stalls, so that henceforth all four of them could ride.

The new horses' characters emerged as the days went by. Pogo was a flighty grey, inclined to shy at trifles whenever he was bored. Levanter was an amiable idiot. If a horse could get something wrong, he got it wrong. Rocky was manifestly glad of their company, but at the same time tolerated no nonsense from either of them, and kept them in line quite as much as their riders did. Pogo was immediately besotted with him, while after a few days Levanter seemed to decide that his best hope of doing the right thing was to copy whatever Rocky did. This worked reasonably well once Ribek had learnt to allow for it if he wanted him to do something else.

Late that first afternoon the road reached the southern limit of the plain. They had just moved in under the first trees when Maja stiffened, suddenly aware of something large and powerful coming swiftly from the south. It was horrible. She recognized it at once, the same sudden nausea of the spirit that she had felt just before the explosion back at the sheep pasture, while she, Ribek and Saranja had been waiting to cross the old ford.

'Benayu!' she shouted. 'Watchers coming! Fast! That way!'

He stared south for a moment, then slithered from the saddle, closed his eyes and stood motionless, pale with concentration. Maja could sense his protective network weaving itself around him. Still concentrating, he reached out and pulled her inside it.

'All right,' he said. 'Grab hold of Jex in your other hand, Maja. Hang on to your feathers, Saranja. You should be all right, Ribek. Just take Pogo . . . Now!'

The wave of change swept down over the woods and broke across them like silent thunder, felt as a sudden electric tension in the air, enveloping Benayu's screen for one aching moment, and then was gone. The jar of it pulsed down Maja's arm to the hand that held Jex, who seemed for that moment to soften into living flesh and then was granite again. Rocky neighed and kicked. She opened her eyes to see Benayu close beside her, breathing heavily, pale and sweating, and beyond him Saranja and Ribek struggling to control the horses. That wasn't the only reason why they looked shaken.

'They're doing a sort of generalized sweep as they go,' muttered Benayu. 'Checking out any serious magicians they pick up. How did it feel, Maja?'

'Your screen? All right, I think. Not as if it was anywhere near breaking.'

'Why now, all of a sudden?' said Ribek. 'It's four days, isn't it?'

'I don't get it,' said Benayu. 'And Maja says that second Eye on the southern gate was new. I don't think that first fellow I trapped in the cottage would have been up to putting it in. You'd have known, Maja, wouldn't you, if any more actual Watchers had shown up?'

'Yes, I think so. Only not if they came in secret.'

'They weren't making much of a secret coming just now,' said Saranja.

'Somebody put the new Eye in,' said Ribek.

'I don't think it was Watcher stuff,' said Maja. 'That's got a funny yucky feel. I felt it just now when they went over.'

Benayu sighed in anxiety and frustration and shook his head.

'No point in guessing,' he said. 'All I know is the further we are from Mord, the better.'

The road wound mainly uphill through wild country, ancient woods, tangled with undergrowth and half-fallen trees, alternating with stony, scrub-covered hillsides. They met a few travellers going north but, apart from one or two battered roadside sheds, didn't see a building until they came in the dusk to an official resting camp, with fees and bribes to pay, but food and fodder to be bought, and other travellers for Ribek to question casually about the possibility of crossing the country south-eastward to visit a sister he hadn't seen for sixteen years. She lived at a town called Parangot, down beyond Tarshu, he said. He was told he'd need to make a long twelve days' journey south before he found a good imperial road, twice as much making the crossing and then, well, it depended how far south of that his sister lived. They hadn't heard of Parangot. Not surprising, as he'd made it up, but someone happened to mention that it was a good thirty days on from where they were to Tarshu.

As they slept under the stars Jex spoke in Maja's dreams. His voice seemed only slightly less faint and strained than before.

'*I have important news. Some of my friends are now aware of me, and have spoken directly to me, though I still cannot answer or question them. Our road south is closed to us. The Watchers have been wholly preoccupied with preparations to meet the coming attack on Tarshu, and were not prepared to lose any more of their number until that was finished, so sent only a junior magician to investigate the loss of themselves beyond Mord, and then a more experienced one to investigate his disappearance.*

'*This work is now finished. My supposition is that meanwhile this second man must have discovered something that they believe to be connected with the coming assault by the Pirates. Hence the urgency with which fresh Watchers have now arrived. Once at the pasture, they will speak with the shepherds and look into their minds, and search for magical traces in the cottage where Fodaro lived with Benayu. I think we must assume that they will then know whose brother Fodaro was, and from that perhaps guess whose son Benayu may be.*

'*Furthermore, they have set up checkpoints on this road at which all travellers are rigorously examined. You must leave it as soon as you can. Other roads south are less strictly watched, apart from random checks at*

*way stations of licenses to practice magic. Tell the
others.'*

'Yes, of course. You sound stronger.'

'*I am, a little. Fortunately I was prepared for the
moment when the Watchers passed over us south of
Mord, or it might have been a setback.*'

'Benayu pulled us inside his screen, but I still felt it.
And you changed for a moment, didn't you?'

'*It was useful to me. I will be able to protect you more
effectively.*'

'Can anyone – one of the Watchers, for instance – tell
that you're there, tell you're doing that?'

'*Not as far as I know. Over the generations we have
learnt to hide ourselves. It is essential for our survival.*'

'And supposing I don't want to be shielded for a
bit . . . ?'

'*Tell me so in your head and I will withdraw for a
while. Farewell, Maja.*'

'Goodbye, Jex. Come again when you can.'

The others heard the bad news without surprise.

'They must have found the picture of the airboat
Saranja drew,' said Benayu.

'Fodaro would have destroyed it, surely?' said
Saranja.

'When I last saw him he was scratching magical signs
round it – at least that's what they looked like,' said
Maja. 'Trying to put them off the scent, I suppose.'

'Good idea,' said Ribek. 'Just like him to think of it.
Not his fault it didn't work out. You know, Benayu, the
more I learn about Fodaro, the better I like him.'

At a lonely place south of that camp Benayu dismounted and climbed a little distance from the road. Maja sensed a steady, prolonged tremor that seemed to move in a circle around him but then none of the expected shock of magic as he became a raven. He rose, circling, and flew south.

They had their midday rest on a grassy bank beside the road. A few travellers passed in either direction. Some of them were wearing the standard dress of the Empire, familiar from the story told in the Valley, the men in little conical caps with upturned brims and a tassel, loose brown jackets and baggy knee breeches; the women in long skirts and long coloured scarves with tasselled ends wound twice round over their heads. The tassels on both caps and scarves were decorated with blue beads, by which one could tell the wearer's grade in the elaborate social system of the Empire.

'I suppose we're going to have to dress like that,' said Saranja.

'I don't know,' said Ribek. 'Nobody seemed to bother with it much up in the mountains. I expect Benayu can easily fix it if we have to.'

The horses grazed contentedly in the noon stillness. Saranja sat, chin in hand, brooding. Ribek now slept, snoring lightly. Maja was happily exploring the new fantasy life that had been gradually growing in her mind over the last few days. It was very different from her usual fantasies, because this time it actually seemed possible. She wasn't a dashing adventuress with her own wonderful charger and magic sword, nor the poor captive of some evil slave trader, who made a daring escape from his clutches and became a key witness to bring him to justice and free his other slaves. It was far simpler than that: she was only a few years older, and Ribek had asked her to marry him and come and live with him at Northbeck and share the place where he belonged. From time to time as they journeyed she'd asked him an innocent-seeming question and he'd answered unsuspectingly, giving her another detail to flesh out the fantasy.

Now she was busy forming a picture of his older niece – not the one who had lent her the warm coat, but the one who looked after the ducks that lived on a platform in the stream to keep them safe from foxes – when she sensed a familiar blip of magic somewhere behind her and knew from the feel of it that Benayu had returned. A few moments later he walked out of the trees.

'I've found something,' he said. 'I don't know that it leads anywhere. It keeps seeming to peter out, but then it picks up again. We'd better take it anyway. There's a barricade at the next village. This isn't an Imperial Highway, so you don't normally need a way-leave to use it, but that's what they're demanding.'

The path certainly didn't look very promising when they reached it – a rough logging track, with a stack of felled trunks beside it, waiting to be picked up by the timber-wain. Sure enough, it seemed to end at the place where the trees had been felled, but they pushed on between the tree stumps and came out on to an open hillside, trackless but easy going, climbed to a ridge and found what seemed to be a footpath winding southward into the hills, though there was not a building in sight or anything to show who might have made it.

The same for mile after mile, their path time and again seeming to stop in the middle of nowhere, only to renew itself. It was well into the afternoon and Maja was deep in her fantasy again when she realized that for some time now she'd been growing increasingly uneasy. The others seemed to feel it too, Benayu with surly silence, Ribek with pointless chat, answered by Saranja with an indifferent shrug or grunt. The horses and Sponge plodded listlessly on. Something was wrong – something missing, Maja eventually decided. It was like total silence. Even in ordinary silence, when there's no particular noise reaching your ears, there are always very faint background sounds – nothing you'd normally notice, but there. Total silence is a blank, so empty that you can almost hear it by its very absence. So now. All natural objects have magic in them, too faint to notice but still giving out their own slight vibration. Not here. Nothing from the boulders, nor the patches of scrawny shrubs and coarse grass.

Emptiness, barrenness, silence. It was like the landscape of some of her dreams. *They* were behind her, snuffling along her trail. She had to know.

Can you stop shielding me, Jex?

She felt the change in her head, but not in the unnatural stillness.

They passed a shallow steam, winding down over water-worn rocks.

'Can you hear what it's saying, Ribek?' she asked.

He cocked his head to listen.

'Nothing,' he said. 'That's odd. I've never come across it before. Sometimes they don't make much sense, but they're babbling away all the same.'

'I think perhaps there's some kind of screen – or do I mean ward? – over the whole area,' she said. 'I can't feel it at all, but it's blanking everything out. I think someone's watching us and doesn't want us to know.'

Benayu roused himself, reined Pogo in, closed his eyes, bowed his head and concentrated.

'Not a screen,' he said at last. 'I didn't think it could be. And it isn't like any kind of ward I've ever come across, but there wasn't much serious magic in the mountains. Anyway, there's something. I can feel it stopping me getting through, but that's all. It's just playing with me. It's a lot stronger than I am.'

'I don't think it's anything to do with the Watchers,' said Maja. 'It doesn't feel . . . *bad*. Or good. It's just there.'

'It doesn't scare you?' said Ribek.

'No. It's a bit like being back in the Valley, only more so.'

'I'd better scout ahead again,' said Benayu. 'Ready, Maja?'

He bowed his head and she steeled herself for the shock of magic. Nothing happened. After a few moments he straightened and looked around as if half stunned.

'It won't let me,' he whispered.

They looked at each other in silence.

'Nothing else for it,' said Saranja decisively. 'We know we can't go back to the road. Might as well carry on.'

They did so, Maja hunched in the saddle, eyes closed, shutting out everything except the magical silence, feeling for the slightest variation in it . . . a faint magical twitch from somewhere ahead . . . later another . . .

'It's choosing where the path goes,' she said.

They halted and looked at each other. Ribek shrugged.

'If Maja's right, it doesn't make much difference what we do, does it?' he said. 'Suppose we try to turn round, whoever's doing this can still choose where the path goes, and we'll finish up where we would have done anyway. So we might as well push on and get it over with. If it's a trap, it's a trap.'

'I don't think it's a trap, exactly,' said Maja. 'It's just . . . interested in us.'

'The horses don't seem to be bothered by it,' said Saranja. 'On we go, then.'

The sun was almost on the horizon when they came to a place like any other they'd seen all afternoon, a shallow fold in the ground, the nearside scrub and boulders, a dismal little stream dribbling along the bottom and a scree-strewn slope beyond. Sponge trotted ahead, tail high, ears pricked, alert and interested. He splashed through the stream, started up the slope on the other side, halted, crouched a moment, turned and slunk whimpering back. Benayu dismounted and knelt to comfort him. Sponge huddled into his arms like a frightened puppy.

Again the others looked at Maja. She shook her head.

'I didn't feel anything,' she said. 'Only – I don't know

– perhaps the ward or whatever it is is hiding something stronger now.'

'Well, there's one way to find out,' said Ribek, dismounting.

They watched him cross the stream and start confidently up the other slope, only to stagger suddenly, as if he'd been struck by an invisible fist, duck down, covering his head with his arms, turn and rush back towards the stream. Almost at once he caught his foot on a boulder and fell sprawling but crawled frantically on.

Saranja ran to help him to his feet and bring him shuddering and sweating back to the others. They waited while the shudders died away. At length he straightened and shook himself.

'Pure nightmare,' he said. 'Nothing there, no monsters, nothing like that, just – just the thing itself. Anyway I can't face it again, and nor can you. Looks like we're going to have to go back after all.'

'There's a stone in Zald, isn't there, Benayu?' said Saranja, starting to pull the jewel out from under her blouse. 'Why don't I give it a try?'

'It's that one there,' said Benayu. 'Ready? Now, touch it with the middle finger of your left hand – no, keep it there, and circle the fingertip over it, three times to the left and then three to the right. You won't feel anything yourself – you'll just have to hope. I don't know if it's strong enough, mind you. That's really powerful stuff making this happen, and a really powerful ward stopping us feeling it.'

'No harm in trying,' said Saranja.

They watched her cross the stream and start up the slope. About where Ribek had crumpled she slowed, not, apparently, because there was anything slowing her but out of natural caution. Nothing visible happened, but Maja sensed a surge of complex energies moving with her up the slope. After a little while she turned and came back.

'Didn't feel a thing,' she said. 'Perhaps it's stopped, or perhaps it just doesn't like men. It wouldn't be the only one.'

'It was trying to get at you,' said Maja, and explained.

'Perhaps I'd better lend you Zald,' said Saranja. 'Then you could go and see if you can tell where it's coming from.'

Inwardly Maja cringed. Even protected by Zald-im-Zald, to face what Ribek had faced! And alone!

'Wouldn't work,' said Benayu. 'Zald is yours, Saranja. Apart from the woundsain, it's imprinted on you, since you almost sacrificed your life to it before. I'll see if I can get it to release the stone, and then you can go together, holding it between you. Do you think you can cope with that, Maja?'

'I'll be all right, with Saranja there,' she muttered.

But what about Jex? Better not start shielding me again, Jex, or perhaps the stone won't work. It may be too much for you anyway.

Hand in hand, the two of them crossed the stream and started up the slope. The little stone lay comfortingly against Maja's palm. She could sense the quiet flow of magic streaming up her arm, spreading through her body and radiating out a little way beyond. There was an almost musical chiming, a complex pattern of inter-woven threads of power, as they passed through some kind of magical barrier, and then the wave of terror surged round them. Innumerable talons of power clawed at their protecting aura. Answering power flowed from the stone and stood firm. With an effort Maja ignored the storm around her and concentrated on the source of the attack. There seemed to be nothing hiding it from her now.

'There,' she said, and led Saranja up and to the left.

They reached a shallow basin a few paces across, lined with almost identical round smooth stones, each about the size of a man's head. All but one of them, half way up the further side of the basin, seemed inert, but the whole attack flowed from that one.

Amazed at its power, Maja led Saranja towards it and pointed. Saranja gazed at it, shrugged, stooped and touched it tentatively with the fingertips of her free hand. The surface of the stone trembled, seemed to melt and flow, and became a face, both childish and ageless, soft, smooth, the colour halfway between flesh and stone. The full lips parted and a narrow, tubular, dark purple tongue slid out and extended until its tip could probe into nostrils and ears, and delicately pick the sleepy-dust out of the corners of the golden eyes, and then withdrew. Without the fear-defying stone against her palm, Maja would have found the whole process too horrifying to watch.

'Yes?' whispered the sweet lips.

'Will you let us through, please?' said Saranja.

'Who are you and what is your purpose?'

'We're Saranja and Maja Urlasdaughter. The others are Ribek Ortahlson and Benayu. I don't know his parents' names, but his uncle was called Fodaro. We're on our way to Tarshu.'

'Fodaro we know of. You say "was". He is dead?'

'The Watchers killed him. They're looking for us. We don't want them to find us. That's why we came this way. Will you let us through?'

'Go back a little. Watch.'

They climbed to the rim of the basin and turned. Maja clung to Saranja's hand to steady herself against the whirlwind of magic that formed as the rocks that lined it began to flow and change shape. They became mason-hewn stone that piled itself rapidly into a building. The basin widened and filled with water, and now she was looking at a squat grey tower rising from the middle of a circular lake. The keystone of its arch was the face that had spoken to them from the boulder, carved in stone.

The doors opened and a woman stood under the arch. She was dressed in a plain brown cloak, and apart from the blue jewel suspended from her neck she looked like some farmwife who has just brought a load of produce to a country market, middle-aged, short, plump, round-faced but small-featured, smiling. She would not, Maja thought, have looked out of place in the Valley, where no magic had ever been known.

A bridge appeared at her feet and she stretched out both arms in greeting but made no move to cross it.

'Welcome, cousins,' she said. 'There was a woman once called Tilja Urlasdaughter. I am her remote descendant. My name is Chanad. I will call your friends.'

Her voice was soft and level, the words very precisely spoken, as if every syllable was precious. They turned and saw Ribek and Benayu look suddenly towards them, and then start to lead the horses confidently up the slope.

They ate in a comfortable room with a steady fire glowing in the grate. Chanad carried in plates, mugs and cutlery on a tray. Maja was puzzled. Even with Saranja holding her steady she had barely withstood the swirling blasts of magic that had accompanied the appearance of Chanad's tower and continued with increasing force as they had crossed the bridge towards it. But once in under the arch, all that was gone. All she could feel was the faint background buzz that told her that outside the tower it was still there. The answer, when it came to her, was so unexpected that she blurted it out.

'It's got a ward on the inside too!'

Chanad looked at her, eyebrows raised.

'Indeed it has,' she said. 'But I'm surprised you're aware of it. A ward that betrays its existence is as useless as no ward at all.'

'I'm not,' said Maja. 'I mean, I can't feel the ward itself. But I can just feel all that stuff going on outside it, so I guessed it was there. It was like that coming here. Everything's got a bit of magic in it – rocks, trees, animals, streams – it's so gentle you don't notice it, but I noticed when it wasn't there, so I knew there had to be something.'

Chanad stared at her.

'I have heard of such people,' she said. 'Magicians, of

course, can sense the presence of magic, but they need to create the means by which they do it, and then to learn how to use it. A few people are born with your ability, as a natural gift, but they very seldom survive infancy. The magic around them – the magic in everyday things, and simple hedge magic – is too strong for them to endure at that age.'

'There wasn't any magic where I was born,' said Maja. 'I never felt it till just a few days ago, when I watched Saranja putting Rocky's wings on. That really shook me. I'm getting used to it, I think, but just coming across your bridge – I couldn't have done it without Saranja.'

'You will meet far stronger than that where you are going, if you are who I think you may be. If I am right, I will provide you with what help I can. I am the last of the group that called ourselves the Andarit, the Free Great Magicians. I knew Fodaro, and grieve for him. A good man to the last – a very good man. Too good to be a good magician. Benayu's mother and father were my colleagues. When we made our move against the Watchers we knew that we might not succeed, and I was chosen to survive until another chance should come. Ancient tradition told us that if it came at all it would be from the north.

'So between us we devised this tower, where I am able to ward myself from the corroding power of my own magic, which, with nothing else to practise upon, would otherwise have eaten me away over the years. I have an unwarded workroom at the top of the tower, but I perform no magic anywhere else within these walls, and do not even step onto my bridge if I can help it. We made all the area around into a magical blank space, as seen from elsewhere in the Empire, large enough to absorb and dissipate any magic I might perform from this centre. If the Watchers in Talakh were to concentrate their attention on the area they would find me, but they rely on their Seeing Tower, which is not designed to respond to an absence of magic.

'From here I watch the roads leading east and south out of Mord, and bring towards my tower any travellers who interest me. Almost all I return to their road fairly soon, taking from them any memory of where they have been.

'You were unusual, in that one of you – Benayu, I now know – became a bird and began to explore in this direction, so I laid a path for him to find, and you followed it. Later, to my surprise, you seemed to become aware of what was happening. When Benayu tried to take bird form again I stopped him, but nevertheless you came on. Finally, I put a barrier of terror in your path, to see how you would react before I let you through. You not only overcame the barrier but came directly to my place of hiding. Only when Saranja told me your names did I understand who you are and why you are here, and know that my time of waiting is at an end. So welcome again.

'First, you can tell me your story while we're eating. Easiest, perhaps, if we all fetch our own food and carry it through. Since I knew you were coming I've had time to prepare something. I like to cook, and I seldom get the chance to do it for anyone but myself.'

They helped themselves to a pungent-smelling stew, hunks of coarse fresh bread and green beans. There was sharp pale cider or water to drink, and a creamy mix of honey and brandy and soured goat-milk and spices for afters.

'I think you take more pride in your cooking than you do in your magic,' said Ribek.

'I suppose I do,' she said. 'It is one of my ways of staying human. Now, tell me what brought you here. Perhaps you'd better start with what you know about our ancestor Tilja Urlasdaughter. Everything begins with her.'

They took it in turn, first the story from the Valley, then what had happened since they had all met, and then their own plans. She stopped them only once, to ask them, just as Fodaro had done, about Faheel's time-controlling ring, of which she too had never heard.

'Yes,' she said when they had finished. 'All that fits in with what I already know. It is astonishing how remembered truth comes down through time. As I said, the only major exception is Faheel's ring, on which your story hinges. You tell me it stopped the movement of the sun across the sky, the march of the waves across the sea, the breath in the mouths of all the living creatures in the world, for the length of time it took for the roc to fly Tilja and Faheel from his island in the southern ocean all the way to Talakh. And yet when Tilja, with her gift of annulling magic, closed her hand around it, in that instant the sun and the waves moved on and the creatures of the world went about their business, unaware that there had been any interval between one breath and the next.

'That must be an object of prodigious power. I have never heard of anything remotely like it. I wonder if the Ropemaker ever used it again, after that first time. It sounds as if he may have been a bit afraid of it.'

'That's what Fodaro thought,' said Benayu. 'He'd never heard of it either. And he was a scholar of magic, he used to say. He knew it all, but he couldn't do it all. Do you think the Watchers know about it?'

'If they do, and if they can find it, then there is no hope,' said Chanad. 'That brings me to the chief thing that I have to tell you, which is that the nature of the Watchers has changed from that in your story. Those had been set up by Faheel to police the use of magic throughout the Empire, but they failed in their task because as time went by they became savagely compet-ing powers. Such is the corrosive effect of strong magic. Even among the Andarit I could see this beginning to happen. I could feel it in myself.

'Very few of us are free from it. Faheel had known it in his youth, but had put it aside, and in the end was forced to destroy his own creation because he could not control it in others.

'The Ropemaker was different. He was never inter-ested in power. His passion was knowledge. He would far rather have remained a free agent, wandering the Empire at his own will, seeing and hearing. Until you told me your story I had not known how he was forced to take control, and begin to sort out the chaos that fol-lowed the fall of those earlier Watchers – other magicians warring for power, in their ignorance and frenzy releasing forces they could not control, demons roving the land unchecked, sand dunes threatening to engulf whole cities for ransom, and so on. He could not do this without helpers, so he chose those who came to hand and whom he thought he could trust.

'To begin with they worked as an informal group, but when the first urgent tasks were done some decided to leave, while most agreed to stay and help to maintain the order they had achieved, each with their own responsibilities in a more formal structure, though they did not then call themselves the Watchers.

'Knowing how the original Watchers had become corrupted he persuaded them to bind themselves into a magical covenant to cooperate for the general good of all the peoples of the Empire. This worked well enough, thanks – I now realize – to his mitigating presence in the covenant, since they did not feel him to be in competition with any of them. Then, some two hundred years ago, he told them that he would be away for a while. He gave them no explanation other than that there was something he must do, and do alone. Months went by, and seasons, and years, but still there was no word from him. They searched by all the means at their disposal, but he seemed deliberately to have left no trace.

'So the covenant remained in force, and their natural urge for power was constrained into a joint urge of ever-increasing force, until the time came when they put their individual selves aside and became what they are now, a single entity, a single shared nature and thought-system. What one knows, they all know. What one desires, all desire. Their joint mind creates a single purpose. They cannot be destroyed one by one. They replace a missing member with a fresh recruit who cannot help but join them and then becomes identical with all the others. And thus conjoined they are far more powerful than the Ropemaker, or even Faheel, or any of the other Master Magicians in their prime. The Emperor and his officials function as they have always done, only where Watchers allow them to do so.

'Elsewhere they ruthlessly adapt the system to their own needs. It is still the case, as it was in the time of your story, that nobody can die within the Empire without a licence to do so, in order that the Empire should not be flooded with the natural magic released into the world at every human death. Those who could not afford the licence and the cost of the rituals to control that magic had to travel to Goloroth, the City of Death, in the far south, where they boarded rafts which were floated out on the Great River and were carried out into the ocean. There they died and their magic was harmlessly released. The first part of this system remains as it was, but now when they pass through the inner gate of Goloroth their lives are simply taken from them, and their personal magic is funnelled back to feed the power of the Watchers in Talakh while their lifeless bodies walk on into the Great River and are carried away.'

'That's the nastiest thing I've ever heard,' said Saranja. 'I've always thought the system in our story was bad enough, but that's obscene!'

'I suppose they say they haven't broken the covenant,' said Ribek, 'because they exist for the good of the peoples of the Empire, so the greater their power the greater the good?'

'Exactly,' said Chanad. 'But it is the general good, remember. They will ruthlessly sacrifice any number of individual citizens of the Empire, just as an individual Watcher will sacrifice himself or herself, in order to achieve it.

'They are like the demons of old. Demons are, as it were, embodied lusts, rage, greed, cruelty, spite, brains without minds – terrible. The Watchers are an embodied lust for domination. Limitless domination, first of the Empire, then of the other nations of this world, then of worlds elsewhere in this universe and universes beyond it, if any there be. Somewhere along that course they will meet their match and destroy themselves, and the Empire, and perhaps the whole world with them. They must be stopped. You set out to find the Ropemaker, three of you for the sake of your Valley, and Benayu to take his revenge for the death of Fodaro, but you are here for greater purposes than that. Even the Ropemaker cannot stop the Watchers on his own, but somehow, between us, we will achieve it.'

Maja looked at her friends, appalled. She had simply not thought about it like that. At the start she had just been running away, as she had done all her life in her dreams. Only by accident had she found that she was now looking for the Ropemaker, and then by further accident that she was going to help Benayu destroy the Watchers. Even at their most frightening their adventures hadn't mattered much to anyone except themselves. Who else cared all that much about what

133

happened to a miller and a farmer's daughter and two children?

But now there was a world to save. Finding the Ropemaker would be only the start.

Ribek must have had the same thought. For several moments he looked unusually serious, then shook his head in disbelief.

'It's a bit more than we bargained for,' he said, smiling slightly, as if at the absurdity of the enterprise.

Saranja flushed and tilted her head defiantly.

'Well, if it's what we're here for we might as well get on with it,' she said.

'I'm going to destroy the Watchers,' said Benayu firmly. 'When I've done that I'm going to go back to shepherding, and a bit of hedge magic. Anything that happens after that – someone else can deal with it.'

'I wish you well, Benayu,' said Chanad. 'But you will find that you are unable to do as you wish. Your own powers will either compel you or destroy you. But first, as I say, you must find the Ropemaker. Where do you propose to start? You have some kind of plan, or clue?'

They looked at each other, uncertain.

'We have a plan of a kind and a clue of a kind, but I'm afraid we've been told not to tell anyone what they are,' said Ribek. 'Not even someone like you. All I can say is that we need to get to Tarshu.'

Chanad actually laughed.

'Let me guess,' she said. 'Benayu has some major magic to perform, connected with your search, and instead of attempting to hide it from the Watchers in some remote province you are taking the risk of disguising it as part of the explosion of magic that will erupt when the Watchers try to repel the coming Pirate invasion. I agree with you. It is much your best chance. But you will need to hurry. Tarshu is almost a month's journey from here.

'It is no use my coming with you. My presence would betray you almost at once. I dare not even watch your progress for fear of leaving a trace. The best I can do for you is to open a road for you to leave here, and to give the two horses you bought greater speed and strength, and fetch you way-leaves to allow you to use the Imperial Trunk Road to Tarshu. You will need a story to account for your journey. Suppose you older two are brother and sister, taking your younger sister to a betrothal ceremony in Tarshu. This is a common practice among the great trading clans. It is a way of keeping the bloodlines pure when the clan is scattered throughout the Empire.

'I'll also prepare an amulet to shield Maja from the effects of magic. What she has faced so far is already wearing her out, and she certainly won't survive the storm of battle magic you're going to find around Tarshu, not to mention whatever Benayu will be up to. Even my amulet may not be proof against such shocks, but it will be a lot better than nothing.

'Now, out of curiosity, I would like to know how Saranja and Maja came so easily through my barrier of fear. You were holding hands, and I think you were carrying some kind of magical object between you. Is that right?'

Saranja took the fear-stone out of her wallet and laid it on the table.

'I've got a sort of all-purpose amulet,' she said. 'It's called Zald-im-Zald . . .'

'Zald-im-Zald!' whispered Chanad, shaken for the moment out of her composure. 'How on earth . . . ? That I *have* heard of. It is said that Asarta made it when she first came into her powers, but it has been lost for centuries. May I please see it?'

Saranja drew Zald out and laid it in front of her. Like Benayu, Chanad didn't immediately pick it up, but sat in silence, simply studying it as if it had been a book, while Saranja told her how she had come by it.

'Benayu must put the fear-stone back,' she said at last. 'There is an intricate balance of the constituent parts, which it is dangerous to disturb. It is an extremely useful object, and you should know as much about it as possible. Benayu can tell me what he has found out and I will see if there's anything I can add. While we are doing that perhaps you others will take the used dishes back into the kitchen.'

They did as she asked, and Maja was amused to see that Ribek was very pernickety about getting things clean, while Saranja was the slapdash one. They came back to find half a dozen books piled on the table. Chanad had two open before her and kept referring back and forth, reading from one and then leafing to and fro through the other. Benayu was looking listlessly at a third one, obviously passing the time while he waited for her. They settled down and waited too, until Chanad sighed and looked up.

'It must be over two hundred years since I last tried to read Solipsi,' she said. 'And it was never an easy language at the best of times. But let's start with the big piece of amber at the centre, because it's so different from the rest. At a guess it's a summoning stone of some kind, but it would take more time and effort than I can spare to overcome the locks and find out what it summons. Something hugely powerful, but it would be extremely dangerous to try to use it without knowing its purposes.

'This one that puzzled Benayu is rather amusing. It's an old demon-binder. You wake it in the ordinary way, and then it will tell the wearer how to use it.'

'I wouldn't worry,' said Benayu. 'It isn't going to happen to us. There aren't any demons to bind these days.'

Ribek laughed.

'In my recent experience *anything* can happen to us,' he said.

'There were demons in the story, weren't there?' said Saranja. 'When Tilja and the others were on their way home, all sorts of horrible monsters appeared, and even on the Imperial Highways people had to travel in convoys with a good magician to guard them.'

'Those were just petty demons,' said Chanad. 'Mostly they were raised by inexpert magicians, ignorant of what they were dealing with, and their first act was to destroy those who had raised them. But there were worse than that. A few really powerful hidden magicians, like the one Tilja called Moonfist, refused to accept control and wanted all the power for themselves. But the Ropemaker and his helpers were too much for them, so as a last throw they deliberately summoned some of the great demons from deep under the earth and tried to use them against him. But demons are not like that. They cannot be used or controlled. They too destroyed their summoners and stalked the Empire, until the Ropemaker and his friends bound them one by one, and split the earth apart and cast them into its innermost fires and sealed them there.'

'That's one of the reasons the Watchers gave for destroying my mother and father,' said Benayu. 'They said they were planning to loose the demons again.'

'And if they catch me they will destroy me and say the same thing,' said Chanad calmly. 'You too, Benayu. You are in revolt against their rule. They are clearly too powerful for you. When you see your cause is hopeless, why should you not attempt to loose the demons? That is their argument.

'But now I have work to do. I must make Maja's amulet, and fetch your way-leaves and so on. It is better for me to do these things from the safety of my tower than for Benayu to continue to risk them on the open road. And you must rest, and in the morning I will set you on your way to Tarshu.'

Chapter 6

GRADUALLY THE NIGHTMARE of pursuit faded as the road flowed backward beneath the horses' hooves, at first as a strange smooth path snaking through the wilderness that they had been crossing since they left the road – never visible for more than a few hundred paces ahead of them and behind them as the folds in the ground hid it and revealed it again, as if it existed only in the stretch they could see. Indeed, after a while, Maja began to realize that this was indeed the case.

Chanad had told her how to use the amulet she had given her as she left. She realized at once that it was going to be a wonderful help. She was growing erratically into the use of her extra sense as it increased. The amulet was a way of controlling that. It looked like a simple bracelet of coloured glass beads and was mildly elastic so that it would stay wherever she put it on her arm. The higher she wore it the less protection it gave, so that when she pushed it a little above her wrist she became faintly aware of the presence of magic, while worn just above her elbow, which was as far as the thickness of her arm allowed it to go, the magical signal became almost as strong as it would have been if she had been wearing it on her left arm, where it had no effect at all.

Now, as they travelled eastward through the deserted landscape, she was able to adjust it until she could sense two steadily moving waves of magic laying and then removing the path before and behind them, leaving nothing to show that anyone might have passed that way. There was even a clean, dry cave with a stream beside it as the sun sank that first evening, which looked and felt as if it had been there for centuries, but for all they could tell hadn't existed an hour ago and would vanish next day as soon as they had rolled up their bedding and gone. Inside, it felt disturbingly magical, but she moved the amulet down her arm and slept there untroubled.

Early the following afternoon they came out onto a public road and turned south. Then several days of farming country, increasingly rich and fertile, with quiet villages and busy little towns, and once the estate of some great lord. Here almost everyone wore the standard dress of the Empire that they had first seen on the road south of Mord. Maja began to recognize the various arrangements of patterns and beads that showed which grade in the elaborate social order of the Empire the wearer belonged to.

It was as though nothing at all had changed in the

twenty generations since Tilja's time. Coming from the Valley, where nothing had changed either until the dreadful irruption of the wild horsemen from beyond the mountains, Maja didn't find this strange.

They slept in farmers' barns or inns. Night after night Maja waited for Jex to speak to her again in her dreams, though he had told her he was unlikely to. She woke each morning to find that her hand had crept under the pillow while she slept and was clasped around the little granite lizard, warm only with the warmth of her own bloodstream. And so it remained during each day, dangling from her neck beneath her blouse.

Everything seemed utterly peaceful and ordinary. Ribek relished every trivial happening or encounter along the way, and when nothing else took his attention was happy to talk about his mill, and didn't think it at all strange that Maja should be so interested. It would have been easy to let their pace slacken, but for Saranja's determination to drive them on. She seemed unafraid of what they were going to attempt at Tarshu; if anything, eager for it.

'You've been given a purpose, haven't you?' Ribek told her one evening.

She shook her head.

'Not given,' she said. 'It was there all along. I've found it.'

They heard no news from there, or any of the doings of the Watchers. Only twice, when they asked their way through the network of little roads that covered that whole tract, their informants hesitated and looked at them oddly before they answered.

'Is there a problem?' Ribek asked the second time.

The man shrugged and shook his head, as much in warning, Maja thought, as refusing to reply.

'It's like that in the Empire,' said Benayu bitterly, as soon as they were out of earshot. 'Fodaro had lived in it, remember. He used to say that however peaceful things seem, fear is never far below the surface. They're content because they have to be, but that isn't the same thing as being happy. These people have picked up somehow that the Watchers are active. They'll whisper about it among themselves, but not to strangers.'

On the fifth day their road joined one of the Great Imperial Trunk Roads that linked the major cities of the Empire together. It took them on in the same direction, a little east of south, but was very different from anything they'd used so far: two broad highways running in opposite directions, with way stations spaced along it where all travellers must stop for the night and pay the fees and bribes to have their way-leaves inspected and stamped.

Now, and more and more as they journeyed, they became aware of the immense and complex thing that surrounded them and called itself the Empire. To Maja it seemed half-creature, half-machine. Every one of the travellers Ribek talked to at the way stations – and he talked to scores of them because he was like that – was a separate cell in that creature, a tiny piece of that immense mechanism. Every one of them had the Emperor's permission to be there, coming from one specified place, going to another, their passes stamped, their movements recorded, their regulated bribes taken by the way-station clerks, who were themselves also just cells or cogs in the creature-machine's labyrinthine intestines.

From their long acquaintance with the story, the three from the Valley were more familiar with all this than Benayu was, though he had lived all his life in the Empire. This was just as well, for now that he had no magic to perform or deal with he became an even more difficult companion, sitting listless and silent for hours on end, surly at any attempt to comfort or distract him, barely muttering his thanks when Saranja groomed Pogo for him, or Maja brought him the meal that Ribek had bought and prepared. His only relationship seemed to be with Sponge, who would lie with his head in his master's lap when he brooded by the fire in the evenings, mourning with and for him.

Day followed day, and the journey became a routine. The clerks tried to cheat them in various ways, which Ribek dealt with wearily, as if he'd been travelling Imperial Highways for half his life. Levanter and Pogo seemed to be thriving on the journey, happy to canter mile after mile, and flagging no more than Rocky did in the heat of noon.

They regularly covered the distances between three, and even four way stations in a single day. The air became warmer, the orchards grew peaches and pomegranates rather than apples and cherries. The individual farms gave way to vast estates, with gangs of serfs working fields that reached as far as the eye could see, where the sluggish rivers were lined with water-hoists worked by patient oxen to feed the irrigation channels. The road doubled its width and still was busy, wagons or mule-trains laden with merchandise, slave masters marching their men to some fresh task, a whole circus on the move, nobles and their trains trotting through along the special lanes kept clear for them, all the fizz and buzz of a contented and prosperous people. It was difficult to remember the bedrock of fear lurking below the surface.

Each evening, as they settled down in their plot at the way station, Maja would practise using her amulet to check around among their neighbours for any possible magical activity. There was almost always some minor hedge magic going on somewhere nearby, causing one of the beads on her amulet to glow faintly, and then more strongly as she rotated it on her wrist, until the glowing bead was pointing towards the source of the signal. Different beads would glow according to the type of magic in use, and perhaps glimmer or pulse to some rhythm inherent in it. No doubt Benayu, if he had chosen, could have picked up the same signals, but with a conscious effort. He needed, so to speak, to open the door of his attention. For Maja, they were simply there, like birdsong.

Ten days or so into their journey they reached a small town where two Imperial Highways joined and continued south together, and here there was a larger than usual way station. All way stations had the same layout: a courtyard, roughly square, with a colonnaded arcade running round all four sides. Richer travellers could rent one of the spaces beneath the arches; the poorer or meaner ones slept in the open. A row of food-stalls ran either side of the entrance. Unless it was raining, which it had done only once so far, Maja and the others slept in the open with the horses tethered beside them.

This evening they were close to the back wall of the way station, almost opposite the entrance. As the dusk thickened and Saranja nursed the fire she had just lit, Maja felt, like a sudden rap on the door of her mind, a quick pulse of magic from somewhere close to the entrance. A pause, and then another. And another. Each time a bead blinked brightly on her wrist, showing the source was moving steadily along parallel to the front wall. It reached the side wall and started back. She told Benayu and he roused himself from his torpor. Together they rose and looked.

Lamps were being lit under the arcade, and silhouetted against these she could see a single man working his way steadily across the courtyard, pausing before each group of travellers, emitting his pulse, and moving on. Halfway back he paused longer. One of the travellers rose and handed him what looked like a document. He glanced at it briefly, handed it back and moved on.

'Random check on magic-users at way stations,' said Benayu. 'Jex told you they were doing it, remember?'

'Will you be all right?' said Saranja.

'Should be. If the Watchers didn't spot me up at Mord . . . It doesn't look the kind of job they'd waste anyone above second level on. There'll be someone more powerful he can call on if he runs into trouble.'

Now he sounded completely confident, like Saranja, almost eager. This was his first real test against his enemy, and he was going to pass it. There was even a hint of the cocky young know-all he had seemed when they had first met him back at the sheep pasture.

It never came to the trial. Maja continued to watch, readying herself for the quick pulse of magic every time the man paused. He was only a couple of rows from them and was checking a licence when there was a sudden, intense flare of power from immediately behind him. A bead on the amulet blazed bright enough to cast shadows. Ribek caught Maja as she fell sprawling. By the time she recovered the man had disappeared and there was a clamour of panic from where he had been, fading to a mutter of rumour that spread through the courtyard and died away. The silence was as dense as a marsh mist, dense with shock and fear.

'What on earth . . . ?' whispered Saranja.

They looked at Benayu. He shook his head, perhaps in warning, perhaps in disbelief. He didn't answer, but instead turned to Maja and muttered to her to protect herself. She slid her amulet down her arm. Even in those few words she had heard the strain in his voice. His lips began to move steadily, and his fingers danced through a pattern of small, precise gestures.

They waited, it seemed, forever. On the other side of the courtyard somebody began to scream and couldn't be stilled, but only one or two stars had pricked through the darkening sky when the Watcher came, and the nightmare was real.

Maja found herself locked into place. She couldn't have moved a finger if she'd chosen. But she'd been looking directly towards where the magical explosion had occurred, so she saw him appear out of nowhere –

a tall figure wearing a pale unornamented cloak and an ivory mask with only two round eyeholes and a dark slot for a mouth. Shuddering at the nauseating impact of the Watcher, she slid the amulet up her arm as far as she could bear. It was important to know, to understand.

The space around him shimmered and became a sphere of light. He raised both hands head-high with fingers spread and spoke five ringing syllables. The sphere rose and grew until it was large enough for everyone in the courtyard to see the scene it held, an upland pasture with a brown hare loping across it.

The viewpoint withdrew, enlarging the scene to show a stretch of sky from which a lion-headed thing, winged and taloned, came hurtling down. A bolt of lightning lanced up at it from where the hare had been. The winged creature absorbed it, plunged and struck, apparently at nothing, and then rose with the naked body of a man writhing in its clutch.

A voice spoke coldly in Maja's head.

'This man chose to use unlicensed powers to take vengeance on a servant of the Emperor, and then to attempt to hide from the Emperor's justice. He will now die slowly over very many days. Continue your journeys in peace, and let one of each party tell all you meet what you have seen. It will not go unnoticed if you fail to do so. Farewell.'

As he spoke the Watcher turned slowly on his heel. His empty eyes raked the courtyard. When he had completed the full circle he vanished.

There was a long, soft sigh as the air was released from several hundred lungs. Mutters and whispers followed. The screaming began again on the far side of the courtyard.

'Never thought I'd be seeing one of *them*,' said a voice nearby.

'Don't mind if I never do again,' said another.

'You all right, young Ben?' said Ribek.

Benayu gave a shuddering sigh.

'They're looking for me too, remember,' he muttered. 'I never imagined power like that . . . and the horror . . . I never imagined it.'

Maja unlocked herself from her own nightmare, instinctively trying to join him in his, to tell him he was not alone. She reached to grasp his hand, clay-cold and clammy with sweat. He didn't respond to her touch, nor come with her when she slowly surfaced into the here and now. He ate not a mouthful of his supper and seemed not to hear their voices, but sat all evening shuddering and staring into the fire. In the end Ribek went to one of the food-stalls and bought a phial of sleeping draught and forced it between his lips. Then he took off his boots and with Saranja's help straightened his body out – he seemed powerless to do even that for himself – and slid him into his bedroll. Sponge settled beside him and quietly licked his hand.

He was little better next morning. Ribek needed to support him to the latrines, and as soon as he returned he curled up again in his bedding and lay motionless until it was time to move. Pogo, aware through some weird horse sense that something was amiss with his usual rider, was in a skittish mood, so they heaved Benayu into Levanter's saddle, where he sat hunched and listless all morning. Saranja led him, with Maja on the pillion, while Pogo took it out on Ribek by shying at trifles by the wayside.

Benayu sat with them silent at their midday rest, ate a few mouthfuls and slept in the shade, but when they moved on began to show signs of life – mutters and sighs and shakings of the head. But he ate steadily that evening, emptied his plate and set it aside, then spoke in a quiet, deliberate voice.

'It's got to be done. It's got to be done.'

He couldn't hide the fear underlying the words.

It remained with them as the days went by, an unseen companion on their journey, as if the ghost of the Watcher walked beside them, invisible to all of them but Benayu. Mysteriously, this made Maja's own private nightmare easier for her to deal with. Compared to the almost solid reality of Benayu's fear, hers seemed little more than a childish terror of the dark. *He* was the Watcher's enemy, the one they were pursuing. Their prey. They probably didn't even know of her existence. Without noticing, she found that she had started being afraid for him, not herself.

'Can't we do *anything* to help?' she said one morning while Benayu was at the latrines.

'It's hard on you,' said Ribek.

'It's hard on all of us. It's like being back at Woodbourne.'

Saranja glanced at her and nodded. She knew what Woodbourne had been like.

'We've got to bear with it, I'm afraid,' she said. 'For

one thing, we gave him our word, and for another we aren't going to get anywhere without him. But we don't all have to put up with it. Pogo will behave himself best alongside Rocky, so I'll go ahead with Benayu and we'll fix a seat for Maja behind Ribek.'

'We could take turns,' said Ribek.

'Let's see how I get on,' said Saranja.

She got on very well, it turned out, simply by being herself. She didn't try to cheer Benayu up, as Ribek might have done, or sympathize with him, as Maja would, but snapped at him if she felt like it, made his decisions for him, ordered him about. This seemed to suit him. Not that he became any less withdrawn, but less morose, more settled.

'Just what he needed,' Ribek told Maja. 'He was pretty well on the edge of madness, I was beginning to think. His world had fallen to bits, and she's put a little bit of it together again for him, a hut in a storm.'

'Her too, I suppose,' he added after a pause. 'She needs somebody outside herself. Not just a purpose, a person.'

Maja knew what he was talking about. It was one of the reasons the change suited her too. Maja wasn't exactly afraid of her cousin, but she always felt on her best behaviour with her. She was so strong and direct and unafraid. She couldn't imagine what it was like to be timid and unsure, as Maja felt herself to be. Or perhaps that was just a mask. No, more than a mask: armour. An armoured knight with a fiery sword, the sword of her anger. How could you know what she was like inside?

Ribek was different, not timid either, but open and

easy. And he liked to talk. He was, simply, more companionable. So Maja perched happily on a folded bedroll behind him, with her arms around his waist to steady herself, and listened to his account of life at Northbeck. He still didn't seem to find it at all strange that she was so interested.

Looking back much later on their adventure she decided that it was because of this closeness that the nature of her fantasy life began to change. So far it had all been about building up a picture of a place where she could belong in the same way he did, at Northbeck mill, imagining the people who lived there, and her dealings with them, and the animals and neighbours and customers who brought their grain to be ground. Being married to Ribek had so far simply been a way of making this happen. He was there, of course. In her fantasy, he set the broken wing of the owlet she found in the woods (it never learnt to fly and rode around on Maja's shoulder instead). He helped her rescue a child from the mill-race. (Whose child? Theirs, of course, but she didn't think about how they'd come by it. Like Ribek, it was simply there for the fantasy, but less real than him, or the mill-race, or the yellow cat.)

Now, though, the balance started to shift as the picture solidified. She found herself more and more reluctant to fiddle around with details once she'd decided on them. In real life, once something's happened it doesn't unhappen. There was no magic in her imagined world, apart from Ribek's ability to hear what the mill-stream was saying, so no absurdities. Following this logic she found herself in a double bind. She couldn't go on being the in-between sort of Maja-now/Maja-grown-up she had hitherto been. Maja-now had no place in her imagined Northbeck, where Maja-grown-up belonged. How grown up? She decided she'd married Ribek when she was sixteen – he wouldn't want her before that: she remembered the jewel-seller at Mord, but he also liked farmers to send their prettiest daughters with the grain, though of course he only flirted with them. Or did he? . . . Anyway, they now had two children, the toddler who'd fallen in the mill-stream and the older boy she'd already arranged for because he could hear what the mill-stream was saying, so she'd be about twenty-two and Ribek a bit over fifty, but just as lively as he was now – having a much younger wife was really good for him – and they were still deeply . . .

Her imagination refused to make it happen. It wasn't interested. No, more than that. She really didn't want to think about falling in love, and kissing and cuddling and lying together naked and their children growing inside her body and so on. All that must have happened for her picture living at Northbeck to become as real as she'd pictured it, but she couldn't make it happen. It was as though some magician had deliberately put a ward round it, to prevent her seeing inside. In the end she gave up. Ribek was a lovely man, so of course Maja-grown-up loved him. That would have to do.

She didn't notice when Maja-now started loving him too.

Steadily the climate changed again as they journeyed on south. They were already resting out the heat of each noon. Soon there were different crops in the fields, with different trees by the roadside, different shrubs and weeds in the patches of wilderness. For a while a huge river ran beside the road, with crocodiles basking on its mudbanks and buffalo wallowing in its shallows. Long-tailed monkeys begged or thieved for scraps in the coppices by the highway. Trained dogs kept them clear of the way stations.

And still Jex did not speak.

The moon had waxed to full, dwindled to a sliver and waxed almost to full again when the clerk at a way station glanced up from their way-leaves and said, 'Journey's end, friends. Tarshu road's closed. Another half day to Samdan, and then you're stuck.'

'How long for, do you know?' said Ribek.

'They've been evacuating folk out of Tarshu this last month,' the man said. 'And there's still a few dribbling through. But nothing's happened yet, far as I've heard. When it does, mind, it's going to be big. Good idea to be someplace else.'

'We've got to get to Tarshu somehow or other,' said Saranja impatiently.

'Well, madam, you're just going to have to enjoy the bright lights of Samdan for a while. Though it'll be packed solid with Tarshu folk waiting to get back in.'

'How much further to Tarshu after that?'

'Two days when the road's clear, but it's going to be jammed solid a good while after they start letting folk back, so you'd best allow three.'

*

153

Across country they took six. Strange hawks quartered the sky by day, so between dawn and dusk they lay up in evacuated farms, then travelled on by moonlight. Benayu pulled himself together now that they were so near, and the danger so real. He dared use very little magic. All he could risk was putting a screen round himself each sunset and transforming himself into a pigeon, so as to scout out a route for that night's journey.

At first he kept them as far as possible in or near shadow, but on the second night, as they were making their way along a shallow, part-wooded valley, Maja sensed a faint magical force approaching rapidly from some distance ahead. From the feel of it she recognized it as having something in common with the hawks that she had tracked all day. It seemed to be coming not directly towards them but as if to cross their path a little way ahead. She whispered her news to the others and they turned aside into the shade of a coppice to let it pass.

Soon Benayu could pick it up too, and they felt it cross the further ridge in a broad line and, still invisible despite the moonlight, sweep down into the valley. On it came in absolute silence until it was near enough for the others to make out, first as a few moving blobs of darkness, then as a whole line, which in a few heartbeats more became about forty wild dogs of some kind, spaced several paces apart so as to cover a broad swathe of grassland as they raced along, noses down, whimpering faintly with the excitement of the chase.

The near end of the line passed about a hundred paces from the coppice. One of them checked, raised its muzzle and sniffed the air. A couple of others joined it. Saranja seized Maja, ready to heave her into the saddle. It was no use, they both knew. Once they were spotted this near Tarshu, the Watchers would be on them in an instant. And then, as suddenly as they'd halted, the dogs gave up and moved on. They began to breathe again.

'Not good,' said Ribek. 'They could still cross our scent anywhere and be after us.'

'Either we've got to find some way to hide our scent, or we've got to choose ways where they won't be looking for us,' said Saranja.

'As well as keeping out of the open?' said Benayu. 'It can't be done. It's difficult enough as it is.'

'I don't think we need worry so much about that,' said Ribek. 'Night hunters like owls fly low. However good your eyesight is, you can't see far at night, even in bright moonlight, but if you want to watch any kind of area you've got to fly high. That's why the Watchers are using dogs. Best they can do.'

'I'll think,' said Benayu.

They moved on in silence, expecting any minute to hear the sound of baying coming from somewhere back on their trail, but the night stayed silent until the stars began to pale.

Next night Benayu led them on a slow and twisting course over broken foothills, though there was far better going on the plain below. At one point they waded for a while up a stream, until they came out on a wide upland dotted with abandoned sheep. Here he used Sponge to round up a dozen sleepy and bewildered beasts and for a couple of hours drove them behind the travellers, blotting out the human scent-trail. Then it was broken ground again for a weary while. Once they heard distant baying and guessed that somewhere the dogs had found quarry. Almost at once Maja sensed something magical joining the pursuit. The feeling ended abruptly and the dogs fell silent. At last they reached an empty farmstead with food for the humans in the larder, mostly mildewed or stale, and fodder in the storage bins. And sleep.

The farmstead was on high ground looking east. Maja was standing in the doorway next evening, watching the movement of hawks as she waited for Benayu's return. She'd seen only one in an hour or more, where there'd been at least one constantly visible on the day they'd started. She was distracted by a sense of something unfamiliar ahead and to her left. Far off, she decided after a while, and therefore powerful for her to feel it at all. And muddled, as if there were several kinds of magic going on at the same time.

Moving into the greater darkness inside the door she found that several beads on her bracelet were glimmering erratically, to no pattern that she could make out. She showed Benayu when he returned. He in his turn stood in the doorway and concentrated.

'Yes,' he said after a while. 'I can feel it, just. I wonder. Perhaps something's started to happen at Tarshu. It can't last forever. We'd better get on.'

'And there've been almost no hawks in the sky, either,' she said.

'Perhaps they can't spare the magicians to control them and use their eyes,' said Ribek. 'Now things have started they need them all at Tarshu. Let's hope it's the same with the dogs. It's going to take forever at the rate we've been going.'

So that night they started to take risks for the sake of speed, travelling on easier ground for a while until the chance came to lose their trail for a bit, and, weary as they were, carrying on into daylight until the first hawk appeared. Both they and the horses needed rest and food before that happened, and by then the storm of magic round Tarshu had so intensified that, even with Jex's steady mild protection, it would have been more than Maja could have endured without her amulet. They continued on this pattern for three more nights and by the third morning they could smell the sea.

They were all now tired beyond belief – even the horses were weary – but that evening they drove themselves on as before, until they crossed one of a series of low, long hills, like gigantic ocean waves, and around midnight looked down into a valley and saw that from over the hill beyond rose astonishing bursts of light accompanied by thunderous explosions, that ran as violent tremors through the ground beneath their feet.

Desperately frightened, and with the horses on the verge of bolting, but at the same time buoyed up by the knowledge that they were almost there, they hurried down into the valley. Maja was wearing her amulet adjusted to the point where the main magical turmoil around Tarshu was as much as she could endure, with her sleeve pulled down over it because the almost continual brilliance of its beads might have drawn the attention of any watcher.

There was a belt of trees at the bottom of the valley, with a river running through it, too wide to ford. As they waited while Ribek listened to the rustle of its flow, Maja became aware of something sweeping towards them, high in the air along the further slope.

They moved back into the shadow of the trees.

'Stand close,' said Benayu, and muttered and gestured. Maja felt his screen build itself round them.

'It's coming,' whispered Maja.

They stared up at the patch of sky visible between the branches. Against another brilliant flare from beyond the hill they saw the thing go by, the reptile head held low, scanning the hillside as it passed, the taloned forelegs, the vast webbed wings, the stubby hind legs, the trailing serpent tail, all enormously too large for any bird. Dragon.

Ribek returned to the stream, listened again and came back.

'There's only one of them,' he said. 'I suppose that's something. It just flies to and fro all night. There's another one all day. And there's a mill a mile and a half downstream. We should be able to cross there, if they haven't got it watched.'

They worked their way along beneath the trees, halted to let Benayu build his screen again while the dragon swept south, and again while it returned. By this time they had reached the trees immediately above the mill.

They watched it pass, and pass again, noting that its return from the north took only half the time of its longer southern beat. Meanwhile with sinking hearts they studied the slope that faced them. Time and again the flare of the explosions from Tarshu lit the whole valley, making every rock and thorn bush on the almost bare hillside stand stark, with its ink-black shadow beside it. They could all see that it would take far longer than the time of the dragon's going and return for them to scurry between the scant scraps of cover.

'Looks as if the mill's near as we can get,' said Benayu. 'Should be enough. There's magic and to spare, even down here.'

'Wait a moment,' said Ribek, pointing. 'See there? That kind of a fold in the ground, running slantwise up the hill? This is a mill, remember – an old one by the look of it. There'll have been carts coming and going for hundreds of years. It was the same at home, and the lane there was feet into the solid rock in places. These hills are chalk – we used a sunk lane a couple of nights back, remember? I'll lay you that one'd hide a loaded haycart, and it'll be shadow all along that far side. We can at least look.'

As soon as the dragon had gone by they crept down towards the shadowy pile of buildings. The mill-race thundered over the weir, glittering in the light of the explosions, which all but drowned out the water's deeper thunder. The windows of the mill were black slots. Someone or something could have been watching just inside any of them. Ribek headed for the upstream side of the building, where a railed walkway close against the mill wall spanned the current. They led Rocky and Levanter across, and Saranja coaxed and bullied Pogo to follow. The water raced beneath their feet, drawn taut like stretched silk towards the rush of the weir. In the yard beyond, a scrawny hound scurried out to challenge them, but Sponge saw it off. They crossed the worn cobbles, went through the gate and almost at once entered the sunk lane.

It was just as Ribek had promised, a deep cleft running sidelong up the hill, wide enough for a heavy cart, its walls almost sheer, its chalk floor rutted by year after year of passing wheels into two great trenches, wide as a man's body and knee-deep or over. The glare from explosions at Tarshu, joined now by the steadier, more orange glow from the burning city, cast a narrow strip of dense shadow all along the right-hand wall.

Maja saw little of this, riding with her eyes half closed as she concentrated on reaching out through the chaos of magical impulses from beyond the hill so that she shouldn't miss the far fainter signal of the dragon's return from the north.

There! Was it? Yes.

'It's coming,' she said.

They reined the horses in and lined them up to huddle along the chalk wall. The shadow here was barely wide enough to hide them. They held their breath as the dragon passed almost directly overhead. A fresh burst of light illuminated it so brilliantly as it passed that Maja felt she could see every separate scale on the sinuous body – beautiful, monstrous, deadly. The powerful, steady wing-beat did not falter, and it was gone. They relaxed and climbed on.

Twice more they paused and hid while the dragon went by, and then they were at the top.

They stood and stared.

Where the lane actually crossed the ridge it bit less deeply into the chalk, but a stand of warped trees grew beside it, blown almost horizontal by the sea winds, roofing them over from above but leaving a good, wide view out to sea. After the enclosed, shadowy hiddenness of the lane there was so much going on, so strange in such a blaze of light, and at such distances, that it was difficult to take in. The reek of burning floated up the hill, carried by a tangy, salty, fishy-smelling breeze.

Almost immediately at their feet, it seemed, lay Tarshu.

Maja had expected to find the whole city ablaze, but it was not. In two large patches the fires raged, golden and orange, with swirling masses of smoke pouring upward and then spreading into a dark, sagging layer tinged purple and orange with the light of the fires below. The columns of smoke rose through two great rents in an intricate network of glimmering violet lines that roofed the whole of the rest of the city. The edges of these rents writhed and reached inwards, as if trying to re-weave themselves over the holes. Even through the protection of her amulet, now worn only just above the wrist so that it almost totally screened her from the immediate effect, Maja still felt dazed by the huge out-pouring of magical energy from a dozen separate sources as the Watchers in the city struggled to repair the damage. Above this extraordinary scene hovered an airboat.

It was enormous, unbelievable. The airboat they had encountered in the Valley would have seemed a toy beside it. A dozen arms on either side of the great bag bore the propellers that were moving the vast craft slowly over the city. Other projecting structures interrupted the smooth curves of the bag. Slung beneath it was the sleek gleaming gondola that carried the Sheepface crew.

The airboat slowed, swung and halted above the edge of the larger of the two rents. From the top of a mast above the bag shot a dozen gleaming metallic streamers, which arced out and dangled down through the rent below and into the flames. Hatches opened below the gondola, releasing a stream of dark missiles, which tumbled end over end a couple of times and then, as they gathered speed, were steadied by the fins at the rear end and plunged on down, some through the gap in the web and on into Tarshu, others on to the web itself. Wherever they struck a colossal explosion followed. The ones that landed on the city below sent shards of flaming debris hundreds of feet into the air, only to rain back down and start new fires where there was anything left to burn.

But that, Maja realized, was not their purpose. It was the ones that landed on the web that struck home. Somehow the web absorbed the shock. The violet network blazed around each explosion. For a moment the brightness spread like ripples in a pool, and then it was gone. But the patch of web through which the brightness had dissipated was in ruins. As patch joined to patch the rent extended while the shattered lines strove to rejoin and re-roof the city.

Meanwhile the airboat itself was under attack. Around it, seeming tiny against its bulk, though in themselves monstrously larger than any normal bird or beast, circled a dozen dragons, flying in V-formation like migrating geese. Suddenly, as if at a word of command, they swung from their course, spread apart and hurtled towards the prow of the airboat. They were met by streaks of dotted brightness emerging from two slits in the front of the gondola, and two more from projections on the bag itself. The dragons wove from side to side, and ducked and climbed, trying to make themselves harder targets. They moved all at the same moment, as if joined by a single will. Sometimes a turn came at exactly the wrong moment for one of them, bringing it straight into one of the lines of light. The bright dots passed harmlessly through it and it raced on towards its target unperturbed.

They had almost reached it, and the first jets of flame were beginning to blast out of their mouths when it happened again. This time the dragon died almost instantly. Maja felt the jolt as its magical being blinked out of existence. Its wings crumpled and it plummeted down, tumbling over and over into the fires below. The other dragons had already vanished.

'There was only one of them,' said Benayu, in an awe-hushed voice. 'The others were simulacra, decoys, to give it more chance of reaching the airboat. Fantastic power it must take to do that with a dragon.'

Fantastic power, yes, Maja thought. And still it churned up out of the city. But in all the swirling chaos of magic Maja could detect no impulse of any answering magic from the Sheep-faces' side. All their weapons – the astounding airboat, the missiles they poured down on the city, the stream of fiery projectiles with which they had destroyed the dragon – were devised out of the materials of the natural world, like Ribek's mill, back in the Valley.

'Well, this is what we've come for, isn't it?' said Ribek. 'Let's get on with it. And then we clear out, quick as we can. Back down the lane, through the mill and up into the woods. Right, Benayu?'

'I suppose so,' Benayu answered.

He sounded listless, dazed, suddenly overwhelmed now that he was confronted by the sheer unmasterable power of the thing that he had vowed to destroy. Maja could sense the upward surge of the returning terror that he had been struggling to suppress ever since the episode in the way station. She put her arm round his shoulders and tried to steady him as a fresh outpouring of magic gathered itself overhead.

The cloud-layer split. A shaft of lightning, wider and more intense than any natural bolt, lanced down. But it never reached the airboat. Somehow the mast above the bag attracted it and then passed it down the glittering filaments to the ground below. They blazed for a moment, blinding bright, and then, though the thunder roll had barely begun, the lightning was gone and the airboat floated on undamaged. Again, Maja could sense no magical impulse in the Sheep-faces' response. It was simply a device, like the engines that drove the pro-pellers, that they had invented themselves.

She felt the lightning-magic gather anew, but there was something odd about it this time, almost as if its heart wasn't in it, as if whoever was doing it wasn't really concentrating, was thinking about something else.

But the bolt flashed down undiminished, and the mast caught it and sped it on its way to earth.

And yet again.

But now Maja picked up something different, something really huge, gathering itself not in the cloud-layer but ahead of her, out to sea. She sensed a mighty stirring, a vast whirling mass drawing steadily nearer, growing in power as it came.

'Get ready,' she said. 'Something's happening. It's bigger than the lightning or the dragons. I think the Watchers are just keeping the Sheep-faces too busy to notice till it's too late. What do you want us to do, Benayu?'

'Do?' he muttered in a dazed voice. 'Anything . . . anything.'

They looked at each other. Saranja took charge.

'All right,' she said. 'Ribek, you manage the horses. Better take them a bit back down the lane. Maja, hold Jex and when the time comes – you'll have to tell me when – put your hand in mine, with him between us, like we did with the fear-stone . . . I think I'm beginning to hear it – sounds like the father and mother of storms . . . Cedars and snows! Look at that!'

For an instant another bolt from the clouds lit the whole scene, far out to sea. By its momentary glare they saw the coming monster, a dark, whirling, tubular cloud-shape reaching up from sea to sky and rushing towards the shore, shrieking and roaring as it came, and sucking the water around its base into a foaming tumble of mountainous waves. The sky overhead was black as pitch. Huge drops of salt-tasting rain poured suddenly down. The Sheep-faces on the airboat must have seen the danger, but too late, for even as the great bag, now dwarfed by the onrushing tower of storm, swung itself round and began to rise, the whirling giant engulfed it and tore it apart.

'Now!' cried Maja.

She waited a moment for Saranja to unwind the Ropemaker's hair from the quills of the roc feathers, then grasped her hand, with the stone lizard nestling in between their two palms.

With her free hand Saranja raised the feathers high above her head.

'Ramdatta!' she cried above the clamour of the storm.

Before the world went black Maja felt the granite pendant she held stir and become live flesh.

A stone voice spoke in the darkness.

'*We must go at once. The dragon guarding the valley is aware of us.*'

Still she couldn't stir, but someone else must have heard that voice, for now as she swam up into consciousness Maja felt herself to be lying face down and half bent over something that jolted unsteadily into her stomach, and with something that held her fast when she tried to stir . . . Yes, lashed on to a saddle – they were already hurrying away . . .

'Awake?' said Ribek's voice. 'Hold it a moment – we're in a hurry. Jex . . .'

'I heard him too.'

The lashings eased. Ribek steadied her as she sat up.

They were already well into the sunk lane. The others were a little way ahead.

'Great you've come to,' said Ribek, panting as they hurried to catch up. 'We're going to need you to tell us where the brute's got to. Something's happened to Benayu. He's pretty well passed out on his feet.'

Maja managed to pull herself together. The magic-storm over Tarshu seemed to have lessened with the destruction of the airboat. She felt for her amulet.

It had changed. The cord was there, but strung through only four or five beads, and those chipped and sharp-cornered. Dimly she remembered a series of snaps and crackles close above her wrist as the amulet had fought to withstand the immense impulse of Jex's return. She pushed what was left up her arm. Nothing happened. It wasn't working. But, but . . .

'*I am shielding you. Is it enough?*'

'Less! Less! . . . There!'

Laid open now to more and more of the tangled magical flow around, reaching out through it with all her soul-energy, she picked out the single strand that came from the guardian dragon.

It was still some distance to the south, but racing towards them. There was a change in it. When they'd watched it from the woods above the mill its power had seemed somehow diffuse, because its attention had been spread over the whole valley. Now it was concentrated, aimed at a single target . . .

'Hurry!' she yelled. 'It's coming! It knows where we are!'

They stumbled down the track. It was dangerous

going, trenched as it was by the axle-deep ruts. Saranja was dragging Benayu by the elbow. The only hope Maja could see was the shelter of the thick stone walls of the mill, but they weren't going to make it, nothing like. Pogo had vanished. Rocky was on the verge of bolting, just as he'd been at Woodbourne when he'd seen the air-boat. Maja slid herself down just in time, and he was away, with Levanter behind.

The dragon . . .

'Get against the wall!' she yelled. 'It's almost here!'

They huddled against the chalk wall and stared up. The pelting rain had stopped as suddenly as it had begun. The fringes of the whirling storm that had destroyed the airboat were screaming overhead, shred-ding the cloud-layer into racing tatters, suddenly hidden behind a glare of blazing orange, lighting the whole lane. Desperately Maja flung herself down into the great rut at her feet and huddled there as the dragon's blazing breath blasted against the far chalk wall. She felt her hair beginning to frizzle in the roasting air, and then it was over.

Shakily she climbed to her feet. Everything was pitch dark after the glare, but the others must have hidden in the rut, as she had, because now she heard Ribek's voice asking if she was all right, and a moment later Saranja's furious yell.

'Benayu! Benayu! Wake up! Pull yourself together! Do something! You're our only hope!'

And then the double crack of flesh on flesh as she slapped him twice on the cheek, and Benayu's dazed voice.

'What . . . ? Where . . . ?'

'The dragon! It'll get us next time! Do something! You're our only hope, you and your stupid magic!'

'Oh . . . Sorry . . . Right.'

'Where's the dragon, Maja?'

That was Ribek. She tried to concentrate.

'It's starting to turn . . . It's not coming back! Yes, it is, only it's circling so it can come *down* the lane next time.'

It would be no use hiding in the rut again when it did. The flaming breath would scour the floor of the lane and they'd all four of them be roasted where they lay.

'Right,' said Benayu's voice, firmer now. 'I think . . . yes . . . Tell me what it's up to, Maja.'

She felt his magic beginning to gather itself, and further off the dragon nearing and nearing, fighting all the while to hold its course through the screaming wind. Steady-voiced she called out the news of its approach. It was at the top of the lane, plunging down the slope . . . any moment now . . .

She reeled as Benayu's magic intensified, but Jex's shield caught her, steadied her. The magic built to a single intense, directed pressure, not against the dragon, but . . .

The wind fell suddenly still, as if the whole world held its breath for the encounter . . .

And now they could all four see the monster against the glare from Tarshu, hear the booming bell-beat of its wingstrokes, watch as it lowered its head for the blast that would roast them alive . . .

Benayu switched off his powers and at once the tempest they had been holding back for those short moments screamed in again, its fury doubled, tripled in intensity by being so pent. It snatched the dragon from its course and whirled it away like a blown leaf. Maja felt its powers flare up and vanish as it was smashed into something unseen.

Jex's shield enveloped her in a bubble of calm.

Dazed by the sudden come and go of those immense forces, it took her a moment to gather her wits. Benayu lay in a huddle on the floor of the lane, with Ribek stooping over him. Now he knelt, expertly hoisted Benayu across his shoulders as if his inert form had been one of the heavy grain sacks in his mill, and rose.

Shakily they hurried on down the lane while the tempest roared inland. When they reached the mill they found that half its roof had been ripped clean off, and beams had fallen across the walkway by which they had come. As they worked to clear them, the horses came nervously into the mill-yard, their panic-flight halted by the river. Levanter must have stayed with Rocky, as usual, and Pogo then found and joined them. Now, stumbling upon their human friends, and being offered a feed of grain from the store-bins, they seemed to decide that sanity had been restored to the world. While they ate, Ribek and Maja rifled the larder for still-edible stores. Ribek heaved Benayu across Levanter's back, and then, weary beyond belief, they crossed the river, worked their way back along beside the splintered woods until they came to a stretch that the tempest had left comparatively undamaged, and there slept dreamless under the trees.

PART TWO

Barda

Chapter 7

'**M**aja.'
    The voice in Maja's head seemed as level and toneless as ever, but somehow different, as though the rock from which it came was no longer granite, but something lighter and less enduring.

'Oh, Jex, thank you! We'd all four be dead without you.'

'*No thanks are due. I in my turn would be dead without you. In human terms I am now convalescent. Until I regain the true balance between my two modes of existence I will return to the form of a pendant that you can wear around your neck.*'

'But it will be you now, not just an, um, extension of yourself?'

'*Yes, I will be fully there, but protected from excessive magical input, but that will also mean that I am unable to protect you from it. However, I will automatically be shielding you from everyday magic more effectively than I have recently been able to do.*'

'I'm getting stronger, I think. I like being able to feel what's going on, most of the time.'

'*Wear me against your skin and I will give you all the protection I can. With clothing in between I will give you less. If you do not wish for my help at all, put me in your wallet. One more thing. I still cannot act with confidence in the material world of either of my existences, so except in an emergency I will continue to speak to you in dreams.*'

'This isn't a dream. You make dreams up, though you don't realize that's what you're doing. This is happening while I'm asleep, but it's real.'

'*Yes, it is real, just as the danger we are in is real. Two dangers. First, since I was unable to prevent it, the Watchers must surely have been aware of what Benayu did last night. They still have to recover from the major effort of summoning their storm, and then for a day or two they will be fully occupied in repairing their protective web over Tarshu. We must be far from here before they start to look for us, leaving no magical trail. Benayu would leave such a trail, faint but not too faint for a good magician to detect if one were to come looking, as one surely will. So would Zald-im-Zald and Rocky . . .*'

'What about the other two? Chanad did things to Levanter and Pogo . . .'

'*Chanad?*'

'A magician we met on the way. She was all right. She said she was the last of the Andarit. She . . .'

'*Tell me later. I cannot keep contact with you very long. The horses. Yes, probably they will now leave a faint trail. But if you and I follow last of all I will absorb all such traces. That is the best we can do.*

'Secondly, I myself am a source of danger. Another creature of my kind may by an error of judgement have betrayed our presence in this universe to the Watchers, so . . .'

He paused for two or three seconds, and went on as if there'd been no interruption.

'. . . if that is the case, they would be hunting us by every means at their disposal, but for their preoccupation with repelling the Pirates. If they were to find me, they would find you. As it is, all of us of my kind are in hiding for the time being and dare not communicate with each other as we are used to doing, so I can no longer bring news of the Watchers' activities. We will henceforth have to guess. Do you understand?'

'Yes. But I still want to say thank you. And I'm glad it's me you can talk to.'

'I reciprocate your gladness.'

'Wait. Now we've got to look for the Ropemaker. How do we do it? Where do we start?'

'I had intended to ask among my friends. I cannot now do that. I will consider the matter.'

She slid back into dreamlessness until something began to snag at her sleeping mind. She woke, and knew it was something Jex had said. Just one word. She had a vague feeling it was something she wasn't supposed to know. He'd made a mistake, hesitated, and then gone on. Perhaps she'd remember in the morning, when she was telling the others. She lay for a while looking up at a few stars shining through a gap in the branches overhead, and wasn't aware of falling asleep again, but she must have done, because now the trees were gone and the sky was full of stars, far, far too many of them.

In her dream she pushed herself up and looked around. She'd been lying alone on an empty hillside. Close beside her in the turf glimmered a little circular pool. She put her hand on the rim and leaned over the pool, propping her weight on her arm. The reflected sky seemed to rush towards her. Pool and hillside were gone and she was falling into the sky. Moons and stars streamed past. Great cloudy masses, dark or glowing, floated by. Now all were gone and she was falling towards the last star of all, the very end of the universe.

Now she was standing on a hillside much like the one she had left. Directly in front of her rose the doorway to Chanad's tower. There was no tower, though, no moat, only the wooden door itself, the arch that held it and the carved face above.

She watched the door open of its own accord. Immediately beyond was another door, so close that they must have been almost touching. It was made of . . . she didn't know what. A sort of solid mist, it looked like, twinkling all over its surface with innumerable flickers of light, no sooner glimpsed than gone. She became aware of the magic of the universe rushing past her and on through the closed door as if it wasn't there, like the tumbling flurry of a mill-race through a sluice. That was what caused the door to flicker as it did.

But it wasn't a door, in any case, she realized. It was only as far as she could see. It wasn't dark beyond that point. There was light there, but it wasn't her kind of light. There was stuff beyond, and movement, and happenings, but . . .

'Your eyes were not made for such seeing,' said a sweetly soft voice overhead. 'Nor your mind for such imagining.'

She looked up expecting to see that the stone face at the top of the arch was flesh now, but the arch was gone, and the door, and she was awake under the trees, looking up at some different stars shining through a gap in the branches.

The word that had snagged on her mind had been 'universe'.

'Another creature of my kind may by an error of judgement have betrayed our presence in this universe to the Watchers.'

With that knowledge safe in her mind she fell asleep, dreamless once more, and when she next woke it was broad daylight.

She was still blinking in its brightness when she realized that something important had changed. Though she was still being gently shielded from all the magic around her, that must be Jex, because her amulet wasn't doing anything. She forced her eyes open and peered mistily at it. Last night she had felt its beads splintering under the magical stress they were trying to shield her from. Now they were all gone but one. That remaining one was a dull black sphere that had never shown any sign of life at all. She had sometimes wondered what it was for. Perhaps a quite different form of magic, something they hadn't met yet, so she'd better go on wearing the amulet, just in case. Anyway, it would do as a sort of luck charm.

The others were talking in low voices. She groaned and sat creakily up. Saranja had a fire going and Ribek was gutting a fish to grill over it. Benayu was staring at the thin smoke, pale-faced and troubled-looking, but apparently fully aware and listening to what Ribek was saying.

'. . . but if they've got it right – rivers don't always, this far from the source, and they'd only picked it up from some gulls who'd flown in to escape the fighting – three of the Watchers and several other magicians who were helping them died in the battle and the rest are too busy repairing the damage to do anything else, so with a bit of luck there won't be any dragons for a bit, or hawks or wild dogs, and we can take the easiest route out, though I've no idea where we are going now.

'Hello, Maja. Ready for breakfast? I hope you slept well. You needed it.'

'I still do – I could sleep forever. But I've got something important to tell you. It's from Jex.'

She explained, again somehow remembering every word.

'He's right, of course,' said Benayu. 'It's not just the dragon. I messed around with their tempest. They'll have felt that . . . Oh, yes, they'll have felt that.'

Something about him had changed in the night. Two things. He now looked openly scared and wasn't trying to hide it, but under the creakiness of his voice there was a note of satisfaction. Last night, up on the naked hillside, he had fought the first skirmish in his war against the Watchers, and won. If he could do it once, he could do it again.

'You're not going to be tackling the Watchers all by yourself,' said Saranja briskly. 'We're going to find the Ropemaker before that.'

'It'll take more than him.'

'Then we'll find more than him,' said Saranja.

'Perhaps the Sheep-faces have been sent to help too,' said Ribek.

'Look,' said Benayu impatiently. 'The one thing we do know is what Jex said – we've got to get away from here before the Watchers pull themselves together enough to start looking for us. We can think about what happens next when we've done that. Till then it doesn't matter which way we go, provided it's as far from Tarshu as possible and as quickly as possible. And we'd better keep well clear of the way we came, because there'll still be a bit of a trail there.'

'That's a thought,' said Ribek. 'Jex is going to wipe out our new trail, so suppose we follow the old one for a bit and then branch off, with luck they'll think we're still going back the way we came.'

'Right,' said Saranja, rising fluidly to her feet. 'Come along, horses – finished your breakfast? Lazy times are over . . . We're going to have to let them take it a bit easy to start with – they'll be stiff as timber after last night, and it looks like Levanter's a bit lame in his off fore.'

Twenty minutes later they were on their way.

The horses were in better shape than Saranja had feared, apart from Levanter's lameness, so to spare him and at the same time put as much ground as possible between themselves and Tarshu, Ribek and Maja rode Rocky while she activated the jewel in Zald and loped unwearying beside them. Still half shattered by yesterday's efforts Maja dozed most of the way, with shreds of her dream sifting again and again into her sleep and the same thoughts and questions recurring when she woke. She kept in particular remembering Benayu once raising his two hands in front of him, palm to palm and almost touching, and then, when he noticed what he was doing, snatching them apart and laying them in his lap.

Two hands, two doors, two universes.

He'd been about to explain how Fodaro had caused the explosion, and then decided it was too dangerous for them to know. Something had to be got just right. Too little, and nothing would happen. Too much, and you got what Fodaro had got. The two things – not hands, not doors – they were just ways of picturing it – the two *universes* must barely touch for the briefest possible instant. But Fodaro had overdone it – overdone it on purpose, perhaps – just to make sure.

And the reason why it was impossible, even for Fodaro, to imagine the reality behind his equations was that what the equations described was the reality of an unimaginable universe. This was part of the hidden knowledge, the truth that it was too dangerous for her to know. She was guessing, of course, but at the same time she was certain. And certain too that she needed to know it.

The storm must have travelled far inland. They slept that night in the still-standing half of an isolated barn. A falling beam had broken the back of one of the sheep that must have taken shelter there when the storm struck, so they ate fresh roast meat for the first time for many days, and Maja snuggled down into the straw dozily content despite her weariness and anxiety, and fell asleep to the sound of Sponge gnawing the chopbones.

'I've been trying to think about the story,' said Saranja as they breakfasted off sheep's liver and kidneys. 'I've never done that before – it was just a stupid story, as far as I was concerned, but until Jex tells us what to do, it's pretty well the only clue we've got. What I was thinking was that Tilja and the others were in exactly the same fix as we are, looking for Faheel when he could have been anywhere in the Empire. I always thought that one of the stupidest bits was the way they did it – with a wooden spoon, for angels' sake! The point was it had been carved from a tree which had grown from the stone of a peach from Faheel's garden. That was enough of a connection for the thing to know where he was and point that way. We can do better than that. We've got an actual hair from the Ropemaker's head.'

'Of course!' said Ribek. 'And right at the beginning he'd hidden it in the Valley, where there aren't any other magicians. A clue we were the only ones could find. Just in case it was needed. What about it, Benayu?'

'Well,' he said slowly, 'it would be worth a try . . . Yes . . . If Maja . . . No, doing it isn't a problem, apart from one thing. Hiding what we're doing from the Watchers is something else. For a start we wait till we're a lot further away from Tarshu. Even then it's going to be tricky. Saranja will have to take the hair off the feathers, and that will make both of them strongly magical, but I think I can screen that. Jex and Maja – it's got to be her, and that's the other problem – will have to wait outside the screen and when everything's ready Saranja will bring the hair to her and whisper the name. That's going to send out another colossal signal, and Jex is going to have to try to stop it getting through to the Watchers while Maja follows what happens. But you can't do that if you're screened or shielded, that's the problem. It will probably lay you out for a bit, like it did at Tarshu, but maybe when you come to . . . I don't know.'

'It's a lot to ask,' said Saranja.

'I could hear Jex then, even when I was unconscious,' said Maja. 'Perhaps it will be like that. Anyway, we've got to try. I'll talk to Jex, if he'll come.'

She called to him as she lay down to sleep.

'Please come, Jex. I need to talk to you.'

He answered, again in the pit of the night.

'*Maja? What is it?*'

She explained.

'*Yes,*' he said, after a pause. '*It would be possible, but very dangerous. And Benayu is right, it will be too great an output for me to absorb completely. Nor do we want to confine the magic only to the area around us because we need it to reach as far as where the Ropemaker is hidden. I can perhaps hide what you are doing from the Watchers in Tarshu, but not from anywhere else. But I*' *cannot at the same time give you, personally, any more protection than I am now doing.'*

'I don't want to be shielded. I've got to feel what the hair does when Saranja says the name. I think I can stand it, if I'm ready for it.'

'*We have a little time, since we need to be further from Tarshu before we make the attempt, and I hope to be stronger by then.'*

'So do I. Don't go, please. I've worked something out. It's stuff you and Benayu said was too dangerous for us to know. I'm sorry. I couldn't help it.'

'*What is the nature of this knowledge?'*

She told him. He paused before answering.

'*It is not your fault but mine, for using the word. I was tired, and did it inadvertently. If the Watchers discover what you know, they will eventually seek both to use it in this universe and to dominate others. You observed the effect of Fodaro's causing a minor contact between two universes. Imagine the possible effect of the Watchers' meddling. They could destroy the world by one mistake, or they could deliberately destroy other worlds that refused to accept their domination.'*

'What shall I say to Ribek and Saranja?'

'*I suggest you wait until we have seen the result of your experiment with the Ropemaker's hair.'*

'All right.'

Four days later they crested a line of hills and looked down on an Imperial Highway running along the bottom of the next valley. It was a warm, still afternoon, with a few slow cloud islands floating slowly towards the unseen ocean.

'Left or right when we get there?' said Ribek, and pointed eastward. 'Tarshu's back that way – right, Maja?'

The flare of continued magical energies around the besieged city was fainter now with distance, but still vivid to her extra sense the moment Jex relaxed his protection. She nodded. The road below ran roughly north and south, so either way would be equally likely to take them further from it. Benayu sighed heavily.

'Better get it over, I suppose,' he muttered. 'We don't want a lot of people milling around us when we give it a go. There was a place a little way back.'

'You're sure you're up to this, Maja?' said Saranja.

'I've got to be. It's what I'm here for.'

The place was a long-abandoned sheepfold. On Benayu's instructions, he and Saranja and Ribek settled with the horses in a corner formed by two of the rough stone walls, and he constructed a screen around them. Maja stayed close outside the fold, where a slab of fallen masonry made a level surface. She checked the position of Tarshu, walked a dozen paces towards it and settled the little stone pendant that was Jex on to a boulder. He seemed to quiver for a moment, and became the blue and yellow lizard she'd last seen on the mountainside.

Much encouraged, she returned to the slab, spread her spare blouse across it, and sat cross-legged on the ground.

'Ready,' she called, and waited unshielded. She could feel the blank space that Benayu's screen made in the busy shimmer of general background, but because the screen was there nothing of the moment when the hair was unwound from the quills – only the appalling jolt of power when Saranja hurried out through the screen with it.

She reeled, but somehow held on, sensing rather than seeing Saranja's movements as she crouched, laid the gold thread out across the coarse green cloth of the blouse, and hunkered round to put her arm round Maja's shoulders.

The hair blazed in Maja's mind, a single narrow streak, without light, without heat, but still with the ferocity of the blast from a roaring stove when the door is opened a crack. She flinched from it, and would have reeled away, but Saranja's strong arm held her steady. Slowly she schooled herself to endure the blast, as a smith learns to endure the white heat of the metal he draws from his furnace so that he can hammer and shape it to his purposes.

Now, knowing what she could stand, she drew a deep breath and squared her shoulders.

'Ready,' she said.

Saranja breathed the name.

As the world went black Maja felt her shudder with the jolt of power. Then sight, smell, hearing, touch, taste, all were lost. But something remained, something beyond the reach of any normal sense. The single thread of the Ropemaker's hair still blazed in her mind with its strange, dark fire. And since it was all that there was in her universe she clung to it, studied it, reaching out along it to wherever it led. It was a streak of pure power,

power with life, a single living purpose. It yearned for one small spot in all the enormous Empire. There.

The power blanked out as suddenly as it had struck. There was a salty, fishy, weedy smell in her nostrils, far stronger than the salt sea breeze that had been blowing up the slope from the Bay of Tarshu.

'*Well done*,' said the stone voice, slow and grating. '*I too am very shaken. That was more than I was prepared for. I could not absorb it all. We must leave. Tell them.*'

Then silence and darkness for a while. She became aware that she was now standing rigid as a stone pillar, with her left arm stretched in front of her, pointing. There was someone either side of her, holding her upright. Saranja's voice spoke urgently in her ear.

'Maja! Maja! Are you there? Oh, Gods! Maja!'

'That way,' she mumbled. 'On the coast. I could smell the sea.'

Her body went limp and Ribek eased her down, then stayed crouching beside her, his arm round her shoulders. She opened her eyes and saw Benayu and Saranja looking down at her.

'Jex says we must go,' she said. 'He couldn't absorb it all. I'll get him.'

'You stay there, said Ribek. 'Saranja . . .'

'No. I want to.'

He helped her rise and she stumbled off. Jex had returned to being the stone pendant, which was lying on its side next to the boulder. She picked it up, dismayed, and cradled it between her two palms. At once a little of his day-long protection closed itself around her, weaker than it had been even immediately after Tarshu. And

186

something else. Normally she could feel none of his alien magic at all, but nursing him like that she imagined she could sense the strange life, electric inside the granite, but only fitfully there.

'. . . judging by the sun,' Ribek was saying when, moving more steadily now, she carried Jex back to the others, 'and Maja was pointing a bit east of that, so it could very easily be on the coast. Any idea how far, Maja?'

'Oh, a long way. It'll take days and days. Jex said it was more power than he'd expected. He couldn't absorb it all.'

'You mean some of the signal could have got through to Tarshu?' said Benayu.

'I don't know,' said Maja. 'He seemed tired. I think he's only just hanging on.'

'What about you?' said Ribek. 'You took a beating too. Can you stand any more?'

'If it's just ordinary stuff. Jex is still doing something. I don't need my amulet. I'll be all right, provided we don't run into anything heavy.'

'I'll do what I can if we do,' said Benayu with a sigh. 'But . . .'

'If we do, you're going to be busy,' said Saranja. 'All the more reason to get away from here. Looks as if the Highway runs pretty well due north. I don't like Highways, but you get along a lot faster.'

'And there'll be more hedge magic for Jex to absorb,' said Maja. 'That's what he needs.'

'Like feeding an invalid?' said Ribek. 'Little and often, no mighty blowouts.'

'We need him well,' said Benayu earnestly. 'Even if he can't talk to his friends and tell us what's happening, he's much more useful than having me keep screening anything I do. I can, but it wears you out after a while. Anyway, let's go.'

It was one of the smaller Highways, with only two lanes of traffic in either direction, one for noblemen and senior officials, and one for everyone else. In places it was so busy that they could only shuffle along, but then the crush would thin and they could make good speed. Most of the people going north were trying to get away from the fighting, while company after company of soldiers marched by on the southbound road.

The way station where they stopped that night was a small and homely one, used to catering to no more than a few dozen travellers, but tonight it was as crowded as a city market. The news was all gossip. According to the official announcements the attack on Tarshu was only another Pirate raid, which the Watchers had well in hand, but the travellers agreed that whole regiments were swarming ashore, armed with weapons just as strange and just as formidable as the airboat. Without their magicians the Imperial armies would have been mown down like grass in a hayfield. One man claimed – he'd heard it from another man whose sister was married to the mayor of a town further south – that the troops they had seen marching by would be paraded in front of three of the Watchers before they went into battle. The Watchers would combine their powers to enspell them, company by company, and send them on to fight, fearless, tireless and invulnerable.

'Yes, it could be done,' said Benayu. 'You'd need to borrow all of each man's future life and pack it into a single day of fighting, so that when the day was over he would be as old as his destiny decreed. He'd not live long after sunset.'

'Well, that's more Watchers too busy to look for us,' said Ribek cheerfully.

'I don't know,' said Saranja. 'If I were a man, I'd be . . . Look.'

She waved an arm towards the crowded way station.

'Notice something? A lot of men on their own, don't you think? If they were just trying to get clear of the fighting they'd be bringing their families. What they're running away from is being rounded up and enspelled and sent to fight. So the next thing that's going to happen is that the Watchers will start raiding the way stations and rounding them up that way. They'd pick you up, and Benayu too. Unless Benayu can screen us.'

Benayu shook his head.

'Not from a Watcher,' he said. 'All right, I've done it once, but they were in a hurry. I'm not ready to try again.'

'Back to the byways, then?' said Ribek. 'Ah, well. I like the road life. Bustle. Gossip. We get a surprising amount of that at the mill, with all the comings and goings. A right old scandal-exchange, we are. I miss it. There's several good juicy stories I left halfway through.'

'Nothing like at my war-lord's fortress, I'll bet you,'

said Saranja. 'Most of the time there wasn't anything else for the women to do, and I don't miss it at all.'

Lying in the way station that night, Maja dreamed her dream again. It began in the same way, waking on an empty hillside, looking up at the stars, turning to look at them again in the little pool, falling into the pool, plunging down between the stars to the very end of the universe to where the magical doorway rose on another naked hillside. This time something began to stir in the unreachable elsewhere beyond the door. A shadowy shape. Monstrous. Human-shaped, but all wrong. Tall as a tall man as far as the shoulders, but the head above that reaching almost to the top of the arch, and twice as wide at the top than it was at the bottom. '*Help me. Trapped,*' it said in Maja's head and at that moment it stopped being frightening. The head wasn't monstrous, it was just huge. In fact it was vaguely familiar. In her dream she searched for the memory.

Then, as happens in dreams, she was no longer look-ing at the door but sideways, across the slope. A Watcher stood there. He could have been the one who had come to the way station, and like him he was turn-ing slowly round, studying the whole scene. At the moment he was sideways on to Maja and turning away from her, which meant that he would see the doorway before he saw her. It was for some reason desperately important that he shouldn't do that. That was why she was here. She did the only thing she could think of.

'Here!' she called. 'I'm here!'

He stopped turning away and swung just as slowly back towards her.

Terror woke her.

That part was only the old nightmare, she thought as the shudders died away. It didn't mean anything. But the part before . . . Awake now, she searched again for the memory, uselessly, of course, until she gave up, turned on her side and drifted back towards sleep. In the shadowy borderland on the edge of oblivion it came to her.

The story. Tilja, bound and helpless in the robbers' cave. The shape of another prisoner, black against the moonlit opening of the cave. Horrifying until he had by his magic set them all free and Tilja saw him again outside the cave and realized that he was only a tall thin man wearing an outsize turban. That had been Tilja's first meeting with the Ropemaker. Satisfied, she slid back into dream and spoke to Jex in her head.

'I don't know if you can hear me, but I need to talk to you. I think the Ropemaker's trapped in the other universe somehow, but when we used the hair it told us to go to somewhere in the Empire. It doesn't make sense.'

'*Tell Benayu*,' came the faint reply.

Waking again in broad daylight she lay for a little while assembling her thoughts. She didn't see how she could tell Benayu about her dreams without telling the others, which was what she wanted to do anyway. By the time she was up they were already halfway through breakfast.

'You still look all in,' said Ribek. 'We left you because we thought you needed the sleep.'

'I'm all right,' she said. 'There's something I've got to

191

tell you. Jex told me to wait till after we'd seen what the Ropemaker's hair told us. He can't help at the moment. He still isn't strong enough.'

She told them about her dreams, and what she thought they had meant. They waited for Benayu.

'All right,' he said with a sigh. 'I suppose it makes life easier. It's a bit of a strain, always having to remember whenever you say anything that there's stuff you mustn't let on about. According to Fodaro there are lots of universes, but as far as we're concerned there are only two that matter: ours and Jex's. They're completely different because ours has four dimensions – length, breadth, height and time – and Jex's has seven. They aren't just our four with three we haven't got, because however many you've got they have to add up to a whole. Our four already do that, so in Jex's universe they have to be different, to make room for the other three. There's something like our length, but it isn't the same, and so on. They have two dimensions of time.

'This is what Fodaro's equations are all about. They are true in both universes. It's no use trying to imagine what a seven-dimensional universe is like, because you've got a four-dimensional mind, four-dimensional eyes and so on. You cannot make sense of it. And you can't go there and find out. If you could somehow get into a seven-dimensional universe the stuff you are made of wouldn't make sense. It wouldn't just cease to exist. It would be destroyed, and all the seven-dimensional stuff it was in contact with would also be destroyed, and there'd be a colossal explosion in both universes. The explosion Fodaro set off was caused by a contact lighter than this . . .'

He raised his two forefingers and lightly touched their tips together for a moment.

'So the Ropemaker can't actually be in Jex's universe, and Maja's dream is only a dream,' said Saranja.

'Yes, he can. He can do it by magic. Magic is a sort of leakage between the universes. It isn't actual material stuff. Fodaro used to say it's a bit like light. Light isn't stuff, but it's there. It does things to stuff. Plants feed on it. If you try to grow plants in the dark they'll grow for a bit but they won't make green leaves and however well you treat them in other ways, they'll die.

'Magic is leakage from the other universe that doesn't make sense in ours, but it isn't destroyed because it isn't material stuff. So if you know how you can use it to change the stuff of our universe in ways that don't make sense . . .'

He picked up pebble, gazed at it for a moment and then put it back on the ground, where it turned itself into a beetle, raised its wing-sheaths and buzzed angrily away, as if far from pleased at being roused from its peaceful sleep as a pebble.

'Like that,' he said. 'Where was I? Yes, well, there are places where the two universes, ours and Jex's, almost touch. Mostly it's only one or two in each world. Or none. But there are quite a few in our world, and they're almost all in the Empire. Fodaro said that there were mathematical reasons for this – something to do with a thing called a nexus in Jex's universe – but it's why there's a lot of magic in the Empire and almost none anywhere else. He called these places touching points. He found one in the pasture.

'Anyway, I think there are two possible ways of getting into Jex's universe, but one of them you'd need Fodaro's equations for, so the Ropemaker must have used the other one. You'd have to be a pretty good magician to do it, but he was.'

'*Is*, if Maja's dream's right,' said Saranja.

'Yes, is. Your anima, your inmost self, is a bit like light. It isn't stuff, but it's there. It can't *do* anything, though – can't act in the material world, like Jex told Maja – except inside a living creature. So what the Ropemaker would have to do is find a safe form and a safe place in which he could leave his material self – it'd have to be somewhere near a touching point – and put his anima into something like a bird, and then fly to the touching point and project his anima into a living creature on the other side, and then use that as his body to do what he wanted there. He wouldn't be able to take anything material with him, mind you, the time-ring for instance, though it'd be a hideous risk to leave that behind.'

'He's a bit of a risk-taker, by all accounts,' said Ribek.

'It's always a risk, whenever you try anything new. But maybe. So if Maja's dream is right, what we're going to have to do is find where he's left his material self – that'll be where the hair was trying to reach to – and then take it to the Ropemaker' anima in the other universe . . .'

'You said you couldn't take stuff – bits of this universe,' said Saranja.

'I've got to take you, haven't I? This is all going to be really big magic, at least as big as anything we've done so far. Bigger than getting Jex back. It'll take all I've got. There's no way I can do it and screen it at the same time, so the Watchers are going to be on to us in an instant. I'm not going to leave you three and Sponge *and* my material self behind for the Watchers to mess around with while I'm gone.

'I tell you, I ought to be able to do it. It's in the equations. But I'm scared. I've been scared ever since the Watcher came to the way station. Saranja had to hit me to make me deal with the dragon back at Tarshu. Sometimes I wish Fodaro had never found the touching point, never worked out his equations. Sometimes I wish I'd never been born the way I was.'

'We don't,' said Saranja. 'We like you the way you are.'

'Nothing wrong with being scared,' said Ribek. 'When things are scary I'd much rather trust myself to someone who knew they were than someone who didn't.'

Maja didn't say anything. She was scared too.

Maja was strongly on Saranja's side about not travelling by the Imperial Highways. For all its life and interest she had soon wearied of the great one they had used on their way south, and even after so short a time on this smaller one she was strangely glad to get away from it. Since, for Benayu, changing his shape to a bird's was little more than hedge magic, which the Watchers weren't likely to notice, he was able to scout out tracks

195

and byways again, and as they wound their way peace-fully north along them, she discovered why she liked them so much better.

Tarshu had changed her. The effect was partly hidden at first as they passed through bare, sheep-cropped downland, completely emptied of people, all evacuated by the Watchers during the siege of the city. Then, as they moved further from the battle, the landscape changed, with the hills less steep and the valleys wide. There were farmhands working in the interlocking stone-walled fields, driving cattle out from milking to the lush pastures, or hoeing amid healthy half-grown crops.

She was wearing Jex with the cord looped round her neck and the pendant tucked into the pocket of her blouse, and enjoying whatever he let pass of the gentle, almost unnoticeable, magical essences in everything around her – an effect like birdsong in woodland, she thought; after a while you don't notice it, unless a pigeon coos right overhead, but it's there, all the time. They were walking along a deep-cut lane, steep banks with walls atop, and approaching a bend. Beyond it, still out of sight, were three people, two men and a boy. She could sense and distinguish their separate essences, even their mood. The men were laughing and the boy wasn't happy.

She rounded the bend with the others and there they were, in a gateway a little distance further on. The boy, about nine years old, must have fallen in a cow-pat or something, because one of the men was crouching beside him trying to clean him up with handfuls of grass from the roadside. Both men obvious thought it a good joke. The boy did not.

Ribek, typically, stopped to chat, offering them his water flask to help with the clean-up. He caught up at a trot a couple of bends further on.

'Nothing new,' he said, panting slightly. 'They keep pretty well up to date. The Highway's only a couple of valleys away over there. They hadn't heard about the Watchers taking men away and enspelling them to fight the Sheep-faces. Perhaps it's only a rumour that fellow we met had picked up. You probably get a lot of that sort of thing in wartime. You should have heard some of the stories that came up to the mill when the horsemen first attacked.'

'If it's only a rumour we'd be better off on the Highway,' said Benayu. 'We'd get on twice as fast. Three times. Saranja?'

'Maja, would you be able to tell from here if a Watcher came to the Highway?' said Saranja.

She didn't even need to move Jex into her wallet. The moment she concentrated, the Highway was there, laid out in her mind as if she'd been standing on a hillside looking down on it. Over to the left a way station, almost empty at this time of day. There was some kind of minor hedge magic being practised there. On either side of that a ribbon of slowly drifting pulses, travellers on the Highway unconsciously beaming out their individual signals, the natural magic that they had brought into the world with them when they were born and that would leave them only when they died. That was what she had picked up a little while ago when they had been approaching the bend and, before she saw them, she'd known about the three people they'd meet as soon as they were round it. She couldn't have done that before Tarshu. Yes, Tarshu had changed her.

'I'd know,' she said confidently.

'Let's go on as we are, then, for the moment,' said Saranja, 'and Maja can tell us if anything like that starts happening. We haven't been doing too badly. These valleys all seem to run roughly north–south, so the lanes do too, mostly. If we get to a point where Benayu can't find a good way ahead for us we can go back on the Highway for a bit.'

All the rest of that day Maja walked or rode in silence, thinking. Her companions seemed to recognize her need and let her be. No, it hadn't been only Tarshu that had changed her. Perhaps the overwhelming blast of the moment when the speaking of the Ropemaker's name had summoned Jex back across the universes had begun the change, but the real work had been done three days further north, by the old sheepfold, when she had laid one strand of his hair out on the rock beside her and let the whisper of a name blast her into a kind of elsewhere. The journey had finished somewhere in the Empire – she was sure of that – but it hadn't gone *through* the Empire to reach it. It had gone through some other *kind* of space. Unimaginable. For a moment she stood on the hillside of her dream staring through the magical doorway at – at but not into – the unimaginable universe beyond.

Whatever else had happened, that was the moment that had finally changed her. She had come into her own, an inheritance that had been waiting, perhaps through many generations, for her to discover and use.

A troublesome gift. In a way she had known that all along, ever since, hiding under the barn at Woodbourne, she had first been overwhelmed by the shock wave of magic when Saranja had given Rocky his wings. Even before they had reached Tarshu, without her amulet to protect her she would have been lost. The same now, if they ran into any more serious magic, without Jex.

Without Jex? She looked around.

For some time they had been climbing in single file up a narrow path, little more than a sheep-track, that slanted up the side of a hill with the valley beneath them on their right, seeming to stretch further and further into the distance as they climbed. Maja was riding Levanter, with Ribek striding just ahead of her. If they continued on this line they would reach the crest and look down on the Imperial Highway. There was a small town there, not unlike Mord. If she concentrated her whole attention on it she could feel the buzz of its comings and goings, with bits and pieces of hedge magic, and a sort of numb spot, perhaps where something more serious was being warded. She could even feel the endless small fidgetings of the magical trinkets in its market. Deliberately she unlooped the stone pendant from her neck and put it in her wallet.

She reeled. Automatically she flung up her right arm to shield her face. All the world's magic seemed to be battering against her. She was crammed into a tiny cell with Ribek and Saranja, Benayu and Sponge and the horses, all bellowing their separate magics into her ears.

She was stripped naked on the hillside with the hail-storm of minor magics of grass and shrub, gravel and boulder and soil, ant and grasshopper and fly, lizard and snail, streaming against her too-tender skin, while her whole body vibrated to the deep, slow pulse of the centuries-enduring hills.

Her hand was already reaching into her wallet. *Not yet*, she thought. *I must learn about this. It is part of my gift. I can use it.*

Slowly she mastered herself, forced herself to ignore the immediate intense assault. To reach out into it, through it and see what she could find. It was like a winter morning once at Woodbourne when she had woken early to look for a hen. It had been missing the night before though she had searched and searched until it was time for her to come in and set the table for supper. It would have meant a word as bitter as a blow from her aunt if she'd been late for that. The hen would have been no excuse – less than no excuse, as it would have been her carelessness to lose it, so she hadn't dared tell anyone.

But it had come to her in the night where the bird might be. So, in the faintest of faint hopes, she had risen and dressed and slipped down the stairs in the dark and lit a lantern and opened the door, into a snow-blizzard.

She had heard the wind in the dark and expected storm weather. But not this. These sudden buffeting gusts from every-which-where, almost solid in their strength, and from the thick, swirling white flakes they bore, hurling into the tiny globe of light from the fluttering lantern-flame and on into the dark. Again and again she had to force her eyelids up as they tried to close themselves against the slashing icy particles that whipped into her face, so that she could peer one pace ahead. She had almost turned back, but she had battled on, mastering her fear, mastering her weakness, mastering the storm, finding the stupid hen cowering in its nook, carrying it back and releasing it clucking into the coop. She had told no one. So now.

Except that there was no hen to look for, no purpose in her struggle against that blizzard of magic except to learn how to survive it. First simply that, and then to have something to spare from the struggle, so that she could actually use this dangerous, terrifying aspect of her gift. She hunched into herself, trying to choose what and what not to feel, to ignore the bellowing voices in the cramped cell, the myriad hurtling fragments from the naked hillside, the deep engrossing vibrations of the underlying hills, to feel through them, and beyond them . . .

'Maja? What's up? Are you all right?'

Somewhere outside the struggle her hand made an impatient gesture. But her concentration held. There! Far, far away, and faint at this distance, but still vibrant with the immense energies of its beginning. She had felt that particular queasy resonance three times before – waiting to ford a mountain river, then on the road south of Mord, then at a way station. A Watcher – no, more than one this time – Watchers going about their sinister business. She unfocused slightly and sensed what lay around that centre, the unmistakable tremor of human life, but chilled almost into stillness, a press of people, several hundred of them perhaps, all locked into the terror of the moment.

Enough.

She reached into her wallet and closed her hand round the pendant. Instantly the shield renewed itself. Ribek had to hold her from falling from the saddle.

'Are you all right, Maja?' he said again.

'In a minute,' she muttered.

She hunched down, breathing slowly and heavily and clutching the pommel of the saddle to steady herself while her spirit found its way back into her body and limbs where it belonged. After a while she shuddered, straightened and opened her eyes.

They had halted on the hillside, Saranja and Benayu, also on horseback, looking back at her over their shoulders, Ribek standing beside her with his hand on her thigh.

'Are you all right?' he said again.

'Yes . . . yes . . . I . . .'

She was too tired to explain. The world began to go dark. She felt herself swaying.

For several hours Maja slept, only half waking once or twice to wonder where she was and why she was sitting sideways in the saddle being comfortably held in place by someone's arm – Ribek's – round her waist, with her head on his chest. She snuggled herself against him and drifted back into darkness.

They must have stopped for the night, but she was only vaguely aware of it, of having a cup held to her lips so that she could drink a little water before sliding down again into the abyss of sleep. Her bladder roused her some time in the moonlit night, and she rose and relieved it and slept again and woke at last, ravenously hungry, to a dew-scented morning and the crackle of a small fire, and mutton chops grilling on its embers. Just as she could smell and hear these things before she opened her eyes, so she could feel the presence of her companions, Benayu's inner turmoil veiled behind the vague buzz of his sleeping power, Saranja's banked furies, Ribek's lovely ordinariness . . .

While they ate she tried to explain to the others more of what had happened to her.

'I asked Jex to stop shielding me. I wanted to see how far I could reach. I could feel *everything*. It was like . . . like . . .'

She struggled to find the words, to help them feel something of the worldwide blizzard of magic that had swept round and through her.

'Anyway,' she finished, 'I think there's one of the big Imperial Highways way over there, a long way off, and some Watchers, two or three, I think, were doing something to a lot of frightened people at a way station.'

'Enspelling them to fight?' said Ribek.

'I don't know.'

'You look all in,' said Saranja. 'You still do.'

'I'm all right now. Just tired.'

'You've got to be careful,' said Benayu earnestly. 'There's always a price. Fodaro told you that. The stronger the magic, the higher the price. There've been beginners who've stumbled into something big and come out raving. I don't think you're actually *doing* the

203

magic, but you're channelling it somehow. And you're doing it more and more. It's bound to have an effect.'

'Yes, I know.'

'Well, you'd better not try that again,' said Ribek.

'I think I've got to,' she said. 'I've got to learn about it. I think it's important. Perhaps it's why I'm here at all, so that I could do this. I've just got to practise, and get used to it, like . . . like learning to kick-box, I suppose. You must have had to practise and practise.'

He laughed.

'Still do,' he said. 'Start of each season. I'd be stiff as a plank, else. Same with your magic, I expect, Benayu.'

'Same stupid little exercises day after day after day,' said Benayu. 'Fodaro kept me at it, no matter how much I bucked. He was right, though. I think Maja's right now. She's got to learn. But only a bit at a time, or you'll wear yourself out. Jex will look after her if she gets into trouble, but he's going to need to be a lot stronger before he can cope with anything really big.'

'And she'd better have one of us with her, always, when she's trying anything like this,' said Ribek. 'All right, Maja?'

'All right.'

Chapter 8

TWELVE UNEVENTFUL days passed. Morning and evening Maja reached back the way they had come, but sensed no tremor of pursuit. The blaze of magic around Tarshu faded into the distance. Or perhaps the ferocity of the battle had dwindled into a kind of stalemate. It seemed barely to matter. Almost, as the miles flowed steadily away beneath the horses' hooves or their own feet, Maja came to forget the frightening purpose of their journey. The journey became all there was. They would never have to reach its nightmare ending.

She used the long quiet hours to think. Her fantasy life with Ribek at Northbeck mill seemed to recede into the remote, unreachable future and became unsatisfying, so she thought about things more near at hand. At first she was preoccupied with coming to terms with her sense of the magical. When its power and reach had first burst on her it had been almost overwhelming, and, except when she steeled herself to face it, she had needed much of Jex's full protection to shield her from it. It had been like the first sudden strong spring sunlight that, carelessly faced, peels and blisters the winter-tender skin to an agonizing scarlet rawness. Now she was slowly becoming hardened to it.

Not merely that. Just as the right level of sunlight, sunlight that greets you when you step outside before breakfast with the dew still on the grass and the night-chill lingering in the air, makes your skin crawl gently and you sigh with sensual delight, so, she gradually came to find, she relished the magic and mystery of the everyday world streaming round her and through her, the continual half-noticed sense that everything in that world, every pebble, every leaf, every midge, had its own individual purpose and meaning. She did too. She was part of the inward wisdom of the universe.

'You're living in a dream, aren't you?' Ribek said, teasing.

'I suppose so. Anyway, you're part of it.'

'Glad to hear it.'

But how could he not be, when his own Ribek-magic, so confident, brisk, easygoing, tingled continually against her consciousness? She rode pillion with him on Levanter most of the day, and when they walked, both for the exercise and to give the horses a rest, he stayed behind with her for company.

This, of course, suited her very well. One morning several days later she started thinking about him again, not fantasizing about her future with him but soberly considering the nature of her love for him. She knew it wasn't a childish crush, because she'd discovered what that was like last summer, when her aunt had at last decided that Saranja wasn't coming back. Or perhaps, Maja now realized, it had been because the unicorn magic was beginning to fail, and it had become urgent that somebody was found who could renew it.

At any rate, a family of second cousins had been invited to stay at Woodbourne – parents, three girls and a boy. Nothing like this had ever happened before, and even Maja had understood that her aunt was hoping that one of the girls might have the gift of hearing what the cedars were saying. The boy had been a friendly, easygoing lad whom Maja instantly had decided was the most wonderful person in the world, and had dumbly hung around him at every spare moment she had. Her aunt had noticed, of course, and had told her in front of everyone it was a silly, childish crush, and then shut her in her room without food to cure her of it. Later her cousins had taken the boy behind the barn and beaten him up. The story had got around, and no more families had come visiting. Her aunt had been right about the boy, but Maja's love for Ribek was not like that.

Nor was it like what she might have felt for the father she had never known. She could only guess, but she knew that it must be different. It was strange for her to be even thinking about her father. Almost before any time that she could remember she had learnt not to ask about him. Her mother would only weep when she did, and her aunt would punish her if she found out, or asked anyone else. It was safer never even to wonder about him, to bury all thoughts of him beneath the stories she used to tell herself of wonderful, impossible adventures among monsters and warriors and mighty sorcerers.

But now everything had changed. Her aunt was gone, and the fears and miseries of her childhood; and the adventure was real and wonderful; and though there was plenty to be afraid of in it, she felt she could face those fears, and wonder about her father if she chose. But it wasn't very satisfying. She knew, or guessed, that the reason she hadn't been allowed to ask about him was that he had done something too horrible for her to be told, so she found it hard to form a picture of him as the kind of father anyone would want to have. In the end she gave up and simply decided that, whatever he was like, any love she might have felt for him would have been different from what she felt about Ribek. The great thing about Ribek was that from the first he had treated her as an equal. Nobody had ever done that before, and her father would always have been her father, never her equal. She needed somebody to love, not as a fantasy, not as a game, but for real, and Ribek was well worth loving.

And even if she hadn't had those feelings, Maja would have chosen Ribek to walk or ride with anyway. She admired Saranja enormously. It wasn't just that she was beautiful. Anybody could have seen she was a heroine – such fire and challenge in her glance, such unconscious pride in stance and movement, even in sleep. Maja was simply in awe of her, and would still have been even if these qualities hadn't resonated from her in the world of magic and vibrated through Maja like continuous trumpet music. But that very fire and fineness made it difficult to be fully comfortable with her all day long, in the way she was with Ribek.

The same was even more true of Benayu. Again, how could it not be? He was a magician. To Maja he crackled all the time, like a fresh-lit bonfire, with his own magical power. The reason they mostly travelled pair and pair, with some distance between them, was to spare Maja the continual mild abrasion of his powers. (Jex could have absorbed these, but he told Maja he preferred a more varied diet. There'd been something about the way he'd said it that made her think that was only an excuse, and actually he was squeamish about feeding off the emanations from a personal friend.) His magic set him apart from ordinary people, and always would do. Poor Benayu.

Late on the twelfth afternoon the landscape changed. For the past two days the lane they had been following had grown in size as other lanes had joined it, all apparently aiming for some point beyond the line of hills to the north. By the time they had finished climbing that last long slope it was a well-travelled road, and when they at last wearily crossed the ridge they discovered in front of them an utterly different world from the placid farming country they'd been travelling through.

'Now that's something!' said Ribek, reining Levanter to a halt. 'Should be quite a bit going on down there, Maja. Nothing by way of Watchers, I hope.'

Maja peered over his shoulder and saw a level plain stretching north, almost a desert from the look of it, burned brown by the sun even at this lush season of the year. As a sort of boundary between the two worlds, green hills and brown plain, a big river flowed from the west with an Imperial Highway running beside its further bank. The road they were on descended the hill to meet it at a large town. Part of the river had been diverted to form a moat round the gated walls, but the main channel ran through the middle of the town, with docks on either bank, and then became the outer harbour, and beyond that flowed into the sea between a rocky headland on its southern shore and a vast stretch of marsh to the north, through which another Highway dwindled into the distance.

This must be a major port. In the centre of the city masts of seagoing craft showed above red-tiled roofs. A faint haze, the dust and smoke of human bustle, lay over it all. And yes, there should be a lot going on down there in the invisible world of magic.

She sensed nothing.

Even at this distance it should be like Mord, twenty times over. Except that at Mord she'd only just come into her new-found sense, and hadn't really been aware that that was what it was. She hadn't *understood* what the sense revealed to her, any more than a newborn baby understands the blur of shapes and sounds and smells that reach it lying in its cradle.

Now, though, she had learnt to look at a town from a distance and read it with her extra sense in much the same way that she could read its larger buildings with her eyes – its turreted walls, its public monuments, its marketplaces and warehouses and so on. Above the buzz of petty magics – made magics, the work of hedge magicians, but still quite different from the natural magics that flowed from tree and stream, companion and stranger – she would be able to sense stronger emanations, or at least the sudden patches of emptiness that showed where some serious magician had put a ward round whatever he or she was doing.

Not here.

Surely, at least, there should have been an Eye on each of the main gates. All large towns had them, often dating from long before the time of the Watchers; but no. From all this city, nothing came back. She took Jex out of the pocket of her blouse and put him in her wallet. Now the natural magics of everything around and behind her came crowding in on her, but she still sensed nothing from down the hill. Nothing at all.

Saranja and Benayu hadn't stopped when Ribek had, and were already a little distance down the slope. Maja felt a brief jolt of magic as, without warning, Rocky skittered sideways and back, something so unexpected from him that Saranja lost a stirrup and was almost thrown. Of course Pogo, a couple of paces behind, shied because Rocky had. He would have had Benayu off if Saranja hadn't managed to grab his bridle, and then dismount. She waited for Benayu to do the same, handed him Pogo's reins, and started to lead Rocky on down the road.

Almost instantly Maja felt another, more violent, jolt. In the same instant Saranja was flung back up the slope, yelling with the shock of the blow and landing flat on her back. Ribek leaped down and ran to help her. By the time

Maja had slid herself to the ground and led Levanter down to join them Saranja was getting shakily to her feet and feeling herself for bruises.

'It wasn't me,' she muttered. 'It was Zald it didn't like. And Rocky. It didn't like him at all.'

'And me,' said Benayu in a low, puzzled voice.

He was standing with his back to the rest of them, as he'd been doing since he'd dismounted, turning his head slowly from left to right and back, apparently oblivious to what had been happening to Saranja.

'I can't feel it. I don't know what it is. You don't get wards that big, far as I know, and if it's some kind of screen it's nothing like mine, and way beyond anything I could manage. It's telling me if I go any further I'll die. It isn't lying.'

'Let's see what it thinks about me, then,' said Ribek. 'You too, old fellow.'

He led Levanter on down the road. At exactly the point where Rocky had shied, Levanter started to do the same, until Ribek halted and turned him.

'Easy, boy, easy,' he said. 'You weren't just copying Rocky again, were you? It's what Chanad did to you. Come and take him, Maja, and I'll try on my own.'

He turned, walked twenty paces down the road and came back.

'Didn't feel a thing,' he said. 'Your turn, Maja.'

She had just enough warning – the light fizz of something utterly new to her waking into life, a burning sensation in her arm – to snatch herself back from the invisible barrier. *It didn't mind Saranja*, she thought. *It was Zald it didn't like.*

The amulet? But it isn't magical at all now. Unless the black bead . . .

There was a large, branched cactus by the road, with a gold ring hanging on one of its vicious thorns and an elaborately decorated headscarf spread across a flat leaf. Both looked far too good to be left by the roadside. The black bead must do something, only she didn't know what yet. She hung the amulet on the cactus and tried again.

There was the same fizz, but no pain in her arm, only a feeling that a hand had been placed against her thigh and was pushing her back. Jex? But his magic (if it was magic) was utterly different. She herself couldn't feel it at all. Nevertheless she took him out of her wallet and hung him on the cactus too. The whole hillside to the left and right of her was alive with natural magic, and she could feel the made magic impulses from Zald behind her, and the permanent light hum that surrounded Benayu, and the rather different ones from the horses, but still nothing at all of that kind from the city below. And nothing from the invisible barrier itself, until she'd passed through it.

Then, instantly, it was all there. And yes indeed, there were Eyes on all the gates, including one set to guard the whole width of the river where it flowed between two massive bastions towards the sea. The Eyes were as old as the walls themselves, and that was very old. But apart from them, nothing man-made. All the natural magics were still there, speaking to her as clearly as those around her on the hillside, the stones of the walls, the majestic, calm flow of the river, the buzz of the citizens' lives, and much more generally, coming from the whole city below, a sense of ease and freedom, that she hadn't felt anywhere else in the Empire. But still no made magic at all apart, perhaps, from one strange, dead patch close to the nearer bank of the river. A ward inside the immensely powerful ward, or whatever it was that closed the city round? What was the use of that?

'Watchers, Maja?' called Ribek's voice from behind her.

She heaved herself back to the hillside and returned to the others. As she crossed the invisible line the small sendings from the city below vanished in the blink of an eye. She picked up Jex and the amulet as she passed the cactus.

'No,' she said. 'They aren't here. They've not been, not for a long while. A very long while. They don't do magic here. It's like the Valley.'

They stood and gazed out over the mysterious city. Behind them, where the road crested the hill, a hoof rattled against loose gravel. They turned. A stout, elderly man was leading two laden mules down the hill.

'Trouble?' he said. 'Something stopping you, right? Must be carrying stuff with powers in it – charms and such. Provosts won't allow that. Best leave it here, pick it up when you come back. He'd be a bloody fool as touched it if it didn't belong to him. Cactus would rip him to bits. I'll show you.'

While he'd been talking he'd rolled up his sleeve and removed an intricately plaited armband and settled it into a crook of the cactus.

'Missus has me wear that to keep me faithful,' he

214

explained. 'Works a treat too. Never want to look at another woman while I've got it on. Not my fault, I tell her, if I've got to leave it behind while I take the wool down to the market, is it? Either that or starve, I say, and you wouldn't fancy starving.'

'Trouble is we're not coming back,' said Ribek. 'We're going on through.'

'That case, one of you'd better go down to the city, hire yourself a pass-box at the gate – costs a bit, mind you – bring it back and put your stuff in it. It'll seal itself shut the minute you're through the barrier, and won't open again till you're out the far side. You'll need to get a move on. Gate closes, hour after sunset.'

'There's no way round then?'

'Not worth thinking about. Easy enough this side far as the river. Back up the hill, right, and right again at the third real road, then down – take you bit over half a day to reach the river. Then you've got to find a boat, take you over to the West Highway.'

'Surely there's a ferry,' said Ribek.

'Provosts won't have it. They want everything going through Larg. But suppose you're lucky, beyond the river it's still three, four times further before you reach the North Highway beyond the marshes, and that's all desert. Spots may look green enough from here after the rains, but that's all gone into the ground. No surface water. No way you can carry water enough for the horses. And there's vicious snakes, and little black scorpions – one sting and you're dead. You'd have to get some of the desert folk for guides. They're weird – not like us, but they can find water anywhere, only they won't do it for chance-come strangers. Worse yet going east. You'll never get your horses down the cliff, you've got to find a boat again, and then it's all marsh and bog crocodiles, and then desert again to the north. Can't be done.'

'Well, thanks,' said Ribek. 'We're going to have to think. Don't wait for us. Best of luck at the market, and tell your wife she married a good man.'

'Long as I'm wearing my armband she did,' said the man, and led his mules on down the hill.

'Brute,' muttered Saranja. 'You too, Ribek, encouraging him. I hate men.'

'Just backchat,' said Ribek, unabashed. 'Bet you he's as fond of his wife as the next man, and doesn't do anything more than glance at the city wenches.'

'*Wenches*,' snarled Saranja. 'Oh, forget it. We're not going to make it down to the city and back up with this pass-box thing and down again before the gate closes. Let's think a bit. They don't want magic stuff brought in. We can put Zald and Maja's amulet and Jex, I suppose, in the pass-box – sounds as if she won't need them again till we're through. But that's no help with Benayu, and the horses. And you'd never get three horses across a desert – they need a lot of water. Unless Benayu can do something about that.'

'I might be able to,' said Benayu. 'Water's tricky stuff – it's a bit different – but if the desert people can find it I should be able to work it out. And I daresay I can undo whatever's been done to Pogo and Levanter, so you could take them through the city. Then it'd be only me and Rocky to find our way round. That's a lot of complicated stuff to screen, and I don't know how much of it Jex is up to absorbing. Maja?'

'I think he'll say yes. He's getting a lot stronger. But we're going to have to spend the night out here anyway, aren't we? Why don't we wait and see if he says anything?'

'Sounds like the best we can do,' said Ribek. 'And I could go down and see if the river's got anything to tell me, supposing it can, and get a bit of fresh food, and maybe I can hire a mule and bring out some fodder for the horses, and then we'll all sleep on it and see what Jex says.'

'Can I come too?' said Maja. 'I like the other side.'

It was wonderfully enjoyable to walk down the long slope with the naked hillside on either side and the town below. The steady, quiet, unconscious sendings from rock and plant and creature blended with more pungent and complex human magics to form a balanced and harmonious whole, like the glorious rich dumpling stews Maja's aunt used to make for special occasions at Woodbourne, which even the permanent rancour and tension of those who ate the food could do nothing to spoil.

The lower slopes were cultivated, with ripening crops. A few sheds and barns were the only buildings outside the walls. Otherwise the fields ran right up to the edge of the moat. The sun was already low before they reached it. Though they were going to need to hurry to buy what they wanted and make it back out of the city before the gate closed, Ribek halted on the bridge and leaned on the rail to listen to see if the waters had anything to say. He had done this so regularly on their journey that Maja had learnt, though not to hear and understand their speech the way he could, at least to sense the tone and seriousness of what they were saying. It was like hearing somebody call from another room. Though one can't make out the individual words, one can hear the emotion that underlies them, anger or amusement or whatever. The moat was only a branch of the main current, but it seemed to be a deeply serious river. Maja leaned on the rail and waited. She was aware of the Eye on the gate. It had registered their presence but not reacted to them.

'They're still fighting round Tarshu, but it looks like they're at a stalemate,' said Ribek.

'How does it know? This water can't ever have been near Tarshu.'

'Clouds have come in over Tarshu and picked up what's happening, in a vague, cloudy kind of way. They condense into rain over the mountains. You won't get much sense out of an individual raindrop, but put a lot of them together into a stream and they begin to gather and shape themselves into patterns which they can put into words. It's mostly just chatter and gossip, like in my mill-race, but as the streams join up and become rivers they make more and more sense of the world, until they reach the sea. Coming from the Valley we don't hear much about the sea, but I'd be surprised if there wasn't a sort of deep, general wisdom in it, too large for our small brains to . . . What's up?'

Maja gripped the rail, gasping and trembling. Two or

three women were crossing the bridge behind her, laughing over some scandal. Their tone hadn't changed, their step hadn't faltered. No new ripple crossed the easy flow of the stream, though if it had felt what Maja had felt, the foam would have been sluicing to the battlements of the walls. Something had struck the surrounding barrier a violent blow, close to where Saranja, Benayu and the horses were waiting. Her heart stopped. No, it can't have been aimed at them. It had come from somewhere far to the south, a single, colossal convulsion, as if a root of the Tree of the World had been wrenched away.

'Tarshu,' she muttered through her daze. 'The Watchers have done something new. Huge. Bigger than that tempest.'

Ribek was watching her, concerned. He looked up over her shoulder.

'Stalemate over?' he said. 'Watchers will . . . Hold it – this may be trouble.'

She turned. Three men had emerged from a doorway under the arch of the gate and were coming towards them. They wore red hats like inverted flowerpots, and dark-blue belted surcoats. Their leader carried a knobbed cane under his arm. Something else . . .

'The Eye's started watching us,' she whispered. 'It knew we were there, before, but it didn't pay any attention.'

The men marched, rather than walked, straight up to Ribek. He faced them, apparently relaxed and untroubled.

'What do you think you're doing, then?' said the leader.

'Resting, looking at the water. I like rivers and streams.'

'More than looking. Doing something to it.'

'Not unless you count listening. The river was doing something, mind you, but rivers do. They talk, only most people can't hear what they say. I can. In fact, I can't help it – it's something I was born with. Runs in the family. I'm not a magician if that's what you're after. Nothing like that, where I come from. We've picked up a few trinkets since we've been in the Empire, and we're on our way to hire a pass-box so we can take them through the city.'

'All that's as may be, friend,' said the man. 'Not up to me.'

His voice became solemn and official.

'By virtue of my office as Gate Sergeant,' he said solemnly. 'I am taking you before the Court of Provosts under Standing Order Number 3a.'

'If you must,' said Ribek with a sigh. 'You'd better go back and tell the others, Maja. I'll join you when I can. With the pass-box, I hope.'

'Kid's coming too,' said the guard, back in his normal voice. 'Maybe she'll tell a bit more about you than you want to tell yourself. Come along then.'

The two other men moved to take Ribek by the arms. He actually laughed, as if this was just the sort of ridiculous minor nuisance travellers have to get used to. Maja guessed he was weighing up whether he could take all three guards on with his kick-boxing. They were large men, but they didn't look particularly tough. Two perhaps, but not three, she thought. She hoped he wasn't going to try it. Anyway, even if he got away with it, it wouldn't help much in getting them all through the city.

He made one more attempt.

'How much to let my niece go back to the rest of our party?'

It was the Gate Sergeant's turn to laugh.

'More than you could pay, my friend,' he said, gripping Maja by the shoulder. 'Come along, then.'

The street beyond the gate was cheerfully busy, with the working day beginning to ease towards the pleasures of the evening. Still half dazed from the shock that had struck her on the bridge, Maja barely noticed the way people stopped what they were doing to stare questioningly at them, as they were led past, as if this was something they weren't used to seeing.

They reached a large cobbled square, with a fountain in the middle and statues dotted here and there. Part of it was used as a market, its stalls still busy. Three sides were occupied by tall but narrow buildings that seemed to have been built in competition with each other over which could carry the most elaborate ornamentation crammed into its restricted facade. Along the fourth side ran the river, as wide as two market squares and busy with boats and barges.

The building at the centre of the side opposite the river was taller and wider than the others, and even more richly curlicued. They climbed the steps. The double doors stood open, but the Gate Sergeant rapped his knob loudly on the right-hand leaf as he went through. The large entrance hall was fully as ornate as the facade, and lavishly gilded. Everything about it spoke of a self-contented wealth accumulated through long, untroubled years. Officials and citizens bustled across it. A functionary moved to confront them, his uniform magnificently swagged and braided. He carried a gold-knobbed staff of office. The Gate Sergeant drew himself up, matching him in self-importance.

'One for the Provosts' Court,' he said. 'Standing Order Number 3a.'

The functionary's eyebrows rose.

'3a?' he said.

The Gate Sergeant relaxed, clearly having won the contest. He let go of Maja's shoulder, drew a small leather-bound book from his breast pocket, found a page, and pointed, forcing the functionary to move round and crane to read, reciting the words as he did so.

'"Apparent magical practices on bridge relating to movement of moat-water. Perpetrator or perpetrators to be taken before the Provosts' Court. If not sitting, court to be immediately summoned." Twelve years, morning after morning, I've been reading out orders soon as I come on duty. Given up wondering what that one's about. Never been invoked before, far as I know.'

The speech had given the functionary time to recover his self-esteem. He swung away, marched to a side-apse, raised his staff and struck it against the bell that hung from the archway. The bell clanged and the bustle in the hall fell to a hush so deep that Maja could hear the last whimper of the vibrations as they died away.

'Standing Order Number 3a,' intoned the functionary. 'The Provosts' Court is summoned into immediate session.'

The bustle restarted, but was changed. Several lesser functionaries spilled from a doorway and raced off, while many of those who a moment before had been hurrying somewhere now waited in muttering groups to see what happened. A rather more plainly clad official, obviously senior enough not to need a fancy uniform, came up and spoke briefly to the first functionary, who raised his staff in salute and went back to the main door.

The official spoke in a low voice to the Gate Sergeant, who showed him the passage in the leather-bound book, but this time allowed him to read it for himself. The official stared at Ribek for several seconds, glanced at Maja, nodded and gestured that they were all five to follow him. He led them across the crowded hall and a wicket set into a much larger double door.

'Thank you, Sergeant,' he said. 'Your men can go, but you will be needed as a witness.'

He led the way through the door into a much smaller, but no less ornate chamber, with a double row of portraits of solemn-looking men running round the walls.

'You two sit there,' he said, gesturing towards a carved bench between two windows in the right-hand wall. 'Keep an eye on them, Sergeant. We don't want any trouble.'

'There won't be any,' said Ribek, amiably. 'We are guests in your city, so of course we'll behave ourselves.'

The official stared at him icily.

'Let me advise you, sir,' he said, 'that you have caused the Provosts of the City of Larg to be summoned from their evening leisure to convene in emergency session.

223

They will not take kindly to any display of frivolity. Ah . . .'

Before Ribek could answer he turned away to greet a plump, bald man who had come hurrying in, panting slightly, and with sweat streaming down his flushed cheeks. The first official beckoned to the Gate Sergeant, and the three of them talked together in low voices.

A younger man came in, placed a ledger on the reading desk by the door and handed a large book bound in black leather to the plump man, who opened it on a table at the centre of the room and started to leaf though it. The pages were thick and yellow, and creaked faintly as he turned them. He found what he wanted and started to read.

A gong sounded in the entrance hall and the big double doors were thrown open by two more uniformed men, who then crossed the room and opened another pair of doors in the wall opposite where Ribek and Maja were sitting. Two older men, wearing golden velvet gowns, despite the heat, and strange, floppy black velvet caps with a jewelled brooch at the centre, walked through. The man at the desk entered their names in his ledger. The plump man bowed to them as they passed. They nodded to him, and he picked up the book and followed them.

'Proctors,' muttered Ribek, and gestured towards the double line of portraits. 'Same outfit all the way along, apart from those fellows in armour over in the corner. Look at the dates on 'em, too. Bottom row's three hundred-odd years later than the top row. Fat fellow will be Clerk of the Court – something like that.'

More Proctors followed, in twos and threes. Maja picked up their feelings as they passed – irritation or anxiety or excitement, but from all of them a sort of bewildered surprise. The last one hurried in and through, followed by the man with the ledger. Two men with short pikes came in from the entrance hall and stood guard, the outer doors closed, then the inner ones.

More waiting. The Gate Sergeant was now too nervous to stand still, and paced to and fro, until one of the inner doors opened and an arm beckoned to him from beyond. He made an effort, squared both jaw and shoulders and marched through, every inch the steadfast man-at-arms. The doors were too thick for voices to carry, but his inner nerves and fright were signals strong enough for Maja to follow as he marched to the centre of the room and halted smartly in front of a long, weighty table – ancient oak, she could tell – and saluted. Someone asked a question. He answered stolidly, telling his story.

More talk, some argument, a decision and an order. The inner doors opened, and a guard gestured to Ribek to come through. Maja followed him.

The room was much as she had pictured it, in the same grand style as the ante-room but six times the size. Tall windows overlooked the square, and yet more portraits of past Proctors lined the remaining walls. Yes, the Proctors sat in a row of throne-like chairs behind the table, with the Clerk of the Court at one end with his assistant beside him. The black book and the ledger lay open in front of them.

The guard who had brought them led Ribek and Maja

to face the Proctors at the centre of the table and withdrew. The Proctor at the centre of the line tinkled a little bell and turned to the clerk.

'Please proceed, Master Tongal,' he said.

'Very good, Master President,' said the Clerk. He looked at Ribek.

'Your name, please?'

'Ribek Ortahlson, and this is my niece Maja.'

'And the purpose of your journey?'

'I and my sister had been travelling south with our niece and nephew to negotiate future marriages for them among a branch of our people who live beyond Tarshu. We were halted by the fighting there and decided to return north. But we learnt that men and boys using the Imperial Highways were being rounded up at way stations and being impressed into the army. To avoid this we chose to use byroads, and so came to your city. We wanted no more than to pass through it, but we were stopped by the barrier because we were carrying a few magical objects.

'We were advised by a passing merchant that our best course was to hire a pass-box at the gate, to enable us to carry them through the city. We were resting on the bridge – we've come a long way, and were tired – when the Gate Sergeant arrested me for carrying out magical procedures and brought me here. May I explain what I was doing?'

'Please.'

With the same quiet reasonableness Ribek told the court what he had told the Gate Sergeant.

'It's a bit like hearing a bat squeak,' he added. 'Most

people can't, because the pitch is too high for them, but I know two or three people who can. There's nothing magical about that. The same about hearing moving water – it just runs in my family. A big river like yours can be really interesting.'

A Proctor near the other end of the line rapped his knuckles on the table twice. The rest turned to look at him.

'This is a crucial point,' he said. 'If the procedures were not after all magical, then there is no need to wake the Sleeper. The Clerk of the Court tells us that he can find no precedent for the use of this clause in the Standing Orders, so we have no guidance. All we can be sure of is that to wake the Sleeper may have the most momentous results, affecting the whole city, our whole way of life. Perhaps the barrier will be removed. Do we really want the dangerous magics of the Empire to come flooding into our pleasant city? Do we want to be drawn into the so-called Watchers' war against the Pirates?'

A second double rap broke into the mutters of agreement. Heads turned towards the sound.

'A further point,' said the rapper. 'If we believe the witness that he can hear the speech of the river – and there is nothing to show that he is not one of the common enough type of lunatic who fancies that he can hear voices – why should we not also believe him that the practice is not magical, or at least not magical in the sense of pertaining to the type of magic against which our city is so fortunately guarded?'

Another rap.

'I wholly agree,' said the new speaker. 'Furthermore,

227

if it were magical in that kind of way, surely it would have been stopped at the barrier.'

Rap after rap, with the Clerk's assistant desperately trying to get it all written down.

'Now look. This won't do. The instructions are absolutely clear. You're just trying—'

'Nonsense. We've got to do what's in the best interests of Larg. Are we going to upset everything for the sake of one madman?'

Maja stopped listening. Something was happening. Not here, but soon. Coming. Distracted by the surface events, Maja had paid no attention to what was happening outside the Council Chamber. It was all there, of course, at the back of her consciousness – behind her the almost empty ante-room, to her left the bustling entrance hall with the river flowing majestically beyond it, opposite and to her right smaller rooms, offices and such, perhaps, but over in the far right corner, though the walls there seemed to be no different from the rest of the room, just panelling and portraits, a small blank patch where everything seemed to stop at the surface of the wall.

By now she'd come across enough wards to be able to tell from the very density of its blankness how powerful this one was, and so guess the immense power of the magic it was warding, here in the very heart of un-magical Larg. And what she had felt, what had drawn her attention, was the first faint beginnings of a change, a weakening of the ward, a faint seeping through of the power beyond it. It was unlike anything she had felt before. She started to shudder.

'Hold me,' she gasped.

Ribek put his arm round her and hugged her firmly to his side, but the shuddering wouldn't stop. Through it she heard snatches of what was going on. The tinkle of the bell – '. . . motion is that . . . as either a product of the witness's lunacy, or not truly magical activity of the sort referred to . . .' – '. . . and those against . . . carried with Proctors Benter and Gald dissenting . . .'

'Hold it! Hold it!'

The Gate Sergeant's bellow overwhelmed the shuddering. He was standing by her side with a pike gripped in both hands as if he intended to use it.

'Orders is orders!' he yelled above the growing hubbub. 'Twelve years, morning after morning, I've been reading out that clause 3a there. Made no sense to me, but when it happened I did what it said, 'cause I know an order when I hear one. Same with what the gentleman there read out of his black book. That's an order, and you don't argue it to and fro, you do what it says. So now where's this Sleeper, and how . . . ?'

Maja raised a juddering arm and pointed at the far corner.

'Right,' cried the Gate Sergeant. 'Out of the way there . . .'

Clamour filled the room, only to be stilled in an instant. A thin whisper came out of the air, faint and dry as the scuttle of a mouse in a hayloft.

'I have woken. Bring the strangers to me.'

'Maja – she can't stand strong magic. It will kill her,' said Ribek in a low, strained voice. He'd spoken to empty air, but the whisper answered.

'I will protect her.'

The shuddering died away. Ribek lifted her into his arms.

'This way then,' said the Gate Sergeant. 'It's where the lassie was pointing, over in this corner. Stand aside, please.'

Maja could have walked, but she needed to cling to Ribek, to his beautiful ordinariness, although something else, something invisible, was now also holding and protecting her. A door had appeared in the corner, its carving and gilding matching the other doors in the Council Chamber. It hadn't been there when she had looked before, but she sensed nothing from it as the Gate Sergeant tried its handle, found it unlocked, opened it and held it for Ribek to carry her through.

'Do I come too, Ma'am?' he croaked.

'No need,' said the whisper. 'You have done well, Sergeant. My blessing is on you and yours, and on this whole, loved, city. Farewell.'

The Gate Sergeant hesitated, turned, stopped, turned back and forced his voice to function.

'You're going then, Ma'am?'

'Yes. The Covenant is broken, and I may go.'

The Gate Sergeant saluted and closed the door.

'Phew!' said Ribek.

'You can put me down now,' said Maja. 'I'm all right. Someone's shielding me. Like Jex. Only . . .' Only so much more powerfully than Jex could have done. He would have been utterly overwhelmed by what now surrounded them.

She looked around. They were in a plain, stone corridor dimly lit by ordinary-looking lanterns. No doors opened off it. They went along it, Ribek moving with short, effortful steps as if he were walking through something much denser than air, and then down a flight of stone steps.

'We'll be well underground now,' said Ribek. 'Land slopes up from the river. Ah, this looks like it.'

In front of them the passage ended, with an open door on the right. Maja had never heard him sound so nervous. Like a shy schoolboy, she thought. She herself felt utterly unafraid. There was a kindliness in the shield around her, like the mother's love she had never really known. Hoping to share some of that with him, she took his hand as they reached the doorway.

'Come in.'

This time the whisper came through human lips, a voice full of human weariness. They crept into the room.

It was a very simple space, stone-walled, windowless, unadorned. But for the vaulted roof it might have been a storeroom in a well-built farmhouse. At the same time, Maja recognized that it was extremely old, far older than the Council Chamber they had just left, older even than the ancient walls of Larg, almost as old as the hills, and despite the shielding that wrapped round her, she knew it for a place of power. There was no furniture in it apart from an iron bedstead. On it a dark green bedspread stitched with what Maja guessed were magical symbols, though she was unable to sense them through her shield. White sheets and pillowcase, looking as if they had been laundered yesterday. On the pillow a skull.

No, not quite. A head next thing to a skull, hairless, the almost transparent skin drawn tight over the flesh-less bone, the mouth a slit, invisible lips drawn in between toothless jaws, the eyes clouded over with a grey, bloodshot film.

The slit of a mouth opened, revealing the two thin lines of the lips, so dark a purple they were almost black. They barely moved to release their whisper.

'Welcome. I am the Sleeper, Guardian of Larg. Two hundred years and more I have waited here for you, though under the Covenant between myself and the Watchers I could not stir to help you. And now, though they have broken the Covenant, there is little I can do. All but the last shreds of my power are gone.

'You, child. What is your name?'

'I'm Maja Urlasdaughter,' whispering too, as if in the presence of the dead. 'My friend is Ribek Ortahlson. We come from the Valley.'

'Of course. I knew your ancestors, Meena and Tilja, Alnor and Tahl. With Lananeth I was the earliest of the Ropemaker's helpers.'

'You're Zara! You're in the story we tell in the Valley! You were Lord Kzuva's magician!'

The corpse-face woke with the ghost of a smile.

'I used that name. When our first tasks were done, and the major demons bound beneath the earth, Lananeth chose to return to natural life and die in human time. I stayed by the Ropemaker's side.

'By then he had other helpers. His is a restless soul.

232

He fretted to be away from his task, back in the life he knew, exploring and learning. With our agreement he bound us into a Covenant that during his absences we should cooperate for the general good of the Empire. Time passed, and all seemed well. Before he last left he told me, and no one else, that he had discovered the gateway into another universe, and there was one extremely difficult task that he could at last accomplish there, and there alone. He could not tell when he would return. I was already old and weary, and asked to be released from my binding and my tasks, and he agreed.

'I chose another course from Lananeth. To preserve what was left of my inward self I came to Larg. Over three years I built a barrier of wards around the city almost as strong as those around the walls of Talakh. That done, I laid my powers aside and surrounded myself with ordinariness, as devoid of magic as I could make it. I healed, and taught others to heal, by ordinary natural means. My old colleagues remained in Talakh, increasing their powers. We waited for the Ropemaker's return.'

The whisper had slowed, become syllable after dragging syllable. It paused, gathered strength and went on.

'He did not return. The Watchers' power grew. Before they could complete the change and become the Watchers, as they are now, they had a need that only I could fulfil, so we bound ourselves under the Covenant, in terms that neither of us could afford to break, that I should fulfil that need and that they should have no power or jurisdiction over my city of Larg.

'Again we waited. I grew older. I could have renewed my powers and prolonged my life, but at great cost to my true self. In the end I could do no more than cast myself into sleep and await the next event. It has now come, twice over. You have appeared at the gates of Larg, and in the very day and hour of your coming to Larg the Covenant was broken with a force that battered against my wards around the city, and woke me from my sleep. The Watchers will say that what they have done is still within the terms of the Covenant, and for that reason I dare not break the pact between us. I know who you are, and what you are trying to do. But still for the sake of this city I dare not help your search. I can give you my blessing, and that is all.'

She paused again. At length, Ribek broke the silence, whispering too in that presence.

'You . . . you can't tell us where this gateway is, the one to the other universe?'

'I dare not meddle. I must recall what is left of my powers, and I do not know if they are enough, and I am old and tired. What the Watchers have done is to wake a great sea demon to use him against the fleets of their enemies. In so doing they have woken others, including the storm demon Azarod, whom long ago I bound and cast into the pit. Before anything else he will come to Larg to take vengeance on me and mine. My barrier is weaker over the sea and it will not hold him of its own. Now you must go, while I prepare to do what I can to protect my city. The Proctors will decide whether to give you passage. My blessing is on you. You may tell them that.'

'Thank you, Ma'am,' said Ribek, low-voiced, and moved towards the door. Maja tugged at his sleeve.

'Perhaps Benayu could help her,' she whispered. 'Tell her about the dragon. And there's a demon-binder on Zald.'

He hesitated, then turned back to the bed.

'I . . . I don't know if it's any use, Ma'am,' he said. 'One of our friends outside the barrier – she isn't a magician, but she's got a demon-binder on a jewel called Zald-im-Zald, if that's any use. And we've got someone with us. He had to stay up on the hill outside your wards, because he's a magician. He knows about storms. We were at Tarshu, on a hill above the town, when the Watchers summoned a tremendous tempest from out at sea to attack an enemy airboat.'

'I saw that tempest. Someone had spoken the Ropemaker's true name, and the shock of it woke me. I saw the airboat's fall. I saw a hunting dragon tossed aside like a leaf on the lashing tail of the wind.'

'Benayu did that. The dragon was hunting us, and it was just going to get us when he used a bit of the storm to blow it clean away and kill it. It took a lot out of him, but he did it. If it's storms you're planning to deal with . . .'

'Perhaps. Zald-im-Zald will work only for its owner, and I cannot work with her if she is not a magician. But your other friend . . . Hold your left hand over my face so that I can breathe into your palm. Now close it, and keep it closed till you see your friend. Tell him what has happened, and if he agrees let him breathe the breath

235

that I have given you. He will then know my need and purpose and be free to refuse.

'Now go. Tell the Proctors to prepare for a mighty storm. Say that with your friend's help I will try to protect the city. In that way, if all goes well, they will have cause to assist you as I cannot myself do. Farewell.'

'Thank you, Ma'am,' said Ribek, and turned to the door once more. Before they reached it, the whisper came again.

'The man you are looking for . . . he was born in Barda.'

Chapter 9

A S THEY CROSSED the threshold into the
Council Chamber the cocoon around Maja
vanished. Instantly a jolt of pure magic from
Zara's chamber overwhelmed her. Utter darkness. No
sight, sound, smell, touch – only that blast of power.
And beyond it, something else, something that was there
and wasn't. Was there and wasn't in a way she knew . . .

And then she was standing, dazed, in the Council
Chamber, with Ribek's steadying arm around her. There
was a blank wall where the door had been.

'I'm all right,' she muttered, but he kept hold of her
arm as he led her towards the centre of the table where
the Proctors were seated.

Everyone in the room seemed to be staring at them, as
before, but the whole atmosphere had changed. There
was doubt, anxiety, interest still, but instead of irritation
with these two troublesome intruders, there was now
something like awe in their faces. Ribek and she had

spoken with the Sleeper of Larg, which no one before had done for who knows how long?

Ribek halted confidently in front of the long table and the President nodded to him to speak.

'Well, we've seen the Sleeper,' he said quietly. 'I can't tell you about most of what she said, except that you've got to make up your own minds what to do about us. But she gave us a message for you to prepare for a storm. It's not going to be an ordinary bad storm, but a real monster. The Watchers at Tarshu have raised a great sea demon to destroy the Pirates' fleet, and that's woken other demons. One of them's about to attack Larg. She'll do her best to protect the city, and we've got a friend up on the hill outside the barrier who'll try to help her, but she's very old and tired and she thinks that it may be too much for her, even with the help of our friend. So if you'll let us go back and tell him . . .'

The President glanced right and left. Everyone nodded. All stood. The Clerk rifled urgently through his folders and passed him a large card, from which he started to read in a carrying voice.

'The Court is adjourned. A State of Emergency is declared. Preparations for a major storm, Category Five, to begin immediately. All shipping to be double-moored. All citizens not engaged in official storm preparations to go to their homes. Curfew imposed. Volunteer Watch and fire crews to report immediately for duty. Watch authorized to arrest persons breaking the curfew on suspicion of looting. Automatic triple penalties imposed on those detected in actual looting . . .'

Everyone seemed to know the drill. Junior officials

were already scampering out of the room, others hurrying in for orders. The President finished reading and put the card down.

'Gate Sergeant,' he called. 'Ah, there you are. We'll forget about your little outburst just now. Will you take our visitors back to the gate, provide them with a pass-box, free of charge in the circumstances, and give them every help you can to get them back to their friends on the other side of the barrier before the storm breaks.'

'Horses, sir?'

'If we can find them in time. See to it, Guard Captain. Two steady horses to the South Gate, an experienced horseman to ride with the girl and bring the horses back, expense to be defrayed from the City Purse . . .'

As soon as Maja stepped out into the open she was aware of the coming storm. There was a sudden chill in the air and fine spray in the freshening wind, which came and went in sudden violent gusts. The bells of twenty towers were jangling at random. A line of uniformed men carrying staves was chivvying the last few loiterers off the square. And out to sea – the great ward was weaker there, Zara had said – something vaguely felt but huge and malevolent was moving towards the city.

They hurried back through almost empty streets the way they had come. It was late evening by the time they reached the gate. The Gate Sergeant left them under the arch while he went into the guardroom for the pass-box. By now Maja felt deathly tired from the magical batterings in the Council Chamber, on top of the long day on the road. She hoped the horses would come. She doubted if she could make it up the hill on her own feet.

They waited. The howl of the wind strengthened, for Azarod himself now rode in it. She could feel Zara's great ward vibrate to his violence. The Gate Sergeant seemed to be taking a long time. A thought struck her.

'Can you ride with only one hand?' she asked Ribek.

'Walk if I have to. Where've they all got to?'

Almost as he spoke the horses arrived, a wizened old groom riding one and leading the other. He was wearing a heavy oiled cloak and a wide-brimmed hat tied under the chin. His vast white moustache was pretty well all she could see of his face.

'Right you are, sir,' he said. 'Wild weather already, and it'll be worse up the hill. Hoist the little lady up behind me and we'll be off.'

'There's a problem,' said Ribek, holding his arm across his body as if he'd hurt it. 'I'm not much of a horseman, and I've only got one hand I can use.'

'That's all right, sir. I'll take the reins and you can hang on to her mane. There's a mounting-block over there.'

Before they could move the Gate Sergeant returned with the pass-box and a couple more oiled cloaks like the groom's. Maja's was hugely too large for her, of course.

'Smallest I could find in the store,' he said, as he parcelled her up in it and belted it round her. 'It's going to be wet up there on that hill.'

He lifted her up and she put her arms round the old groom. He smelt of stables. It was strange not to be riding with Ribek, but it wouldn't have made sense. They moved to the block to let Ribek mount, and then on towards the outer archway.

'Good luck,' said the Gate Sergeant. 'See you in the morning, supposing any of us are still alive.'

'Good luck to you, and thank you,' said Ribek.

The gale seemed to be blowing from the north, so for a little while they were still in the lee of the city wall, but the moment they were off the bridge it slammed into their backs, hissing and shrieking. Even a winter storm at Woodbourne had been nothing like this. If it had been from any other direction it would have blasted them off the road or forced them back. As it was, it seemed to be driving them on up the hill.

Despite that, the horses at once half shied. The groom cursed them and wrenched at the reins and drove them on. The riders bent themselves low over their necks to lessen the pressure on both themselves and the horses. Maja laid her right cheek against the groom's greasy cloak and peered out to sea.

Night was coming early under the heavy clouds, but there was no need of moon or stars. Bolt after bolt of lightning slammed down into the waves, adding their thunder to the roar of the wind. Their glare marked the centre of the storm, whirling the gale around it as it marched towards the land. It wasn't as large as she'd have expected for so huge a storm, but a concentrated swirl of utter blackness in the mottled dark of the hurling clouds. The lightning dazzled down from its fringes. Its come-and-go brilliance blinded her vision and made the dark yet darker until it flashed again, but behind and beyond that centre there seemed to be a different kind of darkness, a huge, squat column rising from the sea. She couldn't be sure.

Rain came, sudden and dense, driven horizontal on the wind, rattling against their cloaks, sending the horses skittering sideways with the shock of it. Again the groom mastered them, coaxing and cursing. They started to climb. *Now we're for it*, thought Maja.

But no. If anything, the wind seemed to ease slightly. It was coming more from the left too, or perhaps the road had turned that way, making it seem so. They plodded on, and yes, though the road began to twist to and fro to lessen the incline as the hill became steeper, checking her bearings with what she could see of the city below, and the sea and headland on her left, she thought she was right. Of course. The wind was only part of the colossal swirl that circled that dark centre out to sea, and the line of the road was taking them more and more across the curve of it.

It was still a mighty gale, wherever it blew, but its power continued to lessen, and she felt that they were climbing not only out across it but also up out of it. And now when she looked out to sea, she was seeing slant-wise to its course, so that the dark column she thought she had glimpsed was no longer directly behind the storm centre and its blinding lightning, but a little to one side.

Yes, there was something there, something solid, not a plain column but a vast, vaguely human shape with a great, snouted, neckless head and something like arms. Between its hands, or paws, it held a long black rod, which it brandished towards the storm. A lash of lightning sprang from its tip, shot out above the surface of the sea, curled around the storm centre and whipped it round, as a child might do with a whipping-top, faster yet and faster, and at the same time drove it towards Larg.

The churning waves around the centre began to shape themselves into a line of swirling waterspouts, taller than the tallest trees, which separated from the steady, implacable march of the main storm and charged towards the shore, all seeming to aim for the point where the two banks of the debouching river funnelled in and became the outer harbour.

They never reached it. Through the weakened ward she sensed an invisible wave of a different order of magic sweep out from the city to meet the waterspouts near the centre of their line and break it apart, and send the ones on either side crashing into their neighbours, and those into the ones beyond, and so on all the way down the line, until they had all collapsed into a tremendous flurry of foam, a white wave that spread outside sideways, lost direction and spent itself uselessly against headland and marsh.

Maja heard Ribek's shout behind her.

'Holding her own against the little 'uns. Big one's something else. We're not going to make it. Horses go any faster?'

'Doing their best already, sir.'

'Let me down.'

Maja twisted her head to see him slip neatly from his saddle, wriggle out of his waterproof and start to run up the hill, awkwardly, with his arm clenched to his midriff and leaning sideways into the buffeting gale.

He vanished into the darkness ahead. The horses plodded on. The storm marched forward, seemed to falter, gathered itself and came on. Faltered, and came on. Faltered longer, but still came on. It was now desperately near.

'Something happening up ahead,' yelled the groom. 'That where we're heading for, Missy?'

She had already sensed the change, urgent and powerful, almost past bearing. With an effort she leaned sideways to peer past him. A pale light glowed up ahead, but everything round it was darkness. A blink of lightning showed her a twisted tree by the roadside. That was where Ribek had turned back, testing what happened to him beyond the barrier. The appalling pressure increased . . . the cactus . . . Jex and her amulet . . . they couldn't be far . . .

'Let me down! Let me down!' she yelled.

Without waiting for him to stop she flung herself off the horse's back, sprawled, scrambled up, gathered the heavy fold of her waterproof up around her and staggered on up the road, driving her feeble legs on and up . . . another step . . . another . . . A hand gripped her arm, helping her on.

'Almost there, Missy,' grunted the groom. 'Look at that, now!'

The light was moving. Against its glow the cactus stood for a moment, a black, gesturing shape which vanished as the light passed on.

'There!' she gasped. The groom hauled her forward.

As they passed through the barrier she was almost over-whelmed by the other tempest that it had been holding back, the buffeting to-and-fro of Azarod's demonic power and the counter-power of the mysterious moving light. She could no longer hear or see or feel, only sense a small, quiet focus of peace and rest somewhere in that turmoil. She wrapped the end of her headscarf round her hand to pick Jex out from among the prickles. The amulet was easier to find, with firelight glinting off its bead. Odd . . . Not now. She looped the cord around her neck, dropped the pendant inside her blouse and slid the amulet on to her wrist.

The world returned.

Gasping, she stared around. The pale light was mov-ing towards the headland at astonishing speed, as if its own separate gale were blowing it into the storm-wind. There was a figure at its centre, robed and still, the folds of its cloak unruffled by the tearing wind. Up the hill, where the light had been, only the reddish glimmer of embers – Saranja could get a fire going anywhere. Now in the lightning flashes, shapes around the fire – the horses, Saranja kneeling, bending over someone lying on the ground – two people lying on the ground . . . Ribek!

She tried to run, tripped on the folds of her cloak, fell, struggled up, wallowing in the wind-driven folds of waterproof . . .

'Easy now, Missy, easy,' grunted the groom, as if speaking to one of his horses. 'Where you trying to get to now, then?'

'Up there!'

'Get you there the sensible way, shall we? What else is horses for, if you don't ride 'em?'

She let him lift her up into the saddle, and clung to the horse's mane, peering into the dark, waiting for another lightning flash . . .

It came, and Ribek was sitting up, head bowed, his arms clasped round his knees. More lightning, and she saw the heave of his shoulders as his lungs gulped air. Benayu was lying on his back, as if fast asleep, Saranja beside him feeling for his pulse. Sponge lay with his head on his master's chest, tense and watchful, ready to take on all the demons in the world.

Maja slid down, staggered to Ribek's side, crouched and put her arm round his heaving shoulders, then looked again out to sea.

The moving light had almost reached the headland. Azarod's whip lashed towards it, and the lightning, almost continuous now, danced around it. The light didn't falter. The roar of thunder seemed to shake the whole hill.

No, the hill had indeed shaken, but not because of the thunder, for that ceased as the lightning died, but another colossal bass roaring was still there, not blast upon blast like the thunder but steady and continuous. The whole hill shuddered to its sound. And by the next flurry of lightning they saw that a full half of the massive headland had fallen away, and the rocks it had been made of, millions of tons of them, weren't simply lying out of sight at the foot of the new line of cliffs, but were shooting out like water sluicing across a tiled floor, forming a kind of causeway through the waves towards the place from which the demon Azarod arose.

Now the pale light came into view, speeding along the causeway towards the demon. Uselessly he lashed with his whip. He turned away, but the rocks closed round his base before he could flee. They surged upward, building themselves into a rugged wall, into a vast rock pillar, encasing him, covering him over. The last howl of his tempest snapped short and he was gone.

The pale light faded. The wind eased and died. The clouds drifted apart, thinned, became silvery with moonlight, cleared away. Four people were left standing on a hillside, another inert on the ground at their feet, horses greeting each other with whickers in the stillness.

'What . . . what happened?' whispered Maja. 'To Benayu, I mean? And Ribek?'

'I don't know what *happened*,' said Saranja irritably. 'Nobody's told me what's going on. I'll tell you what I saw. I was sitting with Benayu, worrying where you'd got to, when Ribek came pounding up the hill. I've never seen a man so shattered with running. He pretty well fell flat in front of Benayu, but managed to crawl forward and hold out his fist in front of Benayu's face. I thought he was going to punch him. "Breathe this. Can't explain," he said. He only just managed to get the words out. He opened his hand, Benayu took a sniff and Ribek collapsed. Benayu looked baffled for a moment, and then he seemed to be listening to someone. Then he thought for a bit and nodded. "Very well, I agree," he said, and lay down like he is now.

'Then there was light all around us, and this woman

standing beside him. I think it was a woman, but there was some kind of veil over her head and her robe covered the rest of her. I couldn't see her feet, but I thought she was floating a little above the ground. She didn't say anything, but she turned and looked out at that monster that seemed to be making the storm. She stood like that for quite a long while and . . .'

She broke off, staring over Maja's shoulder. Maja turned and saw the pale light floating towards them. She helped Ribek to his feet and they stood and waited.

'Well, at least she's coming back,' said Saranja. 'Perhaps she'll do something about Benayu. He's still alive, but I don't like his pulse. It's incredibly slow.'

The light reached them and stopped. The tall, veiled figure within it, neither man nor woman as far as Maja could see or sense, turned, raised an arm and pointed towards the pillar that imprisoned the demon. A light flared from its summit, and continued to burn as the figure turned again and stood beside Benayu. It seemed to shrink a little, and was now clearly a woman. She lifted her veil aside to reveal a calm, pale face, looking as if it had been carved from marble and polished to that unnatural smoothness. Or perhaps that was the effect of the moonlight.

The groom snatched off his hat and fell on his knees, covering his face with his hands.

'Stand, my friend,' said the woman. 'You have done well. While my powers are on me I would like to reward you. I could take twenty years off your age if you choose.'

'More than's right, M'Lady. I'll be happy to go in my

natural time, but a good, healthy life for me and the missus till then . . .'

His voice tailed off, as if he felt ashamed to ask even for that.

'Good,' she said. 'My blessing is on you.'

'What about Benayu?' said Saranja, firmly refusing to be awestruck.

'He must sleep a long while. What lies there is only his physical body, with barely enough of his inward self left to keep it breathing. All of the rest he passed into this form, as I had done out of my own body that still lies sleeping down in Larg, and with our joint powers we mastered the demon. I could not have done it without him. But now, if all that he had lent me, and besides that, all that he has acquired by sharing this form with me, were to return in one rush where it belongs, it would destroy his physical body. He must sleep for all this night, and tomorrow, and another night, summoning it power by power in due order. Then, that next dawn, he can safely wake.

'But even then he must rest. Though he is naturally extremely gifted, he is very young, both for the work we did tonight and for the powers he now possesses. He will need to sleep long hours, and to do no magic at all until he knows himself to be fully ready. And you must care for him in every way you can. He is the Empire's best hope for generations to come.'

She turned to the groom.

'You, my friend, may return to the city and tell the Proctors what you have seen and heard. You others can wait here, and in the morning the Proctors will decide how they can reward you all for what you have done. That will be their choice, not mine. Farewell.'

She was gone, and they were left on the hillside listening to the rejoicing bells of the city and gazing out at Larg's new sea-mark summoning ships to harbour from league on league of moonlit ocean.

Chapter 10

JEX SPOKE BRIEFLY in the middle of the night, in a voice so faint that Maja strained to hear it. *'There is a touching point near Barda. An island off the coast. Angel Isle.'*

The sun was barely clear of the horizon and the dawn still dew-fresh when the old groom rode up the hillside, accompanied by a uniformed functionary and two servants leading pack mules. Maja was already awake, so rose and staggered down to meet them with her finger to her lips.

'Morning, Missy,' said the groom, grinning. 'Thought you'd be fancying a bit of breakfast.'

'Lovely,' she whispered. 'I'm starving. But please don't wake Ribek. He pretty well killed himself running up the hill last night. Shall I get Saranja?'

The functionary interrupted with a pompous cough.

'You have two hours,' he said. 'At that point a

251

delegation from the Court of Proctors will arrive to greet and thank you for your services to the City of Larg. It would be appreciated if you and your friends are ready to receive them.'

'We'll do our best.'

'Furthermore, I am instructed to enquire of you how the City may best reward you for the aforementioned services. We will need to know your names. Perhaps you had better wake your friend.'

Saranja was always snarly first thing, and wasn't at her most gracious as she spelled the names out and the functionary wrote them down. He became steadily huffier, and barely controlled his astonishment at the idea that they couldn't wake Benayu and they'd need a litter for him.

'I will inform the Court of your requirement,' he said stiffly, and bowed and turned away.

'Could have asked a bit more than that, Missy,' the groom whispered to Maja. 'Gave me a medal and a purse of silver without me so much as hinting.'

He glanced over his shoulder at the functionary, already fussing over his horse's harness, making it clear he was too important to be kept waiting.

'I'd better be off,' he said. 'You'll be coming back to Larg one day?'

'I hope so.'

'Look us up, supposing you do. We'll have a lot to talk over.'

He trotted off, cupped his hands to give the functionary a leg-up into his saddle, and then swung himself up as nimbly as if he'd been thirty years younger.

They rode away down the hill, the groom keeping a respectful half-length behind the functionary. The two servants stayed and unloaded the mules. There were fresh logs for the fire, fodder for the horses, cooking utensils and two hampers. Maja opened one, found a long, narrow, crusty loaf, still warm from the oven, and broke a piece off to keep her going till breakfast was ready.

Ribek groaned, yawned, stretched and sat stiffly up.

'I've been dreaming of sausages,' he grumbled. 'Still am. Fat chance up here.'

'It isn't our kind of sausage,' said Maja through an unfinished mouthful. 'But it's lovely. Here.'

She offered him her plate.

'Still dreaming,' said Ribek, and helped himself. Happily she watched him munching like a well man.

'Jex spoke to me last night,' she said. 'He sounded terribly weak. But he says there's a touching point near Barda. It's called Angel Isle.'

He nodded, but his mouth was too full of sausage for him to answer.

'Do you think it's all right to move Benayu, supposing Sponge will let us touch him?' said Saranja as they watched the procession climb the road. 'I mean, does he have to stay where he is till he's got all his whatever-it-is back?'

'Anima, I suppose,' said Ribek, wiping the grease off his mouth and fingers and rising to his feet. 'I don't think there's our kind of here and there where this sort of thing comes from.'

'Anyway, Zara would have told us,' said Maja, rising too and moving with the others to the roadside to meet the procession.

A mounted herald in a splendid surcoat, with a banner sticking up from his saddle, led the way. Behind him came six Proctors and several other dignitaries, all on horseback, and an armed escort on foot. The morning sunlight glittered off their spear-points in the clean hill air. The travellers waited respectfully for the riders to dismount.

The herald lifted a trumpet to his lips and blew a strange, unmusical note: *Paaarrrrrp!* He took a scroll from his pouch and started to read.

'Plenipotentiary delegation from the Court of Proctors of the Sovereign City State of Larg. Occasion – Award of the Freedom of Larg to the following. Saranja Urlasdaughter, please step forward.'

She did so, head high, as if born for this moment of glory. The President opened one of the boxes, took out what looked like a gold medal on a chain and hung it round Saranja's neck.

'Saranja Urlasdaughter,' he said. 'By order of the Council of Proctors I hereby invest you with the state and all the ancient privileges of a Freewoman of Larg.'

He handed her the scroll, and then almost managed to startle her out of her hero-mode by kissing her soundly on both cheeks, but she recovered enough to thank him and say she was very honoured and shake his hand.

Ribek, when his turn came, walked forward with a

different kind of swagger, halfway to a dance step, took his kisses as if this sort of thing happened to him most weeks and winked at Maja as he returned. If she'd been told beforehand that this was going to happen she'd probably have been overwhelmed with shyness, but she managed to carry it off. The President spoke to her in a gentler voice, his kisses were feather light, and he held on to her hand for a moment after he'd shaken it.

'How old are you, Maja?' he asked.

'Twelve, sir.'

'I thought so. I have a granddaughter just your age. If ever she achieves half of what you have done for Larg I shall be proud of her indeed.'

'Thank you, sir.'

Benayu had the same pronouncement read over him. His medal was laid on his chest, but he didn't get kissed – perhaps because it would have been a hands-and-knees job, and Presidents don't do that.

Another Proctor stepped forward, opened yet another scroll and started to make a speech.

'Last night will live in the memory of Larg as long as our walls remain, and with it will live the names of these chance-come strangers, who are now strangers no more, but . . .'

And so on, for some while. When he was finished, servants came round with trays of sweet fizzy white wine in silver goblets, and there were several toasts, after which they stood around finishing their wine and chatting. Ribek was in his element, and Maja stayed close by, not talking much but enjoying his enjoyment. The man who'd lettered the scroll came up and explained what the Freedom of Larg meant. They got a month's free board and lodging whenever they passed through, and if in old age they decided to end their days in Larg, the city would keep them in comfort till they died. Furthermore, Larg had treaties with all the seaports up and down the coast, and if they showed their scrolls at any of these they'd be treated as honoured guests and helped on their way.

'I don't suppose Barda's one of them,' said Ribek. 'I think it's just a fishing village – or used to be.'

'Yes, we have a treaty with Barda. It's certainly a regular seaport, and has been for many years. It's still famous for its oysters, but it's a great deal more than a fishing village these days. After all, Larg must have been a fishing village once. It's a fair distance north. If that's where you're heading for you could consider taking a sea-passage, though the season of storms is approaching, and after what we saw last night . . .'

'That sounds helpful,' said Ribek. 'I'd love to be able to listen to the sea.'

Maja tugged at his sleeve.

'What about Benayu?' she whispered. 'Zara said her powers were weaker over the sea.'

'Good point. Better not risk it,' he said, and explained to the man.

It was mid-morning before they were able to move off with six of the guard to accompany them as they skirted Zara's ward. A handsome barge took them across the river, and on the further shore there were several hundred citizens and groups of schoolchildren lined up to cheer them as they disembarked and a flute-and-drum band to lead them to another feast laid out under a vast scarlet and gold pavilion.

As they were being shown to their places one of the Provosts stopped them.

'One moment,' he said. 'There'll be a few speeches afterwards, and it would be appreciated if one of you would reply.'

'Not me,' said Saranja instantly.

'All right, I'll give it a go,' said Ribek.

'It needn't be more than a few words,' said the Provost, clearly doubting this stranger's ability to produce an oration up to the high standards of Larg. 'And after that you would be well advised to rest. We are arranging with one of the desert tribes to guide you to the Highway, and they prefer to travel by night, when the snakes and scorpions are less active.'

'We won't have much trouble getting to sleep after we've had a share of that lot,' said Ribek, with a nod at the loaded tables.

That was true. Maja, in fact, couldn't wait, and fell asleep during the speeches. She was woken by the sound of laughter. Ribek was on his feet obviously enjoying himself, with his audience in the palm of his hand. He waited for the laughter to die.

'One last thing,' he said, still in his usual light tone. 'We – Maja and I – met and talked to the Sleeper. It's something we'll remember as long as we live. None of you has been so lucky, but you know she's there, asleep. She always has been, and as far as you're concerned, she always will be. But she won't. She's very old, and tired and lonely, and longing to be released from her task and go. It must be terrible to die alone, far from the people you most love. At least she isn't that. She's right here, among them, among you. And the best thing you can do for her is to love her back. I am sure you admire and respect and honour her no end, but that isn't the same thing. Love her. Show your love for her. Plant a rose in your garden for her sake. Teach your children to love her – don't use her to frighten them when they don't behave. That sort of thing. I'm sure you'll think of ways. Whatever it is, she'll know. Even if it's only in her dreams, she'll know.'

He sat down. The first speech, before Maja had nodded off, had been followed by polite applause. This time there was silence. Everyone looked a bit stunned. Somebody started to clap dubiously. Slowly the rest joined in. There was nothing as crude as outright cheering, but it seemed to Maja that the clapping had a different feel about, more than polite: meant, natural. It stopped only when the President rose smiling to thank Ribek and declare the feast over.

A tent had been got ready for the travellers to rest in for the few hours before their guides arrived. Benayu slept unstirring on one of the beds with Sponge curled up at his feet. There was a well-licked dish and a bowl of water for him beside the bed. Maja flopped on to hers fully clothed and was asleep before she had drawn three breaths. The next she knew she was on a horse somewhere – Levanter her extra sense told her – with her right cheek numb from pressing against his mane and neck. The air was cold and dry. The sound of the horses' hooves was no more than a soft *pad, pad.* She opened her eyes, and immediately screwed them shut against the glare of moonlight. In that glimpse she had seen a ghost, black against the glare, swathed from head to foot in a hooded cloak, its only visible feature one spidery arm holding Pogo's bridle. Then she was asleep again.

Next time, she stirred enough for Ribek, riding in the saddle behind her, to realize she had woken and steady her as she sat groaningly up.

'High time,' he said. 'It's past midnight. Best try to stay awake now, or you won't sleep during the day. Stay there a moment.'

He slid himself down, helped her back on to the pillion and remounted. She stared around as they rode on. In every direction the desert stretched away, seeming almost featureless under the big moon. A little way ahead of the party two shadows danced along over the dusty earth. She could barely see the guides who cast them. Saranja and Rocky were on her right, with another guide beyond them. Pogo was still there on her left, led by a guide. For a moment Maja thought the horse was carrying some kind of sack on his back, but then she realized it was another of the tribespeople facing away, hunched down, riding side-saddle. Benayu's litter followed, with another guide leading each pony.

A quiet, throbbing vibration, not like anything she'd felt before, was coming from behind her. Craning round, she saw two more of the guides bringing up the rear, walking with a peculiar gliding pace and carrying short branches. As she was looking at them they halted, turned and waved their branches in the air. A breeze sprang up out of nowhere, picking up little flurries of dust and depositing them over the stretch that the party had just crossed.

Now she realized that the same sort of thing was happening ahead of them. The two tribespeople leading the way weren't merely there as guides – they were using the same sort of magic to do something else. Drive something away, she thought – yes, of course, snakes and scorpions. She shuddered. There'd been only one kind of snake in the Valley, and it wasn't poisonous, but still she had a horror of the creatures. She didn't know much about scorpions, and she didn't want to.

The night seemed endless, the desert all the same, the moon moving oh, so slowly westward, the constellation of the Fisherman in the northern sky circling around the Axle-pin, invisible below the horizon, at the same slow pace as the earth turned over. She felt herself falling asleep again.

'Pinch me . . .' she whispered.

'No fun. Why don't you sing to me? What about "Cherry Pits"?'

'"Cherry Pits"?' she whispered.

'Cherry Pits' was an old, old song, which mothers sang over cradles and children used for counting games. The words, when they meant anything at all, were about two lovers sharing a bowl of cherries and making some absurd promise and sealing it with a kiss for every one they ate.

'What's so awful about "Cherry Pits"?' he asked.

'Nothing . . . Nothing . . .'

'Tell me.'

'I . . . I can't.'

She knew perfectly well what was wrong with 'Cherry Pits', but it was a place in her mind that she didn't go. It had a door like the one in the corner of the Council Chamber at Larg, which she had magically caused to disappear. She had made a gap in time. On one side of the gap she had let the chickens out and scattered their grain for them and collected the eggs and brought them back into the kitchen, and on the other side of the gap, two evenings later, she had put the chickens away for the night and was coming back into the kitchen with the eggs they had laid in their secret nests during the day.

And in that gap Saranja had gone away.

Ribek was silent for a while, then said, 'Well, if you can't, you can't. How about something else? "The Gooseboy"?'

'All right.'

She was astonished to find that Ribek, who could do everything so gracefully, couldn't sing in tune. Never mind. It was still a lot more fun than being pinched. They sang on for the rest of the night, all the songs they could remember. Songs and stories were almost the only thing Maja's mother had managed to give her. Dawn came much sooner than she'd expected, and then, almost at once, it was day.

The tribespeople halted and gathered around. Some of them threw back their hoods to reveal dark, beaky faces, their cheeks patterned with tattoos. By daylight she saw that several of them were carrying stout staffs, pointed at one end. Three of them were only shoulder high to the others – women, Maja knew through her extra sense, but without that it would have been hard to tell. The sack-like figure on Pogo's back was also a woman, but very old. The men lifted her down, set her on her feet, handed her a staff and waited.

She stood for a while, muttering to herself, and then hobbled off using the staff, halted again and drew something from under her cloak. As far as Maja could see, it was just three twigs lashed together to form a triangle with pebbles fastened to two corners and a length of cord to the third. She gripped the end of the cord between finger and thumb, swung the object back and forth a couple of times and with a twist of her wrist set it circling in a vertical plane at her side, raising a thin, throbbing whine as the air whistled through it. More of the same mysterious desert magic began to flow.

Maja heard Ribek gasp beside her.

'She's calling to the water!' he muttered.

The woman turned slowly. The note changed, rose shriller and shriller, almost beyond hearing, began to fall again. She turned back a little, until the pitch was at its highest, and pointed.

Two of the men stood side by side with their arms round each other's waists. A third man placed a leather pad on their shoulders, lifted the old woman, settled her on to the pad and took her staff from her. It was all quickly and easily managed, as if they'd done it many times before. They strode off, black against the glare of the risen sun. Everyone followed.

Twice they stopped to let the old woman, without dismounting, swing her water-charm again and correct their course. The third time they let her down and she hobbled

262

forward and swung her charm again. The whining note didn't vary its pitch as she turned. She took her staff back and prodded it feebly into the ground.

Five of the guides gathered round, three using the pointed ends of their staffs to loosen the earth, and the other two scooping it away. The old woman took out her charm and swung it again. The rest stood by, humming in the backs of their throats, varying the sound in time with the pulsing throb of the charm, as the old woman spun it faster and faster.

'There's some kind of water-spirit hiding here, I think,' said Ribek. 'She used her charm to find it, and now they're summoning it up. I can hear the charm talking to it, not in the water-language I know, but it's words all right. It sounds as if they're bargaining. Maybe the spirit doesn't want to come, and the charm's saying it's got to unless it sends us some water . . . Ah, here it comes.'

Silently the hole that the guides had been digging filled from below with beautiful clear water. Smiling, the tribesmen stood aside and gestured to their charges to drink.

Everyone drank all they could and filled their gourds and water-bottles. Then the horses drank hugely, but the pool stayed full. The old woman swung her charm briefly while the tribespeople chanted.

'We, from the north, would also like to add our thanks, O spirit of the desert,' said Ribek formally.

As he spoke the water seeped away as quickly as it had come. The tribespeople filled in the hole they had dug and tamped the earth carefully down.

'Shade for the horses is the next thing,' said Saranja. 'You can't tell with Rocky; the ponies look pretty tough, and Pogo's got desert blood in him. My war-lord used to ride a beast like him, and it was astonishing what it could put up with. But Levanter's really going to suffer. I'll try and explain to the tribespeople. I'm not sure how much they know about horses.'

Enough, it turned out. According to the functionary at Larg who'd made the arrangements, the tribespeople understood as much of the language of the Empire as they needed to know what was being said to them, but refused to speak it themselves. They nodded as soon as Saranja pointed at the horses and the sun and then the shadow of her hand held over Levanter's flank. Everyone formed up as before and they headed off north-west. The only difference was that four of their guides now led the way. Every hundred paces or so, all at the same time, they broke into a little dancing shuffle, gesturing in front of them with a pushing-apart motion, and now and then Maja could sense some poisonous creature scuttling or slithering out of their path. But nonetheless the ones with the main party walked with bent heads, as if scanning every step of the way ahead, and from time to time would use their staffs to tip a rock over, in case anything might still be lurking beneath it.

The sun was already seriously hot before they reached the place they were apparently heading for, a low, rocky outcrop, promising little relief, but it turned out to have a narrow gully on its northern side. A few wizened bushes clung to the rock in what shade there was. The tribespeople broke off enough branches to light a small fire in the middle of the gully, and once it was going twisted scraps of oily rags round the ends of short sticks, got them smouldering and worked down the gully poking them into crevices in the rock. They used the butts of their staffs to squash whatever came scuttling out.

That done, they placed the rags carefully against the embers so that they would continue to smoulder without actually burning, and then rigged up a remarkably effective awning over the gully, using their robes and the rugs from the travellers' saddlebags laid across cords weighted with boulders at either end and propped here and there by a couple of staffs lashed together to form a pole. Stripped off, they seemed astonishingly skinny, with tough little nodules of muscle clinging to the narrow bones. Every inch of their skin was covered with patterns of tattoos. They obviously preferred to eat separately, so the travellers settled at the other end of the awning, with the horses in between, and picked and chose among the excellent fare provided by the citizens of Larg.

'I've been thinking about the Covenant,' said Saranja in a low voice, though there was no one to overhear. 'The one between Zara and the Watchers, I mean.'

'So have I,' said Ribek. 'I don't get it. All right, we can guess what's on her side of the bargain. Larg is a sort of hostage. Her wards round the city are obviously pretty impressive, but the Watchers must be strong enough to deal with them if they want to . . .'

'And they must want to,' said Saranja. 'They aren't

going to stop until they control everything in the universe.'

'So what's Zara got by way of a hostage to stop them?' said Ribek.

'That's what I've been thinking about,' said Saranja. 'Do you remember Benayu telling us that serious magicians had to find somewhere safe to put their . . . what's it called? . . . anima outside themselves so it didn't get in the way of their magic?

'The Watchers do everything together, Chanad told us. Perhaps they did that together too – put all their animas into one safe place . . .'

'Larg?' said Ribek. 'Larg isn't exactly out of this universe. This curry comes from Larg. And . . . What's up, Maja? Come on, tell us. Don't leave it all to Saranja and me. Your guess is as good as ours. Better, probably.'

Maja couldn't open her mouth. An odd little buzzy feeling had woken in the back of her mind while Ribek was talking, like the warning noise a stinging insect makes when you try to swat it away. She was thinking of what had happened when they'd just come back into the Council Chamber, in that instant before the door vanished – the appalling brief jolt of magic, the sense of something hidden beyond Zara's chamber, a secret inside a secret, in a place that wasn't there, a place that was somewhere else. A way into another univ . . . the buzz was louder now . . . louder, closer . . .

'Stop!' she croaked. 'Don't talk about it! Don't even think about it! The Watchers . . . !'

They stared at her. Saranja started to say something, but didn't. The muttered talk of the tribespeople did not

266

falter. The horses fidgeted. The strange, bitter smoke from the smouldering rags drifted slowly through the gully in the oven-like heat. Ribek nodded, serious-faced for once.

'I want to tell you how my cousin Arissa was murdered,' he said. 'We don't usually talk about it. It's a terrible story . . .'

It was – tragic, appalling, filling the mind, leaving no room for thoughts of the Watchers, or what might lie beyond Zara's cell. The strange, menacing buzz lost its intensity and died away. When the story ended they sat in silence, letting it find its place in their minds, unforgettable.

'You can never tell what people will do,' said Saranja at last, 'however well you think you know them. One of my war-lord's other women . . .'

The story wasn't tragic, just extremely strange, with a sad ending. Maja found herself on the edge of tears for two people she would never know, but who were probably still alive, somewhere on the other side of the great desert.

'Better, Maja?' said Ribek when the story ended.

Maja probed cautiously southward, and withdrew the moment she felt the buzzy sensation starting to wake.

'I think so,' she said. 'It's like . . . my uncle's old dog. She'd be lying in her kennel, fast asleep, not taking any notice of anything, but the moment she heard a stranger's footstep she'd be up and barking.'

'Is it just what we were talking about?' said Saranja. 'I mean can we talk about where we're going, and what we're hoping to find there?'

'I don't know. I mean, yes, I suppose so, if we're care-ful. But not now, not here.'

Ribek chuckled.

'So we continue to pass the time,' he said. 'Lighter fare, do you think? This might be a good moment to tell you about the miller's daughter. There was a young mill-hand whose wife bore him a son. Being an honest and thoughtful man he determined to toil night and day at his craft until he had enough put by to buy the mill he worked in order that he could leave it to his son. But a year had barely gone by before his wife bore him a sec-ond son.

'"Very well," he said. "I must buy or build another mill."

'But another year brought another son, a fourth year a fourth, until he had six sons . . .'

This wasn't one of the stories her mother told so Maja hadn't heard it before and was already enthralled. Despite that, her head began to droop. She was cross about it. She wanted to listen to the story. It struck her that she fell asleep far too easily these days, but it was hot, and the night had been endless and her stomach was full of good food. She half woke a couple of times and heard another snatch of the adventure, but by the next time it was over, and Ribek and Saranja were sit-ting on the far side of the gully talking in low voices. It wasn't about Larg, or anything magical. But it was something that mattered, something serious.

When she finally woke Ribek was gone. No, there he was, standing at the other end of the gully, silhouetted against the sunset glare beyond him. The tribespeople were laughing at him as he swung something vertically beside him. He turned, laughing too, and offered the object to them. Now Maja could see that it was a little triangular charm made of three sticks like the one the old woman had used to summon the water-spirit, but a bit smaller. Of course he'd wanted to try her water-magic, so he'd made himself a charm.

Someone took it and passed it to the old woman, who bent over it, then rose and hobbled forward. Her spidery arm reached up and plucked at his beard. He didn't back away or resist. She bent over the charm, peering at it and fiddling with it, then took his hand and pushed it close to his mouth. She spat into her palm to show what she wanted. Obediently he spat, and waited while she smeared his spittle carefully into the corners of the triangle and then handed it back to him. He turned to the desert and tried again.

This time Maja sensed the flow of the magic and the snarl of the water-spirit's response. Ribek let the swinging slow and cease, and the spirit subsided. The old woman clapped her hands together and hooted and the others responded with a rhythmic outburst of clapping and hooting. One by one they rose and touched Ribek on the cheek and returned to their places and fell silent. Ribek bowed to them, making a wide gesture with his arms to tell them how deeply he was honoured. One of the men rose and made signs to him, pointing at the old woman and a boy, who shyly held up his own water-charm, and then at Ribek, and finally made a sweeping, dismissive gesture at the rest of the group.

They murmured quietly for a little while, then rose and began to gather up their things.

Maja was still sulky with sleep when Ribek lifted her on to Levanter's rump.

'I want to know what happened in the story,' she said. 'It wasn't my fault I fell asleep.'

'You were tired, and no wonder, all you've been doing. My turn for a nap now. You'll have to take the reins.'

He had the lucky knack of being able to sleep anywhere, at any time, in almost any posture. He knotted the reins and laid them on Levanter's neck, bowed his head and in a very few strides was asleep, swaying gently in the saddle to Levanter's movement. He started to snore, rather more musically than he sang. Maja huddled against him, arms round his waist, enjoying the pleasant fantasy that she was protecting him, holding him steady, keeping him from falling, while he sat there helpless and vulnerable.

Sometimes she wondered what he thought about her. She was fairly sure he was fond of her, loved her even, but it wasn't the same kind of love that she felt for him. Not that she really understood her own feelings for him. They were love all right, but they weren't the sort of consuming, world-altering passion you hear about in stories. Dimly she could feel stirrings of that kind of love, the love whose language was glance and caress and close embrace, but she pushed them away. Not yet, she told herself, not yet. Not until he can feel the same about me. Till then she wasn't going to think about it.

It would be a nuisance, coming between them, an embarrassment to them both. They were much more comfortable as they were. Why spoil it?

Ribek woke when they stopped at midnight to rest and eat and water the horses. The old woman summoned another underground stream to the surface, while Ribek watched and listened, fascinated.

'Are you still all right?' he said as he lifted her back into the saddle.

'I'm fine. I've been getting a story ready to tell you. It's going to be better than yours.'

He didn't answer until they were on their way, and he had, deliberately, she thought, dropped Levanter back behind Rocky.

'Can we leave the story for another time, Maja? I'd rather you told me about "Cherry Pits". It's something that happened at Woodbourne, isn't it? Saranja's told me a bit about Woodbourne. You've never said a word. No, Maja, tell me. I've told you almost everything I know about Northbeck. It's your turn now. Come on, Maja. You need to tell someone. Please.'

She shook her head. He waited. Levanter plodded on. As if from a long way off she saw a girl standing in an empty room. No, only one corner of a room and part of the two walls that made it. The scene was lit by moonlight and starlight, and the floor was desert. A door shaped itself in the corner, but the girl had lost the key. Now Ribek's figure – Maja would know it anywhere – appeared beside her and put something into her hand. A key. The girl stepped forward.

He's right, she thought. I can tell him because I love him.

'My uncle . . .' she began. 'My aunt . . .'

She stopped. It was too difficult. Even those five syllables.

'I know about them,' said Ribek quietly. 'Saranja's told me. She told me roughly what happened. Your uncle had had one of his rages and stormed out, and after a bit your aunt sent you out to fetch him in . . .'

'Yes. He was in the barn. I'd done it before. I never knew if he'd just snarl at me, or be nice to me. It was all right that morning. He told me to come and sit beside him and he'd teach me a song called "Cherry Pits." He put his arm round me and I put mine round him and we started. I was comfortable, happy . . .'

He waited in silence while she fought for control.

'. . . And then my aunt came in. She didn't say anything. She picked up an old halter and snatched me away from him and tied it round my wrists and then tied it to a ring in the wall so that my arms were high above my head with my face against the wall and she gave him a riding stock and said, "Whip her."

'He whipped me once. "You are never to do that again," she told me. "Whip her again. Harder. And again." Each time he whipped me she said, "Never." He did it ten times. I was sobbing and screaming.

'Then she untied me and took me into the kitchen and told me to strip off my top and lie face down on the floor. She rubbed some salve into my back and told me to dress again and took me out to the old dog kennel and put a collar round my neck and chained it to a ring

272

in the floor so I couldn't stand up. She brought me scraps of meat and bread in a dog bowl and gave me a bowl of water to lap. She didn't say anything till she let me out next evening. "You are less than a dog in this house," she told me. "Remember that. Now go and get the hens in and look for the eggs."

'That night Saranja came to my room and whispered to me that she was going away. She asked if I wanted to come too, but I was too afraid.

'That's all.'

'Thank you for telling me. It must have been hard for you. Did that sort of thing happen often?'

'That was the only time. She never hit me herself.'

'And your father? You haven't said anything about him.'

'I don't know anything about him. I don't know who he was, or where he's gone to, if he's still alive. I think he must have done something too dreadful to talk about. I wasn't allowed to ask. My mother only cried when I did, and my aunt found out and tied me to my bed for a day and a night.'

'Mm. You haven't asked Saranja, she says. She thought you knew.'

'Oh! Does she . . . ? Can she . . . ?'

'Why don't you ask her?'

He pushed Levanter forward till they were alongside Rocky. Maja could tell Saranja had been waiting for them from the way she looked down at her and smiled.

'My . . . Ribek says you . . . my father . . . ?'

Still smiling, Saranja reached out and touched her cheek.

'I'm your half-sister, Maja,' she said. 'I thought you knew but they'd made you too afraid to talk about it. I hope that's good news.'

She didn't understand for a moment. Then she did. Her body went stiff. She gripped Ribek as hard as she could and gulped for breath.

'My uncle . . .' she croaked. 'And my mother . . . That's why it was all my fault!'

Ribek snorted. Saranja pulled Rocky to a halt, and Levanter automatically stopped too. She let go of the reins, leaned across and took Maja's hand between both of hers.

'No, Maja,' she said. 'You must stop thinking like that. You're the only person whose fault it wasn't. My parents never loved each other. She loved somebody else but he didn't want to live at Woodbourne. She married my father because she wanted a daughter who could hear the cedars. He was a poor man and he married her for the farm, but it was never his. It was hers, and she didn't let him forget it. She gave him two sons to go with it, but they weren't what she wanted and he knew they could never inherit the farm. Then she had me. After that she wouldn't let him touch her.

'Something like that has happened again and again in our family, a woman forsaking love and wasting life trapped at Woodbourne for the sake of the story, but it's never turned out so bad. Ever since I was small I've known I wasn't going to let it happen to me, though she was determined that it should. I think I knew in my heart that if it did I would end up like her. Anyway, I believe that by the time I was born she already hated my

274

father. That's why she gave her sister a home when their parents died, though she treated her more as a maid-servant than a sister. She must have known what would happen, and known that your mother was too great a ninny to say no. You were born so that she could hate him properly, and punish him by punishing you. That's their fault, all three of them. Not yours.

'And you still haven't told me if you're happy about being my sister. Because I am. Very.'

'Oh, yes! Yes! But everything else . . .'

She couldn't take it in. It didn't change anything. It had all happened. But it wasn't her fault, and that changed everything. It even seemed to change how she thought about Ribek. If her father had never been allowed to love her, and she'd never been given a chance to love him . . . And what had her aunt done, to make her mother so hopeless . . . ?

'Ribek?'

'Hm?'

'Can we sing "Cherry Pits" now?'

He still couldn't sing in tune. But they were lovers in the song, weren't they? She loved him for that, and found herself singing the song as if it was true. He laughed and did the same, but it wasn't Ribek singing, of course, it was the lover in the song. He couldn't sing in tune either.

When they'd finished all the verses they knew they invented some new ones until Maja couldn't think of any more. Then she told him 'The Owl-Witch' and he told her 'The Miller's Daughter' all over again, which lasted until, just as the eastern stars grew faint with daybreak, something changed. She knew what it was at once.

'Benayu's awake,' she said, whispering as if she'd been in a sickroom.

Ribek leaned over and murmured the news to Saranja.

'I'll tell him what Zara said,' she answered, and reined Rocky back.

Behind them Maja sensed the contact of two hands and heard the mutter of Saranja's voice. She could feel Benayu's almost overwhelming listlessness.

'Good moment for him to wake,' said Ribek. 'Looks as if we're here.'

Concentrating on what was happening behind her Maja hadn't noticed the sudden change ahead. It was a bit like coming to Larg all over again. They must have been climbing for some while back, but on a slope too gentle for her to be aware of it. Now they had reached the summit and were looking down a rather steeper slope into a world where it was already day.

The sun was not yet risen. Below the pale dawn sky lay a level plain, blazing with colour, sheets of scarlet, purple, yellow and clear bright blue, spreading between barren outcrops of rock. Through this glory ran the Imperial Highway, with a way station immediately below them. The amazing dazzle of colours was – she concentrated – flowers!

'What . . . what . . . why . . . ?' she stammered. 'It isn't magic, or I'd feel it.'

'Rain,' said Ribek. 'Fellow at Larg told me about it. It happens for about three weeks this time of year almost every year. Rainstorms sweep up the coastal plain and last year's seeds germinate and grow, and the eggs of several sorts of moth, which have been lying there all through the dry season, hatch and pupate and turn into moths just in time to pollinate the flowers so that they can produce a fresh lot of seeds, and the moths mate and lay their eggs ready for next year, and die. It may not be magic, but it's magical.'

This was as far as the tribespeople would go. Ribek doled out chunks of salt to each of them, which was all they wanted by way of payment. As he did so they touched his cheek and he raised his hand in blessing.

'We'd better do that to the old lady,' he muttered. 'There's not a lot of them can talk to the water-spirit, just her and that lad there in this group. The ones who can – me too now, I suppose – are kind of special.'

He led the way, and Saranja and Maja copied him. The tribespeople responded with a few pleased hoots. The old woman hobbled to the litter, raised Benayu's limp arm and touched his hand against her cheek. He stirred and muttered as if he'd still been asleep. Then they went their separate ways, the tribespeople back to their desert home and the travellers down to the Highway.

Chapter 11

EMISSARIES FROM LARG had come up the North Highway and were waiting for them at the way station with more provisions. They'd also brought fresh ponies, but Saranja insisted that the horses needed a rest. This allowed Benayu to sleep most of the day, so that by nightfall he was sitting up and talking cheerfully, and helping himself generously to the good Larg food. To Ribek and Saranja he must have seemed almost himself again, but to Maja he was deeply changed.

Before Larg, even when he wasn't using them, to Maja's extra sense he had tingled all the time with his magical powers. Now she was barely aware of them. But if she concentrated she could feel them, still there, deep down inside himself. And alongside them, something else, very old, very powerful, much more than a great tool, a marvellous machine, for him to use when he had learnt how. Something that seemed almost alive in its own right. She remembered Benayu explaining that for a magician to make the change from the third to the fourth level was like learning to breathe a different kind of air. It was as if this thing, this power, had come the other way. It couldn't breathe our air on its own. It could only exist inside a magician, breathing with human lungs, seeing with human eyes. It had lived inside Zara for most of her long life, but during that night when Benayu had lain on the hill above Larg it had left her and come to him. Zara must have known that this would happen, but for the sake of Larg she had let the power go. Now Benayu must learn to live with it, and it with him.

The Imperial Highway stretched before them. Even on the cooler coastal plain it was still roastingly hot at noon, but the mornings and evenings were bearable enough to let them travel by day. They would set out at sunrise with the astonishing fields of flowers around them, sparkling with the morning dew. Well before noon that freshness would be gone, sucked away by the overbearing sun, and by mid-afternoon the desert would be desert as far as the eye could see. But as the air began to cool another batch of flowers would be opening and by sunset competing with the golds and crimsons of the western sky. To Maja's extra sense their magic was like a song of exultation in their short, glorious moment of existence, and at night as she lay in the way station under the amazing desert stars she could sense the soft moths floating over the swathes of flowers, and settling to suck their nectar and at the same time smear themselves with the pollen that would produce fresh seeds to lie another year in the parched earth until next year's rains woke them for another burst of glory.

On such a night as this Maja woke, vaguely ill at ease. She had been hoping that Jex would at last speak to her in her dreams again, but he hadn't come, though she could tell from the greater sureness of his protection that he was already stronger. Something was amiss in the magical world, surely . . . but no, it wasn't anything to do with Jex. There was something sickening about it, a bit like the nausea she felt coming from the Watchers, but otherwise different from anything else she'd come across, as different as a plant is from a stone, or a fish from a hammer – a kind of dull, throbbing beat, not a noise, but a feeling, like a pulsing sick headache. It came from somewhere up north, a little east of the Highway, more than a day's journey away still, she decided. She fell asleep, but it persisted through her dreams and was still there when she woke.

It was there all day. Usually, when she chose, she could now ignore whole swathes of the myriad magics that continually assailed her, in order to concentrate on particular ones, but with this she couldn't. Unconsciously she had begun walking to the rhythm of its beat. By noon it was impossible to think about anything else. It seemed to be nothing that Jex could use or shield her from. She called to him in her mind but he did not answer. Not even thinking about it she groped for her amulet and shoved it right down to her wrist.

Astonishingly, something happened. The appalling thud dwindled to a dull throb in the background. She could look around. She could think. She stared at the amulet and saw that the strange black bead had changed. There was depth in its blackness, like that in the pupil of an eye. It was active. Doing something. Shielding her enough from the drumbeat for her to be able to think about something else. But not enough to let her break step unless she willed herself to do so.

She stared around. Saranja and Benayu were walking a few paces ahead. No, not walking, marching. Marching in step, like her. Why wasn't Benayu riding Pogo? A few days ago they had sent the ponies back to Larg with a merchant from the city whom they'd met at a way station, as Benayu was now physically recovered enough to ride a horse, though not yet to dismount and walk when the other three did. But he was on foot now, marching in step with Saranja, in time to that dull, implacable beat. So, she realized, was Ribek. With an effort she lengthened and slowed her stride, but he kept on as before, and as soon as she stopped concentrating on it she fell back into the same rhythm.

But they couldn't be hearing the beat. There wasn't anything to hear. It came to Maja solely through her extra sense, the awful monotonous magical thump. The horses seemed a lot more restive than usual, but their twelve hooves clopped on the paving to no rhythm she could make out.

Why were they walking at all? It was far too hot. They should all be . . .

Hadn't they passed a way station some while back? Why hadn't they stopped to water the horses and rest out the heat of the day, as usual?

And there was nobody else to be seen from horizon to

horizon. The Highway hadn't been busy since they'd joined it, and as most of the people going north went at the much same walking pace they seldom overtook anyone, or were overtaken, but there'd always been dribs and drabs of travellers coming in the other direction. There were none now. Not one.

She couldn't remember if they'd breakfasted at all.

She had to say something. Nobody had spoken a word since they'd left last night's way station. Only now did this seem strange. It seemed a huge effort to break the long silence. Her voice was a croak.

'Why are you taking those silly little steps? Ribek! Listen to me! Why are you taking those silly little steps?'

He answered as if from a dream.

'Comfortable.'

The silence closed round them again.

'Jex! Jex! What's happening?'

No answer.

At last, another way station. It was deserted. The food-stalls were set up but unattended. The horses recognized it for what it was, or perhaps they could smell water, and tried to stop, but Saranja and Benayu strode on unnoticing.

'Ribek! The horses! They must be dying of thirst! Ribek! Saranja!'

'Let them go,' muttered Ribek. 'Can't stop.'

With an even greater effort Maja forced herself to a halt, but her feet continued to stamp up and down to the implacable drumbeat. It was a heavy, continuous effort to prevent them from moving forward, so she let them go, lengthened her stride as far as she could and caught up, first with Ribek and then with the horses. She slowed enough to take one of the big water flasks from Levanter's saddlebag, and then caught up with Rocky. Still marching, though now with the shortest paces the drumbeat would allow, she snatched his bridle and tried to heave him round.

He halted and half turned. She slapped his rump as the rhythm swept past her. He hesitated. But Pogo had no doubts, and was already trotting back the way they'd come. She willed herself to stop, slapped him again and told him to go, and with a whicker of distress he gave in and led Levanter after Pogo. She let the rhythm sweep her away again and fell in beside Ribek and, still marching, managed to drink a few mouthfuls, slopping most of it down her front. The other three did the same, muttering their thanks. Nobody said anything else. The drumbeat was all there was.

The sun sidled west and down, and the shadows stretched across the desert. Dusk came quickly, and was quickly night. The Highway climbed to cross a low rise. From beyond it, a little to the right, came a steady orange glow. This was the place to which the drum was calling them. Under a brilliant moon they left the Highway and started towards it. For a while the rough ground drove them apart, but then it became a strange upward slope, unnatural in its perfect smoothness. The glow came from just beyond it. This, she knew was the end. She would never walk side by side with Ribek again.

Her voice refused to work. She moved closer and put

her hand into his. He twined her fingers into his and with his free hand stroked her arm, downward from the elbow, in a gesture of pure, natural affection. His hand reached the amulet.

He staggered and almost broke step, then stared at the amulet. She looked too. The single bead was glimmering now, as if with reflected firelight. She wouldn't have been able to see the faint glow in the full glare of day. And once before, on the hill above Larg – something almost lost to her memory in the immense wash of magic that had then been flowing around her – it had glinted as if with reflected firelight. But the fire had been embers. And it had been in the wrong place.

Azarod. Only for a moment had she felt the full force of his demonic magic, forgotten till now amid the storm of other happenings that night. That too, she now remembered, had been utterly different from anything else that she had met. But not different from this. And it hadn't been Jex shielding her from it as soon as she had picked him out of the cactus. It had been the ruined amulet, just as it was doing now.

Ribek had already let go of her wrist and was marching on as if nothing had happened. She grabbed his hand and forced it against the bead.

'Wake up!' she said. 'It's a demon doing this to us! Don't let go of my wrist! We've got to get to Saranja! Zald!'

His stride faltered.

'Demon,' he muttered uncertainly. 'Zald. Saranja. Only hope.'

'Come on! No, keep hold of my wrist. Tight. That's right.'

She lengthened her stride and dragged him forward.

'You go other side,' she gasped. 'Get Zald out. I'll get her hand.'

They reached Saranja as they topped the rise and fell in step on either side of her, with their arms stretched behind her back so that Ribek could still grasp the amulet. Maja could feel her inner rage blazing helpless in the grip of her compulsion. When she grasped Saranja's finger the whole arm was as limp as soaked cloth. She lifted it up and waited for Ribek to ease Zald from under Saranja's blouse and lay it against her chest.

'Other way up,' she said, desperately patient with his dazed clumsiness. 'Turn it over. That's right.'

No need to be told which stone was the demon-binder. One was already bright with the same orange glow that half filled the pit below them. It pulsed to the steady drumbeats. Awkwardly, stumbling to keep pace with the others' downward march, Maja gripped Saranja's middle finger. Using her thumb to keep the finger stiff, she pressed it against the glowing jewel.

Life flowed into the arm, into the whole body. Saranja halted in her tracks. The drumbeat faltered, failed and was replaced by an agonizing howl – a real, ear-shattering sound in the ordinary world of the senses. Ribek had halted too, and Benayu, and they were staring dazedly around. The glow was fading, the mist thinning. There was something vaguely tree-shaped at the centre of it.

Saranja drew herself up, squaring her shoulders. She was glowing all over, as if her clothes and skin had become translucent to the anger-fires within. She pinched the fingers of her right hand against the surface of the jewel and drew forth a line of fire, which she began to coil, loop after loop, round the palm of her left hand.

The thing at the centre of the hollow screamed again. Something came hurtling out of the fading mist towards her. With a cat-like sideways leap Ribek caught it two-handed, and dropped it with a yell of disgust. It was a human arm, torn savagely from the body.

'Wait here,' commanded Saranja. 'Maja can hold the end of the cord. You two look after her. I'll be all right – it can't touch me.'

Maja grasped the cord. It seemed to have neither weight nor heat, but the power of Zald throbbed through her, like a blaze that would have been glorious if she'd not been too close to it, until she felt Jex's shield renew itself and close round her.

'*Demon magic. Poison to me in this universe. This thing is one of my own kind, poisoned long ago.*'

There was horror in the voice of stone.

Saranja was already marching away across the slope, playing out the cord as she went. It didn't then fall to the ground, but floated waist high behind her in a fiery line.

The mist thinned further, and Maja could now see what the thing at its centre was – a living creature, as tall as a fair-sized tree and standing on a single dark trunk. But it wasn't a tree trunk. Its whole surface squirmed continually in response to the squirming, chewing motion of the screaming mouth, a kind of vertical gash near the top. Blood dribbled from its lower end. Above that, instead of branches, came dozens of writhing tentacles with crab-like claws at the end, and above them a crown of twenty or more shorter flexible stalks, each bearing a single huge red eye. Two of the tentacles ended not in claws but in hoof-like growths that flailed continually against the trunk, but now produced only the faintest magical pulse instead of the terrible drumbeat that had so mastered and overwhelmed them.

A huddle of spellbound travellers was crowded against the base of the creature, some of them scrambling over each other as they struggled to get nearer, while others, loosened from the weakening enchantment, were beginning to break away and, still in the grip of the nightmare, stagger sobbing up the slope. For a last, awful moment, before everything changed, Maya caught a glimpse of what they were running from, as several of the tentacles closed around a man the monster had snatched from the pile, tore him, still living, limb from limb, and started to cram the pieces into its mouth. It continued to scream as it chewed.

Only when the mist had almost cleared did it seem to wake fully to its danger. Its glaring red eyes craned towards Saranja like weed in a running stream. Several tentacles snatched victims from the pile, swung back and hurled them towards her. Any one of them, if it had reached her, would have knocked her flat, but instead some force seemed to slow them in their sprawling flight and swing them deftly aside and let them tumble gently on to the ground. One by one they picked themselves groggily up, stared around until they saw the monster,

gave a yell of horror, and rushed away. If they had
friends or loved ones still down in the pit they didn't
stay to look. By the time Saranja completed her circuit
almost all of them were gone.

She halted, took Maja's end of the cord, knotted it
round the length she was holding to form a noose and
hauled it in hand over hand until it tightened around the
creature's stem. The clawed tentacles plucked violently
at it, but it held firm.

She drew herself up, threw back her head and gave a
shout, in a voice Maja had never before heard from her.

'Haddu! Ah! Haddu-haddu!'

She turned, and with long, loping strides, dancer's
strides, she circled the pit again, drawing the flaming
cord tight as she went. The creature was too stupid to
recognize the new threat. While its tentacles heaved and
picked at the first loop the second loop enclosed them
and bound them tight.

Twelve times she circled the pit, winding the cord
steadily up the trunk. The monster continued to howl
until the fiery spiral reached its mouth and bound it
shut. By the twelfth circuit it was a writhing column of
flame from the bole to the top, with only a cockade of
eye-stalks waving frantically above.

At the end of the twelfth circuit Saranja halted.

'Up!' she said, and led the way back to the surface,
playing out the cord as she climbed. She turned to face
the pit.

'Haddu!' she called again. She twitched the cord.

Immediately it streamed towards her, and hand over
hand as it came she fed it back into the jewel she had

drawn it from. The process seemed effortless, but the force was enough to twist the monster's stem, faster and faster, through all twelve windings, until its released tentacles flailed helplessly out around it. By the time the end of the cord had disappeared into the fiery gem the creature had twisted itself free of its base, and, still spinning, still on fire, was rising into the air, higher and higher, until its howls started to fade into the sky.

Saranja raised her arms above her head.

'Haddu!' she cried for the third time, and brought them down in an imperious gesture of ending.

Flame like a lightning strike plunged down, carrying the monster with it. In the bottom of the pit a vast, sulphur-reeking hole opened to receive it. Still howling, the monster vanished into the earth and the hole closed over it. The edges of the pit began to tumble down to seal it over and they backed away.

'How did you know to do all that?' said Ribek in an awed voice. 'You don't even like magic.'

'Not me,' said Saranja in her own voice. 'Him.'

She gestured at Zald.

They crowded round to look. For a moment they saw, grinning out from the depths of the jewel, a little scarlet imp-face. Its thin tongue licked its lips in remembered relish, and then there was nothing but the glow of the jewel.

'Back to the road, I suppose,' said Ribek. 'If nothing else as nasty as that happens to us on this journey I shan't be sorry. Bless you, Maja, for remembering the water.'

He was doing his best to speak lightly, but Maja could

hear the deep shudder in his voice. It had been the kind of nightmare it's no use waking up from – you only lie in the dark, remembering it, still too afraid to move a muscle. Benayu was staggering as if still half drowning in the dream. Ribek put an arm round him to help him along. In silence they began to trudge back towards the Highway. Before they had gone far Sponge came racing out of the dark to greet Benayu with puppyish ecstasy – a bit of the real world, a tiny step towards making everything sane again. It was going to take a long, long time.

'Let's hope the horses are all right,' said Saranja. She must be feeling the same, Maya realized, in spite of what she'd done.

'Yes, the Watchers have loosed the demons,' said Benayu in a low, shuddering voice. 'We haven't yet seen the worst of them. They must be mad.'

They walked on in silence. The rocks threw heavy moon shadows, so black that they seemed solid. In that distorting light many of them had demon shapes. A man appeared, walking towards them, leading a mule. This was an ordinary trick of the moonlight, Maja knew, this sudden appearance – or would have been, back at Woodbourne. Not here. The man halted and waited for them to reach him.

Let go, Jex, for a moment.

No. Nothing unusual for miles around, except the residual throb of the buried pit behind them. And not even a glimmer from the black bead on her amulet.

'I think he's all right,' she whispered.

Still, they stopped several paces from him. He stayed where he was, leaning on his staff.

'Good evening,' he said in a mild, precise voice. 'I take it you are returning from that extraordinary and dismaying event. Are you the last to leave?'

'You're not going back!' said Saranja.

'Indeed, that was my intention. I would have stayed to watch, only my legs would not let me. But now I have mastered them, and found my mule . . .'

'There's nothing to see except desert,' said Ribek. 'The thing vanished into the ground and the pit closed up over it.'

'I can still take measurements and readings, perhaps.'

He was mad, Maja decided. He mightn't be any kind of magic worker, but perhaps there was something a little bit odd about his own individual magic. She couldn't think about it, couldn't think about anything. Now that they'd stopped walking she was swaying with exhaustion and hunger. Benayu looked even worse than she felt. He'd been walking all day when he shouldn't have walked at all.

'Please don't go,' said Saranja.

'I appreciate your concern, Madam, but . . . One moment . . . forgive me . . . Yes. I remember being picked up by that thing and hurled through the air. It was difficult in the circumstances to pay close attention to my surroundings, but for an instant I saw – I am almost certain I saw, and that it was you I saw – you hold yourself in exactly that manner – saw you striding across the slope with a line of fire trailing behind you. Forgive my impertinence, but is that the case?'

291

Saranja's mouth was open to answer but no voice emerged. She was not good at lying, let alone inventing a lie on the spur of the moment. Ribek moved easily into the gap.

'I'm afraid my sister is not at liberty to talk about it.'

'I fully understand,' said the stranger. 'It is dangerous to admit to the possession of any such powers, even when the authorities are fully occupied with events around Tarshu. But perhaps, since we are alone in this place, I may be permitted to assume that what I thought I saw was indeed the case, and that I and my fellow travellers have you to thank for rescuing us all from that terrible predicament. I do so from the very bottom of my heart.'

'Oh . . . er . . . thank you . . .' said Saranja.

'And if there is anything I can do in return . . .'

'You don't have any food in those saddlebags, I suppose,' said Ribek quickly.

'Indeed, I do. I'll be only too delighted . . .'

Prattling on, the man moved to the side of his mule and with deft fingers unbuckled a saddlebag. Maja sat down to wait with her back against a rock. An unknown time later she was lying curled on a rug on some kind of swaying platform with a smell of horse and harness in her nostrils and fragments of salt fish and soft bread in her mouth. She had no memory of how they got there but they tasted as if they'd been very good indeed.

Chapter 12

THEN IT WAS day. Maja was lying on the ground now, and in her own bedroll, by the feel of it. Low voices were talking close by – Ribek's and . . . Oh, yes, the stranger they had met last night. Something to do with watermills. The stranger seemed to know a lot about watermills. She groaned and tried to sit up, but every joint and muscle complained, and she let herself collapse and groaned again. Instantly Ribek was at her side, his arm under her shoulders.

'Don't move,' he said. 'We're staying here. Saranja says the horses have got to have a full day's rest. Here, try this. It's something Striclan brewed up. It's good for aches and pains, he says.'

Gently he eased her up enough for her to sip from the mug he was holding to her lips. The blood-warm liquid had a heavenly, rich, autumnal smell, and was both sweet and bitter in the mouth. A tingling glow flowed through her as she sipped, and she lay back down with a sigh.

'My sister's only twelve,' he explained to someone, 'and we must have done getting on two days' march yesterday. She's been doing too much anyway. She was a plump little thing when we set out, but look at her now.'

'Of course she must rest. And your brother too,' said the stranger's soft voice. Striclan must be his name. Something funny about him. Not now. Later.

'A little gentle exercise this afternoon,' the man went on. 'And I will give Miss Saranja an unguent with which to massage her. I would do it myself, but I imagine that as her guardian you would prefer . . .'

'She's a child still. No harm,' said Ribek, obviously relishing his role as official protector of the two women. *Huh!* she thought. *We'll see what Saranja has to say about that!*

'Spiced pumpkin bread for breakfast, Maja,' said Ribek. 'He's got a travelling larder in those saddlebags of his. I'll toast you some.'

It was as near heaven as Maja could imagine, lying in the morning sun – still welcome after the night chill of the desert – with Ribek feeding little squares of Striclan's toasted pumpkin bread, oozing with wild honey, between her lips. Funny name. Funny man. She could sense his oddness through Jex's mild shielding. Forcing herself into something like wakefulness she concentrated on the stranger.

Yes, there he was in his magical essence, just as she'd have expected, busy, eager, interested, self-confident, like quick, cheerful, clever music, music to dance to. But under that, almost unnoticeable beneath the surface dazzle and fizz, something much slower, much more deep and thoughtful, like huge cloud-islands drifting along on a summer day, grand and calm, but full of hidden thunder.

Interesting, but not now. Too tired.

She slept dreamless, and woke again, this time in the evening cool. Her left forearm, lying close beside her cheek, had a pleasant, pungent smell and was faintly greasy to the touch. She eased herself up without a twinge and looked around . . .

Something had woken her – Ribek's voice – 'Hold it!' and a sudden rush of movement.

Benayu was asleep beside her, as if he had never woken. Beyond him, Saranja had been grooming Pogo, but had just turned and was staring over Maja's shoulder. She dropped her brush and broke into a run. Maja turned too.

Ribek was there, sprinting towards three people a little distance away. One of the men was the stranger, Striclan, who'd been talking to Ribek about watermills last time Maja had woken. The other two were squat, dangerous-looking men. Each of them had a knife in his hand. Striclan was holding his staff across his body in both hands as if he was about to try and push them away with it. He gave it a quick twist and it came apart. One piece fell to the ground. He flicked the short piece in his left hand at one of the men. A cloud of powdery stuff shot into the man's face and he staggered back, coughing and choking. The other man had dropped his knife and was backing away because the point of the narrow sword Striclan held in his right hand was pricking into his throat. Ribek slowed, reached them, picked up the two knives and said something to Striclan, who nodded, apparently unperturbed. He spoke briefly to the second man, who walked off, cursing, to help his friend.

Striclan picked up the fallen section of staff and slid the sword blade into it, screwed the bit that had held the powder back into place and was holding his staff again. Saranja joined them and they walked back together to where Maja was sitting.

'. . . on the open road, in lonely places, perhaps,' Striclan was saying. 'But in my experience Imperial way stations are much too well run to allow this sort of thing to happen. The authorities in Talakh . . .'

'They seem to have lost their hold for the moment,' said Ribek. 'They're too busy with what's happening around Tarshu, I suppose. You know about Tarshu, I gather.'

'To say I know would be an exaggeration. I was hoping to go to Tarshu, but was turned away, with no reason given. Since then I have heard only rumours, but they have been consistent enough to compose a truthful scenario. The city is said to be under seaborne attack by invaders generally referred to as Pirates, though they appear to be much more disciplined and organized than any pirates I have had the misfortune to encounter . . .'

'Where we come from, we call them Sheep-faces,' said Ribek.

Striclan giggled, mysteriously delighted. He fished a little pad and stylus out of his wallet.

'That's good. That's very good indeed,' he said. 'I must make a note. But surely that means that someone in your area must have met, or at least seen, some of them, in order to bestow a visual sobriquet upon them. You told me your mill was among the northern mountains, whereas I understood this incursion to be a purely coastal affair . . .'

'Just rumours, same as you,' said Ribek. 'A sort of flying ship with a human crew exploring the passes into the Empire. Fierce fighting the other side of the Great Northern Desert. That sort of thing.'

Striclan nodded, apparently accepting this as a perfectly good explanation, and made another note on his pad. But Maja had sensed a sudden stirring of his deeper, other self, as if what Ribek had told him had been much more interesting and important than a few improbable rumours from a remote corner of the Empire.

'And that unpleasant phenomenon we encountered last night?' he said. 'Some of the others here in the way station escaped much as I did, thanks to Miss Saranja. They are talking of it having been a demon of some kind. Furthermore, travellers from the south reported that some kind of storm demon had recently attacked the City of Larg, and been driven off by magical means. I had been under the impression that demons, if they ever existed, were a phenomenon of the distant past, of the same order as rocs and unicorns, but the consensus seemed to be much what you were saying about that pair of thugs just now, that these two, and perhaps others, had emerged because the relevant authorities were preoccupied with the struggle around Tarshu. Can that be the case?'

'It was a demon all right, wasn't it, Saranja?' said Ribek. 'Or you wouldn't have been able to deal with it.'

'I suppose so.'

Striclan was writing on his pad again, and seemed not to notice the grudgingness of her tone, and the slight headshake. Ribek answered with a nod and a hand gesture to say he knew what he was doing.

'And the possibility of one's encountering further such, ah, creatures?'

'Last time it happened, far as I know, was several hundred years ago. It wasn't quite like this, as what you call the authorities are still there, only they're busy at Tarshu. Last time they'd been pretty well wiped out, and suddenly there were demons everywhere. Even so, I wouldn't think this one and the one at Larg can be the only ones.'

'Ah. In that case, how would you feel about my travelling for a while, if not in your company, at least in your general vicinity? I'm afraid this may seem an impertinent request on so short an acquaintance, but let me explain. I am employed by a wealthy scholar, who has dedicated his life to compiling an encyclopedia describing all the various peoples of the Empire. He is particularly interested in their beliefs about, and interactions with, magical and other paranormal phenomena. No single man could complete such a task in a lifetime, so he employs me, and others like me, to investigate and report on allotted areas, and he then collates our reports. I joined the Highway a little north of here, having completed an investigation of the desert tribes, and was on my way to Larg to despatch my report. But I was very alarmed by our encounter with that creature last night, and if others of that kind are likely to beset the Highway, I would prefer to be in the company of someone who is equipped to deal with them, as Miss Saranja so evidently is.'

'We aren't going to Larg, I'm afraid,' said Ribek. 'We're travelling north.'

'I can equally well send my report from Farfar. I shall have to go there in the end. But please don't feel that you are under any obligation to agree. The obligation is wholly on my side. And of course I won't ask you to make up your minds on the instant. I must water my poor mule, and perhaps we can meet later this evening and you can tell me what you've decided.'

'Of course,' said Ribek, rising with him. Striclan bowed to Saranja, raised a hand in farewell and turned away. They waited for him to move out of earshot.

'Why did you tell him all that?' said Saranja. 'He's been very helpful, but I don't trust him.'

'So that he'd tell us stuff about himself,' said Ribek. 'He's got to have seen Sheep-faces too, or he wouldn't have thought us calling them that was funny. What did you make of him, Maja?'

'He's like what he is, I think. Only there's someone else inside him. Someone secret.'

Ribek nodded.

'Let's go and water the horses,' he said.

'I haven't finished grooming Pogo,' said Saranja.

'Bring him when you've done,' said Ribek, reaching

for Rocky's halter. 'You bring Levanter, Maja. I want to know more about this fellow. We'll probably have to wait in line. See what you can pick up. Come along, old boy, water.'

There were a horse and a mule at the trough, another waiting next in line, then Striclan with his mule, then another horse ahead of them. All these desert way stations had deep wells reaching down to water sources far below, with a horse-trough beside them. The system was that two animals drank at a time while the well-master's slave wound the buckets up and down to keep the trough filled. The travellers waiting next in line haggled over the fee and bribe with the well-master, as Striclan was doing now. Maja could sense his enjoyment of the process. The only strange thing about him was that he seemed absolutely unshaken by his encounter with the demon last night.

Ribek handed Rocky's halter to Maja, unhooked his flask from his belt, emptied it into the sand and hooked it back on. He fished in his wallet and withdrew the water-charm he'd made last evening. Casually he swung it beside his hip, as if he merely needed something to fidget with while he waited. Maja felt the strange magic flow, far gentler than the old tribeswoman's insistent, almost bullying, tone. Ribek wasn't commanding the spirit, he was asking. Maja felt the spirit's weary answer. Ribek persisted, pleading, and it gave in and Ribek looped the cord round his wrist and left it dangling.

The two animals at the trough finished drinking and their owners led them away. The next horse and Striclan's mule moved to take their places, and the man immediately ahead of Ribek began the absurdly elaborate process of dealing with the well-master.

As if for something to do while he waited his turn, Ribek wandered over to the trough, unhooked his flask again and filled it from the flow of the next bucket into the trough. He put it to his lips, swigged, sluiced the water round his mouth and spat it into the sand. As he returned to his place he offered the flask to Striclan,

'Like to make sure,' he said. 'Lot of sulphur in some of these desert wells. Only a trace here, plus a bit of copper.'

'If you say so,' said Striclan. 'I doubt if I've that fine a palate.'

Nevertheless he took a mouthful, sluiced it round as Ribek had done, but then swallowed.

'I can detect the sulphur, of course,' he said. 'Copper you say? Curious.'

He sounded completely casual, but for a moment it was as if that hidden inner self had come alive, full of interest, thoughtful.

'Just a trace,' said Ribek and returned to Maja. As she waited for him to settle with the well-master she wasn't surprised to see Striclan making a rapid note in his pad. The other man's horse finished at the trough and she led Levanter to take its place. A moment or two later Rocky joined him, while Ribek strolled round to the well-head and emptied his flask over the edge, swilling the water round as it gurgled out.

'I'm hoping there's a trace of his saliva round the rim,' he murmured. 'Let's see.'

He took the charm from his wallet again and started

to swing it. The magic flowed, and the spirit answered at once. Ribek listened for a moment, and laughed aloud.

'What's up?' said Maja.

He bent to whisper into her ear.

'He's one himself.'

'One what?'

'Sheep-face.'

'He can't be! Anyway, he doesn't look like one.'

'He wouldn't, because he's a Sheep-face spy. All is explained.'

'He was really interested in what you said about tasting copper in the water.'

'I wonder why.'

'We can't let him go to Larg! If he tells the Sheep-faces there isn't any magic there . . .'

'Shh! Yes, that's a point. We'll see what Saranja says, and then we'll have to wake Benayu up.'

What Saranja said was: 'I'm no good at pretending.'

'You don't have to. Just act like you would do anyway. The poor chap's completely in awe of you. You saved his life and you can bind demons. He absolutely worships you. You're a simple country girl and you don't know how to handle it, so no wonder you act a bit surly.'

'I don't think he's in awe of anyone. What he said was some of the truth. The Sheep-faces want to know all they can about magic, and that's what he's here to find out. I can bind demons, thanks to Zald. If he finds out about Zald he'll grab it and run. Now that the Watchers have woken the demons against them it'll be just what they're looking for. And what about Benayu, when he's well enough to start doing things again?'

'How's he getting on, Maja?'

She concentrated. Benayu was dreaming – a bad dream. She knew because she could feel the horrible strange magic, still potent, even like this.

'He's having a nightmare about the demon,' she said. 'We'd better wake him up.'

Ribek knelt, slid his arm under Benayu's shoulders and eased him up to a half-sitting position. His head lolled.

'I can't do anything,' he muttered. 'I mustn't.'

Ribek put his other arm round him and hugged him to his chest.

'It's all right,' he said. 'Saranja's here. She's got Zald.'

Benayu snorted, sat fully up and stared round.

'Stupid. Stupid,' he said. 'You know it's only a dream, but . . . What's happening?'

'Remember that chap we met in the desert – said his name was Striclan?' said Ribek, and explained. Benayu didn't seem very interested, but thought about it a little while, then smiled sourly.

'Back in the mountains Saranja told me I might need the Pirates – Sheep-faces – whatever they call themselves,' he said.

'That settles it,' said Ribek. 'I'll tell him he can come along. It's not only demons we may be running into, and with you out of action he's got some useful tricks if we hit trouble.'

They barely needed to pretend, even Saranja. Striclan was cheerful, interested in everything, told the most amazing stories, and so obviously liked to be helpful. He took a lot of trouble with Benayu, brewing him healing remedies and strength-giving tonics, and seeing there was plenty of iron in his food, and things with strange names like proteins and vitamins. He exchanged herbal lore with Saranja and persuaded Ribek to teach him kick-boxing. Ribek said he was remarkably good at it for somebody starting so late and with a figure like his.

'You never know what might come in useful,' Striclan said. 'These are dangerous times. And that reminds me. It's all very well for Ribek to rely on his skill with his feet, but the rest of you ought to be able to defend yourselves too. I have a little switchblade knife for Maja – here. I will make an arm-sheath for it, but in the meanwhile put it in your wallet, Maja, and I'll show you how to use it if you have to. You can kill a full-grown man with it if you know where to strike. I believe there are serious penalties for carrying anything like a sword without a licence, which is why I carry my rapier concealed in my staff. It would be difficult to arrange anything of the sort for Miss Saranja and Benayu. The best I can suggest is that I should cut quarterstaffs for them and again show them how to use them. In fact it is possible to strike a damaging blow with a well-balanced quarterstaff. It is certainly far better than nothing.'

So for most of the time, even to Maja using her extra sense, Striclan seemed to be exactly what he said he was. Of course he asked a lot of questions and was always taking notes – a rich eccentric scholar was paying him to find things out, wasn't he? And of course many of them were about magic stuff because that was one of the things his employer was interested in. But almost anything they told him might bring the notebook out. Only at certain times, perhaps with no visible outward sign at all, Maja would sense that stir of inward interest in something that had been said.

He insisted on taking over almost all of the cooking, saying it was a way of repaying Saranja for protecting him against demons. In fact he obviously loved to cook and did it very well. He decided – or perhaps Ribek had persuaded him – that Maja was too thin, and fretted because she didn't seem to be putting on weight, and was obviously tiring herself too much, and falling asleep in the saddle, and so on.

Usually he managed to produce luscious meals from the very ordinary ingredients available at the way station stalls and spices and herbs from his saddlebags, but one morning he took a detour to a village they passed and came back with a fresh chicken and a couple of flasks of local wine, catching them up as they rested out the midday heat. That evening – maybe it was the wine that helped – he got Saranja talking about her time among the war-lords, and then kept her going with just the right question or comment at just the right moment. Maja didn't notice him doing it at first, because Saranja's stories were so fascinating. She told them well, as if she'd been there herself, fought in that siege or made that desperate journey. Maja had never seen her like this, so animated, so clearly enjoying herself, with all her inward furies for the moment sleeping. And then . . .

'Some Sheep-face merchants came to Bilabi Gey and gave him a lot of fancy gifts and said if he let them run his copper mine at Sansan for him they would get a lot more copper out of it and he'd end up with a great deal of money. Tarab Arkan and Arda Gey hadn't realized that copper was actually worth that much – if it had been silver one of them would have grabbed the mine long before – so of course they wanted Sansan and the Sheep-faces' money for themselves. Either of them could easily have done it, except that the Sheep-faces decided to back Bilabi Gey, and that's how they finished up fighting the war-lords. And then they ran up against magicians. Tarab Arkan had a pretty good one . . .'

Ribek touched Maja's wrist and glanced enquiringly towards Striclan. He looked completely as usual, as if all his mind was engaged in paring paper-thin slices from a strong, hard cheese that he liked to sprinkle on to his food. But really his inner self was fully awake, not just interested, as though what Saranja was telling him was seriously important.

As if he was anxious not to force himself on them too much, Striclan usually left them soon after they'd finished their evening meal, and slept in another part of the way station. That night, as soon as he was out of earshot Ribek said, 'Either of you two pick up what our friend made of all that? Maja, Benayu?'

'I wasn't noticing,' said Benayu. 'It's too much effort

with him, anything beyond the surface. He's got a way of closing that part of his mind off.'

'He sort of puts it to sleep,' said Maja. 'But it really woke up when Saranja started talking about the copper mine. Do you remember, when you told him about the copper in the water at that other way station . . . ? And he was very cunning about keeping Saranja talking, asking just the right questions.'

'There've not been a lot of people in my life who I've really liked,' said Saranja quietly. 'But he's one of them. I thought, "What does it matter if he's a Sheep-face spy?" It's nothing to do with us, really. In a way we're on the same side. We both want to get rid of the Watchers. But if he's just pretending all the time . . .

'I wish you hadn't told me,' she added, so sadly that they all fell silent, sharing her disappointment like a shared vibration, mournful bells. It reminded Maja of what it had been like only a short time ago, just before Ribek had touched her wrist, the same kind of sharing, but that time chiming cheerfully together, all five of them. Striclan too, as Saranja told her stories and they listened. Hadn't there been something extra about Striclan's enjoyment?

'I think he likes you too,' she said.

'Oh!'

Maja managed to pinch Ribek just in time to stop him laughing.

Chapter 13

THE NEXT FIVE days, outwardly at least, might have been any other uneventful five days in their long journey. Ribek, Striclan and Benayu kept the conversation going – though perhaps there was a difference in that they stayed completely off the subject of magic. Saranja was very silent, but then she often was. Maja, with Ribek's help, managed to keep her end up – awkwardly, she felt, but her feelings were confused by her knowledge of the inward awkwardness between them. Striclan too. He was as helpful and affable as ever, clearly enjoyed his kick-boxing sessions with Ribek, saw that Benayu and Saranja practised each evening with their quarterstaffs, made a wrist-sheath for Maja's knife so that she could hide it up her sleeve, and taught her how to slip it out unnoticed and how and where to strike a stronger attacker. But he must have been aware that something had changed that evening, because he didn't ask Saranja to tell him any more about the war-lords –

she was both relieved and hurt, and seemed to have lost all her usual confidence in dealing with him – and in general he asked far fewer questions and hardly produced his notebook at all.

On the fifth evening he said, 'Well, it is only a couple of days now to Farfar, and we have encountered no demons. Perhaps the danger is less than I feared, and I no longer have my excuse for enjoying your pleasant company, and we should part there. I will have my report to prepare and send, which will take me a day or two, and you will be anxious to proceed on your journey.'

Ribek was about to say something when Saranja interrupted.

'Let's get to Farfar and see.'

The sixth day was different. There was practically no one on the Highway, as most other travellers preferred to take the longer way round through Agadal, a small hill town which happened to be holding its famous seven-yearly firework festival. Magical fireworks were strictly against the rules, so Striclan decided he wasn't interested. Thus it was that there were no other travellers in sight, either before or behind them, when they walked into the trap.

It was mid-morning. The Highway wound between ragged hills, and they were walking five abreast along it, with Sponge at Benayu's heels and the mule and horses quietly following, when four men rushed out from behind the broken wall of an old roadside shed and barred the way. There was nothing magical in their sudden appearance. Maja and Ribek had been telling each other a story, taking turns to carry it forward and picking up wherever the other one left off, so she hadn't been paying attention to the little inherent magics in her surroundings.

The men were carrying short, improvised spears, or heavy, broad-bladed slashers and hatchets. They swaggered towards the travellers. Instinctively Maja turned to run, but three more men had appeared in the road behind them. She remembered just in time to slip her knife into her hand in the way Striclan had taught her, and hold it there, hidden in her clenched fist.

'Hands above your heads, then,' snapped the man at the centre of the group in front. 'No trouble, and you won't get hurt.'

Ribek already had his arms raised and held slightly forward, palms open in a gesture of appeasement. He took a careless pace towards the men, as if he truly didn't believe they meant him any harm. A pike lowered to point at his chest.

'Hold it there!'

He seemed to halt, but instantly sprang, too quick for the thrust, stooped, swivelled, his right leg swinging viciously to crack into the knee of the man next in line. Striclan was drawing his sword. Saranja had disappeared.

There were yells, shouts, hoarse coughing from someone with pepper-dust in his face.

Maja was grabbed from behind, her arms pinioned, was dragged kicking, struggling, lifted like a sack and slung across Levanter's shoulders. She almost managed to wriggle free as the man mounted, but his grip on her wrists was too strong, and then he was up and wrestling one-handed with the reins as Levanter skittered and shied, and with the other hand still round her wrists, forcing her hard down into the gap between Levanter's neck and the pommel of the saddle.

Twisting her head sideways she caught a glimpse of the struggle. One of the bandits was on the ground, one on his knees, retching and choking. Ribek and Striclan were engaged in individual duels, Saranja up on Rocky, her quarterstaff raised to strike at the man who had grabbed her bridle, and Sponge was leaping to attack the remaining man as Benayu stumbled back before him. Then Levanter wheeled and her captor's knee blocked her view.

He was yelling at Levanter, urging him into a gallop. She could tell he knew about horses. Now she could hear two sets of hooves. He let go of her wrists. She shifted her knife in her fist, found the catch, heard the click as the blade slid out, raised her head to gauge how and where to strike.

In the instant he gave her she saw, close in front of her, his hand unhooking his slasher from his belt and beyond it Saranja bearing down on them, half standing in her stirrups, her hair streaming behind her, her quarterstaff raised two-handed, ready to strike. Then the butt of the slasher slammed into the back of Maja's head.

Blindly in the roaring, agonizing dark her hand and arm finished the movement she'd begun, swinging up and round behind the man's back. She felt the wicked little blade bite deep into the softness below the rib-cage.

The man's yell was cut short by the heavy thwack of Saranja's quarterstaff. She grabbed the pommel of the saddle to save herself as he toppled, lost her grip and fell too, landing with a thump on top of him. His body juddered as a hoof crashed into it somewhere.

The jar of the fall half cleared her head. She staggered up, gasping, saw the man's slasher at her feet and grabbed it. The man himself lay sprawling. The left side of his shirt was already soaked in blood. His other leg was bent sideways at the knee. Saranja was pulling Rocky out of his charge, turning him.

'I'm all right,' Maja yelled, though her head seemed ready to split with pain from the blow the man had given her. Somehow she hefted his slasher on to her shoulder and held it there, poised to strike.

Saranja waved in acknowledgement and sent Rocky charging back, with Levanter now not far behind. The pure pain eased to a heavy throb. Maja shifted round the fallen man to where she could watch and still be ready if he tried to get up. Benayu was down, with Sponge standing over him, snarling and watchful, as the enemy's spear-point neared. Ribek's left arm was red with blood, but he was still dancing round his opponent, light on his feet as a fawn, feinting, dodging, looking for an opening while the man stood stolidly waiting, with his slasher held two-handed across his body, ready to swing to left or right. Striclan's man had a pike, with which he could outreach Striclan's sword. It looked like stalemate, but the man who'd been blinded by the pepper-dust was on his feet and staggering towards them with his hatchet in his hand.

Only Striclan's opponent saw Saranja coming. The distraction was fatal. Striclan's blade was into his throat and his own blood stifled his cry of warning. As he toppled, Saranja drove Rocky straight into Benayu's attacker, struck viciously down with her quarterstaff as he reeled away, and charged on. Ribek's man turned to face her, but Ribek was in and floored him before she reached him. She reined to a halt and gazed around. Sponge and Benayu between them had their man down and helpless. The last man had turned to run, but Saranja sent Rocky hurtling after him, barred his way and drove him back, then circled menacingly, herding the men into a group round the man Striclan had killed. Maja lowered the slasher, knelt and plunged the blade of her knife several times into the dusty earth to clean the blood from it. She slid it into its sheath and then used the slasher to prod the man who had kidnapped her until he rose groaning to his knees and crawled to join the others. That done she gathered the dropped weapons, handed Ribek a long knife and piled the rest together.

Benayu was standing a little to one side, so she offered him another knife. He gestured it away. He was white and shaking – not, she realized, with shock, but with anger and shame.

'I could have stopped them,' he muttered. 'I could have stopped them with a word. Look!'

He raised his right fist. For a moment something seemed to be struggling to escape between his fingers.

Just in time she snatched Jex out of her pocket, but still reeled as Benayu flung what he was holding towards

313

the men. Wind shrieked from his opened palm, became a single, concentrated gust roaring out into the hot stillness of the day, picking the bandits up and whirling them away like chaff before the winnow.

He flipped his left hand dismissively towards the pile of weapons. The steel splintered, the wooden hafts crumbled to dust.

He bowed his head and stood shaking it slowly from side to side. She tried to put her arm round him but he pushed her away . . .

The Watchers! He'd been so angry with himself he'd forgotten about the Watchers! Jex had been growing stronger day by day, but she knew from the way that she had staggered that he'd nothing like absorbed the whole of the shock of power. Even now the force of the magic suddenly woken in Benayu came strongly through.

And Striclan too! He'd forgotten about Striclan! Striclan wasn't supposed to know about . . .

She looked. Striclan was getting something out of a saddlebag. His mule was standing there stolidly, looking as if it hadn't noticed anything unusual happening. So did Striclan when he turned and offered the bandage he was holding to Ribek. Ribek stared at him, for once at a loss for words. Saranja dismounted and joined them.

'Let's get this over with,' she said quietly. 'I think we've all just saved each other's lives, and I can't go on pretending. You're a Sheep-face spy, aren't you, Striclan?'

He blinked, that was all.

'Agent,' he corrected her, sounding as sad about it as she had. 'But perhaps before we discuss it we should deal with Ribek's arm. He's losing a dangerous amount of blood in my opinion. Sit down, old man. I'll need to cut the sleeve off.'

He eased Ribek on to the ground and knelt beside him. Only now did Maja notice how pale Ribek was. And he oughtn't to need to be helped to sit down, for heaven's sake! Anxiously she peered over Striclan's shoulder as he peeled the sleeve away. The wound was right at the top of the arm, a deep, ghastly-looking slash, right to the bone, like a half-open scowling mouth turned down at the corners. Blood was still streaming from it. Striclan pressed the lips together. The flow weakened but didn't stop.

'Trouble is, it's too close to the shoulder for a tourniquet,' he said. 'I don't know how you kept going, fighting that chap – remarkable what adrenalin can do . . .'

He chatted on, not doing anything, just holding the wound closed, watching the blood-flow. Maja concentrated, and sensed that beneath the surface he was as anxious as she was. And there seemed to be only one inward Striclan now, all of him intent on Ribek's wound. She nudged Saranja's arm.

'Can't we use Zald?' she whispered. 'If you give me the healing stone, he won't know it's got anything to do with the demon-binder.'

Saranja nodded, slid her hand inside her blouse and felt her way over the surface of Zald. Her lips moved as she mouthed the simple release formula. She withdrew the jewel and slipped it into Maja's hand.

Maja knelt to whisper into Striclan's ear.

'It's worse than you're telling him, isn't it?'

He nodded.

'There's something I can do,' she said. 'No, don't let go. I'll start at the edge. Please try not to watch.'

'Of course,' he said and shifted to make room for her. A corner of the wound showed each side of his grasp. She put the ache in her head away, still there, but somewhere outside herself, and whispered to Jex to relax his shield. Naked to all the magic in the world she pressed the jewel to and fro around the right corner of the wound, feeling through the slithery blood for the torn edges and easing them together, above and below and back, above and below and back, again and again. Her hand and arm grew warm as the healing power flowed into them and on through the jewel. Ribek sighed and closed his eyes. She could feel his openness to what she was pouring into him, her whole life force, all her love. The wound began to close.

'Where's Pogo?' said Benayu suddenly. Vaguely, concentrating on what she was doing, Maja registered the change in his voice. On the surface, at least, this was the Benayu they had known before Larg.

'Stupid horse bolted almost at once, of course,' said Saranja. 'Nobody'd even made a grab for him. Back the way we came, I'm afraid.'

'I'll fetch him while Maja's doing that. Come on, Sponge.'

Unshielded, Maja flinched to the shock of his changing, but her arm and hand kept their rhythm. By the time she recovered, two identical dogs were loping away down the road. With her free hand she nudged Striclan's fingers to the left to give her more wound to start on.

Saranja appeared and knelt beside her with a water flask and a cloth and started to sponge away the blood from what she had already done, revealing a morsel of pink, new-healed flesh. Maja worked on.

'Perhaps it would help, while we are doing this, if I explained a little about myself,' said Striclan.

'I don't know if it would help, but it would be interesting,' said Saranja.

'I hope both,' said Striclan, chuckling, though he must have noticed the dryness in her tone. 'I am not by birth a Charargalid, though I was partly raised in Charargh.'

'Where's Charargh?' said Saranja.

'Charar means south, and Charargh is the South. It occupies the whole southern half of a continent on the other side of the world, and in fact dominates the northern half as well. Technically it is not a single nation, in the way that the Empire is a single nation, but a community of seven separate nations. Its full, formal name is Storgon Charargha, the Community of the South, but it acts and thinks like a single large nation. We speak of Southern civilization, Southern values.

'But as I say I am not a true native of Charargh. I was born in one of its dependencies because a generation ago the authorities decided that the time had come to deal with what they regarded as the problem of the Empire. For most of their early history the seven nations had been more or less at war with each other . . .'

Expertly, at Maja's gentle nudge, he shifted his grip along the wound, but his voice didn't falter. She stopped listening to concentrate on the healing. This was the difficult bit, where the slash was deepest, severing veins and nerves and sinews. She couldn't reach in to touch them with the jewel, but she could reach through it to them and fill them with her own health and wholeness. She lost herself in a trance of healing. Striclan's quiet voice was just a background to what she was doing, almost as meaningless as birdsong. A sharper interjection from Saranja broke through into her consciousness.

'You mean you've actually fought wars to persuade people to do things your way?'

'I'm afraid so. There was usually some kind of excuse, of course. And to the Southern way of thinking it would obviously be so much better for them in the end.'

'Not the ones who were dead.'

'No. And then they came up against the Empire. It was different from anything they had encountered before – so different and yet so obviously rich and successful that it seemed a threat to their whole way of thinking. They had known about it for centuries, of course, but . . .'

Maja moved Striclan's fingers again and worked on.

Three miles to the south a travelling sandal-maker was riding a horse. He was drunk. Last evening, at a way station, he'd fallen in with a couple of friendly fellows and they'd wined and diced into the small hours, and he'd won heavily. But perhaps they'd drugged his wine, though they drank from the same flask, for he'd slept very late, and when at last he'd woken he'd found his companions gone, along with his winnings and his mule and his stock of sandals and everything else he possessed. All they'd left him was a half-empty flask of wine, so he'd finished it off and started home, drunk again.

And then luck had smiled on him. He'd found a stray horse by the roadside, ready saddled and bridled. It was flecked with dried foam, so he guessed it had bolted from somewhere. It had skittered a bit as he tried to mount it, but in the end he'd hoisted himself into the saddle and persuaded the animal to move. He would sell it at the next market town he came to, he told himself, and if someone claimed it before then, well, maybe there'd be a reward.

Two dogs came loping up from behind him and started to pace along, one on either side. The one on his right raised its head and looked at him.

'That's not your horse,' it said.

He blinked. He'd known he was drunk, but not this drunk.

'I'm taking him to his owner,' he said.

'That's me,' said the dog.

'Don't be stupid. Dogs don't own horses.'

'You live and learn,' said the dog.

Both dogs loped forward, turned and barred the way. The horse stopped. The sandal-maker shook the reins and drummed his heels against the horse's ribs, but it stayed where it was. It lowered its head. The dog licked its muzzle. The horse began to shrink.

In a moment it was no bigger than a pony, and in another his feet touched the ground. Two or three more and he was standing astraddle in the road with a child's toy horse between his feet. The dog which had spoken to him picked it up in its mouth and winked at him. Both dogs trotted off the way they had come.

Distantly Maja felt the tremor of mild, almost playful magic, and recognized it as Benayu's work.

'You can let go now,' she murmured, and moved to close the outer edge of the slash. She was swaying where she knelt, utterly weary, but at the same time wonderfully alive and fulfilled.

'But that's absolutely appalling!' said Saranja. 'You mean that because their own spies kept getting found out they kidnapped several hundred innocent people and took them to Charargh and bred them like farm animals so that when the kids grew up they could send them back to the Empire as spies! That's quite as bad as anything I've heard about the Watchers!'

'In fact not many were kidnapped,' said Striclan. 'Mostly we waylaid coastal shipping and persuaded some of those aboard to purchase men and women in the slave markets and ferry them out. They were then taken and established in a closed community on Palto, the nearby island which they already controlled, and there they replicated as closely as possible the conditions of the Empire. That is where I was born.

'The captives were not required to have children but were given considerable incentives to do so. I am the eldest of four siblings, not all by the same father, and my mother often said that as a result her life had been a great deal more comfortable than it would have been as a slave in Shankrili. She never expressed any bitterness over what had happened to her. Nevertheless, Miss

320

Saranja, I am forced to agree with you that it was morally reprehensible, and even in my earliest childhood I was dimly aware that this was the case. I knew I did not belong on Palto.

'My mother spoke Shankri, a dialect of the Imperial common language, so that was what we spoke at home. She sang us the cradle songs and told us the nursery stories she had learnt from her own mother. She was also encouraged to tell us about everyday life in the Empire. We played the games and ate the food we would have eaten in a well-to-do household in Shankrili – my mother was a very good cook.

'When I was five I was sent to school, where I was first taught formal Imperial and Chararghu as second languages, and then began to be inculcated with Southern values and Southern ideas. I was a ready learner, but at the same time a cautious and secretive child. I found it easy to please my teachers, but I did not reveal to them that I neither accepted nor rejected what they had told me about the superiority of Southern ways over the ways of the Empire. One day, I determined, I would go there and see for myself.

'I came to this conclusion well before I was taken to Charargh to finish my education and formally told that this was what had been planned for me all along. Even then I was careful not to sound too eager. I did not want them to suspect where my ultimate loyalties might lie. Since my earliest childhood I seem to have had a tendency to present a pleasant exterior to the world while concealing my inmost thoughts and feelings . . .'

Yes, thought Maja drowsily. *Yes, indeed. But he isn't*

doing it now. She stared at her hands as they repeated and repeated the same hypnotic pattern coaxing the clean new skin to cover the shiny scar tissue that closed the wound. *Like rolling pastry further and further across the board*, she thought.

There. Finished.

'See how it feels,' she murmured, and slipped the healing stone into her pouch. As she let go of it her hand and arm went numb.

Ribek rose to his feet and moved his arm around.

'Tingles a bit,' he said. 'As if it'd been something that happened years ago. Thanks, Maja. That's wonderful. You look all in.'

'I'm just tired. But it's worth it.'

'Indeed it is,' said Striclan, who had also risen from where he'd been kneeling at Maja's other side. 'I did not like to say so earlier, but in my opinion you were likely to lose the use of that arm, if not the arm itself. May I see? Astonishing. Not even a scar.'

'And now you're going to put it into your notebook and tell the Sheep-faces all about it,' said Saranja.

The sharpness of her tone silenced them all. Ribek bent to whisper in Maja's ear.

'Are you sure you're all right?'

'My arm's gone numb. And my head hurts where the man hit it with his slasher.'

She felt his fingers gently probing the bruise, heard the hiss of his indrawn breath.

'Got anything for a bruised head, Striclan? Maja's got a lump coming the size of an apricot where that bastard bashed her.'

'I'll get a salve.'

'My turn to do a bit of healing,' said Ribek, and settled beside her. He took her forearm into his lap, unstrapped her knife and gently began to massage the inert muscles. Almost at once Striclan returned and knelt behind her.

'Tsk, tsk,' he muttered. 'You carry on with what you're doing, old man. Take a sniff at this, Maja my dear – it'll help with the headache.'

His hand appeared under her nose, holding a small pot containing a bluey-grey paste, reeking with a strange, sweet-sharp pungency. Even before she had drawn it into her lungs the headache was easing. She heard the snip of scissors and then he was deftly working the paste into the swollen flesh. His touch on the bruise made it feel almost pleasant.

'Where were we?' he sighed. 'Ah, yes. I have in fact written nothing about any of you directly. Miss Saranja saved me from a hideous death. Ribek told me she was not at liberty to say how she did it. How could I not respect that, and apply it to the rest of your party? All that I have written in my notebook has been information you have given me that might have come from any fellow traveller. I have not ascribed a particular source to it. Miss Saranja's account of the origins of the desert war is a good example. Chararghi intelligence has a wholly different take on that, claiming, and probably believing, that the desert chiefs were instigated by the authorities in Talakh to attack the Chararghi copper-mining concession.'

Dimly Maja heard a distant whinny, answered by Levanter, almost in her ear.

'Here's Benayu,' said Saranja. 'He's got Pogo back all right. Stupid horse. Benayu's looking pleased with himself, which makes a change. You mean you're not going to say anything about him turning himself into a dog in front of your eyes, Striclan?'

'I see no need. I have already reported on consistent accounts of magicians being able to transform themselves into various animals. I shall simply add that I myself was a bystander at a similar event, and had no reason to doubt the evidence of my senses.

'As for the way in which he disposed of our assailants, which seemed to me, in my ignorance, a much more remarkable exercise of power, I propose to say nothing about it at all.'

Yes, thought Maja, as Benayu rode towards them, smiling and confident. *Much more remarkable*. And he'd done it as easily as flipping a coin. Well before he reached them she realized how much he'd changed. The soundless hum that had come from him all the time, even when he wasn't actually using his magical powers, until he'd lost them at Larg, was back again. It was still quiet, still controlled and contained, but it was no longer mild. There was a depth and intensity about it, like the depths of a clear night sky before the moon has risen, going on forever beyond the stars. The nearer he came the more it dazed her. She was going to have to learn to resist it, or she would need to wear Jex against her skin all the time, and then she would be no use to them at all.

Pogo was in a sulk, and halted untold the moment he reached them. Benayu dismounted, grinning.

'We'd better move on,' said Ribek. 'Somebody may have noticed you getting rid of those fellows.'

'As you wish,' said Striclan. 'I suggest that for the moment I separate myself from you and follow a little way behind, so that you can explain to Benayu what I've told you and you can then discuss it among yourselves and decide, among other things, whether I can be trusted.'

'That's all right,' said Benayu, smugly. 'I've been listening. He was telling the truth.'

'You mustn't do it!' said Saranja, instantly furious. 'I said so right at the start! Looking into our heads!'

'I didn't think he counted . . .'

'Well, he does! And anyway I don't need a mighty magician to tell me someone's telling the truth! And what's so funny about that, Ribek?'

'Just that it's so wonderfully unfair.'

'Please,' said Maja, before she could blast him too. 'I'm tired.'

Saranja sighed and turned to Striclan.

'Suppose we needed to talk to the Sheep-faces,' she said. 'Could you fix that? What do you think, Benayu?'

'It might be useful. I don't know yet. There's a lot of stuff I can do now that I couldn't before, but it's nothing like enough, even so.'

'I might be able to arrange something,' said Striclan. 'I would need to give my superiors reasons why they should take you seriously. One of my briefs is to make contact with any groups resistant to the rule of the authorities in Talakh, and I have had to tell them that I have seen no sign of any such movement. Apart from yourselves, of course, and so far I've kept my own counsel about you. Everywhere else, as far as I can discern, the general mood seems to be a curious mixture of fear and contentment. The people, by and large, enjoy peaceful and prosperous lives, but at the same time live in terror of offending the authorities, or even attracting their attention. But I have gathered from things that you have both said and not said that, one, you have already jointly caused offence and, two you are engaged on this journey in an effort not merely to escape but also to resist the vengeance.'

'Let's get moving, anyway,' said Saranja. 'I'll explain on the way.'

'Tell her to be careful,' Maja muttered as Ribek helped her on to Levanter's back. 'That night in the desert, when you told us "The Miller's Daughter" – just before that, what we'd started talking about, and I said don't – don't even think about it. It's still like that. And I can't tell you whether we've been noticed all over again after what Benayu's been doing – not with him so close.'

'I'll tell her,' said Ribek, smiling. 'Then we'll drop back and you can see if that makes enough difference. If all's well I'll wave to Saranja and you can have a nap. You're dead beat. All right?'

It came in her dream – one of those ones that you know are a dream because you know you're lying in your own bed and you're having a dream there, but at the same time you're in that dream and somewhere else, walking, talking, listening. So Maja knew she was half lying face down on Levanter's back, with a strap round her to keep her from falling, but at the same time she was sitting upright in the saddle in the Council Chamber at Larg, watching Ribek explaining something to the Proctors behind the long table, only when she looked at them again she saw that they weren't the real Proctors, though they wore the Proctors' gowns and hats, but they all had the same expressionless smooth ivory face or mask that the Watcher had worn when he came to the way station all those weeks ago.

She was aware of an odd little buzzy feeling at the back of her mind. She couldn't hear what Ribek was saying, but when he pointed at the corner of the room that held the hidden door to Zara's chamber, the buzz instantly became louder, closer . . .

'Stop!' she shouted, shoving herself violently up. The strap bit into her shoulders. She wriggled herself out of it, sat up and stared round. Ribek had halted and was looking at her. The sun was high. They were alone on the Highway. There was a way station a little further on. The others were nowhere to be seen.

'Where are they all?'

Ribek gestured towards the way station.

'Gone on ahead to get some food ready. I was just about to wake you to see if it made any difference not having Benayu around. Well?'

'I don't know . . . Yes, I think so . . . I had a dream . . Wait.'

She concentrated, focused back to that moment in her

dream, the sinister buzz. She grasped it with her mind, let the real world expand around her, followed it as it faded off to the south. It didn't dwindle completely away, but stayed faintly there, in the far distance, like the quiet tick of a clock somewhere in a house, a sound you've grown so used to that you never notice it. Only when you think about it, there it is, ticking endlessly away.

'I don't think they're actually there looking for us now,' she said. 'But . . . It's like . . . sometimes when I went fishing with my cousins there'd be a man there. He used to have three or four rods sticking out over the pool. He didn't hold any of them in his hands, but he watched the floats and the moment one of them bobbled a bit he'd know there might be a fish nibbling the bait. He just waited and watched until the float bobbled a bit more and then he'd know the fish had taken the bait and he'd grab that rod and strike. I don't know, of course, but I'm scared that that's what we're doing when we start talking about . . .'

Even to name the city where Zara lay sleeping now seemed charged with danger. She jerked her head round towards her shoulder, indicating something behind them. Ribek nodded, understanding.

'We're nibbling the bait when we do that,' she said. 'If we do it for more than a moment, they'll start watching, ready, and as soon as we actually start talking about it seriously they'll know where we are, and strike.'

Chapter 14

ONCE AGAIN, DAY followed day and week followed week as they had on the way south. The season changed as the world started to tilt towards winter. And it seemed to change faster than it would have if they had been staying in one place instead of travelling north, away from the sun. The grapes had already been beginning to ripen on the vines around Farfar. Now the vineyards were rare, and cattle grazed in kempt pastures, and the streams and rivers they crossed were already, to Ribek's delight, beginning to foam and roar as the autumn rains that had fallen on the inland hills flooded back towards the ocean. Though they were still far south of the Valley, Maja began to sense, as she lay in the dark at the way stations, that she could smell the mountains.

Vaguely she wondered what was happening there. Had the horsemen burned or smashed or killed or stolen everything they could find and then melted away through the northern passes? Had the people of the Valley driven them off? No knowing. She realized she was strangely uninterested. She had never been happy in the Valley. Almost the only happiness she had known in her life had been on this journey, despite all its terrors and hardships. The reason the Valley mattered to her was that one day she was going to live there with Ribek, in peace at Northbeck mill. That made it worth saving. Apart from that, she would almost have liked the journey to last forever.

But Saranja boiled with impatience to press forward and her mood infected them all. They were reluctant to leave Striclan behind, but there was no way his mule could have kept up if Benayu hadn't endowed it with extra speed and energy, just as Chanad had done for the horses. It must have been almost as ingratiating an animal as Striclan was a person, for it soon struck up an unlikely friendship with Pogo, which seemed to have a calming effect on him.

The pattern of their lives changed in other, less tangible ways. They had become more unsettled, less easy with each other. Even when Benayu had been at his most moody and difficult there had from the start been a unity of purpose between the four of them, an immediate friendship, though they had been strangers to each other only a few days earlier. This did not now sit so easily around them.

At first Maja thought it was something to do with Striclan. Not with the travelling scholar they had met after their encounter with the demon north of Larg – they had all liked him then. Saranja had actually said so.

They no longer had to pretend they didn't know he was a Sheep-face spy, and that should have made things easier, but it didn't seem to. He still didn't share their purpose. He didn't even know about it. The barrier of secrecy and deceit had altered, but it was still there.

Later she decided that there was more to it than that, and they would have changed anyway. Maja herself was certainly changing, after what Saranja had told her in the desert. It was surprisingly difficult to get used to the idea that everything wasn't her fault. That had been such a habit of thought she couldn't suddenly start thinking differently. She ought to have felt new-born, freed from the mysterious prison of guilt and shame, ready to start her life all over afresh, with Woodbourne only a hazily remembered dream, but she didn't. There was old Maja and there was new Maja, and one was the shadow of the other, but which was which? They kept switching places, and this made her moody and jumpy in ways that she hadn't been before.

Benayu had changed even more. They were all aware of it to some extent. To Ribek and Saranja there probably seemed now to be two Benayus. One was the boyish, confident young magician, delighting in his own powers, whom they had first met with Fodaro on that mountain pasture. In this mood some evenings, to Saranja's undisguised irritation, he would chat happily about magic to Striclan while he filled page after page of his notebooks in his private unreadable code. It was mainly gossip and anecdote, and always couched in the language of levels and powers – no hint of Fodaro's equations, or the possibility of other dimensions, other universes.

The other Benayu was a brooding presence, riding or walking or staring into the fire of an evening in day-long silence. Over the long weeks of their journey the anguished, passionate lad, who had sworn his oath with them to destroy the Watchers and avenge Fodaro's death, the terrified boy who had cringed before the Watcher in the way station, had recovered his poise and purpose. Saranja no longer nannied him and ordered him about. They all respected these silences and withdrawals as part of that purpose, strengthening exercises, as he continued to absorb into himself and come to terms with the enormous powers he had inherited from Zara on the hill above Larg.

Ribek and Saranja knew this was what was happening because Zara had told them it would. But Maja, through her extra sense, could feel it to be so, and realized that it was more than that. For her, sometimes, they had a stranger sitting with them in the evenings, breathing the air they breathed, eating the meal that Striclan had prepared, but only partly human. This was the third Benayu. It was something she had first sensed soon after they had left the desert north of Larg. It had been half dormant then, waiting until he was ready to receive it, but it was now fully active in him, wholly absorbed, as much a necessary part of his spiritual self as his liver or his spine were parts of his body. She couldn't observe or examine it because it was warded within and without, like Chanad's tower. If it hadn't been, she couldn't have lived long in its presence. All that she could tell for

332

sure was that it was there, and it hadn't been before. Dimly, also, she could sense, as she had when she'd first been aware of its presence, that it wasn't an inert thing, like an heirloom passed from Zara to Benayu on her deathbed. It was a living entity that had of its own will chosen to make the transfer, like an Imperial messenger leaving an exhausted horse at a way station and taking a fresh mount for the next stage of his journey.

Ribek, of course, hadn't changed at all. Maja couldn't imagine him doing so. He was what he was and always would be. It was one of the things she loved him for. And Saranja was still very much herself, only more so, her patience shorter, her temper trickier. She tended to pick on Striclan in particular, explosively condemning something he'd told them about the Pirates and having no patience with his explanations of the complex web of facts and motives that had brought it about. For her, anything the Pirates did was a thoroughly bad business, and that was that.

'They simply don't think the same way,' Ribek said. 'She's got a black-or-white, all-or-nothing way of seeing things. He's more of a shades-of-grey in-betweener. Me too.'

'I'm a don't-knower, I suppose.'

'Problem. If you are, you can't know you are.'

'Then I can't know I can't know.'

'You win.'

And Jex? How could you know whether he had changed, apart from growing steadily stronger? After they had eaten their midday meal Striclan would disappear to write up his report, so on fine days this allowed

Jex to return to the form in which they had first seen him and bask, blinking in the sun, like any normal lizard. But he was reluctant to speak in their minds because doing so sent out a signal he was unable to reabsorb. It was very faint, but even so sufficiently different from other minor magics to attract attention if the Watchers were hunting for creatures of his kind.

The way stations were full of whispered rumours about the Watchers. They had withdrawn from Tarshu and were preparing to defend Talakh with mighty feats of magic while the Pirates flooded inland. No, it was the Pirates who'd run away with their collective tail between their legs, while the Watchers were re-establishing their control over the Empire – why, hadn't two of them appeared in the nick of time to deal with a gigantic hog-demon who was uprooting whole hillsides of the Stodz forest, first binding the creature in a lattice of woven lightning and then hurling it down into the innermost fires? In a west wind, the speaker said, you could still smell, as far off as Gast, the reek of roast crackling as it seeped though crevices in the rock where the hills had closed back over the pit. No, said others, the Pirates had merely withdrawn and were regrouping out at sea beyond the reach of the Watchers' magic, while the Watchers attempted to make contact with the mysterious powers of the ocean in the hope of forming an alliance. And so on.

Some of the rumours about demons Maja knew to be true, because she had several times sensed their curiously sickening magic somewhere in the distance. It was strange that none had manifested themselves nearer than a full day's march. She wondered if they were somehow aware of what Saranja had done to the demon in the desert north of Larg, and were staying well away from her and Zald.

Not that the journey was without more ordinary dangers. Brigands abounded, mostly more sophisticated than the ones they had fought earlier. These set up roadblocks and claimed to be acting on the authority of the councillors in some nearby town. They demanded astounding levels of tax to pay for repairs and maintenance of order on the Highways, which they said was now the responsibility of the town in question. Highway-users responded by openly carrying weapons and travelling in groups large enough to overwhelm any such gang, but this meant moving at the pace of the slowest. So Maja's party pressed on, with Jex keeping Maja barely shielded, and her senses feeling ahead for the presence of ambush.

Twice that happened, and twice the Highway was openly barred. Each time Benayu flicked a screen around the area – he seemed now able to do this almost as easily as raising a hand to scratch his nose – and cast the bandits into a magical sleep. They left them for the next party of travellers to find and despoil of their weapons and loot. Each time, Maja turned her attention south to where, she was sure, their true enemies were still searching for them. Perhaps it was this endlessly wearing attention forward and backward that hid from her something that had been quietly happening all the time since that first ambush.

It had been a long, hard day's travel, across an

endless-seeming plain, all boringly the same, with a scattering of hamlets among huge square fields almost ready for harvest, but nothing as interesting as actual harvesters to look at. There'd been a wearing wind in their faces, carrying vicious little showers, the last of which had drenched them just before they reached the final way station. And then there'd been the hassle of getting their wet cloaks hung to dry in the inadequate space of their booth. Saranja for some reason had been unusually on edge all day, biting Ribek's head off whenever he opened his mouth, almost, and now she was driven to fury by the way-station ostler. Ostlers never did anything for the horses in their charge, other than allocate the stalls and take the fees and bribes, so on fine nights most travellers stabled their beasts in the open, but at times like this the ostlers could charge pretty well what they chose, and would insist that the stable was already full until they got what they wanted. Saranja knew from experience that there was no way round the system, and usually paid up grimly, but tonight she raged as if it had never happened to her before.

Her fury filled the booth. It was like Woodbourne on a bad day. Nobody, not even Striclan, dared say anything. She insisted on getting a fire going in the covered hearth in front of the booth but the wood was damp and at first wouldn't do much more than smoulder until Benayu woke up from his day-long trance and set it ablaze. They ate their supper late, and in silence. Maja must have fallen asleep halfway through.

She'd been trying to stay awake because it was her turn to help Striclan wash his cooking pots at the well.

He insisted on doing most of that himself as he had a strange superstition about something he called bacteria which he said lived in the tiniest scrap of rotten food and made you ill if you ate them. No one else came up to his standards of what counted as clean, but it still seemed unfair to leave it all to him. Then he'd go off to his booth to work on his notes and repair his kit and do his exercises and prepare for the next day's travel. At least, that was the reason he gave, but Ribek said it was mainly to leave them alone for a bit, in case they wanted to talk privately.

She woke with a start and pushed herself up, filled with guilt at having slept at all. How long? Somebody must have tucked her into her bedroll. The fire was mostly embers. By their faint light she could see Ribek and Benayu getting ready for bed.

'Wh—? Where . . . ?' she mumbled.

'Saranja helped Striclan with his pots, and she's staying on to help him with some stuff he's writing about the desert magicians.'

'But it was my turn!'

'You're too far gone to be any use. You'd have dropped things down the well.'

'Oh. All right. Tell her thank you.'

She flopped back down, but as she was about to plunge back into sleep a strangeness struck her. Almost before she'd woken she'd been aware that Striclan had left because she'd had no sense of his presence. But Saranja . . . Surely she'd felt her, still quite near . . . No, only part of her. Zald. Saranja wore the great jewel both night and day, and the quiet pulse of its many sleeping

magics registered more strongly on Maja's consciousness than Saranja's own natural magic. For Maja, Zald
had come to mean Saranja, and Zald was still nearby,
but Saranja wasn't. She concentrated. The saddlebags.
Zald was in the back of the booth, in one of Rocky's
saddlebags.

'She's left Zald behind!'

Benayu chuckled.

'Has she now? Has she now?' said Ribek, sounding
both surprised and amused.

'What are you laughing about?'

'Think it out. Or go to sleep. Anyway, it's none of our
business.'

She did her best, but sleep took her while she was
sorting through as many as she could remember of
Zald's various jewels, trying to imagine which of them
could possibly possess properties that prevented Saranja
washing the pots right. The answer came to her in her
sleep. She and Ribek were riding Levanter. She had
her arms round Ribek's waist and was leaning against
his back. He seemed unusually hard and bony. She wriggled, trying to make herself more comfortable. Ribek
glanced round, and it wasn't Ribek at all. It was the imp
from inside the demon-binder. The imp winked, as if
sharing the joke that had amused Ribek and Benayu.
And then she was standing in an empty street clutching
Zald to her chest, still very hard and knobbly, and wondering hopelessly why Ribek had left her alone in a
place like this.

Her unhappiness broke the dream and she woke,
knowing the answer. However useful Zald might be in

other ways, you don't want something like that in between you and the person you're hugging. Yes, and the fire had been embers. It didn't take that long to wash the pots and talk about a few magicians.

She lay in the bedroll listening to the rip and rattle of the wind and thinking, *How strange. Saranja, of all people.* Never in a million years would she have guessed that was going to happen. But Ribek knew already, and so did Benayu. And yet Ribek had been surprised that Saranja had left Zald behind. Had she done that before? No. Maja would have noticed, surely. So this was the first time they'd . . . *That's* why Saranja had been in such a foul temper all day. Maja could understand that, though it wasn't anything like what she felt about Ribek. But she'd always been a yielder and hider – that was how she'd survived – and for her, among other things, Ribek and his mill meant safety, protection, a place where she could stop hiding and be herself. Saranja wasn't like that at all. She'd always been a battler, fighting her rough brothers as often as they'd fought each other, giving as good as she got.

That was why Zald suited her so, belonged with her as if it had been a suit of armour made for her, and now she'd made up her mind to take it off for Striclan. She said she hated men, and no wonder, seeing what had been done to her, but she'd put her hatred aside too, and was trusting herself to him, unarmoured. So she'd been scared, and furious with herself for being scared.

And why hadn't Maja felt *that*, for heaven's sake? You'd have thought something like that . . . Or perhaps they weren't actually in love, but were just taking the chance to give each other a good time, like Ribek and the jewel-seller at Mord.

No. She'd have known about that, surely. It was the sort of thing she couldn't help feeling, even if she didn't want to pry. And it would have been part of Striclan's outer self, which she could reach easily enough. But what he felt about Saranja took place in his hidden, inner self – the real Striclan. Yes, he loved her, and she loved him. How strange. How wonderful.

But . . .

But what did it mean for the rest of them – Ribek, Benayu, herself and Jex – and for their whole purpose in being here at all? Was Striclan one of *them* now? Could they trust him as much as they trusted Saranja?

Had trusted Saranja, was it now? What had she told him? Was it even possible (horrible thought!) Maja had been wrong about Striclan, and what he was hiding in his secret inner world wasn't his love for Saranja at all, but that he was still really a spy who'd somehow tricked Saranja into falling in love with him so deeply that he could coax out of her everything she knew, all about the Ropemaker and the Ring and Zara and Larg and Jex, and then betray them all to his Sheep-face masters?

She couldn't believe it. But she wouldn't have been able to believe that Saranja might fall in love with Striclan. And here, in the pit of the night, where it wasn't only moon shadows that take strange and frightening shapes, she couldn't stop thinking about it. Worrying whether it was true kept her awake for the rest of the night, or so it seemed, but in the end she was woken by sunlight full in her face, and immediately knew the whole idea was nonsense.

Nevertheless she asked Ribek about it later that morning, when they were riding well out of earshot behind the others. To her surprise he didn't laugh at her.

'Yes, I've been wondering about it too,' he said. 'Saranja? I don't believe it. She's got too much sense of her personal honour. She's touchy enough about it for a whole fellowship of noble heroes. She'd feel utterly guilty and ashamed if she'd been telling him anything. I know you try not to pry, but you'd be picking that up, surely.'

'I suppose so. I can tell she's hiding something, but I don't think she's ashamed about it. Not that sort of ashamed, anyway. More like shy. Does she know we know?'

'I doubt it. He probably does. He's very sharp. Of course we can't tell how much he's picking up from her that she doesn't realize she's telling him, but however much in love she is she isn't a fool. If she thought he was simply using her she'd be outraged.

'No, that's not the main thing I've been worrying about. It's more what we're going to do about him when we get to Barda. It's only another few days now. Assuming that what we're looking for – the Rope-maker's physical being in some form or other – is actually there, and we don't know that for sure, we've still got to find it, or do you think you'll simply be able to sense where it is when you're near enough?'

'I don't know. He's got to have hidden it so carefully.

We're going to have to use his hair again, like we did by the sheepfold after we'd left Tarshu.'

'So that's one great burst of magic. Do you think Jex is up to dealing with it yet? Can you ask him?'

'He can hear what we're saying. He'll probably tell me tonight. But last time it laid him out for weeks, though he's a lot stronger now than he was then.'

'And if we're on the right track that's only going to be the beginning. There's going to be another great burst when we find this thing, whatever it is, about as much as happened when we got Jex back, at a guess, and we went all the way down to Tarshu just to hide our doing that. There isn't going to be anything to hide us this time. And then we've got to use it somehow. That's three huge explosions of magic. Tarshu's going to be small stuff beside it. And you're going to have to stand it all.'

'I'll manage. Don't worry about me. The Watchers are going to be on to us almost at once, aren't they? There's no way Jex can screen all that.'

'I *am* worried about you. We all are. We worry about you every time we look at you. You're skin and bone, almost, in spite of what Jex is doing to shield you, and your eyes are pits and you're sleeping fifteen hours a day. The only good thing is that you eat like a lumber-jack, but you're still burning yourself up.'

'I'm all right. I'm happier than I've ever been in my life.'

'I know you are, and I'm happy for you. But listen. Yes, you're right about the Watchers. Anything we do has all got to happen extremely quickly, so that we can be away and out of this universe, whatever that means, before they catch up with us. We can't take Striclan without him finding out all about other universes and so on, and we can't just leave him behind at Barda because then the Watchers are going to get hold of him and squeeze everything they can out of him. He's a tough little guy, but that's not going to do him much good. Or us.

'I like Striclan. It isn't only for Saranja's sake that I don't want anything like that to happen to him. But we're talking about you, Maja. I don't believe that even if Jex was fully fit, he'd be up to protecting you against this sort of magical cataclysm. It may very well knock us all out. I know I was pretty shaken by Tarshu, and again by what happened at the sheepfold, and I know what that did to you. So if we can persuade Striclan to leave us I'd like you to go with him.'

'I can't. You won't find the Ropemaker without me.'

'You can't be certain of something like that.'

'Yes, I can. I just know. It's what I'm here for.'

And if you're going to be there, so am I.

Ribek started to say something and stopped. He sighed heavily, gazing down at his hands. It was strange to see him looking so unsure of himself.

'Let's see what the others say,' she said,

'I doubt if Benayu will even hear me asking. He's been in a complete dream these last few days, in another universe, almost. I suppose that might even be true.'

'He's doing a lot of stuff inside himself. Getting ready for Barda, I think. Let's see what Saranja says about Striclan.'

What Saranja said was: 'I've already told him he can't come. He wants to talk to you about it.'

'After supper tonight?'

'I'll tell him.'

What Striclan said was: 'Miss Saranja tells me that I cannot come to Barda with you. I have pleaded with her before now, but she has just told me that it is also your joint decision, made independently from her, and coincides with her wishes. So I am forced to accept it. But I have a favour to ask, nevertheless.

'She has told me nothing about your reasons for going to Barda, but I have deduced that what you are proposing to do there is extremely dangerous, probably involving a direct confrontation with the authorities in Talakh, whom you call the Watchers. I am of course well aware of their power and their ruthlessness. I believe you must have some hope of success, some factor they have not taken into account, but however good a hope that is, you think it very likely that you will all perish in the attempt, and that you accept the risk.

'That is your right. But I think I also have acquired some minor rights from our association. I assume that you are aware that Miss Saranja and I have become emotionally involved with each other. Since my mother died, there has hitherto been no one in my life about whom I have cared deeply. I have met and liked many people, but there has been no one, until these last few weeks, whom I have loved. If she is now to be taken from me, am I to live out the rest of my life ignorant of why this was necessary?'

What a strange man, Maja thought for the umpteenth

344

time. Here he was, desperately in love with Saranja, worried to bits about the unseen dangers ahead of her, yet talking about it like a fussy schoolmaster.

'We can't tell you much, I'm afraid,' said Ribek. 'It isn't that we don't trust you. We didn't, at first, of course, but we do now. It's just that some of what we're trying to do means that we know stuff it's extremely dangerous for anyone to know – dangerous in the end for everyone in the Empire. I'll give you an example. We'd barely started on our journey, in fact we'd only just met Benayu, when something happened to attract the Watchers' attention. It was no use running away. They had the power to trace us wherever we went. A very dear friend of Benayu's, a sort of middle-range magician, stayed to confront them, deliberately destroying himself in the process. He did this partly to make it seem that he alone had been responsible for the magical activity they'd noticed, so that we could escape, but partly also because he knew a lot of the stuff I was talking about, and he was determined not to let the Watchers get hold of it.

'So I think the best I can offer is that you tell us what you know or have guessed – I bet it's a lot more than you've let on – and then we'll decide what else we can tell you.'

'Very well. I have already told you that I believe you are expecting some kind of confrontation with the Watchers at Barda, but I will start at the beginning. We have been maintaining the fiction that the four of you are close kin, but for some time I have not believed this to be the case, though I detect some family likeness between Maja and Miss Saranja, and you have just now told me that you met Benayu after your journey started. There is a further anomaly about your party, in that Rocky could well be a horse from a prince's stables, and it is unlikely that a group of your apparent social standing should possess such an animal. This leads me to suspect that he has magical qualities that have not manifested themselves in my presence.

'Ribek has some kind of minor magical affinity with water, but not much else, I believe. Miss Saranja, of course, has her ability to destroy demons, but I think that is not a direct attribute of hers, but is associated with the object she normally wears beneath her blouse. There is something mysterious about Maja but I have had no indication of what it might be. Sometimes she seems to be listening to voices no one else can hear. Once or twice I have noticed one of you glance enquiringly at her, and her reply with a slight nod or headshake. This may be connected with her lizard pendant. I suspect that there is more to that than meets the eye.

'Benayu, on the other hand, already has considerable powers, and when he is older will be a remarkable magician, even by the standards of the Empire. This raises the question of why he has not used those powers to facilitate your journey. No doubt he could have transported you all to Barda almost instantaneously. I presume he chose not to do this because magical activity at that level would have been certain to attract the attention of the authorities, but I have been wondering why, apart from the minor change in my mule, he has done nothing that

I can perceive to hasten your daily progress beyond what is natural. It is true that you have made rapid marches, and yet, except for our encounters with groups of brigands, as far as I have been able to perceive he has not exercised his powers at all.

'The only explanation I can think of is that you fear you are already being watched, or watched for. For some days after the first episode with the brigands you were extremely apprehensive, and Maja almost exhausted herself with constant listening for hidden voices. If this is the case, I have something to contribute. I am a fully trained agent, and almost the first thing we were taught is to act on the assumption that one is being constantly sought for. The fact that one has not been apprehended does not mean that one has not been observed, because one's opponents will prefer to delay until they can strike with maximum advantage.

'In your case, this would be not until you have reached Barda and found the object or person you seek, but before you can make use of that against the Watchers. You should therefore act on the assumption that this is going to happen, and that they will give you very little time in which to act. If that is impossible for you, then your only hope is somehow to elude their watch, or mislead them into believing that you have not yet found what you are looking for. Failing that, you must try to prepare defences that will protect you long enough for you to put your plan into action.

'If I thought that I could help with any of this I should insist on coming with you, but if my guesses are anywhere near the truth I would be no more than a distraction and encumbrance. But can you wonder that I am extremely anxious, not only for Miss Saranja, but for all of you?'

They sat in silence. If Striclan knew so much, thought Maja, how could the Watchers not know it also? And of course they'd wait until they knew where the Ropemaker was. Why hadn't she thought about that before? There simply wasn't going to be time. They'd pounce at once. It was all, suddenly, hopeless.

'At least I can tell you you're a very good spy,' said Ribek after a while. 'If their other spies are that good, your Sheep-faces must know practically everything there is to be known about the Empire.'

'Alas, no,' said Striclan. 'Information from agents on the ground often appears contradictory, and the tendency of the authorities is always to believe what they want to believe, even when the weight of the evidence is against it.

'Well, I will do what you ask me and leave you. I shall set out early in the morning, and get as far away from you as I can before you reach Barda. And I must thank you yet again for your companionship and wish you a successful outcome to your perilous undertaking, and so bid you farewell.'

He rose and helped Saranja to her feet. She didn't let go of his hand. Ribek also rose and Maja scrambled up, but Benayu stayed where he was, dazed with his long dream, looking as if he hadn't heard a word.

'Good luck to you too,' said Ribek. 'I really hope we'll see you again.'

'I've given him one of the finder stones,' said Saranja.

'When all this is over he's coming back to live in the Valley. And thank you for not asking any questions till now.'

Still holding hands they walked away and vanished among the shadows of the way station. There was no more nonsense that night about Striclan taking Maja with him when he left.

Chapter 15

COMING TO BARDA was very different from coming to Mord, or Tarshu, or Larg, or anywhere else they'd been. For two whole days the road crossed an utterly flat landscape, drearier even than desert, scraggy little fields with reed beds here and there, sighing in the steady wind from the ever-nearing ocean. Bank after bank of low clouds rolled in on it, endlessly threatening rain, but not a drop fell. No houses, only a few tumbledown sheds and sties, built where they were for no purpose Maja could imagine, and apparently abandoned years ago.

Once, on the first morning, they passed a sad old yellow horse in a small paddock that it had grazed almost bare. Pogo, prepared to flirt or gossip with anything vaguely horse-shaped, whinnied a greeting, but it didn't even raise its head. Seabirds glided on the wind, hawks hovered, and there were waterfowl on the innumerable sluggish rivers and streams, all flowing from the west, which the road had begun to cross. Otherwise the landscape seemed almost completely lifeless.

But not the road. This was busier than they'd seen it at any time since they'd left Larg, apart from the two narrow strips down the centre that had been set aside for nobles and other grandees, which had very few users. On the other hand there were two extra lanes in either direction for slow-moving ox-wagons and the only slightly faster horse-drawn carts, and by the time three major Highways had joined the one they were on – two on the first day and one on the second – these were pretty well nose-to-tail with traffic. The frequent bridges boomed and thundered to the steady drub of wheels.

Ribek no longer bothered to stop and listen to every bit of water they crossed.

'It won't have anything new to say,' he explained. 'It's just an arm of a delta – all the same river. It's brought down a tremendous load of silt, which has spread further and further out into the sea, with the river breaking up into different channels to find a way through it.'

'So the actual village where the Ropemaker was born won't be on the coast any longer?'

'I suppose not. Even since he disappeared the coastline will have shifted further out. Come to think of it, that may have made things more awkward. Well, we can only see when we get there. What's up?'

Maja clutched him to stop herself from falling from Levanter's back. For a moment she was back at the sheepfold north of Tarshu, almost drowning in darkness as she clung with her mind to the fiery streak of the

Ropemaker's hair. It was a smell, a reek, that had carried her there, salty, fishy, weedy, stronger than any mere sea smell. She shook herself back into the here and now and stared around. The reek was still in her nostrils, beginning to fade.

'What's that smell?' she said.

'Came from one of the wagons on the other side. Oysters, I should think. Remember that fellow at Larg said Barda was famous for them?'

'It's what I smelt when I used the hair.'

'Are you sure?'

'Almost.'

'Interesting.'

Now that Striclan had left them, Jex had returned to his natural form. That evening, as they sat round the fire, he spoke in their heads. Benayu woke from his long half-trance to listen.

'*I do not know, any more than you do, what will happen at Barda, other than if we find the form into which the Ropemaker has put his physical self it will involve an explosion of magic far more powerful than any you and I have so far endured. I must return to an inert form before that happens, or I shall not survive. But we cannot find what we are looking for without Maja's help, so she must stay in her own form until that is done, and I will protect her as best I can. Benayu must then immediately endow her with an inert form in which she no longer needs protection.*'

'Any ideas, Maja?' said Benayu.

Maja hesitated. It was difficult to think. To leave her

own body, which had always seemed to be so much a part of her, who she was, all that made her Maja, always there, ready and waiting when she woke from dreams . . .

How could she do that and still be the same person . . . ?

If she must, she must. She mastered her reluctance.

'Will I be able to see and hear?'

'If you've got eyes and ears.'

'Whatever's easiest, then. Something Ribek can carry on a loop round his neck.'

'I'll think about it. Go on, Jex.'

'That done, both Maja and I will for the time being be helpless, but we must all instantly escape to Angel Isle and into my alternate universe, where the Watchers cannot follow.'

'I've been bothered about that,' said Benayu. 'I could take us there, of course, but it's a risk. It doesn't get us there all in a moment, quite, and if the Watchers show up in time I won't be able to stop them grabbing us back. They've got the power. The sea won't make any difference. They can do it from dry land.'

'Fortunately we have other means of escape at hand. A roc is a creature from my other universe, and therefore an impossible creature in this universe, where it can survive only as a magical animal. Similarly, a horse is a creature of this universe and cannot survive except as a magical animal in the other. It follows that a horse with the wings of a roc is an impossible creature in both universes and can survive as a magical animal in both. So, immediately before we attempt to locate what we are looking for, you must screen us while Saranja restores

Rocky's *wings. Using him as a basis you will be able to create the means to give the other two horses and the dog the power of flight, so that when the time comes they will be able to carry us to Angel Isle and through the touching point.'*

'Won't the Watchers be able to interfere with that too?' said Saranja.

'I should be able to think of ways to fight them off for a bit,' said Benayu.

'*You will need to prepare all that you can in advance, before your powers are weakened over the sea. The Watchers will face the same difficulty, but they will have come in haste, without time to prepare specific weaponry to use in such circumstances. They will certainly deploy thunderbolts, and send a dragon in pursuit. Probably no more than one, since they have lost several over Tarshu, but they may well produce simulacra.'*

'You might think about trying to hide us and laying a false trail. Like we did when we left Tarshu,' said Ribek.

'*And finally there is the problem of how we can survive as four-dimensional creatures in a seven dimensional universe,*' said Jex.

'I've been working on that,' said Benayu. 'I can do it all right, in theory. I'll get some of that ready tonight too, but I can't finish it off till we get there. I'm bothered about this business of being weaker over the sea.'

'*Angel Isle itself is different. It is a major touching point, a source of great power.'*

Maja was woken in the dawn by a stir of magic and found Saranja and Ribek still asleep, but Benayu sitting up, staring at a pattern of what looked like coloured rice-grains he had laid out on the tiled floor of their sleeping booth. Every now and then he would point at it and more grains would appear under his fingertip, forming another swirl in the pattern. He had screened himself closely round, so that Maja could feel no more than a whisper of something immensely powerful and complex being brought out of nowhere and woven into the fabric of reality.

He'd continued to work throughout breakfast while Saranja fed him morsels which he chewed without noticing. When they were ready to leave he spread both hands over the pattern, which flowed upwards from the centre, maintaining its swirls and windings as it followed the movement of his hands as he twisted them, palms inward, until they were cupped around a shimmering egg about the size of a baby's head. He moved them together until he could fold his fingers into each other and clasp them tight, absorbing the egg into himself.

The screen vanished.

'Done,' he muttered. 'Help me up. We must go. Wake me when you see the garden.'

There was no particular moment at which the town of Barda began: sheds and barns slightly more frequent, slightly less ramshackle; a patch where someone had been trying to grow vegetables; a row of sties with actual pigs in them; a shed, not apparently more habitable than any of the sheds they'd passed earlier, but with a line of laundry flapping in the breeze; and then, astonishingly, beside yet another slow-oozing mud-rimmed river (the tide apparently reached far enough inland here to expose a few feet of the bank), a seriously grand house with two pleasure yachts moored at a jetty and gardeners working its carefully symmetrical gardens.

Ribek booted Levanter forward until he was alongside Benayu on Pogo, leaned across and shook him by the elbow.

'Ready to wake up now?' he said. 'This looks like your garden.'

Benayu snorted, sat up, squared his shoulders and looked around.

'That's it. Thanks,' he said, speaking as cheerfully and confidently as he had done when they had first met him on that mountain pasture north of Mord. There was a blip of magic, and a screen enclosed a section of the garden. He raised his right hand towards it, palm forward, fingers spread, and closed it in a slow, grasping motion. The whole section – a small raised pond and the strip of lawn around it, with a few small trees and a curving, bed of rose bushes with a close-clipped yew-hedge behind it – shimmered for a moment, disappeared, and returned unchanged.

'All set now,' he said. 'I think I'm as ready as I'm going to be. Anything else I'll have to improvise. Any suggestions about where to start looking? We really don't want to use the hair again until we have to. Maja?'

'The oyster beds? That's what I smelt.'

'There'll be a lot of them,' said Saranja. 'I've lost count of the reeking wagon-loads we've passed.'

'The first thing is to find out what Barda consisted of around when the Ropemaker disappeared,' said Ribek. 'I thought we might take a leaf out of Striclan's book. Suppose I'm doing the same sort of job he was, and I've come here to compile a report on the history of the oyster trade. If I find the right official and show him the scrolls they gave us at Larg, there's a good chance he'll be helpful.'

A trivial, irrelevant thought came into Maja's mind.

'I wonder what oysters taste like,' she said.

'Now's your chance to find out,' said Ribek. 'I'll ask the fellow I see for a recommendation.'

The street where they waited for Ribek to reappear was utterly different from the tatterdemalion outskirts of Barda. Those had been like that because they had been long ago abandoned as the town had moved steadily eastward to stay near the sea that was its livelihood, keeping up with the unstoppable growth, inch by inch through the centuries, of the delta upon which it stood.

This was a broad, cobbled thoroughfare lined with stolid-looking brick buildings, mostly large and plain, with only here and there a flourish of ornamentation around the main doors. Ribek was inside one of these slightly fancier ones. Maja and the others waited in the shade opposite. The horses fidgeted and stamped. Saranja was almost as restless. But Benayu seemed to have retired into his trance and stood with his head bowed and his eyes half closed, swaying very slightly from side to side, as if he had fallen asleep on his feet. Only Maja could sense the steady, purposeful activity inside as he gathered and ordered the powers he was going to need.

Maja herself was almost sick with anxiety, so obviously that Saranja noticed and moved to her side and put a comforting arm round her, but even that didn't stop the spasms of shivering and the endless, useless swallowing of saliva that wasn't there. She wasn't afraid of dying, or of what the Watchers might do to her if they caught her, but of the task ahead. No, she wasn't going to bear the brunt of it, as Benayu would have to, but only she could find the Ropemaker. They'd talked about this on their way into the town. As Jex and Ribek had said, it would all have to happen in an instant, before the Watchers were on them. Ribek would be holding her. Saranja would unwind that single golden hair from the roc feathers. There would be the double blast of magic, leaving Maja blind and deaf but tracking that intense thread of golden fire through the darkness between the universes . . .

Would she survive even that far? Jex would do what he could, but . . . But if she did, then what? At the sheepfold she'd had time to recover, to come back into the here and now, to point the way they must go. This time, somehow, in that instant before the Watchers came, she would have to act, to tell or show Ribek what to do, where to go. It could only be him – Benayu would be facing the Watchers and Saranja wrestling with the panicking horses – and still she would need to endure, endure . . .

She tried to distract herself by studying the scene before her. What were all the wagons doing, trundling thunderously to and fro over the cobbles? Not difficult. At the far end of the street she could see masts and cranes, and the now familiar odour of oysters told her what most of the ones going in that direction bore, and what many of those coming back, only a little less thunderously and reekingly, had unloaded at the harbour. But a far greater variety of cargoes returned from there, in different carts, because you wouldn't want your corn or your carpets or expensive luxuries impregnated with the basic Bardan odour, would you?

That man there now, bustling out of a door, dodging between the wagons, pausing anxiously to check through the file of papers he was carrying, as if searching for a document that should have been there and wasn't, sighing with relief and hurrying in through another door – not difficult either. Or that grander gentleman stalking up from the harbour, listening haughtily to the expostulations of the seamanlike figure beside him, and followed by a porter wheeling a trolley with a brass-bound sea-chest on it . . . All so everyday and impossibly different, almost in another universe from the one she knew, the one that had the Watchers in it, and winged horses, and Jex, and the unimaginable terrors of the next few hours . . .

'At last!' said Saranja. 'Look at him! He's been spinning it out, enjoying himself! He drives me mad sometimes!'

Maja looked, saw Ribek, sane, beautiful, everyday Ribek, coming out of the door opposite, and instantly felt better. Jex wasn't the only one who could live in two universes, she thought.

A large man with blubbery lips was talking volubly to him as he held the door, and talked on as they wound their way between the wagons, though most of what he was saying must have been drowned by the wheel-thunder. He approached them reaching forward for a hand to shake and starting to introduce himself before he was fully in earshot.

'. . . Adorno Dorno, Oyster Magister of Barda, at your service. And you three are also Freepeople of Larg, my friend Ribek tells me. Honoured, honoured indeed . . .'

Ribek managed to get the introductions in while the Magister was vigorously shaking their hands. If Sponge had known to hold up a paw he would no doubt have shaken that.

'And none of you has ever tasted an oyster! You have waited until you can start at the pinnacle of excellence. Wonderful! Wonderful! Perhaps as a preliminary – ahem – taster to your inspection of our oyster beds you ought to have your first experience of this wonderful delicacy. You have come to the right man. It is part of my official duties to inspect and license the commercial outlets of Barda, and there are two on our way to the oyster beds that I would especially recommend . . .'

Maja quailed. How could she get *anything* down her throat with the terror of the event so close upon them? And Ribek had said that oysters were slippery blobs that you ate not just raw, but *alive*!

'I . . . I'm not very hungry,' she blurted.

The Magister stared at her, pop-eyed with astonishment, as if he couldn't imagine the circumstances in which somebody might not want to sample his oysters.

'I'm afraid we made the error of partaking of a substantial repast shortly before our arrival,' said Ribek in his Striclan voice. 'We did not foresee our good fortune in encountering such a fountainhead of knowledge so immediately. Perhaps when we have had our fill of the oyster beds we will be in a better frame to have our fill of the oysters.'

'Excellent! Excellent!' crowed the Magister, covering Ribek with saliva in his excitement. 'I shall certainly enter that among the Remarks of Visitors that I publish in the Town Year Book. Well then, shall we stable your horses and take my barge? Fortunately the tide is flowing towards the full. Or would you prefer to walk? In which case we could save time in stabling the horses and leave them at the gate. We have a strict rule against allowing animals in the oyster fields for fear of contaminating the purity of the waters. The same ruling also applies to those with magical powers, but for different reasons, of course.'

'Of course,' agreed Ribek. 'What does everyone feel about that? Saranja?'

'Um . . . er . . .' said Saranja. Maja sensed a brief pulse of magic from Benayu, and words seemed to come into Saranja's mouth, unwilled.

'Let's walk,' she blurted. 'Benayu and I can stay with the horses.'

'It would perhaps be more stimulating to the appetite,' said Ribek, as if he'd noticed nothing remotely odd about the exchange.

361

'True, true,' said the Magister. 'Well, if you're ready to depart . . .'

He had a surprising turn of speed for so portly a figure. Even Ribek had to stride out to keep up with his vigorous waddle. Maja started to fall behind and broke into a trot to catch up, almost running headlong into one of the Magister's sweeping gestures. Instantly she started to fall behind again, trotted, caught up . . . No, too tiring.

She halted and waited for the others and let Saranja lift her on to Levanter's back. Benayu had come back into this world to greet the Magister and now took the chance to mount Pogo. Saranja seemed to be in a bad mood, probably cross about Benayu telling her in her head what to say just now. And perhaps it was also her way of dealing with the coming crisis. She was scared, and no wonder, and she was ashamed of being scared. It didn't fit in with her idea of herself and that made her furious.

'Look at him!' she snarled suddenly. 'Oozing charm at that appalling man as if he's having a lovely time!'

'Ribek's doing fine,' said Benayu absently. 'He's got him eating out of his hand.'

'Yes, of course he has. But he doesn't need to enjoy it so much! And talking in that stupid voice! I think it's grotesque!'

She strode on, seething. It was the Striclan voice, of course, that got her goat, Maja realized. She glanced at Benayu, hoping to share the joke, but he was deep in concentration again. Without warning a wave of apprehension washed over her. She felt utterly alone. Jex . . .

'I am here in the saddlebag, still in my living form. I will at least partially protect you until the last instant. There will not be three separate magical impulses for you to endure. They will be almost simultaneous, and then Benayu will convert you into your inert form. It would be as well to remind him.'

'All right . . . Benayu? Can I bother you? It isn't important if you're busy. Jex says I've got to remind you about changing me as soon as it's over. He says he'll look after me till the last minute. Something with eyes and ears, you said.'

'Don't worry. You won't be able to move your eyes, so you'll only see what's straight in front of you.'

'That'll be fine.'

He nudged Pogo closer, leaned over, plucked at her sleeve and effortlessly drew out a single dark green thread, which he coiled carelessly round his thumb.

'Listen,' he said. 'I'd better tell you what's going to happen. This business about the horses actually helps, because it's the same as at the sheepfold. You can't do it if you're screened, but if Saranja and I stay with the horses I can screen what I'm doing to them separately. I'll get everything set, so I can do it in a flash, and I'll keep in touch with you and Ribek in your heads. One of you just tell me when you're ready. Count ten, and Saranja will take the hair off the feathers. That'll activate it. We won't be as close as we were last time, but you'll still be able to feel the link between it and what we're looking for, won't you, Maja?'

'Yes, I think so.'

'Right. Then while you're busy your end Saranja and I will put the wings on the horses and Sponge – I'll speed that up – and I'll bring us. I've got everything ready to change you into your inert form the moment you've found what we're looking for. I'll do it whatever else is going on. All right? I've told Ribek in his head.'

'I've got to have Jex close. Do you think he counts as an animal?'

'*I am stone again until you are through the gate. Take me out of the saddlebag and put me in your wallet. Put me on the ground when you tell Benayu that you are ready to proceed.*'

Before Maja had finished putting Jex away Benayu was back in the maze of his own mind.

She gazed around. They were travelling up a broad path beside a brick-banked canal, whose waters looked very different from the opaque and sluggish streams of the inner delta, clear and clean enough for her to be able to see a school of silvery minnows scuttling along beside the dark green weed that cloaked the further embankment, all the way from the canal bed to the high-tide mark a few inches above the surface.

The buildings either side were solid but elegant houses that somehow announced their owners' richness without any parade of wealth. From snatches in the conversation ahead of her Maja could tell that the Magister was telling Ribek about those owners, and the trades that supplied their wealth, and Ribek was making Striclanishly knowledgeable remarks about those trades and at the same time trying tactfully to get the subject back to the history of the oyster beds.

Yes, of course he was having a good time, and she was glad for him. But underneath, she guessed he was as scared as the rest of them, and this was his way of dealing with it, just as Saranja's way was to be furious, and Benayu's was to work on his magic, and hers – hers was to think about Ribek.

There was a bridge across the canal, at which the two rows of handsome houses stopped abruptly. A road crossed the bridge with a ten-foot brick wall on the far side. An iron gate barred the path they were on. There was an odd little Eye on the gate.

As Ribek and the Magister approached a man appeared, uniformed like a soldier and armed with a pike. He opened the gate and saluted the Magister, but then moved as if to bar the horses.

'The animals are remaining outside, Gidder,' said the Magister. 'Two of our honoured visitors will remain with them. Supply them with anything they may need as befits free persons of our sister city of Larg.'

'There's an Eye on the gate,' Maja whispered to Benayu.

He considered a moment.

'There to spot magicians,' he muttered. 'Wouldn't have let me through anyway. I wonder why. You'd better go. Don't want to keep him waiting.'

She hurried to join Ribek, but she needn't have worried, as the Magister was still impressing the guard with the importance of his visitors. Then all three walked on together through a landscape so different that Maja was tempted to look back and check that the roofs of Barda were still there beyond the wall. This was the same level, stream-threaded delta through which they had arrived, but here as kempt and tidy as that rich man's garden with the pleasure yachts beside it had been. No tumbledown sheds and barns, no miserable horses in paddocks, only, a few hundred yards ahead of them now, an organized line of sturdy timber buildings along the banks of one of the larger waterways. There seemed to be no one apart from themselves anywhere in all that flatness and emptiness.

'. . . established seven hundred and fifty-eight years ago,' the Magister was saying. 'I am the sixty-third to hold the office of Magister. The oyster beds themselves are owned by the individual members, but the Guild supervises the processing, checking and marketing. It was set up during the great oyster plague, when all the beds down the whole east coast of the Empire were ravaged by oyster worm. Only Barda escaped. Prices went sky high, our oyster beds expanded out of all recognition and we have never looked back.'

'How exceedingly fortunate for you,' said Ribek. 'Magical, almost.'

'Certainly not,' snapped the Magister. 'Our competitors have many times accused us of employing rogue magicians to inflict the plague on them while sparing ourselves, but the authorities in Talakh – as you no doubt know, extremely strict in such matters – made a thorough investigation and cleared us completely. Exceedingly fortunate, yes. According to our records we have nineteen times over the centuries been spared such plagues, while

366

others have suffered. It is thought to be something to do with the quality of the water, which is another reason for our security precautions. Lunatics believe that their ailments will be cured by immersion among the oysters. There is a flourishing illegal trade in bottled Barda water – much of it fake, of course. We attempt to prevent it. That is not the sort of publicity we want to encourage. The excellence of our oysters is advertisement enough.'

'And has that always been the case?'

'Indeed it has. Our earliest records include regular orders from the Emperor's kitchens.'

'And those actual beds still exist, you tell me? I should very much like to see them with my own eyes.'

'So you shall, so you shall. We will do that first of all. You will want to talk to some of the old oystermen later, but it is high tide, and they are taking their rest. They won't be returning till the tide is well into the ebb, when the work begins again. Now these beds here on your right . . .'

He burbled on. Ribek answered just enough to keep him going, but his mind was no longer on it, and he'd almost stopped using his Striclan voice. Maja could understand why. Most of his attention was absorbed by what the waters were saying, or rather singing. She could almost hear it herself, an endless, slow, wavering chant, repeating and repeating itself but never quite the same each time. Utterly, utterly peaceful.

Of course, she thought. The same pattern as everything else that had happened. The Ropemaker would have hidden his material self in a place which only someone from the Valley could find. Only someone from Northbeck. Only Ribek.

They came to a slightly wider stretch of water, almost a pool, where two streams joined and flowed out as one. The floor of the pool was grey with layers of oysters. The tide was almost full, barely moving, but there must have been some faint current because she could see a white down-feather moving very gently along, close by the near bank, away from the sea, and she realized, from her sense of the secret sound that only Ribek was hearing, that the whole body of water was quietly rotating round some central point, an unending ritual dance, the slowest of slow measures to the soundless chanting.

'Marvellous,' said Ribek in his own voice, his awe wholly genuine. 'I was born by a mill-stream, high in the mountains. I have always had a kind of feeling for water. Never anything like this.'

'How strange,' said the Magister dreamily. 'You have never tasted oysters and I have never seen mountains. Ever since I was a boy I have longed to see mountains.'

They stood together in silence, lost in their separate trances.

'*Wake up, Maja!*'

She shuddered herself into the here and now, tugged urgently at Ribek's sleeve and felt him do the same.

'Sorry,' he whispered. 'Ready?'

She nodded. He took her by the elbow, led her to the edge of the bank and crouched beside her, pointing, as if he was showing her something in the water. She slipped the stone pendant out of her wallet and laid it on the ground.

'Just show me the way,' he muttered. 'I'll find it. Hold your breath when I say . . . I'm going to push you in. Don't try to swim. Now!'

She filled her lungs and stopped breathing. Two thundering heartbeats and the world went black. The hair blazed through that dark. She was jerked forward, was falling, distantly heard Ribek's shout of alarm, heard the Magister's yell, met the shock of cold, automatically clung on to her breath, but barely noticed any of these things as the blazing strand streaked onward, filling her consciousness, all there was. Her hand must have been already pointing when Ribek gripped her wrist and dragged her down, but she didn't feel him doing so. All she knew, all that held her together, was that single intense line of fire seeking its home.

And then, in another colossal explosion of power, it was gone, and she was bursting apart, rags and splinters of what had once been Maja, whirling away into the never-ending blackness.

And then . . . But there was no then. Not any more. Never.

Then there was now. Now was extremely strange. She had no sense of herself, Maja, existing in that nowness. There was sight, there was hearing, but nothing to tell her who or what was doing that seeing, that hearing. And even they were strange. The hearing was the sound of a heavy, windy thud or boom, repeated and repeated, strangely familiar, though only a few times heard by the Maja that once existed. The sight was of a dim, greyish something – more than just a grey light because there

369

was texture in it, mottlings and grains, moving erratically around, uninterpretable.

For a moment the greyness moved away and she saw a dark, reddy-brown surface, slightly curved, moving upwards, only to vanish as the greyness returned. It had something to do with the thud . . . Yes! – Rocky, flying towards mountains – wing-thunder. But wrong colour, not Rocky, Levanter.

The greyness vanished and for a moment she saw his vast neck stretching away from her, and then that swung aside and she saw sky, and then, for another moment Saranja, hair streaming behind her, riding Rocky, golden-winged, glorious, and behind and beyond them white-winged Pogo with Benayu in his saddle craning backward and upward, and Sponge at their heels streaking along in the winged equivalent of his normal easy lope.

They too swung out of sight and everything was blanked out by something too huge and close to recognize, which pressed itself briefly over her eyes as she heard a faint familiar noise such as two moist surfaces make when being gently pulled apart. *What was it? What was it? It was important.*

Everything wheeled around and briefly she could see the sky, hazy blue with a strange black cloud in it, streaming towards them far faster than any wind could have carried it. She seemed to be seeing sky and cloud, everything in her restricted field of vision, through some kind of transparent mesh, but all that was blanked out as the cloud became blinding to her unclosable eyes and the thunder drowned her hearing.

Lightning! she thought. *The Watchers came! This is the end.*

It wasn't the end. Sight returned, hearing more slowly, only to be lost again in thunder-bellows. Lightning poured around them, but eyesight remained since she wasn't looking directly at it. She couldn't see Benayu, but she guessed he was somehow warding it off. And Levanter flew steadily on, apparently not even noticing it. Amazing, considering how Rocky, prince among horses, had shied and bolted at the appearance of the airboat. Benayu must have thought of that too, and done something to the horses.

Lightning and thunder weakened and ceased. She had time to think, time to look properly at what she could see – frustratingly little since she couldn't turn her head or even move her eyes in their sockets. At the lower edge of her circle of vision she could discern a greenish grey expanse stretching away into the distance. They must be out over the sea.

Rocky and Saranja were moving out of her line of sight as Levanter edged closer to Benayu. Ribek's shout came faintly through the thunder-deafness.

'. . . only a lull. Like at Tarshu. Then more lightning, to distract you while they get the next thing ready. A dragon, Jex said. Simulacra, but if you can sort out which is which it'll be one-to-one. Maybe it'll sail straight in. But they must get it by now, what they're up against. My bet is it'll feint and wait for you to respond so it can catch you off balance with a sucker kick.'

She couldn't see or hear Benayu's answer, but he must have gestured understanding or something because

Ribek swung Levanter away and back to Rocky's other flank. They waited. It was strange not having a heart to pound, breath to come quicker, palms to break into sweat, at a moment like this.

Her mind wandered. She was still seeing everything as if through a transparent mesh. And why was her hearing so strangely woolly? It had been like that before the thunder, when all she'd been able to see was a moving greyness.

Oh, of course! That had been Ribek trying to clean and dry her with a bit of cloth after her immersion in the oyster pool. And then he'd lifted her up and round to loop her over his head and now she was dangling on his chest, but on the way . . . on the way . . .

That funny sucking noise had been his lips kissing her.

And she hadn't even felt it.

It wasn't fair!

More lightning streaming harmless round them as Benayu swept it away. In the middle of it a yell from Ribek, words lost in the rolling thunder but voice full of urgency and danger.

'Ribek! Can you hear me? Ribek!'

If he answered she couldn't hear. No. He'd never have kissed her if he'd remembered she could see and hear. She'd never reminded him! She hadn't had a chance. Desperately she tried again.

'What's happening? I can't see. I can't move my eyes. Turn me round.'

The world wheeled and steadied, and she was looking back and to their flank. Saranja and Rocky were at the right-hand edge of her vision; Benayu had fallen back a little and had twisted round in his saddle to face the danger; Sponge was darting to and fro behind Pogo's heels, snarling defiance.

Beyond and above them them, dwarfing them, loomed the dragon, twice the size, at least, of the monster that had patrolled the valley above Tarshu, gnarled and scaly, dark-hued, mottled brown and green like lichened rock. Maja could see it clearly only in glimpses as the rhythm of Levanter's flight brought her centre of vision to bear on it. A huge round eye with a black vertical slit for a pupil, the rest of the eye glowing smoky-pale like a harvest moon, as if lit from within; the vicious spike that ended a rib of one of the vast leathery wings; a taloned foreleg tucked cosily for flight against a chest like the hull of a warship; a double puff of black smoke from the hummocked nostrils at the end of the long snout. The dragon hovered a long moment, half folded its wings and plunged.

Benayu was ready. He flung out both hands and a bolt of darkness, sudden and swift as the lightning, streamed from his fingertips. It wrapped itself round the dragon in a swirling cloud of absolute black that carried the beast backward and at the same time seemed to shrink and solidify as if it were about to squeeze it out of existence.

Another intense shaft of lightning, dazzling even in daylight, but aimed this time not at Benayu and his companions but at that sphere of midnight. With a bellow and a blast of flame it burst apart, and out of the dazzle emerged five separate but identical dragons, wings half folded, plunging down. No knowing which was the real one.

Benayu shouted and flung out an arm, and Sponge was climbing to meet the attack, double, four, eight times his real size, great black wings pumping him upward. All five dragons bellowed flame, but only one, fourth in the line, directly at him. The other four, constrained to do exactly what the master dragon did, blasted the unreal flame in lines parallel to the reality. By its own fire it had betrayed itself.

Immediately Sponge turned towards the single blast that engulfed him and now flew directly into it, relentless and untroubled as it streamed round him. The dragon had no other weapon. Sponge was almost muzzle to muzzle with the monster when he dived, rose, gripped the immense scaly gullet in his fangs and started to wrench and worry at it like one of the Woodbourne terriers worrying a rat. Black wings and gold buffeted the air as he wrestled for purchase and the dragon writhed and scrabbled at him with its puny forelegs. On either side of it four simulacra dragons towered, writhing and scrabbling at invisible Sponges. Above the individual struggles, seen and unseen, the agonized heads bellowed unavailing flame, and below it dangled the pale, vulnerable underbellies and the endless writhing tails.

Now something invisible, something Benayu must have prepared in those long days of meditation, struck home. Black blood spurted from all five underbellies. He shouted a command and Sponge released his hold and drew clear as the four simulacra blanked out of being and the master dragon plummeted out of Maja's vision towards the ocean.

374

Ribek whooped in triumph. Benayu held up a hand in acknowledgement and pointed ahead. The horses, who had flown steadily on through the turmoil as if nothing was happening, began to descend.

'*What is it? Are we there? Say something. I can hear now.*'

No answer.

'*Turn me round. Please.*'

Again, though she was now half certain that Ribek couldn't hear her, the world swung, and she was looking past Levanter's neck at the immense expanse of ocean. Out of it, not far off now, rose a single broad pillar of rock with the ocean swell breaking into foam all around it. Angel Isle. The touching point.

The horses glided towards it like gulls, wings barely moving. Without being asked Ribek turned Maja so that she could see the wave-ravaged cliffs, fissured into immense, irregular columns, slide past. *Why Angel Isle?* she wondered. She had a vague idea that angels were a kind of good demon. There were plenty of demons in the old stories, but no angels as far as she could remember.

Halfway round the island a crevice between two pillars widened into a dark slit. The horses swung past without hesitation and circled on. But second time round Rocky led them out and away, swung back and headed directly for the slit. At the last moment he half folded his wings and disappeared into the cliff. Pogo followed, and Levanter, and they were in darkness. The opening must have widened considerably the moment they were inside, for now she could see Rocky and Pogo gliding on, silhouetted against a pale light gleaming ahead.

Darkness again. No, Ribek had twisted right round in the saddle to look behind him, so she perforce had done the same. The slit must have closed. Or something.

He turned back, and she watched the light increasing and increasing until they glided out into the daylight of what she instantly knew to be another universe.

PART THREE

Angel Isle

Chapter 16

THERE MUST HAVE been some kind of night in this different universe, because now it was dark, and the others were all asleep. Maja knew that because the darkness seemed to come from the outside, so it wasn't anything Benayu had done. Everything else was, here inside the eggshell he'd made to keep their own four dimensions safe from touching the seven dimensions of this other universe.

Maja wasn't asleep, because rag dolls can't shut their eyes. All they can do is lie and stare into the dark and wait for it to be day again.

She knew what she was now because as soon as they were off the horses, Ribek had unlooped her from round his neck and propped her against something, and for a moment her head had flopped forward and she'd seen her muddy legs sticking out in front of her with a bit of the hem of her skirt, dark green like the thread Benayu had pulled from her blouse. Her stockings were green and yellow stripes and her round puppy-paw feet were purple. The stockings were knitted, but the shoes and skirt were fabric, so she supposed her face must be fabric too, with her features painted on to it. She was pretty certain her eyes must be blue because of the way everything she could see looked a bit too blue, and the transparent mesh she saw through came from the weave of the fabric, and of course her hearing was woolly because wool was what her head was stuffed with.

Then Ribek had straightened her up and she'd been able to see everything in front of her. Benayu was explaining how he'd got all the four-dimensional stuff ready in those last hours when he seemed to be three-quarters asleep, and hidden it inside himself so that he could bring it out as they passed through the touching point. There, as soon as it came into contact with the seven-dimensional stuff of this other universe, it started to explode, but then stopped and became the place where they were now.

It was very pretty. She'd watched him steal it from the rich man's garden they'd passed just outside Barda, with the raised pool rimmed by a low stone wall and a stone mermaid in the middle, and the turf and the trees and the rose bed with the neat clipped yew-hedge behind it, though there was now a neat pile of horse-dung on the perfect turf beside it (*Tsk, tsk*, as Striclan might have said). The horses were drinking from the pool, and Benayu had 'fetched' fodder for them from somewhere.

Immediately beyond the yew-hedge was the shell of the egg that enclosed it all. Or was it so close? For all Maja could tell, it could have been half a mile away. It shimmered, but it shouldn't have because it didn't seem to have a surface and it was all one colour, a kind of extra-grey grey. (White can be dazzling white and black can be pitch black, but grey . . . ?) Benayu said that this was because it was made of the two kinds of light, one from each universe, tangled into each other and forming a shell of solid energy to keep the actual stuff of which the universes were made from touching and being destroyed in the explosion.

Ribek, of course, had moved into sight from beside her, gone through a gap in the yew-hedge and tried to touch it. She'd seen him jerk himself back and stand wringing his hand as if he'd jarred a nerve in his wrist. Benayu had laughed. Maja hadn't been able to see him from where she'd been sitting but he sounded utterly exhausted and at the same time triumphant. It had been a frustratingly long time before anyone thought to ask what Ribek and Maja had found in the oyster pool.

Ribek was out of sight again, but Saranja had been sitting on the wall of the pool, almost at the centre of her line of vision, with Jex on the coping next to her.

'Well, what happens now?' she said. 'I'm afraid we haven't got the hair any more. I'd laid it out on Rocky's saddle and was holding it in place with a fingertip in case it blew off when Benayu told me to say the name. The moment I did so it got hot enough to burn and I snatched my hand away before I could stop myself, and when I looked it wasn't there. Not that it would do us much good without Maja to tell us which way it wants us to go. Aren't you going to show us what you found in the oyster bed? Perhaps we can use that somehow.'

'Trouble is, I don't know if it's the right thing,' said Ribek. 'I'd got hold of Maja's wrist and I was letting her show me the way down and at the same time helping her get there. She seemed to know exactly where she wanted to go. She pushed her hand down through the oysters into stuff beneath – loose sandy gravel – and then just went limp and the breath started bubbling out of her mouth and any moment she'd've started breathing water. I had to get her out. I only had time for a quick grope where her hand had been. Anyway, this is what I found. I don't think there was anything else.'

A long pause. Saranja stared, frowning.

'Show me too! Ribek, please! Jex . . . !'

Why couldn't even Jex hear her?

'Let's have a look,' said Benayu. 'I should be able to tell . . . Yes, this is it! By all the levels, this is it! There's the hair. Woven itself right in . . . No, there are two of them . . . Jex! Are you all right, Jex? . . . Must've been too much for him. He should be fine – he said he'd be ready for it this time. But he was right, it would've destroyed Maja.'

'Almost did, I think,' said Ribek. 'In the oyster pool, the moment she touched it. You're sure she's really all right in there?'

'Should be. Pass her across . . .'

'Can you clean her up a bit? I suppose I could rinse her in the pond and wring her out, but it doesn't feel right.'

Benayu laughed again. Ribek's vast hand appeared, closed round her body and swung her through the air. Briefly the contents of the eggshell wheeled past, Ribek himself, serious and anxious, more lawn, three narrow cypresses, Sponge fast asleep with his muzzle on his paws and his wings folded behind his back, the horses nuzzling into their fodder as if they'd worn wings all their lives (and Pogo was really beautiful. Talk about dazzling white!), Benayu reaching to take her . . .

His hand closed round her and she felt the touch of his mind.

'Benayu?'

'*Good, you sound fine, Maja. You heard all that?*'

'Yes, but Ribek doesn't remember. I forgot to remind him I'd be able to see and hear. What's happened to Jex? He can't hear me either.'

'*He's resting. That was all a bit much for him. I think he'll be all right.*'

'And I want to see what we found.'

'*This.*'

He adjusted his hold to turn her and with his other hand picked up from the grass beside him a piece of old rope, about as long as the real Maja's foot and as thick as her two thumbs laid together. The strands at the lower end had unravelled into a fuzzy tangle.

No. They were meant to be like that.

'You're holding him upside down. That's his hair.'

'*Ah.*'

Benayu laid the rope down to reverse his hold and picked it up again. He must have done something, though Maja couldn't feel it, or see one single strand of the rope stir or change colour, but now, though still rope, it seemed to have a definitely human shape, a tall, thin figure with a wild shock of hair concealing the neckline, and body and limbs hidden beneath a long robe.

Huh, she thought. *That makes two of us, one rag, one rope.*

Benayu must have heard that, because he laughed as he settled the manikin carefully against the rim of the pool.

'Say thank you to Ribek for looking after me. And remind him to show me things. He's been doing it sometimes, but sort of by accident, I think.'

Ribek didn't say anything for a moment when Benayu passed the message on, then chuckled. (What did that mean? Relieved? Embarrassed? No telling.)

'Glad you're still with us,' he said. 'I'll try to remember.'

'So far so good,' said Saranja. 'We got what we came for, and that's great. Now what?'

'Let's talk about it while we're eating,' said Benayu. 'I've fetched something from that restaurant the Magister was going to take us to. It's all right. I've paid for it.'

That meant the others had all got to taste oyster-and-bacon pie, but Maja hadn't even been able to smell it. If Ribek had thought to smear some of his supper on to her painted lips she still couldn't have tasted it because she hadn't got a tongue. Life as a rag doll isn't all kisses and cuddles.

'How long have we got, d'you think, Benayu, before the Watchers find a way in?' said Ribek.

'I don't know,' said Benayu wearily. 'I'm not sure they even can.'

'The Ropemaker got in somehow.'

'The touching point was still open then. I closed it as soon as we were through. I had to use Fodaro's equations for that. So first they'd need to know a lot of other-universe stuff to open it again, and if what Jex heard is right they've only just found out about that. If they have, and that's not certain.

'Then they'd have to have thought about it a lot, the way Fodaro did, from what Jex had told us. There's all sorts of really difficult mathematical relationships you have to sort out before you come up with the equations. You can't do that by magic. It's pure brain stuff, and it took Fodaro years. So I doubt if the Watchers can do anything about it from the other side, except trial and error. That'd be wildly dangerous.'

'So you don't think we'll see them again before we go back to our own universe?' said Ribek. 'Never mind that they'll be waiting with everything they've got, ready for us to come out. We can think about that later.'

'But we're stuck in the same kind of bind, aren't we?' said Saranja. 'We've got to find the Ropemaker somewhere out there, and we haven't got Maja to help us do that, and then we've got to get him out of whatever's he's stuck in and bring him back here to join up with what you found in the oyster pool, but none of us can go outside the eggshell to do any of that without being destroyed . . .'

'The horses can, as far as I can gather,' said Ribek. 'And Sponge, I suppose. They're magical animals now. And Jex's other self must be somewhere out there – I imagine he'd help – but . . .'

'It's not even worth thinking about until I've talked to

Jex,' said Benayu. 'Getting us here was as far as I've worked out, and it took everything I've got. I'm practically dead on my feet. The first thing is for me to have a good night's sleep, and after that I'll need to get a lot of new stuff out of Jex and see if Fodaro's equations still apply, and then, well, it'll still be a question of finding the Ropemaker without Maja's help. That's going to be the hardest bit.'

'It would kill her to bring her back, even for a few moments?' said Ribek.

'Yes.'

'All right,' said Ribek. 'Let's sleep on it.'

'Not until we've said thank you to Benayu,' said Saranja. 'He's done absolute wonders for us today. Back at my war-lord's they'd have held a feast and filled his cup with rubies and had the poet compose a praise-chant.'

'At least he did get oyster-and-bacon pie,' said Ribek. 'Even if he had to fetch it himself.'

So now they were all asleep, people, horses, dog. All except Maja. Ribek had wished her good night and kissed her forehead and laid her beside him on the rolled-up cloak he used as a pillow. She couldn't see him, couldn't feel if he was actually touching her, but she could hear the steady whisper of his breathing close beside her, and that was enough.

He began to dream. She knew that because she caught faint glimpses of what he was dreaming about, a large dim space with heavy sacks stacked against one wall – it must be his mill. He was looking for someone or something. His breathing changed, became heavier, and now, still in the same dim place, he was leaning on a rail, desperate with worry and loss, staring down into a torrent of foaming water tumbling into a series of scoops attached to the rim of a great wooden wheel that was turning, turning . . . Something soft and green floated for a moment in the pother in one of the scoops, then was carried down into the mill-race. Loss and grief like a spear in the heart . . .

'Ribek! It's all right. I'm here, me, Maja, on the pillow beside you.'

He snorted and half woke. She heard him turn towards her. His breathing faltered as fragments of the nightmare returned and trailed away.

I'll wait till he's stopped dreaming, she thought. *Jex never came to me in the middle of a dream. But he really minded. Only it probably doesn't mean what I'd like it to. He'd feel like that about a pet dog, or something.* She lay there, perfectly happy, thinking about what she was going to say.

His breathing steadied and slowed. She counted fifty breaths. Now.

She started carefully.

'Ribek.'

'*Maja? I was dreaming about you.*'

'Good, we can hear each other when you're asleep. We couldn't before. It was maddening. I kept yelling to you to turn me round when the dragon was chasing us so I could see what was happening, and sometimes you did, so I wasn't sure you couldn't hear me some of the time.'

387

'No. I just had a sudden feeling you'd have wanted to watch if you'd been able to. I suppose I did it for luck, as much as anything. You've brought us luck so far. I don't know . . .'

'Perhaps you just somehow felt what I wanted. Anyway I saw almost everything. Benayu was wonderful. And Sponge. Tell me what I look like. I've seen my legs, so I know I'm a rag doll.'

'*Cute. No substitute for the real thing, mind you, but nice and light and easy to carry around. You look reasonably like yourself too, apart from the blue eyes.*'

Now or never. No way she'd be able to do it when she was back in her own shape, speaking the words aloud. Don't rush it. Start gently, somewhere else.

'What happened back at the oyster pond? I was in the water. I think you got hold of my wrist and were helping me down, but I couldn't see anything or feel anything except the fire line I was following. Then everything went black.'

'*Like I said. We'd reached the bottom but your hand was like a dog pulling on a leash. You weren't doing it yourself. Your arm would've been completely limp, except that it was being dragged down by your hand. It pushed on down between the oysters into the gravelly stuff and then – you saw me trying to touch Benayu's eggshell earlier?*'

'Yes.'

'*It was like what happened to me, only a hundred times more so. My own arm went numb. I saw the breath bursting out of your mouth so I had a quick grope with my other hand and found the bit of rope and*

388

hauled you up to the surface. I was desperate to get you ashore and tip the water out of you, but the moment I broke the surface I was snatched into the air and deposited on Levanter's back. I seemed to have lost you somehow. So I started yelling to Benayu to turn back and find you, but then I realized I was holding something and got the water out of my eyes and saw what it was.

'You looked absolutely pitiful and my heart sank, but I just hoped that Benayu and Jex had got it right between them and I stuffed you into my shirt for the moment – I was sopping wet too, remember – and looked to see what we'd found. I hadn't given it a thought till that moment. I could perfectly easily have dropped it in the excitement. My heart sank all over again, but all I could do was shove it into a saddlebag and sort myself out, get hold of the reins, sit properly and so on.

'As soon as I got the chance I looked behind us, but there wasn't anything to see at first because Benayu had made a dense fog over the whole area. It wasn't anything to bother the Watchers, really, he says, though it gave us a few more seconds to get further out over the sea before they swept it away, but that wasn't the point.

'I saw that happen. One moment the fog was there, the next it was thin mist, except for a dense patch over the harbour. Benayu had made that to still be there when the fog was gone. There was a screen round us, he says, but of course I couldn't see that. And down at the harbour he'd built a good strong ward round a flock of sheep waiting to be shipped, and then "sent" them –

that's the opposite of fetching – somewhere up the coast. And he'd put it into the poor old Magister's head that he'd seen us heading off in that direction. That was part of his false trail, like the extra bit of fog.

'Anyway, what I saw looked like a ripple of sunlight sweeping up from the south and rolling the mist away in front of it. A bit of the mist seemed to stay round us, enough to hide us from the shore, I guess, but I could just make out the Magister standing by the oyster pond staring back towards Barda. Six or seven Watchers appeared out of nowhere – they all looked exactly like that one who came to the way station. The oyster pool exploded. The Magister fell flat on his face. Everything in the pool fountained up into the air and rained down through a glittering net, which I guessed was there to sieve out anything magical in the pool.

'Then the Magister was stood up like a doll – sorry about that – no offence meant – and just dropped after a couple of moments, and the Watchers disappeared. They must have gone down to the harbour because there was a colossal explosion and a swirling dark cloud which was sucked up into the sky and just vanished.

'By this time I was absolutely shuddering with cold. I was still wearing my wet clothes, and the wind was whistling past at the speed Levanter was going. The only thing that stopped me freezing solid was a bit of warmth coming up from him through my legs. Having you dangling against my chest, sodden as a sponge, wasn't helping, so I fished you out and squeezed the water out of you best I could and cleaned you up with

390

a dry shirt out of my saddlebag and hung you round my neck . . .'

Now!

'Before you did that you kissed me, didn't you? Not on my forehead, like last night. In the middle of my face. On my mouth.'

'Well . . . I just felt like it. I'm fond of you. I didn't realize you'd notice. Your face is a small target and there was a lot going on. I didn't take careful aim. I'm sorry.'

'I'm not, except that I couldn't feel it. I want to marry you when I'm old enough. What do you think?'

Long pause. She'd got it all wrong, and plunged right in. If she'd been in her own body she'd have been plumred with embarrassment. Poor Ribek.

'You don't have to answer. It probably isn't a fair question.'

'I was thinking how to put it. The answer is no, but it isn't as simple as that.'

'No, it's all right. You don't have to explain.'

'I want to. I've been thinking about it, because I was aware you might have feelings like this. Nothing to be ashamed about. It happens. But if I had the same feelings about someone your age I'd be sick in my head. I knew a chap once, farmer, used to bring his wheat to the mill . . .'

Another pause.

'Go on.'

'All I'll tell you is that when I found out what had happened I told him he was sick in his head and he could take his wheat somewhere else to be ground. He would have been better dead.'

'I wasn't talking about me now. I said, "When I'm old enough." Suppose I was six years older . . .'

'*Make it eight. I'd be fifty-two.*'

'I don't mind how old you are.'

'*I do. I've seen what can happen. When I was sixteen my sister married a farmer from down the valley. She was three years older than me, and he was a bit past fifty. That's about two years more than the gap between you and me. He was a big, strong, friendly man – we all liked him. Five years later he had a stroke. The worst of it was that he lived for another twenty-two years, an almost helpless wreck of what he'd been. My sister had the farm to manage, three children to raise, and him to look after night and day. You'll meet her one day and you'll see she looks a good twenty years older than I do. Two of the three girls don't want anything to do with her. They feel that between them their parents managed to blight their own childhoods . . . oh, my dear. All that good young life my sister should have had, wasted and blasted! I'm not going to do that to you. Or to me. Do you see that? I think it was worse for my brother-in-law than it was for my sister.*'

There wasn't any point in arguing, though Maja could think of plenty of arguments, but not now. Perhaps if she talked to his sister. For the moment it was enough that he'd really been thinking about it. Even that was more than she'd hoped for. Best thing now was to make it easy for him.

'It's a good thing for you I can't cry, or you'd be having to wring me out again.'

'*There's that.*'

'How much younger would you have to be, d'you think? Five years? Ten? Fifteen?'

'Ten at least. But . . .'

'. . . and if you tell me about this nephew you've got who's only sixteen and the spit image of you at that age . . .'

'How did you know?'

He was teasing, of course. He'd already told her he had just five nieces, two living at the mill plus the three he'd been talking about. But so was she. Why couldn't he see it? They were so right for each other. *Not now. Change the subject.*

'This is only a dream, isn't it? We won't talk about it when I've changed back.'

'Right. Thank you, Maja.'

'Wait. There's something I do want you to talk about. To the others, I mean. It's about one of us getting outside the eggshell. Ask Jex and Benayu if I'm a sort of magical animal, like Sponge and the horses.'

'No!'

'Or if I'm not, can they make me into one?'

'Absolutely not! It would kill you.'

'You can ask them about that too, and then we can decide. There are five of us, so Jex can have the casting vote if he wakes up. You've got to ask them, Ribek. It isn't fair if you don't, because I can't talk to them myself. You can tell them what you think, of course, but you've got to tell them what I think too. I'll be listening, remember, and if you don't play fair I'll get into your dreams and give you horrible, horrible nightmares.'

'If they let you go I'll be in one already.'

393

'It's what I'm here for, to find the Ropemaker. It's why I'm like this now. I'm still the only one who can do it, the way I did in the sheepfold and the oyster beds. It's all meant.'

'All right. We'll see what the others say.'

Chapter 17

B Y MORNING JEX had recovered enough to talk and listen so he was there when Ribek told the others about that part of the conversation over breakfast (oyster kedgeree). He put Maja's case fairly enough but then argued so passionately against it that she wondered whether the others might guess something about the part of the conversation he hadn't told them.

'I don't like it either,' said Saranja. 'She's been wasting away as it is, despite what Jex has been doing for her. It all depends whether there's anything else we can try first. If there isn't, then it's a question of whether Jex and Benayu think they can actually do what Maja suggests. But if it's our only chance then I think we've got to let her try. Benayu?'

'I don't know. I hadn't thought of doing it like that. Out of the top of my head I think it might be possible, not quite the way she says because a rag doll is four-dimensional and she wouldn't survive like that. So she'd have to do something like the Ropemaker must have done and put herself into a different form for the other universe . . .'

'Could you protect her at all while that's happening, Jex?' said Ribek.

'*No more than partly. And remember that she would also need to endure the stress of following the line left by the Ropemaker's hair when his name is spoken by one of you. Both the previous times that that has happened she has been very near the limit of what she can stand.*'

'Then that's out,' said Saranja and Ribek together but in different tones.

'Anything else?' Saranja added. 'I mean, could you move the eggshell about, for instance?'

'Not a hope . . . But . . . Wait . . . I think there's just a possibility . . . If we combine that with Maja's idea . . . It's going to take a lot of thinking. Pure brain stuff, like I said. No short cuts. And I'll still need to talk to Jex. I wish Fodaro was here . . .'

'*Do not forget that I also exist on the other side of your eggshell. I do not understand the equations, but I may still be useful.*'

'We wouldn't have a hope without you. Let's talk about it when I've finished eating.'

The morning passed slowly. When breakfast was over Ribek propped Maja into the crook of a small tree, where she could see almost everything that happened inside the eggshell. Then he brought the saddlebags across, unpacked their contents on to the turf, spread the bedding out to air and sorted and repacked everything else.

Saranja groomed the horses, combed their manes and tails, cleaned a small cut in Pogo's hock – and goodness, did he make a fuss about it! – and checked the harness. The horses preened their wings with their front teeth as far as they could reach, and then took turns to spread them so that the other two could finish the job. They did this as naturally as if they'd had wings all their lives. So did Sponge, though with his more flexible neck he didn't need help.

When Ribek had finished he settled to sleep against the rim of the pool, close to where Benayu sat gazing into the depths of the still water as if he could read the answers to his equations in them. Jex squatted opposite him on the stonework. Maja could sense the murmur of his stone voice in her mind, in much the same way that she could faintly hear the rhythm of what Benayu was saying without being able to distinguish the individual words.

After a long while Benayu rose, stirred Sponge with his foot, lifted Jex down onto the turf and all three came across to Maja's tree. In the normal course of events Jex didn't move about much, but when he chose to he did it with an easy, fluid motion, unexpected in so clumsy-looking an animal. Ribek looked up, saw what was happening and called to Saranja, who came across too.

'You talk to Maja, Jex, and I'll explain to the others,' said Benayu and turned to meet them. Jex spoke in Maja's head.

'*Maja?*'

'Yes. How are you getting on?'

'*There is something we would like to try, but all this is unknown territory. The difficulty is that what we are thinking of will become inoperative if I shield you, and you will also need to be to some degree sensitive to external magic if you are to follow the trail to the Ropemaker. So you will have to tell me the moment you feel that it is becoming too much for you.*'

'All right. What do you want me to do?'

'*Benayu believes that he can construct a much smaller version of what you have been calling the eggshell, just large enough to contain you and therefore light enough to be transported. The form in which I exist in the universe outside the eggshell is largely sedentary, like a sea anemone in your universe. In that form I can, after some preparation, relocate myself over considerable distances. Indeed, I have only a short while ago arrived immediately outside the eggshell, which will make the transfer of large magical impulses between the universes very much easier for me.*

'*But I cannot follow a trail, as you will need to, to an unknown destination, nor relocate other objects with me except by swallowing them. We doubt whether Benayu's eggshell would survive the strength of my digestive juices. Our solution is that the dog should carry you, since, being a magical animal, he can exist in both universes.*

'*The problem then—*'

He stopped abruptly and became stone. Something like an immense but soundless explosion battered against the eggshell. Maja couldn't feel it, but she saw

398

the ground judder, and the whole enclosure seemed to heave around as the tree in which she was seated swayed violently to and fro. The stone mermaid toppled into the pool. The horses squealed and reared, wrenching at their tethers and spreading their wings for panic flight. Weird rainbow lights swirled across the surface of the eggshell. Benayu was on his feet, obviously pouring out magical energies but Maja was impervious to them in her doll form. Saranja was shouting to Ribek to come and help with the horses.

Slowly the turmoil stilled.

'Trouble?' said Ribek mildly.

'The Watchers have found the touching point,' said Benayu. 'That was their first shot at breaking through my barrier. I reckon they'll have suffered, but it was much sooner than I'd expected. Much stronger too. They're not going to give up. I was wrong. I think they might make it after all. I'll do something about the horses, like I did yesterday, in case it happens again.'

'How long have we got?' said Saranja.

'I don't know. But we can't afford to hang about. Where've you got to, Jex? Jex!'

The stone Jex flipped back into its living form.

'Let me try,' Maja told him. 'You want to do something to me so that I can tell Sponge where to go? All right. See if it works. I'll tell you if I can't stand it.'

'*Maja agrees*,' said Jex, speaking now to the others.

'Wait,' said Ribek. 'I accept that nothing that can happen to her here will be as bad as what would happen to her if she fell into the hands of the Watchers. You're sure there's nothing else we can try?'

'I can't think of anything, and nor can Jex,' said Benayu. 'This is by far the best chance we've come up with.'

'All right,' said Ribek. 'You're going to hang her round Sponge's neck, I suppose. I'll do that when you're ready.'

'This is only a trial,' said Benayu. 'I'll set Sponge up first, and then I'll do her as gently as I can. Jex will keep in touch, so she can stop the process whenever she wants. If that goes all right she can try guiding Sponge around in here. No point in building the little egg if that doesn't work, and it's going to take a bit of time, in any case.'

Ribek grunted and lifted Maja down from the tree. He settled himself down with his back against the trunk. She could just see the back of his right hand across her legs, holding her steady in the crook of his left arm.

'Might as well be comfortable while we're waiting,' he said. 'See all right? Start telling you the rest of "The Demon Baker" while we're waiting, shall I? I need to take my mind off things just as much as you do. More, probably.'

It didn't really work. For the first time since she'd known him he let her see how worried he really was. The natural little pauses that storytellers use to sort out in their minds what comes next kept stretching into longer gaps, and then he'd shake himself, say 'Sorry,' and go on with the story. Maja didn't mind. She was aware of being strangely unscared, for someone who had always thought of herself as timid, by what she was soon going to have to try to do. The fact that Ribek really cared about her took up most of her attention.

So she half listened to the story while she watched what Benayu was doing by the pool. He spent some while kneeling with Sponge sitting opposite him. At first he simply cradled Sponge's head in his hands, looking into his eyes and muttering. Then he asked Saranja to fetch one of Maja's human socks and gave it to Sponge to sniff. He told Sponge to stay where he was, fetched a handful of soil from the rose bed and dribbled it in a thin stream all the way round Sponge, muttering as he did so.

He was halfway round when another silent explosion battered against the eggshell, but his hand didn't falter. As soon as the circle was completed it began to glow with a steady pale light, not bright but still visible in the sunless daylight. He straightened, squared his shoulders like someone momentarily easing powerful inward tension, looked briefly round at the eggshell, where the swirls of strange light that had followed the explosion were still dying away, and came across to the pool.

'We're going to have to speed things up,' he said. 'I think that was only a try-out. I took them by surprise first time, and they didn't get a chance to study what I'd done and start working out how I'd done it. They'll try something different next time and I'd better be ready for it. I don't want to be still messing around with this.

'You're going to have to be able to see what's happening outside your little eggshell, Maja, and there's no way I can let you see through it without weakening it fatally, so you're going to have to see everything through

Sponge's eyes. Of course he's seeing in seven dimensions, but his brain does its best to switch them into four, as far as it can. It doesn't bother him, but you'll find it pretty confusing.

'I'm telling you that now because you'll be testing the connection here, inside the big eggshell, in our ordinary four dimensions. You won't find out what it's like till you're on the outside. Ready? Just hang her round Sponge's neck, Ribek.'

Again the scene swung and tilted as Ribek carried her across the lawn and knelt just outside the circle of pale light. She was facing him now. He was doing his best to smile through his anxiety as he eased her loop over Sponge's neck. He stood and moved back. Benayu took his place and reached towards her with both hands. She couldn't feel his touch or see what he was doing, but she guessed it was the same sort of thing he'd been doing to Sponge, because almost at once something started to happen inside her.

It had the familiar tingle of magic, which she hadn't felt at all in her rag-doll shape despite everything that had been going on around her. It started slowly, becoming steadily stronger, but with nothing like the dizzying impact of powerful magic happening outside herself that she'd learnt to bear in her true Maja form.

'All right so far?' asked Benayu. 'Tell Jex if you're not . . . Now I'm going to make the connection. I've only done it for myself before, and with you as you are . . . well, it's a bit tricky. Here goes.'

He rose and stood. She could just see his feet, with an arc of the glowing circle running close in front of them.

The glow became stronger, rose, moved inward and passed out of her vision. But now she could feel it, not as though it was touching her on the outside, but moving up inside her body, so that as it passed over her she began to feel for the first time since Ribek had carried her out of the oyster pool where the bits of that body were – something she'd felt all of her life without noticing, knowing the position of each of her hands and feet, even with her eyes shut.

So now she could tell where Sponge's four paws – *her* paws – were, and actually feel the pressure of the ground on her hindquarters where she sat with her tail curled round to her right . . .

The glow passed over her eyes, too bright for her to see anything but the weave of the fabric on which they were painted, but after a few moments it changed to a darker colour and then faded and she was seeing again, only very differently from either of the ways she had seen before, Maja or doll. The colours had changed, become much duller. The whole rose bed was now various tones of browny-green, with a few pale blobs and patches to show which were the white flowers, while the darker and browner bits might be the red ones. She couldn't tell from their shapes which of the rest were leaves or flowers they seemed to fade into each other.

On the other hand she could smell all their intense individual scents, and could at the same time tell that the enjoyable reek of the dollop of horse-dung behind her on the other side of the pool had been dropped there by Levanter.

'Still all right?' said Benayu (wonderful, godlike Benayu) in a curiously deep voice.

She hadn't really thought about it, because the change had been all-absorbing, but, yes, the magic was still there, twice as strong now, half of it coming from within her and half from outside, two steady powerful vibrations which might well have been too much for her if they hadn't balanced each other so well, like the two pillars of an archway, each of which can only stand and bear the weight above it because the other one is there.

'Tell him, yes, I think so, Jex. It depends what else happens. Shall I try and get Sponge to do something?'

'Try not to think of it like that,' said Benayu, when Jex had relayed the message. 'I don't tell my hand to scratch my ear – I just do it. So it'll be you doing it, with Sponge's body. You'll get used to it. On his own he'd sit there all morning until I told him he could get up. I'm not going to, and you couldn't make him break that rule simply by telling him to get up. He's sort of dormant. He thinks he's dreaming all this. So you're going to have to break it yourself. Just see how it goes.'

It wasn't as difficult as it sounded. *It isn't a rule for me*, she thought and got up, and then for a while did whatever the body wanted without thinking, eased her muscles after all that sitting by reaching forward with her front legs and then transferring her weight on to them so that her back legs stretched luxuriously out behind her. She unfolded her wings and resettled them, scratched under her chin with her right hind leg and looked around. *What next? Ribek, of course. Give him a good lick to show him how much I love him. Oh, nice!*

404

'That's enough, Maja,' he said, trying to push her away. 'That's *enough*!'

No, it wasn't. She might never get another chance. Somebody was laughing. She stopped licking and looked over her shoulder. Saranja and Benayu, both of them, looking as if for the moment they'd totally forgotten the urgency and danger of what they were all four trying to do. She realized that she'd never seen or heard Saranja laughing before. It was an odd sound, almost a guffaw, the strangeness enhanced by her own strange dog-hearing. She realized without any embarrassment or shame that they were both well aware of her besottedness. Had been, probably, for a long time. Never mind. She had another good lick.

'Now stop it!' said Ribek again, struggling with his own laughter. 'That's enough, I tell you, Maja! Can't you see you're making Benayu jealous?'

She broke off and trotted over to Benayu, lifting her left wing so that she could rub her flank against his knee without it getting in the way, to show him that she knew perfectly well where Sponge's own affections belonged. He bent and teased the sensitive area behind her ear. *That's nice too*, she thought. *Something you miss, being a human.*

'So far so good,' said Benayu. 'You've obviously got the idea. But that's all dog stuff. Try doing something Sponge wouldn't normally do.'

The pool was close beside her. She skipped up on to the coping of the wall, but it turned out to be narrower than she'd thought and she had to spread her wings for balance or she'd have toppled in. Once steady she

405

trotted round the rim, still using her wings for balance, hopped down and sat where Sponge had been sitting in the first place.

'All right,' said Benayu. 'It's not going to be so easy outside, mind you, and I can't help you as I've never been there myself. It isn't just that there'll be strange things there. You'll be seeing them strangely. They won't fit together the way you're used to. It'll look something like the bit in your story where Faheel destroyed the Watchers. I'll give you a few minutes to get used to that, and then I'll send a warning pulse, so you can count to ten and be ready when Saranja says the name. Then it'll be up to you. If anything goes wrong just think *Home* and Sponge will bring you back.

'Assuming you manage to follow the trail, I don't know what you're going to find or what to do about it when you find it. You may have to come back and tell me and I'll try and work something out. Probably your best bet is to say the Ropemaker's name again. You can't actually say it out loud, so you'll just have to think it as hard as you can.

'Now you've got a bit of time while I make your eggshell. Don't worry about not touching it. It's going to be small enough for me to put a kind of four-dimensional lining into it. Any other questions you come up with I'll try and sort out when it's ready.'

Ribek was still sitting against the tree, so she trotted over and lay down with her head in his lap. His hand teased gently at her ears. *Lovely, lovely. This stupid adventure is just an interruption*, she thought. *Perhaps when it's over he could get himself a cute puppy, and*

406

Benayu could put me into it, and I could be his dog. That would be better than nothing, a lot better. And at least it wouldn't matter then that he's so much older than I am. We'd be growing old together and I'd probably die first. We wouldn't be able go back to Northbeck, though, because that sort of thing doesn't work in the Valley.

'Don't you want to watch what Benayu's doing?' he said.

Not if it means stopping doing this. He must have guessed her thought.

'Shift round so you can see, shall I?'

They resettled comfortably, but there wasn't much to see because Benayu was kneeling. At the moment he was kneeling with his back towards her in the gap in the hedge beyond the rose beds, close to the shell of the egg. His head was bowed over some object he seemed to be holding between his hands, judging by the position of his elbows. His shoulders heaved regularly as if he was taking a series of deep breaths, or more likely blowing onto or into whatever he was holding.

At length he rose and turned, and she was able to see that he did indeed have an egg-shaped something about the size of a man's head floating between his hands without their quite touching it.

'Sponge! Maja!' he called, urgency in his voice. 'Come over here. Hurry. I haven't got it quite right. Some of our air is getting through to the surface, and it won't stand a lot of that.'

She let her body react instantly to its own name and was with him before he'd finished speaking. Close up

407

she could see that the surface of the egg was sprinkled with come-and-go sparks of light – tiny bits of air getting through to it and exploding against it, she guessed, and nibbling away at it as they did so.

'Good boy – I mean girl,' he said. 'This is the tricky bit, for you, Maja, as well as me. I'm going to have to tinker with your rag-doll shield a bit so that you'll be able to sense the trail. No one's ever done this sort of stuff before, so I'm just going to have to guess. I won't be able to do that once you're inside the eggshell. But what I'll be doing is fairly powerful stuff close up to you, about as much as you can bear, I should think, and you're going to have to keep old Sponge absolutely stock-still while it's happening. If you kneel that side, Ribek, you can hold his collar with one hand and use your other to keep Maja steady. No, put your fingers together round her cord, close against her head, and keep the rest of your hand as high as you can. That's better.

'And as soon as I've sealed you in, Maja – you'll feel that because the magic will mostly stop and Ribek will let go of your collar – get up and go and nose your way out through the main eggshell as if you were nosing a door open.

'Ready, everyone? Off we go.'

He knelt and held the egg only a few inches in front of her dog nose, then bowed his head and began to blow on it, a series of slow, deep breaths. Through her dog eyes she watched a hollow appear in the top, which deepened and deepened as though the shell was folding in onto itself without becoming any smaller, until it was

408

like the empty shell of a boiled egg. He lowered it out of sight of her dog vision, but she could still watch its shadowy shape pass downward in front of her faint doll vision, now that those eyes were seeing it separately. Then the other side of it moved upward, nearer, as the shell enclosed her.

'So far, so good,' said Benayu. 'Now I'm going to unshield you. Let go of her, Ribek, but hang on to the collar. Ready?'

The impulse came not as a violent blow nor a piercing thrust but as a sudden intense pressure, a pattern of innumerable strands that ignored the fabric and stuffing of her doll form and closed round her inward self and squeezed her yet further inward, smaller and smaller . . .

She willed herself into utter stillness, not fighting or wrestling against it but simply resisting it, refusing to allow herself to be squeezed out of existence, though by now all there was left of Maja seemed no larger than a single droplet in a haze of fine drizzle. *But it's all here,* she thought. *Everything. Not just me, Maja. Two whole universes, the one I've known all my life – Woodbourne and the Valley, the Empire and all its cities, all its marvels and magicians, the Pirates and their far country, the whole world, and the stars beyond the sun and moon – and the unknown universe I'm about to enter.*

Sustained by that knowledge, she endured until the pressure eased, and all that she had gathered in flowed out again beyond her and became itself again. She could still feel the magical pressure, but with little more discomfort now than she might have felt from too-tight clothing. She must be still inside the egg, she realized, because all that she could see though her doll eyes was the bluish weave of her eye-fabric against a vague pearly background.

But Benayu was there in front of her dog eyes, looking anxious but at the same time more relaxed.

'That's all,' he said. 'See if you can still talk to Jex.'

'Jex? Can you hear me?'

'Faintly, but well enough. Are you all right?'

'Yes. It was hard for a bit, but it's better now. Will I still be able to talk to you from outside the big eggshell?'

'Not to me in here, we think, but I will also be there outside, in my other form, so we should be able to continue to converse until you set off on your mission. You will find it difficult to see me at first, but your dog nose should be able to smell me since it is not dimension-dependent in the way that sight is, and I presumably smell much the same in both my forms. You are familiar with my odour?'

Of course she was, now. She hadn't noticed it before, since it was too faint for human nostrils, but for Sponge's nose almost everything had its own odour. Jex smelt a bit like old sheep-droppings mixed with pine needles, a pleasant, homely smell to a sheepdog, but she didn't like to say so.

'I'm sure I'll know you, then.'

'Good. You had better leave now, before your shell weakens any further.'

'All right. Say goodbye to them for me.'

She allowed herself the last luxury of leaping up to put her paws on Ribek's shoulders and lick his face once more. He didn't resist. His fingers teased gloriously up

410

and down her spine. She dropped, wagging her tail, turned to the outer eggshell and pushed firmly into it. There was a sharp tingling in her nose, making her sneeze violently. She closed her eyes before the tingling reached them as she pushed on. Her fur stood up stiffly the moment it reached the barrier, and the tingling flowed on down the skin beneath it, a strange feeling, too intense for pleasure but still just less than pain. It had reached her ribcage by the time her muzzle emerged on the far side.

Chapter 18

S HE OPENED HER eyes in a truly different
universe.

It made no sense at all. There was stuff out there
to look at, but far too much of it, and none of it seeming to fit with anything else. Bits of it appeared to have
some kind of shape, bulges and edges and planes, but
they didn't fit together into anything she could think of
as a *thing*. And all of it seemed to be moving, flowing,
but she couldn't tell in which direction or what was
nearer her than what was further off, because it seemed
both near and far, and the whole scene was criss-crossed
with dark lines, tense as winched cables, connecting one
non-thing to another, but not seeming to slacken at all if
the non-things moved together or to resist at all if they
wheeled apart, or did both at the same time.

Odder still was that, though the lines seemed to be
more understandable, more real, more *there*, than the
non-things they connected, and to carry such tension

412

within them, she wasn't sure that they were real, or there at all. They were like narrow beams, not of light but of darkness, full of intangible energies.

She felt helpless, crazy. How could she do anything in a world like this?

'Jex! Jex! What's happening? Help!'

'*I am here, little one. Come fully clear of the eggshell. That is confusing you. Good. Now move to your left. Trust your dog senses to make the movement, since his brain is adapted to interpret the phenomena of this universe. Use his smell sense in particular, since it is not dimension-dependent. Simply by moving through the phenomena of this universe you will begin to perceive it more clearly. I will wave my arms as you approach, to help you. To you I will seem to be something like a dead tree.*'

'All right. I'll try.'

She moved out of the eggshell and automatically gave herself a good shaking, as if she'd just come from a dip in a pond and was shaking the water out of her pelt. That done, she raised her muzzle and sniffed. She'd been trying so hard to see that she hadn't paid much attention to her other senses, but yes, this universe was full of smells. They were odd, weird, different, but not incomprehensibly different the way the sights were. Without her thinking about it her dog brain was already sorting them out. There! Slightly different from his smell in his other form but still unmistakably Jex. Sheep-droppings and pine. To her left, like he'd said.

Find, boy.

Her dog body trotted eagerly off, at last in this long

adventure doing something it had been trained to do. Sponge had known every sheep in his flock by its separate smell, Benayu had once told her. Sheep droppings and pine needles – pup's play. And even as she moved among the no-things of this no-sense universe they began to acquire their own crazy logic. She wasn't seeing them as they actually were, she realized – as the this-universe form of Jex saw them, for instance. Her brain wasn't the right shape. She wasn't even seeing them as Sponge saw them. The images that came to all three pairs of eyes (supposing this Jex had two eyes) were the same, but Jex's brain could process them in seven dimensions, and Sponge's brain could magically process them into four, but hers hadn't learnt to do that yet. Jex had told her that actually she'd be seeing them somewhere along that process, or she wouldn't have been able to see them at all.

Once again she was reminded of the story in the Valley about the woman who'd been blind all her life and suddenly began to see, who could perceive the shape and colour of a mug, for instance, but couldn't at first tell that it was a mug until she'd touched and handled it. She was just beginning to do that. Distances were still very strange. The no-things could seem to be both behind and in front of each other. A bit of the edge of one could turn out on its other surface to be a bit of the edge of a quite different one.

She wondered if the strange rays of darkness connecting the no-things were where Sponge's brain had put the extra dimensions, so that it had only four to deal with, though the rays didn't really fit with each other now.

Even when she seemed to be loping towards one that barred her way it was somewhere else when she reached it, without having moved or lost its tension.

A new no-thing loomed in front of her, clear enough to be almost a thing – a dead tree with wildly waving branches, except that the branches moved both behind and in front of each other and some of them might be off to one side, or the trunk itself, though still attached to them, was somehow much further away. For a moment she saw it clearly, and with a shock of horror realized that it must indeed be some kind of distant cousin to the appalling demon that had so nearly destroyed them all, north of Larg. She had to will herself to speak to it.

'Jex?'

'*Welcome, little one. I wish I were seeing you in your own form. You have done very well yet again.*'

The voice in her head wasn't the granite one she knew so well, but had the quality of good timber, cut from a great tree and then sawn and planed to show the clean, smooth grain. She thought of the mighty cedars in the forest behind Woodbourne, whose voices her aunt had been able to hear when the wind stirred their branches. The memory banished the spectre of the vanquished demon.

'I wish I could see you properly too. I'm very fond of you in your other shape. You've really looked after me.'

'*The affection is reciprocated. But are you ready to go, Maja? It is now of some urgency. I can sense that our enemies are preparing a more sophisticated assault.*

415

I have told the others, and Benayu is ready, but he needs to have you on your way before the attack begins.'

'Yes, I think so.'

A pause. Then . . .

'I have told them. You will feel a brief pulse of magic, and then Saranja will count to ten and say the name.'

'All right.'

The pulse came almost at once, brief and blinding as lightning, and then was gone. She held herself steady and started to count.

. . . nine, ten . . .

And there was total darkness, with the trail blazing through it. Only that single dimension of distance. She was barely aware even of Sponge's physical solidity enclosing her as she spread her wings and raced along the trail. Its power was appalling, not shaped and controlled by some magician to a specific purpose, but a shaft of pure magic. It was like the light of the sun must be before it strikes the atmosphere of earth and softens into daylight. She felt herself shrivelling in its intensity, wasting away. She was at the limit of what she could endure.

Not long now, please!

Oh, finish, end!

Ramdatta!

Darkness. The trail gone with its unendurable power. Gone. Lost.

No, it was she who was lost and gone. The trail would still be there, skewering its seven-dimensional universe, but there was no one to follow it. Nobody now could. Benayu couldn't. The Watchers might break through and overwhelm him, but they couldn't either. Only she, Maja, could have done it and she had failed.

Ramdatta!

Nothing. Not a quiver of change in the emptiness.

Thinking the name wasn't enough. To be truly powerful it had to be spoken aloud. If only Saranja had been here instead of her, to cry it into the void, as she had done on the hill above Tarshu.

But here there was only a useless rag doll, with no lips to shape the syllables, no lungs to give them their power. Only a useless rag doll . . .

. . . and a dog . . .

Sponge.

'*Try doing something Sponge wouldn't normally do.*'

Somehow she forced herself into awareness of him, of Sponge himself, not just of his body as an extension of herself. He was still there, patient and accepting of what was happening to him, but at the same time vaguely bewildered by it all, and longing for Benayu, with a grassy hillside and a flock of sheep to herd.

Good boy, she thought, trying to comfort him. *Won't be long now.*

Three syllables, then. Three sharp yaps. A bit of a growl at the start of the first one to make the R shouldn't be too difficult, and then . . .

She experimented, moving the long tongue round inside the narrow mouth, touching it against palate and front teeth in various positions, trying to imagine the explosion of the yap forcing its way through. Nothing was the right shape. Her lips wouldn't make the M. The closest she could come was a sort of humming noise in her throat . . .

It's all right. Good boy . . .

She raised her muzzle.

'RRAGHnng! dhAGH! dtAGH!'

The fierce, urgent bark shattered the immense silence into shards and fragments. In the selfsame instant those particles were reborn into unnumberable universes, exactly as they had been before. And in that instant Maja was caught up and whirled away, back on to the trail and shuddering under its ferocious power.

But now she was at the longed-for end. The trail reached it and stopped. She hovered for a moment, staring at the object, bewildered. It was utterly unexpected, but yes, of course. If this was the only way to do it, then this was how he must have done it.

A four-dimensional thing hanging above the shadowy landscape of no-things.

Another egg.

Unable to hover for more than two or three wing-beats she began to circle, and found that once she was round the other side it screened her completely from the intense input of the trail. No impulse whatever came from the egg itself. She backed away a little until she could circle in that shelter, studying the thing.

It was about the size of the one she was in, and it had the same odd solid-mist surface, but rougher, as if it hadn't been shaped out of something smooth, like a clay pot, but had been woven or knitted from fine cord. One bright point of mauvish light was moving across it, trailing a short glowing tail, like a comet. It moved out of sight on one side and reappeared, crossing the surface at a different angle this time, and again, and again, once more at a different angle. It was oddly hypnotic. It meant something.

I was wrong, she thought. *This wasn't the only way he could have done it, if that's him in there. Jex told us that he thought he must have put the essence of himself into a creature of this universe, and then he could have gone where he liked and done what he wanted and the seven dimensions wouldn't have mattered. Benayu could have done that too, he'd said, if it had only been him. It would have been much easier than making the eggs, but he couldn't do it because he had to bring the rest of us so that the Watchers couldn't get us.*

That means that the Ropemaker must have needed to bring someone or something from our universe with him. Something small. And he'd made himself small too so that his egg wasn't too big to move about.

Round and round, round and round, round and round as she thought it out. She found that she'd unconsciously started to time her circlings so that she was facing the egg each time the light crossed its surface. Round and round, round and round, round and round. She couldn't stop. She wasn't doing it. The light was doing it to her. Round and round . . .

It was like . . . like . . .

Something horrible. Some old nightmare, just beginning . . .

No, not a nightmare. Real.

She and Ribek, Saranja and Benayu, all walking in

419

step along the Highway north of Larg, because the demon was forcing them to do it.

But the light wasn't horrible. It was trapped too in the egg, going round and round and round because it had to, making her do the same not because it wanted to but just because it was there.

The Ropemaker, trapped, helpless, in his own egg.

She didn't need to think what to do next. She drew a deep breath of the strange seven-dimensional air into her lungs, raised her muzzle, and bayed.

'RRAGHnng! dhAGH! dtAGH!'

If she'd been expecting anything it was that the eggshell would shatter, but instead the light began to spin faster and faster round its surface and the comet-tail remained behind it longer and longer, covering the surface in a net of lines that joined together into an intricate dense mesh. A moment or two and the last gaps closed and she was staring at a shell of glowing light . . .

The egg hung there, bright enough to cast dense, wrong-shaped shadows over the landscape of no-things as far as her dog eyes could see. And at the same time the compelled rhythm of her own circlings was broken and she could swing round to the far side of the egg and watch the trail she had followed streaming into it, with all its immense power.

Gone.

Once more she circled the egg, watching and waiting.

Relief flooded through her as a voice spoke in her head, quiet but slightly gravelly, and jerky with suppressed energy. *Done it!*

'Thanks. Been waiting for that. Didn't even know I

was waiting. Knew it was a risk, of course. You found my bit of rope, I take it.'

'Yes. In the oyster beds.'

'And you'll be one of the Urlasdaughter lot?'

'I'm Maja. But I've got my cousin Saranja with us – she can hear the cedars – and Ribek Ortahlson.'

'You can't have got here on your own, though. All three from the Valley. No magic there.'

'Benayu did all the magic. He made the eggs.'

'Let's have a look . . . Hm. Nice bit of work. Eggs, you said?'

'There's two of them, this one and a big one. It's near the touching point on Angel Isle. It's too big to move around because he had to bring all four of us and the horses to get us away from the Watchers. They were try-ing to get through the touching point when I came to find you.'

'Can't have that. Better get back. Tell me the rest on the way. You're inside that egg, but you're in control of the dog, right? Did the same sort of thing myself. Used one of the local life forms. Must've got tired of waiting and pushed off. Dog pick this egg up in his mouth, d'you think, if I give him something to get hold of? Doesn't weigh anything. Tell me the rest on the way. Now . . .'

A small area right at the top of the globe sprouted into a mass of bright threads that immediately started to plait themselves together as they rose and became a glowing rope about as thick as her forefinger. When it was a foot or so long it stopped growing, looped itself over and wove its tip neatly into itself about halfway down to make a carrying handle.

'Try that, then.'

She stopped circling, swooped in, snatched up the loop in her jaws and swung away with the second egg dangling beneath.

Where now? This time there was no trail to follow through this meaningless, no-thing world.

'Home, boy. Find Benayu.'

Good old Sponge, she thought, as the strong, confident wing-beats hurtled them though the meaningless maze.

'This Benayu fellow. How old? Since my time, but could still be getting on a bit.'

'No, he's only fourteen or fifteen.'

'Hm! Would've been way beyond me when I was that age. Tricky business, dimensions.'

'His Uncle Fodaro – he's dead now – the Watchers killed him – he worked out the equations. Benayu says he still doesn't understand them, but he knows how to use them.'

'Ah. Thought there'd got to be something like that. Did it trial and error, myself. Not much room for error, mind you. Right. I've got it about the Watchers. Anything else going on?'

'Well, there's the Pirates, I suppose.'

'Always been Pirates. What's new about this lot?'

She was describing the attack on Tarshu when the first blast hit her. One moment she was back in imagination on that bleak hillside, watching the monstrous airboat hovering over the burning city while the lightning played around it, and the next she was tumbling helpless through darkness.

Something caught her, held her, shielded her round, beat her wings for her while she gathered herself together. She was aware of a close presence, inside Sponge's body now, sharing it with her, looking out through the same eyes, seeing the whole muddled scene ahead lit by pulsing and flaring light, brighter even than the glare over Tarshu.

'Sorry. Strong magic does that to me unless I'm shielded. I wasn't, because I had to follow the trail to find you.'

'Right. Better see to that for you. Lot of stuff going to be happening in a minute or two. You take over now?'

'All right. Do you think they've broken through?'

'Looks like it. Should be there in time. Speeded him up a bit. Nice dog.'

The presence withdrew. As before she let Sponge's own instincts and perception pick their way. He was indeed now flying at unbelievable speed, banking almost vertical as he swung and curved his way through the backward-racing no-things, with wing-beats so rapid that they became a blur, like those of a flying insect. And now they were lit not only by the nearing glare of the landscape ahead but by a steadily brightening glow that could only come from the Ropemaker's egg, dangling below her head.

'Up now. Get above them.'

Obediently she climbed into the magical glare, and now from this height she could see Benayu's egg, flaming like a furnace, with all the strange vague colours that had swirled through it and gone at the Watchers' earlier assaults. Around it, circling it completely, lay the body of an immense dark dragon. As Maja watched, it raised its head, and breathed out a single blast of oily orange fire, overwhelming the egg's pale flames and totally engulfing it.

'Down. Straight through. While they're busy.'

Three powerful beats of her wings drove her into the dive, and then she folded them and plunged like a stooping hawk into the heart of the inferno. It had barely begun to singe her fur before she was through and frantically buffeting the air to brake their onrush.

They hit the turf with a thump. The egg she had been carrying in her mouth detached itself, rolled across the turf to where the little rope manikin stood against the rim of the pool, and exploded into human form.

She felt she had known him all her life, though she had seen him only once before, and only in a dream, and then just as a shadowy shape beyond a magical doorway – tall, oddly gawky, with what at first glance seemed to be an unnaturally enormous head but she knew from the story to be an elaborately folded turban.

He glanced around and pointed a finger at her. Her own egg fell apart and a tremor ran through the hitherto insensate body of the doll, without even feeling the change, apart from that she was back in her own true shape, too dazed with weariness to open her eyes. Only someone's arm around her shoulders held her from falling.

'Welcome back,' said Ribek's voice in her ear. 'Nick of time, by the look of it.'

He'd tried to speak lightly, but she could hear the strain in his voice.

'What's happening?'

Before he could answer Saranja shouted a warning. An instant later the ground juddered beneath her. She felt Ribek stagger as he rode the shock wave and held her upright. By the time he'd recovered their balance she seemed to be standing ankle deep in a rushing stream. With an effort she heaved her eyes open.

The beautiful garden was a ruin. The trees were all leaning awry. The perfect turf looked as if it had been rootled through by a gigantic hog. The inner surface of the egg flared and glimmered as it had seemed to do from the outside. The wall of the pool had split apart and its water was sluicing over her feet. The horses, over to her right, were deep in Benayu's magical coma but still with instinct enough to have spread their legs apart and spread their wings to ride the quaking ground. Saranja waited beside them, tense and ready, watching the Ropemaker strolling long-legged towards Benayu . . .

Benayu?

The figure was wearing Benayu's clothes and Sponge was there beside him, teeth bared, hackles raised, poised ready for the word to spring to the attack against whatever came. But the face was no longer that of Benayu, or of any particular human. It was a moon-pale mask like the one Zara had worn on the hillside when she had returned from the destruction of the demon Azarod.

He stood perfectly still, seeming to be floating a little above the ground, so that he didn't even stir as another shock wave juddered across the arena. Nor did the

Ropemaker falter in his stride, but reached him, moved behind him and placed a large, bony hand on either of his shoulders. Benayu crossed his arms over his chest so that his palms covered the Ropemaker's knuckles. There was a moment of stillness and everything changed.

Or rather, it both did and didn't. The garish lights in the eggshell died away as the fabric rapidly repaired itself, but otherwise nothing much happened that Maja could actually see. The trees didn't magically right themselves, the water didn't flow back into the pool, the turf didn't return to its perfect smoothness, but at the same time it was all different. What must have happened, Maja realized, what she would have known for sure if the Ropemaker hadn't mercifully numbed her extra sense (though she wouldn't have survived the experience), was that the turmoil of magical energies that had been throbbing through the egg had now moved outside it, leaving a bubble of sanity and peace within.

Ribek breathed out a long sigh of relief.

'That's a bit better,' he said. 'Couldn't have stood much more of that. At least it gives me some idea of what you have to put up with. How've you got on? Let's have a look at you, then.'

He took her by the shoulders, turned her round and held her at arms' length. The smile of welcome vanished from his face.

'Oh, my . . . dear! What have we done to you?'

'I'm all right. I'm just tired.'

'You are not all right! Look!'

He let go of her shoulder and almost snatched at her wrist as he lifted her hand and arm for her to see.

They weren't hers. They were . . . they were Zara's hand and arm, lying on the counterpane of her bed in the stone cell behind the Council Chamber in Larg. There seemed to be no flesh at all between the sagging ivory skin and the bird-thin bone. With an effort, though it should have weighed nothing at all, she raised her arm further and spread her fingers against the light. Yes, she could see the shadowy shapes of the finger bones through the translucent membrane.

'I'm just tired, so tired,' she muttered, and allowed herself to collapse.

Ribek caught her on the way down, effortlessly scooped her up and cradled her in his arms. She had never seen him looking so grim. She didn't like it.

'And I'm hungry,' she whispered. 'Is there any oyster pie left?'

He managed a smile – for her sake, she guessed – and started to carry her over to the pool. Saranja met them on the way.

'What's happened to . . . Oh, Maja!'

Even Benayu must have heard the horror in her voice, for he turned his head to look. His face was his own now, but it too changed, as Ribek's and Saranja's had, the moment he saw her.

And the Ropemaker was looking at her. She stared back at the narrow, long-chinned face framed by the extraordinary turban – bristling fire-red eyebrows, pale eyes set close together beside the bony nose, all strangely out of place with the wide and mobile mouth. He didn't seem to have aged at all over the centuries, certainly not the way Zara had.

'We've got to get her out of here,' said Benayu. 'She can't stand any more of this, however she's shielded.'

'Sooner the better,' said the Ropemaker. 'Not much we can do here. One more jolt, Maja. Put you to sleep first, eh?'

'I'll be all right. I want to see.'

And to be here, knowing I'm in Ribek's arms, awake and aware, and with him if anything goes wrong and this is the end.

'Tough as they come, these Urlasdaughters. Right. Anything you want to take?'

'We're all packed and ready,' said Saranja.

'Fine. You three take the horses. I'll shift for myself. Line 'em up by the touching point. Moment you hear my voice, go.'

'Where's Jex?' whispered Maja, as Ribek carried her over towards the horses.

'There was more going on than he could cope with, so he turned himself into stone again and I put him in the saddlebag.'

'Oh, look! The Ropemaker's going to turn himself into a lion. That's what he did in the story!'

Craning weakly past Ribek's shoulder she watched with growing excitement as the Ropemaker raised a hand, twitched out a loose end of his turban and with a flick of the wrist sent the intricately woven structure floating into coil after coil of cloth around himself. She never saw what happened to it after that because almost at once it was hidden beneath an immense mane of flame-gold hair, reaching almost to the ground, but then gathering itself back upwards, revealing first four vast

428

animal pads covered in flame-gold fur, then the muscular legs and the solid mass of the body and the skinny tail with a tuft of darker fur at the end. Within two or three heartbeats it had become the bushy mane of an enormous winged lion, big as a barn.

It waited, motionless except for the to-and-fro flicker of its tail tip. Its huge yellow eyes watched while Benayu woke the horses. Saranja held Maja while Ribek mounted Levanter, then passed her up to him and swung herself into Rocky's saddle. Benayu was already up.

'Ready?' he said, and led the way across the crumpled turf and the fallen cypresses. They lined up with the horses' noses almost touching the eggshell. Benayu raised an arm.

'I want to watch what he does,' whispered Maja, and Ribek adjusted his hold to let her see past his shoulder.

The lion swung ponderously away from them and paced towards the further side of the egg. Halfway there it halted and stared slowly around as if it could see through the barrier and was studying something beyond it. It raised its head and roared.

The sound was all there was, filling the universe. The eggshell blazed with light and melted inwards. A few more moments and it would shrink to nothing. But the horses were already airborne and driving into the vague dark opening that led from universe to universe. Now there was only a glimmer from behind, a glimmer that vanished as the body of the lion filled the narrowing gap and burst through.

A pale, faint light, marvellously familiar after all that

strangeness, gleamed ahead. They were gliding peacefully towards it when Maja heard Benayu's shout from ahead.

'Down! It's too narrow!'

A thump and a clatter, and Pogo's squeal of hurt and outrage, and Benayu's voice again.

'Hold it! Let's have some light.'

Immediately the walls of the tunnel glowed, and there was Saranja picking herself up and helping Pogo struggle to his feet and then starting to feel him over – before herself, of course, though she was clearly limping. The floor of the tunnel was strewn with broken boulders and its walls seemed to have been scorched with fire.

'He'll do,' said Saranja. 'Oh, come on, you stupid horse, it could've been a lot worse. What's happened here? It wasn't like this when we came through.'

'That was the Watchers getting through,' said Benayu. 'I told you there'd be an explosion. At least I got one of them.'

He gestured towards what looked like a bundle of charred grey cloth lying among the tumbled rocks. A skeleton hand protruded from between its folds.

'We're going to have to lead the horses, and take it slowly,' said Saranja. 'They're no good on this sort of footing. They're not goats.'

'Wait,' rumbled a deep voice behind them. Maja wriggled herself round and saw the lion's body filling the tunnel. It opened its jaws and blew out a long, slow breath. A warm gale swept along the tunnel, picking them all up, horses, people and dog, and floating them out over a moonlit ocean where the animals could once

430

again stretch their wings and fly. Behind them the tunnel collapsed in thunder.

They rose, circled and landed on the summit of Angel Isle.

Chapter 19

'WAKE UP, MAJA,' said Ribek's voice. 'Benayu wants to know what you'd like for breakfast.'

'Oyster-and-bacon pie,' she mumbled.

'Bit rich for an invalid?'

'I'm not an invalid. I'm just tired. I only want a little to taste.'

'Provided you have some chicken broth first. Your stomach's shrunk too, remember.'

'All right.'

'Good as my grandad made, I'll have what you leave, well as my own,' said the Ropemaker.

'Two oyster-and-bacon pies,' said Benayu's voice. 'One chicken broth, three lots of lamb chops, one raw and two medium-rare, one spiced kidneys. Lime water, ale and coffee. Fodder for the horses. Anything else?'

'Rhubarb and ginger crumble,' said Ribek. 'Milaja Finsdaughter at Frog Bottom does a good one.'

'Coming up. There'll be a ten-minute wait on Saranja's kidneys.'

'They taste best if you can make them disappear from under a war-lord's nose,' said Saranja.

'Look, I've got an Empire to sort out,' said Benayu, obviously delighting in the challenge.

'First things first,' said Ribek.

An extraordinary sense of well-being pervaded the little encampment. They were in a smooth patch of thymy turf ringed by a wall of the jutting rocks of which Angel Isle was made. Maja had seen the place only briefly last night, by the light of the pale glow the Ropemaker, back in his human form and wearing his turban, had shed around him as he had knelt by her side and stared down at her. Now, even with her eyes shut against the morning glare, Maja could hear the exhilaration in everyone's voices. Not wanting to miss a moment of it she opened her eyes, rolled on her side and tried to push herself up. Instantly Ribek's arm slid under her shoulders to help.

'I can do it,' she said crossly.

But she couldn't, and in the end was forced to let him lift her and resettle her in a nest he'd made out of the bedding rolls with her back propped against one of the rocks, arranging her limbs much as he'd done when she'd been a rag doll inside a magical egg in that other universe. *Not enough stuffing*, she thought, gazing at the stick-thin legs stretched out in front of her.

'How are you doing?' he said quietly.

'Better. I think it was that extra-dimension stuff that wore me out. I could feel it eating me away. It wasn't

Benayu's fault, or Jex's. They had to let it happen so I could follow the trail. I'll be all right now we're back in our own world. Look, I'm a rag doll still. Floppy legs.'

'We need Striclan back to feed you up. Can't keep asking Benayu.'

'What about the Watchers? Won't they notice?'

'The ones who came after us are still trapped on the other side of the barrier, and he's put a ward all round the island. He seems to think it's all right. Ah, this smells like your broth.'

'First things first, you said,' said Benayu, not bothering to hide the boyish pleasure he felt in showing off, just as he might have done on the mountain pasture where they had first met him all those months ago. The soup tasted as good as it smelt. She sipped it with dreamy relish as the warmth flowed into her bloodstream. She let Ribek have a taste of it and drank the rest herself. The next course arrived as she put the mug down.

'I could show you the war-lord's face if you like,' said Benayu as he handed Saranja her pungent-odoured bowl.

'All right . . . Oh! That's Tarab Arkan. He was a real beast. He treated his women like trash, punched them and kicked them when they had daughters and then gave them away to his bodyguard to do what they liked with. Nobody dared suggest it might be something to do with him that he didn't have any sons. He'd have had them flayed alive! I'll savour every mouthful.'

They ate in contented silence, apart from Sponge's joyous snarls as he wrenched at his raw chops. Ribek had been right, though. Maja could tell she would have enjoyed the pie if she'd been well and strong, but now it was far too rich. For a while she dipped corners of bread in the sauce and chewed them slowly, but in the end passed almost a whole bowlful over to the Ropemaker to finish. Then she closed her eyes and drowsed against Ribek's shoulder, half listening to the Ropemaker telling the others in short, jerky sentences about his childhood in Barda. His father was a fisherman who had drowned at sea when he was a baby and his mother had married a man who didn't want him in the house, so he'd lived with the grandfather who'd made the oyster-and-bacon pie. But he'd died when the boy was six and he'd been sent to live with the village ropemaker, more as a child-slave than anything, though he'd been called an apprentice. He'd picked up the trade simply by watching what his master did, and this included using a few simple spells to supple a rope or strengthen a splice and so on.

He grasped them instantly, and worked them almost without thought, and when his master realized this he told him other charms that he knew of but couldn't do himself, and they too came to the boy as easy as breathing. Soon he could rig a fishing smack in a morning, or tie two ends of cord into a pattern of knots that would of its own accord repeat and repeat itself until it was a full-size fishnet.

He got no thanks. The reverse, if anything. He was still his master's apprentice, and so still a slave, but now a valuable one. For fear that he might be kidnapped by a rival, or run away and look for a kinder home, his master kept the boy locked up when he wasn't under his eye, leaving food for him when he went to carouse with his cronies. A rat arrived, searching for scraps, and the boy made friends with it, studied it, searched out its inner nature, and as if by instinct turned himself into a rat. He crept out by the hole through which his friend had entered and scuttled down to the foreshore, where there was a skiff waiting ready for him to rig it next morning.

He did the work by moonlight. At one point he was aware of a wind-charm blowing in the breeze off the ocean, so he wove it into the halyard. When he'd done, he winched the skiff down the slipway, let the incoming tide set it afloat, for no reason that he knew of loaded several coils of spare rope aboard, hoisted sail and told the wind-charm to take him wherever it had come from. Unhesitating, it took him to Angel Isle.

On the way over he unravelled a spare length of rope, knotted a few strands into a pattern of squares and set it to grow into a bag-net, which he trailed over the stern and scooped up a couple of plump sunfish. But at Angel Isle his luck seemed to run out. All round it the cliffs ran sheer down to the water with the ocean swell foaming against them. There was no possible anchorage or landing place.

He sailed as close as he dared to the cliffs and asked the wind-charm to hold the skiff steady in one place against the current flowing past the island. Then he took four of the coils of rope he had brought and flung their ends up against the cliff, telling them to lodge themselves in crannies, wriggle on up and find somewhere to

436

secure themselves. That done he dropped their lower ends into the water, two on each side of the boat, telling them to float themselves below the hull, knot themselves to the rope opposite, and then tighten their weave along their whole length so that as they shrank they lifted the skiff clear of the water while he used an oar to stop it scraping against the cliff face.

He was nine years old, and none of this was anything he'd thought of, let alone tried, before. It was just there, on Angel Isle, waiting for someone who knew about ropes to use it.

'Swarmed up and found this place,' he said. 'Changed me. Didn't realize it, then kids don't. Cooking my fish, all I thought about. Told the ropes to fetch me drift-wood, caught in the rocks. Piled it up. Lit it by snapping my fingers – hedge magic, of course, but I'd never seen it. Good fish, mind.

'Dropped off when I'd finished – dog tired – working all night, remember. Strange dreams, shapes, distances, all wrong. Nothing fitting with anything. Know why now. Maja will tell you. Eh, Maja?'

She opened her eyes to see him sponging the last morsels out of his bowl – her bowl – with a hunk of bread. Jex had changed back into his proper shape and crept out of the saddlebag and was now squatting on a sunlit boulder, staring at him with unblinking eyes.

'Woke up feeling nothing I can't do,' said the Ropemaker as he chewed. 'Only got to find out about it. Twenty years I spent, just finding out. Best time of my life.'

He had changed, she thought, since she had first seen

him yesterday, in Benayu's egg. There was something slightly different about him, but she couldn't think what. He swallowed the last spoonful and gave a long, satisfied belch. As if at that signal the rhubarb and ginger crumble appeared on the turf. Maja smiled at the familiar smell. Even the dread and misery of life at Woodbourne couldn't spoil the excellence of her aunt's cooking.

'I could eat a little of that,' she whispered.

'A little,' said Ribek.

It was as good as her aunt's had been, but no better. Strange to think of her aunt never making it again. When they were back in the Valley, she decided, she'd go to Frog Bottom and ask Mrs Finsdaughter to show her how. Then she could make it for Ribek as often as he liked.

'Want you to understand,' said the Ropemaker. 'That's why I've been telling you all this. Next thing, Tilja and the others show up in my life. Won't bother you with all that – you know the story.'

'I'm not from the Valley,' said Benayu. 'I only know what they've told me.'

'Ring Faheel passed on to me? Know about that?'

'You can use it to change time, so you can undo something that's happened and do something else. You'd need to get outside time to do that, so it's got to have something to do with other universes, where time's different.'

'Mphm. Fourteen, and you've figured that out. Took me getting on a couple of centuries. Didn't start thinking about it straight off, of course. Too busy getting things straight in the Empire. Good people helping me, mind you. Tilja, Lananeth, Zara . . . You met Zara at Larg, Maja says. Waiting for me to come back. Good, brave woman. Let her down. Any of the others, they'll be gone. Or turned into Watchers. Worse, that. Ah, the things you do for the best. You think.'

He took a small black box from the fold of his cloak and sat staring at the ground, juggling it up and down in his hand. The mood and posture made him look somehow older. She could almost feel how long he had borne his burden. Yes, that was it. He did look older. Yesterday, in Benayu's egg, he'd seemed about Ribek's age. Now she'd have guessed at a good ten years more.

He sighed and straightened.

'Never used the ring unless I had to,' he said. 'Scared the hell out of me first time I tried. Still does. Maybe if I'd practised a bit more, wouldn't've got into the mess I did. Ah, well.

'Getting worse, if anything. Time's like that. Every day goes by, another lot of complications weave themselves in. Things old Faheel did, I doubt he could do now. Ring only makes it worse. Every time you use it, you mess with time itself. Does a bit of that, even when you're not using it. Like a rock in a river – sets up an eddy, just by being there. Round and round, round and round, can't stop. And after all that, who d'you hand it on to? Really want it, you're not fit to have it. Wrong people get hold of it – Watchers, way they're set up now – these Pirates of yours – either of them – doesn't bear thinking about.

'Decided, better get rid of it. Once and for all. Hide it,

someone'd have found it. Melt it down, smash it to bits, no chance. Only hope was unmake it, same way it'd been made.

'How? Saw I'd got to get outside time somehow. Tried using the ring – takes you some place else – sort of nowhere – can't explain it – all there is is this rope thing, everything ever happened, happening now, going to happen, this and that causing this and that, all woven together, stretching on and on each way, forever. Been there before. So that's time, I used to think. Started nosing around, up and down time, see how it all worked, how it was made, how to unmake it.

'Took me a while to see I'd got it wrong. Rope isn't time. Time's always out there – things happening, kid swinging on a branch, star falling, chick hatching, arrow on its way, blink of an eyelid. Rope I was looking at – that's only a *model* of real time, time out there. Ring's inside time, and you're in there with it, and the rope you're looking at, all inside the ring, still inside time. You can mess with it inside real time, and somehow it reaches out, outside real time, and messes around, messes with stuff that's happened, changes what's going to happen.

'No use trying to unmake the ring from inside real time. Wasn't made that way. Made from outside it. Got to be unmade same way.

'How do I do that, eh? Thought about it all day. Got nowhere. Woke up next morning thinking, Wrong question. Not how? Where? Where's outside time? Thought about that all day. Still got nowhere. Had a dream that night. Strange. Nothing happened in it. Just kept seeing shapes, distances. All wrong. Nothing fitting with any-thing. Remember? Same dream here, on Angel Isle.

'Never been back till then. Didn't want to spoil it for myself. But came here and nosed around. Found the whatchamacallit . . .'

'*Touching point,*' said Jex in their heads.

'Right. Made of the wrong stuff somehow. Didn't get it about different universes, different dimensions, all that. Trial and error. Blasted myself clean out of the tun-nel a couple of times. Must've been mad to try it.'

He laughed, shaking his head at his own folly.

'Did it in the end,' he went on. 'Made a sort of pocket in the barrier. Put a lining into it – wove it out of same stuff barrier was made of, way I do with a net. Made it small, easier to move around once I was through. Came out egg-shaped, like Benayu's. Seemed to be the only way. Don't know why.'

'Nor do I, really,' said Benayu, 'But it's in Fodaro's equations, so I knew it had to be like that.'

'Right. Had to leave something behind to come back to – know about that too?'

'Jex had told Maja there had to be something,' said Saranja.

'Worked it out for myself. Made a couple of little dol-lies, put one in my egg, sent other off to the oyster beds. All ready now. Lot of weird creatures had shown up other side of the barrier while I was at it. Knew some-thing was up, I reckoned. Got inquisitive.'

'*They were feeding on the energy seeping through the touching point from what you were doing.*'

'Right again. Wish I'd had you there to tell me what's

441

what. Saved a lot of trouble. Anyway, took over one of these creatures, way Maja did with Sponge here. Great lump of a thing. Lots of eyes.'

'*A fufu. More intelligent than it appears.*'

'Take your word for it. Got it to pick the egg up and ferry me around. Used the ring to work back through time, find out where it came from, first place. Tricky work, different rope from the one I knew.'

'*There are two dimensions of time there, which have to fit with the other five dimensions, which are also different.*'

'No idea about that. Still, found where the ring was made – when in time, where on the rope. Must've been blind luck, but I thought that meant I'd got it all sorted. Bad mistake. Nothing special about the place, I could see, but the whatchamacallit, fufu, didn't want to go near it.'

'*You had reached a dimensional node, a point at which the seven dimensions lock themselves together to hold the structure of the universe firm. Considerable secondary forces are generated, which could have been used in the construction of the ring. Proximity to such points arouses sensations of extreme anxiety in the creatures of my universe.*'

'Second mistake. Tried putting it to sleep. Shouldn't've been a problem, but soon as I got one lot of eyes shut another lot opened.'

'*That is how a fufu sleeps. Serially.*'

'Know next time. Didn't have anything to spare to hold the creature hanging around when it was crazy to be off. Had to let it go.

'Problem was, couldn't have the ring unmake itself there – place it was made, time it was made. Do that, there'd be no ring, so no Tilja story. You wouldn't be here. Had to set it up there to destroy itself – only place I could have done that – then forward into the future, beyond the time when I came in, time now. Leave it there, all set to send me back to time now, and then unmake itself when I gave the word. Pick up another creature, give the word, out through the touching point into my own world, before anything happened.'

'*Let me understand you. The ring cannot be destroyed in your universe, because it was made from outside the time of your universe. So you were planning to use it to travel to some time in the future of both universes . . .*'

'Didn't get it they were that different.'

'*Yes, very different. And then you were going to arrange for the ring to destroy itself at the dimensional node where it was made in that universe, but not to do so until you had used it to return to the time you had come from in both universes, which you assumed would remain identical with each other, and escaped into your own universe?*'

'That's about it.'

'*It is just as well you failed. The convulsion at a dimensional node would have caused a major change in the structure of that universe, with unpredictable results in other universes, including at the least a major irruption of demons into this one.*'

'Bad as that?'

'*Yes.*'

'Doesn't bear thinking about.'

443

They sat in silence and thought about it. To Maja the dismaying thing wasn't the chance-averted disaster – that seemed so remote as to be unimaginable – but that the Ropemaker, whom she had been vaguely assuming knew almost everything and could do almost anything, could have come so close to such a blunder. Even going backward and forward in time hadn't warned him.

'Wonder I'm scared of the thing?' said the Ropemaker. 'Too dangerous to have around. Got to get rid of it. Beyond me. No time, anyway. Think you could do it with these equations of yours, Benayu?'

Benayu shook his head.

'We've done the first part of what we came to do,' he said. 'Now I'm going to destroy the Watchers and then I'm going back to shepherding. I'll show you how Fodaro's equations work, if that'd help.'

'And you've got to get Maja and Ribek back to the Valley,' said Saranja. 'She can't do it the way we came. It'd kill her.'

The Ropemaker stared at Maja, his face unreadable.

'Not enough time,' he muttered, as if he too had been in the same state as she was, just a tired old man.

Yes, thought Maja. *I'm very close to the edge.* She could sense the coming fall, her almost weightless body floating down into darkness. Won't be long now. No time.

'Well, you're going to have to make time,' snapped Saranja. 'You can use that ring of yours, can't you? Look, Ribek. You can take Rocky. He'll be quicker than Levanter. I'll leave the wings on him. It'll only take . . .'

She didn't finish the sentence. She knew too. Not enough time.

'Ribek,' Maja whispered. He looked enquiringly down at her.

'He's got time to tell us how the story ended. How did he get himself stuck?'

The Ropemaker's whole mood changed when Ribek passed the message on. He laughed.

'Time for that,' he said. 'First bit was the tricky bit setting the ring up to unmake itself. Managed it in the end. Rest should have been easy. Relaxed a bit, maybe. Bad mistake. Came forward, reached time now, where I came in. Uh-uh, there I was, coming in again, going back again, setting the ring up to unmake itself. Then forward, time now, and same again. Still got ring, no memory of where I'd just been. Went forward again. And again. And again . . .

'Didn't know it was happening. All fresh every time. Then somebody spoke my name. Farmyard long way off, horse, roc feathers, hair from my head. Forgot about it next time round. Same stupid business, over and over and over.

'Happened again. Still long way off. Mountain pasture, sheep, same hair, roc feathers. Big convulsion close by me, connected with other place. Couldn't make it out.'

'My selves in both universes were adversely affected by the magical overload emanating from the utterance of your name.'

'Uh-huh. Remembered first time for a moment, then forgot 'em both starting next time round, remembered 'em halfway through. Got an idea what was up. Forgot and remembered that too.

'Happened again. Had to be a while later because it was someplace else again. Hilltop above the sea. Big magic, dragons, burning city, flying battle-wagons, monster storm, convulsion close by, same rum connection. Jex here, of course. Roc feathers, hair – got it this time. The Valley. Urlasdaughters and Ortahlsons, coming to look for me . . .

'Then the same stupid cycle again, remembering and forgetting. Tried to think about it in the remembering bits, pick up where I'd left off, get through to you somehow. Frustrating, forgetting and forgetting. Just one glimpse, once. Doorway, kid standing far side, watching me – you, Maja?'

'Yes, but there was a Watcher there on the hillside, looking for you. I shouted at him to stop him seeing the doorway.'

'Felt that. Got us both clear somehow. Didn't want to risk it again. Big help, all the same. Remembered longer each time round. Same again when you found my dolly at the oyster beds, again when Saranja called my name from inside the egg. Still that last little bit of forgetting each time I started again. Still couldn't break right out, not till Maja barked my name right there, close outside my egg. That did it.

'Story over. Stop now, Maja?'

'Thank you,' she whispered.

Satisfied, she closed her eyes and felt herself floating away, down and away. She was dreaming, strange, shadowy moments: a kiss beside the mill-race; a wedding feast, herself at the heart of it; a caress on her naked flesh in the warm dark, with the race roaring beneath the window; the stir of a child inside her own ghostly body; two children fishing on a green bank, their reflections steady in the stillness of the mill-pool; a shaft of sunlight slanting through gloom, a slowly turning millwheel clear in its brightness, the shapes of a man and a half-grown lad dark against it as they watched the steady trickle of flour down the chute. Hauntings from the promised life she would never now be given. Vaguely through this she was aware of her exhausted body being laid gently on the turf, of hearing the murmur of voices, receding, almost gone . . .

Chapter 20

CHANGE. WHAT . . . ? HER hands . . . a flow of warmth . . . feeling . . . other hands gripping them, the warmth pouring through, into her arms, spreading through her body . . . A voice, known but strange . . .

'Maja! Wake up! Come back! You're going to be all right!'

She opened her eyes, clenched them shut against the morning glare, and forced them open. Ribek was kneeling over her, a dark silhouette, features almost invisible. But . . .

She snatched her hands free and pushed herself violently up, almost clashing heads with him.

'You couldn't've done that a few minutes back,' he said.

His voice had a strange, effortful wheeze in it. She stared.

Stared at an old man, stoop-shouldered, rheumy-eyed,

with a bald, mottled scalp fringed with wispy, silvery hair; smiling lips thin and purple, with a dribble of spittle at one corner; wrinkled cheeks sunken above toothless jaws. She flung out an arm to support him as he sank on to the turf beside her, laid her head on his shoulder and wept for both lost lives. He caressed her shoulder with a trembling hand.

'It's all right,' he said. 'I've just lent you a little of my life until we can get you home to the Valley.'

'It isn't a little!' she said furiously. 'It's all of it! Good as, anyway. I don't want it! You didn't ask me! I'm going to give it right back!'

'You were dying, Maja. You were very nearly gone. And you've got to have more than just enough to keep you alive. There's no way they can shield you completely from everything that's going to be happening here when the Watchers arrive.'

'When the . . . No, tell me later. I don't need it all. I really don't. I'll be all right. I want to give some of it back.'

'Got what you're going to need,' said a voice above them – the Ropemaker. 'I've got the rest.'

'No!'

She shot to her feet. So far she'd had eyes only for Ribek, but now she saw that the others were standing close in front of them, watching and waiting. She swung round to the Ropemaker. He'd changed too – changed back to the age he'd been when she'd first seen him.

'Give it back if you say so,' he said gently. 'Tell you first?'

'Oh . . . All right.'

'Kept saying, not enough time, remember?'

'I thought you meant time till whatever was going to happen next.'

'That too. But talking about myself, mostly. Time's almost up. Back there trapped in my egg, wasn't any time going by. Same time over and over. Each time I went round, back to the same age I'd been last time. Didn't get any older. Back here – you've seen Zara – that's how old I am.'

'But you don't look—'

'Angel Isle. Betwixt and between. Wouldn't last even here. Feel the pull of it already. Couple of days, at most. Still got to disempower the Watchers, right? Think Zara could take that on, the way she is now? Me, like this – need Benayu's help, as it is.'

'But . . . but . . . Why Ribek?'

'Because,' said Ribek and started to struggle to his feet. Saranja moved to help him.

'I'll do it,' said Maja furiously.

Oh, he weighed so much less than he should have!

He turned to face her and took her hands.

'Listen, my dear,' he said. 'Back there, in Benayu's egg, it was the other way round. You wanted to go and follow the magical trail to the Ropemaker, unshielded from its power, because it couldn't be done any other way. I said no – I care deeply about you, and I knew what it would do to you. I was right. You said you had to do it. You were the only one who could. It was why you were there. And if you didn't, the Watchers would find us and that would be even worse for you, as well as for the rest of us. All that was true, but I still didn't want you to go. I simply had to accept it.

'And it's true now, only the other way round, except for one thing. It won't be as bad for you as it was for me. I knew that you might find him but we might still lose you – that very nearly happened. Now if we fail, that will still be unspeakable for all of us. But if we succeed, he will repay his loan, and I'll have lost nothing, so nor will you. Please will you accept this? I did.'

By the time he'd finished he was wheezing for breath between every few words. Maja couldn't speak. Weeping again, she nodded and helped him ease himself back on to the turf.

Maja settled again beside Ribek, put her arm round him and curled herself up next to him with her other hand on his thigh. He laid his own hand on hers and squeezed it gently. *Good practice for later*, she thought, *when he really is old*. She knew she was cheating as she cuddled against him. He cared deeply about her – he'd said so, but not in the same way she cared about him. He was an old man, needing human comfort, closeness, love, and was letting her fulfil that need, as well as her own.

She glanced across at the others to see if they'd noticed, but they seemed to be taking it for granted that that was how she felt about Ribek. Benayu and the Ropemaker were talking together, low-voiced. Benayu was trying to explain something about Fodaro's equations – for what was going to happen next, probably. Jex was on a boulder beside them. Every now and then both human voices would stop, and Maja could hear,

451

faintly, his granite murmur inside her head. Saranja was listening.

Now they moved apart. The Ropemaker raised his hands, touched the ring on his left forefinger and spoke quietly. The pale, cloaked figure of a woman carrying a narrow-necked urn in the crook of her arm appeared in front of the encircling rocks. Even in the full light of that stormy morning she seemed to glimmer as if lit by a full moon under starry skies. She stood the urn on a flat boulder beside her and turned. It was Zara, Zara in the form she had assumed on the hill above Larg when she and Benayu between them had bound the demon Azarod into the rock. But she too had changed. Now she looked wraithlike, almost transparent, though the urn she had carried seemed solid and heavy enough.

The Ropemaker took both her hands in his and kissed her on the cheek. She greeted the others and joined the discussion.

Maja was distracted by Ribek, who had fallen asleep almost instantly, the way old people do. He was mumbling something uninterpretable. Maja wished she could have got into his dream, the way she'd been able to do in the egg. Not in this universe, even on Angel Isle. Probably just as well. There was a movement on the rock behind her. She glanced round and saw Jex. No, Jex was still where he'd been, with Benayu and the others, and this one had purple blotches.

'Hello,' she whispered. 'You must be one of Jex's friends.'

'*Greetings, Maja. We are here to help you destroy the*

452

Watchers before they themselves destroy both your universe and ours.'

We . . . ? Yes, there was another one, a little further along. And another and another. All round the arena they were flickering into existence. Scores of them now. Hundreds. Crouching there, waiting.

Waiting for what? For the Watchers to arrive. Whatever powers they poured out against the Ropemaker, the massed Jexes would simply absorb and channel them away, while he, thus shielded, destroyed them. And she and Ribek and Saranja, Benayu and the Ropemaker, were waiting for them too, not running away any more, not hiding any more, but waiting to destroy them, here, on Angel Isle. Soon.

Saranja's voice broke through.

'Wait! Something's happening to Striclan . . .'

She pulled Zald out from under her blouse.

'I told him how to call for help,' she said. 'He wouldn't do that, unless . . . I could take Rocky. Do you need me here?'

'Know where he is?' said the Ropemaker.

'Zald will find him.'

'Let's have a look . . .'

He craned over Zald.

'Hm. Fair distance. Demon stuff. You'd better deal with it. Nothing much you can do here. Going to have to hurry. Can't come myself. Lot of stuff to get ready here. Tell you what. No, keep it out. Hold it steady. Right.'

Maja saw him draw the black box he'd been playing with earlier from under his robe, open the lid and hold the box cupped in his right hand. He laid the forefinger of his other hand on one of the stones in Zald and curled the middle finger of his right hand over to touch whatever was inside the box. It was only for a moment, and then he closed the box, put it away and laughed.

'Even that simple, still makes me sweat a bit,' he said.

'What did you do?' said Saranja.

'Held time still where your fellow is till you show up. Get there, touch the stone, whisper my name, start time again.'

'Shall I bring him back here?'

Maja didn't hear his answer, because Ribek had muttered a grunt of discomfort in his sleep and shifted his position as if to ease an aching hip. By the time she'd worked the bedrolls round him to cushion him as much as possible and adjusted herself to the new position, Saranja was mounted and ready to leave. She was making no attempt to hide her eagerness and excitement, and Rocky seemed to share her mood. In the strange light of Angel Isle horse and rider glowed like a cloud at sunset.

She gave the reins a shake. Rocky settled back on to his hindquarters, spread his wings ready for the first driving down-beat, sprang into the air, and they were away, dwindling fast beneath the stormy sky.

'Amusing collection of stuff, Zald,' said the Rope-maker casually, as if this was any ordinary day and there was time for chat. 'Tricky locks. Take a bit of thinking about to get at the amber.'

'Do you know what it's for?' said Benayu. 'Someone told us it's for summoning some kind of major power.'

'Not to say know. Have a guess. Amber's from the north, right? Cold there. Ice and snow all year. Would've saved me a deal of trouble, Maja's time.'

'Oh yes, of course. That's what . . . You don't think we could've used it now?'

'Too much to handle, everything else going on. All set then?'

'I still need the staff. Shall we do that now?'

'See how it goes,' said the Ropemaker.

He turned to face Benayu, who nodded to show he was ready. They crouched side on to Maja and facing each other, and placed their right hands together, palm to palm, close above the turf, then moved them steadily back and forth as if they were rolling a cylindrical object between the two palms. A swirl of light, bright in the cloud-gloom, appeared above the two hands. The Ropemaker grasped it with his left hand and fed it in between their palms, apparently twisting it between his thumb and the side of his forefinger like a housewife feeding wool on to the spindle of her spinning wheel.

At the same time Benayu was doing something very similar from below, close against the turf, seeming to draw his material directly out of Angel Isle itself. Shielded though she was, Maja felt the steadily growing pulse of powerful magic – two separate magics, utterly different from each other yet steadily weaving themselves together, like two different tunes being played at the same time and somehow weaving themselves together into a single piece of music.

Slowly the four hands rose upward, and now Maja could see the second swirl, not of light as she knew it, but of something else that Benayu was feeding into the process in the same manner, non-light, light from another universe, drawn somehow through the sealed touching point below them and into this one.

It continued to stream upward as the hands rose further, difficult to see, never what or where it had seemed to be only a moment before. But through its vagueness she thought she could sometimes discern some kind of central shaft, extending and extending from the steadily rising hands down to the ground.

When the two magicians were standing erect with their hands level with Benayu's shoulder, the two swirls, light from above and non-light from below, dwindled and vanished in between the moving palms, allowing Maja to see the staff they had created between them. She recognized the pearly, half-luminous glimmer of the substance it was made of, greyer than grey, the light of two utterly incompatible universes so entangled together as to compose a single solid object – an egg, a staff – that could survive in either set of dimensions.

Benayu and the Ropemaker were fully upright and the staff rose vertically from the turf between them, but its vertical was visibly not the same as theirs. It obeyed some other set of physical laws.

Benayu grasped the top of the staff with his right hand. The Ropemaker clasped it in both of his and Benayu laid his left hand on top. They closed their eyes and stood for a while, Benayu pale with concentration, the Ropemaker's restless energies stilled to a single focus. Then they let go, leaving the staff erect. It struck Maja that the turf of Angel Isle was far too thin to hold it steady. It must penetrate well into the underlying rock.

'Should do,' said the Ropemaker. 'Couldn't have managed it on my own.'

'Nor me,' said Benayu. 'And anyway, it was Fodaro, really. And Jex, of course.'

'Right. All set, then? Ready, Maja? No telling how this'll turn out. Surprise 'em a bit, maybe, but they'll have stuff to spring on us too. Better have the horses over with you. Sponge too.'

Maja started to scramble to her feet, but as if led by invisible grooms Levanter and Pogo came ambling over and lined themselves up beside Ribek. Sponge trotted across and settled at her feet. Disturbed by the sudden bustle Ribek grunted, opened his eyes and peered blearily at the scene in front of him. It seemed to take him a moment or two to remember where he was.

'What's up?' he mumbled.

'I think the Watchers are going to arrive soon.'

'Right. He told us while you were asleep earlier. He's going to summon the Council and tell them he's back so they aren't bound to cooperate any more and they can have their animas back. Zara's brought them. In that urn. Bargaining counter if the worst comes to the worst. He doesn't think they're going to accept it.'

'And then what?'

'He didn't say. It'll come to some kind of pitched battle, I should think. Close call. He's stronger than any one of them – any three or four, I daresay. But all twenty-four, even with Zara and Benayu to help . . .'

'And the Jexes.'

'Jexes?'

'Look.'

She pointed. He peered, frowning. It was as bad a moment as any she'd experienced since she'd first woken to find him so changed. That those keen and cheerful eyes should have become so blurred! But before she could begin to explain, the Ropemaker nodded to her, turned, moved a couple of paces away from Benayu, squared his shoulders and with a series of sweeping and deliberate gestures transferred one of the several rings on his left hand to the centre finger of his right.

He changed neither shape nor size nor stance, but instantly he was a different man, no longer the eccentric, quizzical wanderer, but a focus of authority and power, with knowledge of and command over things seen and unseen. He gestured to Benayu, who gripped the staff, raised it a foot or so clear of the turf, struck it down and let go. The jar of the blow spread through the rock beneath with a steady roar, not the grinding thunder of collapse but a purposeful rumble as the rocks beneath returned to their places and rebuilt the tunnel between the universes.

The Ropemaker nodded and turned slowly, moving his arms in front of him as if he was coiling in an invisible rope, and Maja could sense the magic of the whole world streaming in once more as the ward that had protected them since they had returned to Angel Isle was taken away. When he had finished, Benayu touched the staff gently and stilled the thunder from below. The Ropemaker raised his right hand, palm forward.

'As Chief Magician to His Imperial Majesty,' he said, 'I summon the Council of the Twenty-four to convene this day on Angel Isle.'

He used his ordinary speaking voice, as if confident that his words would reach the ears they were intended for anywhere in the Empire.

Twenty leagues inland the villagers of Obun were celebrating the departure of their new god. They had very little experience of gods, and perhaps this new one would have been better than the previous one, but they were happy not to have to find out whether this was the case.

They had met their first god a little less than a month earlier, when almost all of the inhabitants of Obun were trooping up the road to start the melon harvest. As they reached the melon fields a strange creature barred their way, a pink lizard with a body the size of a hay-wagon and an absurdly small head with a human face that could have been male or female. It was wearing a golden crown.

'I am your god,' it had told them in a prim little voice. 'You may worship me by the name of Slowoth. I like a quiet life, and will see that you get the same provided that you cater for my simple needs. All I ask is one human sacrifice every month at the full moon. Man, woman or child, in reasonable health and not already at death's door. It does not need to be one of you. A passing stranger will do. That is all. It has been a pleasure to meet you.'

There were murmurs of discontent, but before anyone could speak the creature turned its head to one side and exhaled, almost deflating all its gross body. Only a few wisps of its breath drifted towards the villagers, but several of them vomited at the stench, and as for the field by the road which had caught the main blast, every plant withered on its stem and the unharvested melons collapsed into slime.

'I think you would be wise to do as I say,' said the creature, 'or you will not eat well this winter.'

It turned and waddled away, leaving a slimy pink trail.

The villagers discussed the matter unhappily. Several of them were not especially popular, but none was sufficiently hated to be sacrificed without qualms. Two roads led into Obun, both of them joining the Imperial Highway at points several leagues apart, so passing strangers were not an option since nobody came to Obun who didn't have business there, and there wasn't any.

The obvious answer was to kill the creature. Tog remarked that it shouldn't be too difficult, since it had neither claws nor fangs to speak of, and was at once thanked for volunteering to do the job. He was, in fact, the obvious choice, since he was a burly fellow and had neither wife nor children but did have a good axe.

The villagers woke next morning to find their god in the market square with Tog's body on the ground beside it, drained of all its juices. In its chilly, polite voice it thanked them for their zeal in providing a sacrifice so promptly, but pointed out that the full moon had only just passed so it would take Tog as a late payment on that account and would expect another instalment next month. It should be paid at noon, here, in the market square.

The days dragged miserably and rancorously by. A number of families tried to leave rather than risk any of them being chosen, but the monster met them in the road and herded them back. On the eve of the full moon they agreed to draw lots next morning. It was already dark when the exhausted stranger staggered into the village, not coming up either road but down from the hills. He had been in a hurry to reach Barda, he said, and had taken a short cut.

The villagers welcomed him and offered him food and a bed for the night. The stew they gave him was pungent enough to conceal the slight tang of the powder that the herb-mother had added to it. He woke shortly before noon to find himself lashed to a stake in the deserted market square. Nobody had cared to stay in sight, in case the god rejected their offering and chose one of them instead, but many eyes watched through cracks in shutters and doors.

The stranger wrestled with his bonds, not in a mad frenzy but systematically. He loosened a wrist enough to be able to dip a finger into a belt purse, but withdrew it and wrestled some more. He had his left arm almost free and a knife in his hand when the god waddled into the square. The stranger glanced at it and sawed at a rope. If he had woken only a few minutes earlier he would have freed himself in time. As it was, the monster reached him as he was bending to cut his ankles loose.

It paused a couple of paces from him, waiting for him to finish the job, and then exhaled delicately. He collapsed.

At that point the new god arrived. There was a minor mystery about how this happened. According to most accounts she simply swooped down from the east, but the only house in the village with an upper storey faced in that direction, and the witnesses at those windows had a clear view of the sky. They all declared that at one moment there had been nothing to be seen but storm clouds, and at the next that there had been a woman riding a winged horse immediately above the opposite roofs.

That is a minor matter. She undoubtedly appeared, gave a great shout, and as the god reared up to pour out its poisonous breath, lashed out with a fiery whip which curled around it, then swung her horse round and round it in the other direction, binding it tighter and tighter. The gas squeezed from its lungs and ignited into a roaring flare.

She landed, leaped from the horse, heaved the inert stranger across her saddle-bow and mounted. The horse thundered aloft. She shouted again and hauled on the whip, and the god rose spinning into the air. At her third shout the cobbles of the market square split apart, the vanquished god plummeted into the roiling fires below and the cobbles closed neatly together as woman, horse and stranger sped away eastward.

As has been said, the villagers of Obun didn't know

462

much about gods, but they decided that it takes a god to vanquish another god, so the woman must be one. She seemed to have done them a good turn, but perhaps she had simply wanted the sacrifice for herself, in which case they didn't want her coming back for another one. At any rate, they were relieved to see her go.

Chapter 21

S ILENCE ENCASED THE island. Maja clutched
Ribek to her and steeled herself for the arrival of
the Watchers. She didn't have long to wait. A
group of five erupted through the turf and stood in a
line on the far side of the little arena. Benayu, Zara and
the Ropemaker turned to face them. The Jexes scuttled
down from their perches and massed in front of them,
carpeting a great swathe of the turf with a protective
barrier, all set to absorb and channel away whatever
magic they might deploy.

The Watchers paid no attention, showed no sign of
surprise. One of them stooped and laid a limp, pale
object on the turf. Before he was upright it had grown
to the thing Maja had glimpsed in the tunnel, a
Watcher's mask and robe, with a skeletal hand protrud-
ing from a sleeve. So these must be the Watchers who
had been trapped on the other side of the touching
point.

The rest of them appeared rapidly, in ones or twos, or several at a time. One of them was different from the rest, wearing a dark cloak and hood. It was clearly a woman, short and plump, though the hood concealed her features. She moved like a sleepwalker as one of the Watchers took her by the hand and led her to the body on the ground. The pale robe floated up and enveloped her. The Watcher stooped, picked up the mask and handed it to her. As she took it the Ropemaker broke the silence with a snap of his fingers.

The mask crumbled to dust. She raised her hands and threw back the hood of her cloak, shaking her head as she stumbled aside, like someone emerging from a dream. With a shock of horror and fear Maja saw that she was Chanad.

'All here, then?' said the Ropemaker affably. 'One of you speak for the rest, eh?'

'We speak for ourself,' said a bloodless voice out of the air.

'Yourselves,' he corrected. 'Twenty-three of you now. All different people. Bound you to cooperate while I was gone. Back now, so that's over.'

'You are mistaken,' said the voice. 'We are neither twenty-three nor twenty-four, but one. True, with our consent you bound us, and can release us from that binding. But of our own choice we have since bound ourself further and more fully, and there is no power other than our own that can release us. You have made a vacancy in our wholeness. Your choice is either to fill that vacancy and become one with us, or be destroyed. Your time is over, Ramdatta.'

The name took the Ropemaker by surprise. He hesitated as the three quietly spoken syllables woke whispering echoes in the rocks, echoes which reverberated to and fro, growing louder and louder and louder, until they became three gigantic raps on the doors of time.

He flinched, staggered, and at the third blow he reeled back, throwing up his arms in front of his face. His turban unravelled and fell to the ground. His magical mane hung limp around him, a dull yellowish orange, streaked with grey. He fell to his knees and put his head in his hands. Zara was already a pile of silvery fabric on the turf. Chanad had fallen and was struggling to rise. Benayu too reeled, but grasped the staff and steadied himself. As the echoes rumbled into silence Zara's urn cracked apart, leaving a mound of crystal phials lying among the shards.

Soundlessly, one by one, they burst, like soap bubbles. Each time, a puff of pale smoke rose, carrying brilliant flashes of multicoloured light, like sparks flying up from a bonfire, no sooner glimpsed than gone. The smoke streamed away on the gusty wind, and the animas of the original Watchers, the hostages that Zara had guarded through the centuries in the mysterious space beyond her cell, all that had once made them human, her ultimate power against them, were gone.

Benayu was the first to move. He plucked the staff from the ground, strode to the centre of the triangle formed by the three stricken magicians and turned steadily round, with the point of the staff tracing a circle close beyond them. The air seemed to ripple above the invisible line, though the ripples didn't rise steadily, like waves of heat, but twisted and eddied in an increasingly complex, close-meshed pattern, forming a visible surface, a known shape, a shell of the entangled light of two universes. For a short while Maja could still see the four magicians, three of them sitting or lying as she had last seen them, with Benayu still grasping his staff but kneeling beside the Ropemaker. The Ropemaker took something out of his wallet and gave it to Benayu, who hesitated and took it. He was rising to his feet as the shell misted over, was briefly translucent, and finally became that strange, opaque, impossible substance that had kept them safe in a world where they shouldn't have been able to exist. Its near side shimmered, and Benayu stepped through it. He touched it briefly with his staff and watched it sink into the turf, then turned confidently to face the Watchers.

Maja turned too, and stared at them, her heart pounding, as she waited for the next shock of disaster. Why had they done nothing to stop him? Surely they had the power. But they seemed not to have moved at all or even to have noticed what he was doing. Something was happening to them, though. Those smooth, pale masks had a greasy, oily look. Their robes too. Blobs of pale ooze were dribbling from their hems, forming into pools around their feet. Their erect, formal stances were losing their stiffness, sagging as if they'd been carved from butter and left in hot sunlight. And the dribbles were rivulets now, and the pools starting to coalesce as the whole line of Watchers melted slimily away and down and were absorbed into a single smooth expanse.

A faint but cloying odour wafted to and fro on the gusting wind.

The army of Jexes recoiled, jostling to get away from the spreading edges of the pool. A yellow one with bright blue blotches was staggering directly towards her.

'Jex! Jex! What's happening? Are you all right?'

'*Poison to us,*' came the faint and gasping whisper. '*Hold me.*'

Instantly he shrank into his granite form. She snatched him up, looped his cord round her neck and tucked him into her blouse. The rest of the Jexes were already scuttling off to the surrounding rocks and dissolving themselves into patches of coloured lichen. All but three. One of these the liquid must actually have touched. He lay twitching at the edge of the pool until the other two, though themselves obviously already affected, took his forelimbs in their mouths and started to drag him away across the turf.

'Poison?' Ribek muttered. 'He said something about that before, didn't he? Demon magic, wasn't it? I don't like the look of this. And Saranja's got Zald. What's Benayu up to? Talking to someone?'

When she'd last looked Benayu had been standing sideways to them, leaning on the staff, gazing broodingly out over the pool. Now he had half turned his head away as if listening to somebody beyond him. She heard the brief murmur of his voice. The words had the lilt of a question, but at the same time were full of purpose, tension, fire. Peering, Maja imagined for a moment that she could catch the faint outline of part of a human figure, shoulder, arm and flank, shadowy, almost transparent, like the smudge of a finger on clear glass. Then she lost it against the jumble of rocks beyond. A man, she thought, if it had been there at all, the top and back of a head, dense hair stiff as a bottle-brush, a broad and stocky body, some sort of stiff kilt.

Benayu turned back to the pool, drew himself up and waited, intent and watchful.

No wonder. The whole body of liquid had begun to stir, turn, spiral inward, a single huge eddy. But this was no normal eddy. When water eddies in a stream it too spirals inward, but when it reaches the centre it sucks itself downward and is lost. This was doing the opposite, swirling upward into a twisting column, and at the same time sucking itself away from the edges of the pool and leaving behind it not green turf but a swathe of sickly-yellow poisoned grass. As it withdrew it revealed, one after another, a row of fleshless skeletons, sprawled where the Watchers had stood.

Meanwhile, at the centre, it continued to swirl silently and slimily upward. It quivered, and the lines of the spiral fell vertical and became the pleats of an ivory robe. Shoulders formed, and arms, folded across the chest, and, as the last glutinous ooze of the pool was absorbed, the hood of a gigantic Watcher grew from the shoulders, a Watcher as tall as a forest tree, glistening from head to foot with the slime of the pool. This wasn't just a coating, Maja could tell. The monster was made of the stuff. Neither bones nor sinews held it into shape. No heart, lungs, stomach, nerves, brain provided it with the machinery of life. It was utterly dead, more dead than the skeletons it had left behind, more dead than the rocks of Angel Isle, death embodied and held into shape by a single, powerful magical will. This was the One that the Watchers had chosen to become.

It differed from the Watchers as they had been only in one thing. Beneath the shrouding hood there was no mask, not even a featureless blank, but a black cavern, a dark and endless emptiness. Though it had no eyes it seemed to Maja to be looking directly at her, telling her that she must come to it, come and begin to fill that void. Unlike the demon north of Larg it yearned and ached not simply for the flesh of her living body but for her thoughts, hopes, dreams, the small natural powers within her, for all of her. Even before the Watchers had made their choice, she realized, it had been there, waiting. Been there, perhaps forever, an unseen presence, waiting for the body that would give it power to act in the world of things. And now it had not only their physical substance but also their immense magical powers and it could begin to absorb into itself all the spiritual energies of this material universe, to satisfy its infinite, unsatisfiable hunger.

This was the ultimate demon, the demon destined to devour the universes. Starting with her, Maja.

'*Come,*' it told her.

Her shielding faltered. She snatched at her amulet and dragged it down to her wrist. The black bead blazed with smoky fire as it withstood the call. But Ribek had heard it too and was trying to struggle to his feet. She flung her arms round him and forced him down, while he threshed feebly in her grip. The horses were already moving blindly forward in response to the

470

summons. Sponge as well, whimpering miserably at the compelled disobedience to his master's order. Benayu heard, glanced over his shoulder and flung out a hand. Ribek subsided with a groan and the animals stayed where they were.

The demon appeared to notice him for the first time. It turned its hunger towards him, raised a hand and beckoned. Benayu seized the staff, anchoring himself to resist. A gale from nowhere tore at his clothes as if trying to drag him forward. With his free hand he tossed something upward, and the gale became a blizzard, dense, huge flakes streaming in the wind, blanketing the Watcher, melting for a moment and instantly freezing into a carapace of close-packed ice. There had been blizzards like that sometimes at Woodbourne, waking the sleepers in the farmhouse again and again in the night with the crash of another huge branch rent from a forest giant by the sheer weight of the ice that had formed around it.

The demon, though, accepted the blizzard as an offering to feed its hunger. Before it had begun to melt, the ice started to flow, not downward as water would have done, but upward and inward, into the cavern within the hood. If any of the powers that Benayu had used to create the blizzard were still incorporated into it, they too were now lost in that darkness.

The call was universal. Already, creatures that had nothing to do with the struggle against the Watchers were beginning to answer it. The white seabirds that had soared around the cliffs of Angel Isle were streaming towards the cavern, their harsh cries of alarm falling suddenly silent as they disappeared. Four or five small bees that had been busy around a spike of sea holly suddenly forgot their job and followed the gulls. Right out in the open, easy prey to a predator, a family of voles was threading its way over the turf. Nothing was too small to be taken.

The monster raised its arm and beckoned to Benayu again. He answered with a bolt of lightning, blinding bright even by daylight, aimed not at the head but the midriff. In the instant of its flight it veered from its course and followed the gulls.

Maja's ears were still ringing with the thunder when she caught Jex's desperate whisper.

'He needs time, still. Only a little more time. We must all distract the demon if we can. Put me on the ground.'

She hardly had him out of her blouse before he resumed his true form.

A tremor shook him as she placed him on the turf. He turned towards the demon, choked convulsively, staggered a little way forwards and then, with what was obviously an enormous effort, started to back away. Beyond him on the rocks she could see several patches of lichen swelling into lizard form.

'Us too. Did you hear what he said?' she whispered.

'Just about. Help me up. Make as if we don't want to – we're fighting against it. It's got to pay attention to us – force us, step by step. Right?'

A pace. A struggle to retreat. Another pace. Reluctant, fearful. To left and right the Jexes, rank after rank of them, were doing the same. She could see one, a little ahead of her and to her left, that seemed already to have

472

lost the use of its hind end and was using its forelegs to drag itself onward and then force itself back.

Another pace and she and Ribek had no need to pretend. They must have crossed whatever barrier Benayu had thrown between them and the demon, for now, suddenly, Ribek felt the call. His struggle to resist it became real. She forced his hand against her amulet. Nothing happened. No, it had barely worked for him with the demon north of Larg, and this was the ultimate demon.

Only his will remained, as he fought with all the slight strength of old age against every pace forward, groaning and gasping as he was forced on. And Maja fought to help him, fought by fighting against him, or rather against the demon through him. She could feel the already exhausted muscles weakening, and at the same time feel the invisible power that drove them on growing stronger and stronger as the demon answered their resistance.

Nothing else mattered. Vaguely she could hear faint, fluttering pipings of distress all around her as the army of Jexes fought their own individual versions of the same struggle. Hopeless, all of them. Each one less than a pinprick. But all together, perhaps, an itch. That was their only hope. That the demon would lose concentration for a moment, and scratch.

So they battled on, losing all the time, pace by agonizing pace. The nature of the struggle barely altered when Ribek gave a final, dreadful groan and passed out in her arms. His eyes closed, his mouth sagged open and his head fell sideways as if his neck was broken. But still his legs drove them forward.

So far she had been clutching him to her side with her arms around his upper body, wrestling to haul him back. Now she changed her grip, losing a precious couple of paces to do so as she worked herself round to get her shoulder against his belly. His body slumped above her, forcing her to bear half his scant weight. Gasping, she heaved with all her strength against the staggering onward drive of his legs. Her sandals lost their grip on the slithery turf and they toppled in a heap.

He fell on her, half winding her. By the time she'd got her breath back he was on his hands and knees, crawling blindly towards the demon, now desperately near. She saw it stoop, reaching out an arm to scoop him up. The fingers at the end of the ivory sleeve had no knuckles, no bones, but a double row of suckers along their inner surfaces, each like a tiny mouth.

Desperately she flung herself forward, grasped his ankles and heaved him back. Effortlessly the arm extended itself. The talons closed round his waist. She screamed, and her scream was answered.

Answered from high overhead by a sound she knew, a long, clanging neigh, like a war cry. The demon loosed its hold and she tumbled back, dragging Ribek with her.

In the moment that she was facing skyward she saw Rocky above her, wide wings hurling him forward, Saranja and Striclan on his back, the fiery line of the demon-binder snaking out, bright against the storm clouds, curling itself widdershins around the demon's shoulders as Rocky swung the other way to begin the binding. The demon didn't resist. It seemed not to respond in any way, or even to turn its head to watch them go. Nor did Maja. Immediately, with her lungs still heaving, her heart still thundering from her previous struggle, she started to heave Ribek further away.

All round her the Jexes, those who could still move of their own will and not the demon's, were doing the same. She caught a glimpse of Benayu standing in the middle of them, with his staff erect in the turf in front of him. Half blinded with her own sweat she couldn't see quite what he was doing, but he seemed not to be even looking at the demon but at an invisible ball that he was holding cupped between his two hands close above the top of the staff.

She didn't have time to think about it, to wonder what he was up to, or whether there was anything he could do to save them. All that mattered was to drag Ribek further away.

Another wild neigh from Rocky. Different. Terror? Rocky?

She looked up and saw that the demon had moved at last, effortlessly bursting several coils of the fiery binding to raise an arm and beckon.

Rocky was responding, swinging in towards the terrible darkness under the hood, while Saranja fought to turn his head and force him back on to his course.

Useless. He was almost there. Another heartbeat and they would all three be gone.

It never happened. Before it could thud once more Maja's heart stood still. A gulp of air stayed in her windpipe. She could no more look to left or right than she'd been able to do when she was a rag doll. Rocky and his riders remained poised in front of the darkness. The racing storm clouds stayed in their places. Even sound was stilled. Not a mutter from the waves, not a whisper from the wind, broke the silence.

Something moved in that stillness. A small black object floated up at the edge of Maja's vision, surrounded by . . .

By what? Nothing visible, but . . . Nothing, visible because it was less than nothing? Negative zero . . . ?

Something below it now, greyer than grey . . . the top of Benayu's staff, with the black thing floating above it like the dot on an i. Benayu's hand gripping the staff, his other hand just below it, his arms, Benayu himself, floating up and forward into view, locked into total stillness like herself and Rocky and the demon and all the rest of the universe, his face set to stone as he poured all the powers in himself and the staff into keeping that single impossible sphere whole and balanced above the staff.

So in time outside time, the space he had somehow created between two instants of time, he drifted up and forward, past where Rocky and his riders hung timebound, to the very edge of the darkness.

At that point time resumed. Benayu thrust staff and sphere forward with a twist of his wrists. The staff was still in his hands as he plummeted earthward, but the sphere was gone, engulfed by the darkness. Maja's delayed heartbeat thudded within her ribcage. The gulped air poured into her lungs. With a triumphant neigh Rocky swung clear. And the demon . . .

The demon ate itself. The darkness under the hood became an inward-whirling vortex, dragging hood and robes and the whole huge ivory figure into its emptiness, and then was gone. All of it gone into the sphere of nothingness that Benayu had somehow formed and kept in existence in the world of things by creating a space between two instants of time in either of which it would have been an impossibility. All that was left of the Watchers was a patch of dead turf.

Chapter 22

STILL GASPING AND shuddering with effort, Maja got to her feet, heaved Ribek on to his back and felt for his pulse. Nothing. Nothing. Yes – was it? – yes, desperately faint, but there. She looked up for somebody to tell. Benayu was picking himself up from the turf close beside her.

'He's alive!'

He stared at her, dazedly shaking his head, stunned either by the fall or what he'd done.

With a boom of wings Rocky landed beside them. For the first time Maja noticed that Striclan hadn't been riding pillion, with his arms round Saranja's waist, but in front of her, as if he'd been a child who needed to be held in place. Saranja slid down, deftly caught him as he collapsed sideways, and helped him sit. His face was almost the same horrible pale yellow as the poisoned grass.

'Here's your banbane,' she told him. 'No, don't try

and say anything – you're still not making sense. Just keep on breathing it in. It's working. Look, it's changing colour. That's right.'

She turned to Maja.

'Are you all right?' she said. 'I thought we were all done for when Zald wasn't strong enough. What's happened to Ribek? Where's the Ropemaker?'

'He was getting old too fast. Ribek lent him some of his own life so that he'd be strong enough to deal with the Watchers. Then he summoned them, and they came. They knew the Ropemaker's name. They almost got him, but Benayu managed to hide him somewhere. And Zara and Chanad. They were here too. Then the Watchers turned themselves into a demon – the one you tried to bind. It poisoned the Jexes . . .'

'Them too? So's Striclan. He's pretty bad. A demon breathed on him just as I got there. I'd spotted some bog-oaks on the way there so I looked coming back and found him some banbane.'

'Banbane?' said Maja.

'It grows on rotting bog-oaks. It's a bracket fungus. You can use it for snakebite and things.'

'Have you got any more?' said Maja. 'It might help with the Jexes.'

'Not enough for all of them,' said Saranja, fishing in one of the saddlebags and bringing out a fawn-coloured object about the size and shape of a cow-pat.

'I suppose you could try it on Jex,' she said, breaking a piece off. 'If it works I could take Rocky and look for more. Break a bit off and put the broken side under his nose so that he breathes the fumes in. If it's working it'll start to go orange.'

'Can you look at Ribek while I'm doing that? I can only just feel his pulse. He was fighting to get to the demon and I was fighting to stop him. Then he collapsed, but he kept on trying to go forward.'

'He is asleep,' said Benayu in a dazed voice, as if he was half asleep himself. He shook his head, squared his shoulders and gave the ghost of a smile.

'He's dreaming about . . .'

'You mustn't look! It isn't fair!'

Benayu wasn't good at looking ashamed, but at least her snarl had woken him up.

'Sorry,' he said. 'I thought . . . Anyway, it was just an ordinary kind of dream. I don't think he's poisoned, just tired.'

'All right,' Maja muttered. 'I suppose you had to. Thanks.'

Still unfairly furious, she took a piece of the fungus and settled down beside Ribek with her back, deliberately, to Benayu.

'Jex. Jex. Can you hear me? How are you?'

'*Not well, but not as sick as many of my friends. Some of us are dying.*'

'I've got some banbane. Saranja says it might work. But you've got to breathe it in.'

'*Take me out and put me on the grass.*'

She still had him in her grasp when he changed his form. His eyes were glazed and the clear blue and yellow of his scales was muddy and dull. The taut and muscular body was as floppy as dead meat. The broken edge

480

of the banbane was oozing with opaque pale droplets and reeked of rotting timber. Carefully she arranged it close to Jex's nostril slits, propping it in place with her sandal. His neck ruffles rose and fell in time with his deep-drawn breaths.

'Yes,' he whispered. '*Yes, that appears beneficial. Ah, Benayu is fetching some more. Leave me to breathe this piece, while you take pieces to my friends. Some of us are unaffected. They will show you who is most in need.*'

'Striclan's looking better already,' said Saranja. 'He kept trying to tell me something urgent he's got to tell Benayu, but he wasn't making much sense. Ah. His bit's started to change colour. It forms a crust, Maja. When it's bright orange you can crumble that off and start again . . . No, love. Keep breathing. Benayu's busy. There's a lot of stuff going on, but it looks as if he's done for the Watchers. Cedars and snows! Where did you find all that?'

Maja glanced round. Benayu was standing, looking smug, in a pile of banbane up to his knees. It was as if he'd decided he'd fulfilled his vow and destroyed the Watchers and could now keep his promise to himself and revert to the boy he had been not all that long ago, playing with his powers among the sheep pastures.

'Here and there,' he said airily. 'Hope it's enough to keep you busy. Now I'll see if I can bring the other three back. I'm going to have to take it slowly, as I don't know what sort of state they'll be in. They took the full shock of it. I was just lucky I happened to be holding the staff.'

'You're sure Ribek's going to be all right?'

'Pretty sure. He's not been as near the edge as you were. Just let him rest, while you and Saranja do what you can for Jex's friends.'

It didn't take as long as she'd feared, anything like. It turned out that when the Jexes had decided to help distract the demon, they'd agreed among themselves that some of them should remain hidden. These now emerged and thronged round Maja and Saranja as they broke off bits of banbane for them to carry to their stricken comrades.

When the first flurry of distribution was over, Maja fetched Ribek's bedding roll and made him more comfortable. His pulse seemed stronger and steadier and there was a little bit of colour in his cheeks. Striclan was looking a lot better, very pale still, but no longer that ghastly yellow, and holding himself as if he wasn't about to collapse any moment. Between breaths of the banbane he was talking in a low urgent voice to Saranja, and she was trying to calm him down.

Now he fell silent and they both sat watching what Benayu was up to, so Maja turned to do the same. He had moved over to the other side of the arena, and somehow cleared a circular patch among the mass of Jexes. He was leaning on his staff in the middle of it. He had changed again. He wasn't the shepherd boy now, but ageless, human still, but also something other than human, the look that the Ropemaker had worn when he had summoned the Council.

He did nothing for a while, then whispered a few slow syllables. A ripple swept across the Jexes like the ripple of a breeze over ripe wheat. He positioned the staff upright at the centre of the circle, let go and watched it sink for a third of its length into the ground. He grasped its top in both hands, bent and blew gently down it as if he was blowing into a reed pipe.

A bulge formed immediately below his hands, moved slowly down the staff and disappeared into the ground. As soon as it was gone he blew again, and another bulge formed and was gone. And again, and again, for some while. At length he stopped blowing, stood upright, took a fresh grasp on the staff and firmly but without obvious effort drove it right down into the turf. Then, as the Jexes made room for him, he stood back outside the circle.

While he waited, the other-than-human look faded away until he seemed to be just another spectator, waiting to see what would happen. Maja assumed that another of the now familiar eggs would appear, and if all was well the three magicians would be alive inside it. Instead, the turf inside the circle shimmered over and a pool of tangled light formed from which a flock of white gulls emerged, screaming, and fled away.

The surface of the pool stirred and something began to rise from it. Chanad's head, her shoulders, her body down to the waist. Benayu reached out, took her hand and helped her up on to the turf. She turned to wait beside him.

The surface stirred again, but nothing happened. Benayu shrugged and knelt. Chanad knelt beside him. Together they reached down with both hands into the pool, adjusted their grip and with some difficulty lifted out the inert body of Zara and laid her on the turf. The

Ropemaker followed, climbing out without help. He was wearing his turban and looked much more like himself than he had after the Watchers had so nearly destroyed him. Immediately he knelt beside Zara, put an arm under her body and cradled her against his chest. Chanad knelt the other side, took her hands and began to whisper quietly.

Benayu stood watching for a moment, then turned and gave a brief whistle. Sponge went bounding towards him, put his front paws on his chest and tried to lick his face. Benayu pushed him away, laughing, and walked over.

'That's your fault, Maja,' he said. 'He thinks it's allowed now.'

'Could you come, Benayu?' said Saranja. 'Striclan's got something important to tell us. It's a bit complicated.'

'Can it wait a moment? I'm hungry. It seems a long time since breakfast. What do you want?'

'Whatever's quick and easy. Some of Maja's broth for Striclan, if that's not a nuisance.'

'And for Ribek too,' said Maja. 'I think he's waking up, and it's my turn to be tough with him.'

'And if you could do something about the weather,' said Saranja.

By the time the meal arrived the sky was already clearing and the wind abating as it swung round to the south. The smell of food brought the Ropemaker over. He had changed, still friendly and interested, but less eager and inquisitive, and moving more slowly and with the beginnings of a stoop. He seemed to be ageing even as Maja looked at him. It was as though the minutes were weeks and the hours were years. Chanad had stayed nursing Zara, so he carried a bowl of soup over to her, with a chunk of bread and an apricot, and returned. He was frowning, puzzled by something.

'Where's the old ring, then?' he said. 'Can't feel it. Gave it you, didn't I? Memory's going, along with the rest. Got rid of it already?'

'I think so,' said Benayu. 'You'd set it up to destroy itself, and Jex told us the only safe place for that to happen was in the sort of non-space between the universes – what he called ultraspace. I think it's the same thing as the negative zero in Fodaro's equations. Neither of them makes any sense to me, but they work in the same kind of way. Anyway the demon was consuming anything with any kind of magic in it, so I used the equations to fetch a sphere of ultraspace into our universe and keep it there – that was the tricky bit – and put the ring in the middle of it as bait. Then I let the demon have it, but as soon as I released it the sphere had to return to ultraspace. The demon kept right on swallowing so it had to go with it. And then, if I got it right, the ring destroyed the demon along with itself.'

'Tidy,' said the Ropemaker.

'How's Zara?' said Saranja. 'Striclan says the Pirates are all set to attack Larg, so . . .'

'Too late for her. Can't do anything. Ready to go. Me too. Time to undo our days. Didn't want to do it on an empty stomach.'

485

'Oh, but Larg!' Maja blurted. 'Couldn't you stay long enough . . . ?'

He shook his head and finished his mouthful.

'Nothing to give,' he said through the crumbs of it. 'Taking all the magic I've got keeping my teeth in place. Who told you? This chap?'

'He's called Striclan,' said Saranja. 'He was a Pirate spy when we met him, but he's on our side now. He was poisoned by a demon on his way to tell us.'

'Sure about him?'

'Absolutely.'

'Take your word for it. When's this going to happen, then? Soon, you say?'

Striclan tottered to his feet and Saranja rose to steady him.

'The day after tomorrow I believe, sir,' he said in a barely audible whisper, but speaking as formally as ever. 'The battle fleet is already on its way.'

'They need a battle fleet to attack Larg?' said Saranja. 'There isn't any magic in Larg. They could take the town with a couple of barges.'

'That is the point. A delegation of the Syndicary . . .'

'No time for that,' interrupted the Ropemaker. 'When I've gone. Know who's running the show? Be with the fleet?'

'I believe so, sir,' said Striclan. 'They will be aboard their largest vessel, the *All-Conqueror*. Admiral-General Pashgar is the Fleet Commander. Supreme General Olbog, who is in charge of the whole operation against the Empire, will almost certainly be there to make sure

486

the Syndics are impressed by a successful operation against Larg.'

'That'll do. Show up. Stop it in its tracks. Impress them that way. Right, Benayu?'

Benayu started to shake his head and looked away.

'We're talking about Larg,' said Saranja. 'I know you've done what you came to do and destroyed the Watchers, and now you want to go back to shepherding. But we've got friends in Larg. You're a Freeman of the City.'

'Someone else can do it. I'm tired.'

'There's no time to find anyone else,' said Ribek. 'It's already started.'

'Chanad . . .' said Benayu.

'Tired too,' said the Ropemaker. 'Take the both of you, anyway.'

Benayu turned to Maja, biting his lip.

'And you're going to tell me the same, I suppose,' he said.

'Zara gave you something at Larg. It's inside you, part of you now.'

He stared at her, startled.

'Please,' she said aloud.

'You'll enjoy it,' whispered Ribek. 'Impress them, he said. You can do a lot of fancy conjuring tricks. Just your sort of thing.'

Benayu managed to laugh and sigh at the same time.

'Oh, all right,' he said. 'But then we're going home. I'll help you seal your Valley off, if that's what you want, but then that's absolutely and definitely it.'

'Want to talk to you about that,' said the Ropemaker.

'You're right, lad. Too young to take it all on yet. You go back to shepherding and a bit of hedge magic. Let the Free Magicians have a go at it for a while. It'll come for you one day, mind, like it did for me. Bound to. But . . . No, listen to me, lad. And you three too.

'Like it or not, things have changed. We've done that between us, you and me. Destroyed the ring, right? Suppose we'd not done that, whole thing would've started all over again, Valley sealed off, Watchers gone, demons all over the place, magic running loose, new lot of magicians getting together to sort it all out, getting more and more power, changing their nature . . .

'See where I'm going? Round and round, round and round, trapped in a time loop, same as I was in the other universe. Told you, didn't I? Ring does that. Like a rock in a river. Makes a whirlpool. Show you.'

He stopped and sat nodding gently, a tired old man, lost in a dream. Then he pulled himself together and raised his forearm, let his wrist go limp and slowly rotated his hand around it several times, apparently hypnotized by the movement. Maja found herself standing on a bridge over a broad stream, immediately below a weir. Upstream the water flowed smoothly towards the drop. From twigs and leaves carried on its surface she could see where the main current ran between the slacker patches along the banks. Downstream all she could see was unreadable hummocked foam vanishing into a fog bank. She had no need to be told that she was seeing an image of the past changing into the future. The weir was the instant of change. Now.

Close above the weir a boulder jutted up out of the

water. Immediately below it, almost on the edge of the drop, a large eddy had formed. On its wrinkled surface circled a feather. It might have been the selfsame feather she had seen on the pool in the oyster beds at Barda. Round and round, round and round, round and round . . .

The scene vanished, and she was back on Angel Isle.

The Ropemaker shook his head, sighed, and went on slowly, effortfully, with long pauses every few words.

'Bit of a strain. Even showing you that . . . Well, rock's gone now. New times coming. You're in at the start of it. Not famous, not rich, nothing like that. But you're here. Planting a seed. What you do, next few days. How you plant it. That's going to shape the tree. These Pirates. They're part of it too. Not going away. Right, mister?'

'Certainly their whole history would suggest otherwise,' said Striclan. 'Even if Benayu were to destroy their whole battle fleet at Larg, they would try again, and with greater forces, elsewhere.'

Another rock in the stream, thought Maja. Another eddy. Round and round, round and round.

'New times coming, I told you,' said the Ropemaker. 'Now's your chance. Change all that. Won't come again. Good luck.'

In an abrupt gesture of closure he started to brush the crumbs off his robe. Maja stared at him, bewildered. He couldn't leave them like this, right in the middle of what he was saying. And he hadn't even . . .

He looked up, saw her expression and grinned.

'Trouble, Maja?'

'Er . . . Ribek,' she muttered. 'He's . . . Can you . . . ?'

'Better repay him, eh? Don't want you haunting me. Wherever I'm going. Me, I can spare a year or two now. Still got to catch up with Zara. *Pay him a bit of interest, maybe.*'

Maja heard the last seven words inside her head. He laid a bony finger against his nose and winked at her. He had put his last burden aside, and now, as time raced by him, scouring wrinkles and blotches into his skin, rheuming and reddening his eyes, he seemed to be returning almost to his childhood, boyishly cheerful at the prospect of his own going. She smiled understanding and glanced at Ribek, but he didn't seem to have noticed.

'Owe Ribek a year or two, right?' he said. 'Better do that. While I've got any. After that, you five hang around. Get your friend better. Going to need him. Knows what's what with the Pirates. Speaks their lingo. Make a bit of a plan. I'll send Chanad over. President Elect of Council. I'll give her my ring to prove it. Don't go till we're both gone. Zara and me. Dusk, that'll be. Like to have you there. Ready, Ribek? Help me up, someone.'

Saranja steadied him as he creakily rose. Maja did the same for Ribek. They faced each other, stooped and weary, Ribek now looking only barely the older man. Saranja made as if to stand clear but the Ropemaker put his hand on her forearm and stopped her. He took Ribek by both hands, drew a deep breath and closed his eyes. Time spooled between them.

Maja could actually watch the process of change as the once-tall figure opposite her bowed and shrank into itself, and the flesh wasted beneath the mottled and sagging skin. At the same time, with her arm still round Ribek's shoulders, she felt him straighten, felt the wiry muscles reclothing the bones, and the slower, firmer breathing, as the whole joy of being active, healthy flesh returned to the shrivelled carcase.

It seemed an astonishingly short time before the Ropemaker let go of Ribek's hands.

'Back to where you were?' he mumbled.

'I feel fine,' said Ribek cheerfully. 'Ten years younger than that, if you want to know.'

The thin, purple lips of the old man smiled. Maja grinned and winked at him, but she wasn't sure the bleared eyes could any longer see that far.

'Say goodbye to you now,' he said. 'Won't be up to it when the time comes. Good thing someone came looking for me. Lucky for me it was you. Soft spot for Valley folk. Ever since Tilja's time. Very fond of her. Helped me a lot.

'Benayu, lad. Twice the magician I was, your age. Five times wiser. Your friend Fodaro – did well by you. Zara can't speak. Says to renew her blessings.'

Maja couldn't speak either, for tears, but she ran and hugged the old man. Saranja, surprisingly, was also weeping-dumb, but when she had helped the Ropemaker back to where Zara lay and eased him down beside her, she knelt and kissed him, then rose and came blindly back. Nobody wanted to talk, so they sat for a long while in silence. Chanad came across without a word and joined them.

At length Ribek gave a deep sigh.

'Well, I suppose we'd better do as he said and start thinking about what happens next,' he said. 'How are you feeling, Striclan? You're going to have to do a lot of the talking, telling us how the Pirates operate, all that.'

'I am certainly well enough now for that.'

'All right,' said Ribek. 'Let's go back to what you were trying to tell the Ropemaker. Why Larg, when there isn't any magic in Larg?'

'For that precise reason. I think I told you that the Southern Federation was originally an alliance of warring tribes. As time went by these developed into a number of competing interests. There is the Manufacturing Interest, and the Farming and Forestry Interest, and the Military Interest, and so on. However, they have retained the original tribal method of settling disputes. This they call the Constitution.

'Once every six years all the members of each Interest elect a number of Syndics to represent them in the Syndicary, and make the laws and decide what taxes to raise and where the money is to be spent. It was they who decided on the invasion of the Empire, to force it to open its borders to world trade. The invasion was sponsored by the Mercantile Interest and the Military Interest, for obvious reasons, and the Manufacturing Interest, who foresaw vastly increased expenditure in weapons, which they would make, and so on.

'Other Interests were strongly against the war, but the idea was sold to the public at large with the promise of an easy victory against a backward and superstitious nation. But popular support is rapidly weakening in the light of the fatalities around Tarshu, the full extent of

492

which has yet to be revealed. An influential committee of the Syndicary has been sent to investigate and report.

'The military have been aware for some time of the lack of magic in Larg, but have regarded a possible occupation of the city as an unnecessary diversion of resources. Now, though, they see it as a welcome opportunity to demonstrate to the Syndics that the resistance at Tarshu is the exception, and that large parts of the Empire will fall very much more easily into their hands. If all goes well Larg will offer no resistance at all, thus demonstrating to the tender consciences back home that heavy loss of life among civilians is not a necessary corollary of an invasion. Meanwhile the Syndics will have been able to witness a large operation carried out with military efficiency and complete success.'

'And they'll go home no wiser than they came. Less, if anything,' said Ribek. 'Presumably they're the ones we need to talk to.'

'They will be a mixed bunch,' said Striclan. 'Some will be vociferous supporters of the war, either on ideological grounds or because they are actually in the confidence of the military and have their own hands in the till. Others in the Mercantile and Business Interests will have lost their original enthusiasm, and are now more doubtful in view of the unexpected cost. Others, in particular the powerful Homemakers' Interest, will have been against the invasion from the start.

'I gather that we are going to travel magically to the *All-Conqueror* and either persuade them to call off the assault or to prevent it by magical means. Our first problem will be to get any kind of a hearing. For a start, we will need both to claim and to appear much more influential than we in fact are. I assume Benayu can alter our dress and appearance . . .'

'I'd better be grown-up,' said Maja.

'Perhaps the first thing is for Benayu to go and take a look on this airboat,' said Ribek. 'What did you say it was called?'

'The *All-Conqueror*. She is the sister ship of the one you saw destroyed at Tarshu.'

'That's a bit of a risk, isn't it?' said Saranja. 'I mean, if it happened once it could happen again, and with these Syndic people aboard . . .'

'The official version is that there was a freak natural storm, a once-in-a-thousand-year catastrophe,' said Striclan. 'There will be hired magicians aboard the *All-Conqueror*, Benayu, as well as elaborate defences against magical intrusion.'

'I'll be careful. Come along, Sponge,' said Benayu.

The two of them vanished.

'I suppose I shall become accustomed to this,' said Striclan.

'I haven't,' said Saranja. 'Even when I'm using Zald I keep thinking, *This isn't really me*. You'd better have a rest, Strick. You're still looking utterly washed-out.'

'Striclan's not the only one,' said Ribek. 'Yesterday was as hard as they come on all of us, specially Maja, and then how much sleep did we get? Three hours? Four, maybe. We'd all be dying on our feet if this wasn't Angel Isle.'

*

Sleep came early and deep. Maja dreamed of a ruined city. She thought it was Larg, but there wasn't anything she recognized, and the river was much too small. Whatever had destroyed it (enemy attack? Earthquake? Or simply the unimaginable touch of time?) had happened years before. It was utterly deserted – nobody in the smashed streets, no birds nesting in crannies, no lizards scuttling among the fallen masonry. She wasn't even there herself – she was just seeing it from some other place and time. Now something moved, a white horse, Pogo, disconsolately wandering around that emptiness, looking for his wings so that he could find fields and woods and streams, and horses to be friends with. He came to a tall, featureless wall, for some reason still standing. Once there had been a picture on it. A lot of it had flaked away but Maja could still make out some of what Pogo had been looking for, a green slope, two horses grazing beside a lake. Pogo stepped into the picture and joined them. He was a unicorn now, but Maja couldn't see the top half of his horn, because the paint was missing from that bit of the tree.

She stirred in her sleep, distantly heard voices – Benayu's was one of them, so he must be back – and went to sleep again. That dream *meant* something, she told herself as she slid back into oblivion, but she had no idea what.

A familiar voice spoke in her head, faint enough to tell her that Jex wasn't in his live form. *Not the little granite pendant*, she thought. Something softer.

'*Maja.*'

'Jex! What's wrong? I thought you were better.'

'*I am indeed better, but I am resting, as you are. In my live form I continue to experience bouts of nausea, which of its nature lichen does not experience. How are you, Maja?*'

'All right, except terribly tired. What about your friends?'

'*They vary. Three of us have, alas, perished, and eight more will take a long while to recover their full health, if they ever do.*'

'I thought you didn't die.'

'*Not from natural causes, and very rarely from others. It is equally rare for one of us to come into existence, so this has been a great loss and a great grief. I do not know when there was last such mortality among us.*'

'I'm very sorry. I suppose it was all our fault for wanting to find the Ropemaker.'

'*If it was anybody's fault it was mine, for revealing my existence to Fodaro. But I think that when we come to discuss the matter my friends will accept that the increasing power and knowledge of the Watchers was already a serious threat to our way of existence, and would eventually have had to be countered. We could not have done this on our own, so some kind of alliance with one or more human magicians was essential. My choice of Fodaro and Benayu was accidental, but despite these deaths it has turned out to be fortunate.*

'*Be that as it may, I think we will certainly decide that all future contact with humans, indeed anything that might make them aware of our existence, is to be avoided. I must ask you and your friends, including the magician Chanad, never to speak of our existence, even among each other, and as far as possible to forget about us altogether.'*

'Oh, Jex, that's impossible! I won't talk about you to anyone or say anything about other universes and all that. I think Chanad will understand. But you saved my life several times over . . .'

'As you did mine, Maja.'

'I can't forget you! I'll remember you as long as I live.'

'And I you, Maja. Farewell.'

'Goodbye, Jex. Goodbye.'

She wept in her dream, but woke to find her cheeks dry. The shadows of the circling boulders were long across the grass. There was a patch of yellow and blue lichen on the boulder beside her. She stroked it gently but it didn't respond.

The others were awake, still discussing how to deal with the Pirates once they were aboard the airboat. Benayu was back from wherever he'd been. They seemed to have pretty well worked out most of their plans. Maja sat up and nudged Ribek's side.

'Is Benayu going to make me older?' she whispered. 'I won't have to say a lot, will I?'

'You'll be a grown woman, representing agricultural interests in the Empire. I don't think the military will be very interested in that. The Syndics might be, as the Empire's economy is mainly agricultural. Benayu says . . . it's too complicated to explain, but you'll be all right. He's going to do a much trickier version of what we did with the jewel-seller at Mord. They'll have translators aboard, so Striclan's not going to let on he speaks their language. If he wants you to say anything important, Benayu can tell you in your mind. He says the magicians they've hired are fairly good but nothing special. Normally one of them would spot what we're up to, but he'll put them out of action. What do you want to look like?'

'I don't mind. Only not too young and pretty. And not like I'm going to look when I'm forty.'

He raised an eyebrow.

'I just don't want to know,' she said. (*Him* knowing was what mattered, of course. No. She'd got to stop thinking like that.)

'But can I have white hair?' she added hurriedly.

'Tell Benayu.'

He turned back to the others. Striclan was explaining something about how two of the Syndics were enemies in public but were actually both in the pay of the same big mining company, which wanted to start mining in the Empire. Maja's attention drifted. She was sitting companionably with Ribek, but being careful not to touch him. *Perhaps too careful*, she thought. She oughtn't to need to be careful about it.

In that other existence she'd been planning to go back and live at the mill with him. Now she wasn't sure it wouldn't be better to go back to Woodbourne. It depended what Saranja, and Striclan of course, decided to do, whether they simply rebuilt the farm and lived together there. They weren't making much attempt to conceal their delight in being back in each other's company, but it was difficult to imagine them both settling down to the steady, repetitive annual round of life on a farm in the Valley. They were born to be adventurers, both of them. There weren't any adventures in the Valley.

That made her wonder about her dream again. It had been such a strong vision. Pogo without his wonderful wings, just an ordinary sad white horse. Not magical at all, never any more. And then stepping into the picture, and becoming a unicorn. Unicorns are as magical as they come, but this was only a unicorn in a crumbling picture. Half his horn was already gone. The rest of it, the rest of him, the rest of the whole magical world, would soon be a drift of coloured flakes on the cobblestones, until a breeze blew up and wafted it away.

If it hadn't been for Ribek, would she even have wanted to go back to the Valley, once Benayu had sealed it off as Faheel and the Ropemaker had done? Supposing he did. After what the Ropemaker had been saying she wasn't even sure about that now. Anyway, there'd still have to be a way of stopping the horsemen coming through the passes. So Ribek would have to go back to his mill. He'd want to, anyway. It was where he belonged. Where she would belong one day, if all went well. One day.

She thought of all the wonders she'd seen on her journey. Even more she thought of the wonders she'd felt with her strange extra sense. Not the terrible, battering, almost obliterating explosions of pure power, but the little everyday magics inherent in people and creatures and plants and everything in the whole material world. To lose that, now, having only just found it – it would be like losing – no, not her eyesight or her hearing, but at least her sense of smell. Think, the smell of an early morning after longed-for rain has fallen on parched fields – never to have that again in your nostrils!

Of course, even if Benayu renewed the magical sickness that had for generations kept the armies of the Empire out of the Valley, that wouldn't affect her, being female, and she'd be able to come and go through the forest and revisit the world of magic when she wanted, but it wouldn't be the same as living among its day-to-day wonders. And she would never finish learning how to cope with major magic, not just to endure it, but to explore it and understand it, perhaps even to relish its strange and dangerous energies.

Her rough cousins had loved climbing the largest trees on the edge of the forest, whose branches hung low enough to reach, and where they were not affected by the magic sickness. They would dare each other higher and higher, further and further out along the swaying boughs, and descend gleeful and triumphant. Maja could never have done that, but with Jex's help she'd been beginning to do something of the same kind with serious magic until Benayu and the Ropemaker had needed to shield her completely from the huge forces unleashed in all that had happened from the oyster beds of Barda to the destruction of the Watchers.

Suppose she went back to live in the Valley, sealed again into its seclusion, she would never make another wonderful journey. Was that what her dream had been telling her? All she would have was her memory, a flaking picture on a crumbling wall. Suppose, suppose . . .

She must have sighed at the thought.

'What was that about?' said Ribek. 'You can't be that bored with adventures.'

She told him.

'Well, it's worth thinking about,' he said, to her surprise. 'I've been wondering myself, after what the Ropemaker told us. Watchers are gone. Who knows what's happened to the Emperor? Chanad's got the ring the Ropemaker used to summon the Twenty-four, but there isn't a Twenty-four to summon. Not even a One. All we know is things are going to change. It could be wonderful. It could be hideous. And we won't know. Frustrating, very, as our friend would have said.'

'Benayu says he doesn't want to do big stuff, anyway for a while. Suppose he didn't seal us off in the Valley, then we'd still have the horse people.'

'Well, maybe. Let's see what happens tomorrow.'

'What's that got to do with the horse people?'

'You haven't been listening?'

'I told you. I was asleep. I had that dream.'

He grinned at her, but didn't say anything.

Frustrating, very.

Chanad was coming across towards them. She was obviously still very tired and shaken, but apart from that everything about her, the look on her face, the way she moved and held herself, was quietly solemn. She wasn't making a parade of it. It was how she felt. They all rose and waited for her to speak.

'They're ready to begin,' she said. 'They would like us

all to watch, but not to come too near. It will be clear to you how close we may safely get. They will need help to stand at first. I will steady Zara . . .'

'I'll do the Ropemaker,' said Saranja firmly.

'Good. I will give you bread soaked in wine. Put it to his lips before you try to lift him. He will nibble a morsel off and that will give him the strength to stand and move. Then follow me and Zara and we will position them either side of the tablet. When I give you the signal – it'll be when the sun's rim is about to touch the horizon – put the bread to his lips again. As soon as both are ready, we can move away. We will stand and witness their going.'

They walked quietly over to where the two dying magicians lay in the shadow of the rocks. Zara was on her back with her hands clasped across her. The Ropemaker was on his side, facing her, slightly curled up, with his cheek resting on the back of his hand, like a sleeping child. Standing, Maja could just see over the top of the rocks to where the round, smoky-orange sun was settling out of a pale gold sky towards the dark hills. Visibly the gap closed.

Chanad took a roll and a small flask out of the folds of her robe. She broke the roll in two, releasing an odour of fresh-baked bread, and poured a little yellow wine into the soft interiors. She handed one half to Saranja, then bent and breathed gently on each of the still faces. The eyes opened. She placed the softened pulp of her half-roll against Zara's mouth and the shrivelled lips sucked and chumbled at it. Saranja did the same for the Ropemaker until he turned his head away. The helpers stood back, and they all waited.

'I am ready,' whispered Zara.

'Me too,' said the Ropemaker, and pushed himself up on to his elbow.

Chanad had to lift Zara to her feet and half carry her across the turf, but the Ropemaker needed only to be helped up and then steadied as he tottered behind them. The others followed. A hollow had appeared in the centre of the arena, grassed like the rest of the space, as though it had been there for centuries. At the bottom lay a low stone slab, carved with what looked like a letter in an unknown alphabet. Chanad and Saranja helped the two magicians down the slope and positioned them either side of the slab. Without any discussion Ribek, Benayu, Striclan and Maja spaced themselves out round the rim of the bowl. Sponge was already at Benayu's heels and the horses came ambling over and joined them.

Again they waited. Maja was facing west. The sun was almost red now, seeming unnaturally huge and near, but dim enough for her to be able to watch it unblinking. Chanad, in deep shadow at the bottom of the bowl, could not have seen it, but when only a sliver of golden sky separated the rim of the disc from the rim of the hills she nodded to Saranja.

The bread had barely touched the lips of the two magicians when they raised their hands and took it themselves. Chanad and Saranja backed away, turned and climbed up out of the bowl. The sun reached the hilltops.

The magicians didn't stir, but they seemed now to glow faintly as they slowly nibbled the bread, or perhaps that was only an effect of dusk settling into the bowl. They stopped eating, and a rustling whisper rose from the hollow, steady, faintly rhythmic, shaping itself as Maja listened into the sound of two old voices muttering as if in dreams. Gradually the mutter was strengthened into song. They raised their arms in a gesture of invocation. Somehow the space in and above the bowl seemed to begin to revolve, without causing any movement in the windless air, but because it was filled with minute flecks of light, like dust-motes, turning and turning, floating downward and inward, drawn to the two figures standing either side of the slab, drawn in by their quiet song.

Maja knew what she was looking at. It was all in the old story, right at the start of it. This was what had happened to the magician Asarta forty generations ago. She was watching the whirlpool of the years. The motes were all the uncountable instants of those two long lives spiralling back down into the bodies from which they had come. The glow from the two magicians intensified and spread around them, filling the bowl but casting no shadows beyond it. The light contained itself, like a drop of liquid held into a sphere by its own surface tension.

The two voices became distinct. They were almost at the same pitch, but very different, the Ropemaker's a light, slightly nasal tenor, quavery at first, but true, and soon becoming firmer. By the time he was standing to his full stature it rang with his natural energies and zest for life. Zara's was deep for a woman's voice, much darker and sadder in tone, with effortlessly sustained long haunting notes. Their songs were not the same songs, but intertwined gracefully with each other as if they had been made and shaped to do so.

Though there was no wind the whirl of time plucked at their clothing like a fresh breeze, unsettling small bright birds from the folds of Zara's robes, like those in her cell in Larg, to flutter and dart around her. The backward-racing minutes twitched and fingered at the Ropemaker's turban, loosed it and sent it snaking away in a brilliant ribbon of colour, and the birds danced in and out of its windings. Laughing through his song he shook loose his fiery shock of hair and it blazed out like sunlight around him.

Their song became laughter, delight in their own youth and strength and the joy of the living world. Still singing, they held out their arms to each other across the slab, gripped hands with hands, and stepped easily up on to the slab. He knelt, bringing their faces to a level. She moved to him, and they took each other in their arms and kissed. Even to Maja it was obvious, from the sudden slight awkwardness after all their assured and purposeful movement through the ritual, and from the long, intense silence breaking the song, that the kiss was no part of the ritual, and that never before in all their immense lives had either of them done such a thing, done it in the love that magicians can never afford.

They separated. She stepped back and he remained kneeling. They raised their arms in front of their faces and moved them closer to each other, all four hands spread and tilted backward at the wrist, forming a shape like the sepals of a tulip. The light in and over the hollow, without losing any of its intensity, shrank inward to its centre, smaller and smaller, until it became the thing that the hands were holding, all the instants of all their years gathered into a sphere of pure light, that still cast no shadows because it spread no ray beyond itself, an offering up of those lives, the purpose and ending of the ritual.

Quietly they allowed themselves to be absorbed into its brightness, and it floated upward. The witnesses round the bowl watched it go, widening now and fading as it spread across the sky, until it became the light of the newly risen moon. The stone slab vanished and the hollow in which it had lain rose quietly back to level ground.

They stood for some while in silence. Maja's eye was caught by a movement among the rocks on the further side of the arena. A Jex, several Jexes, a whole rank of them, all round the arena, had returned to their living form to watch the magicians' going, much as humans might have risen from their sickbeds to witness some astounding event. Rows of lizard eyes glistened opal in the moonlight. Maja had scarcely noticed them before they began to melt back into patches of lichen.

Nobody seemed to want to move or break the silence. Even Chanad, steeped perhaps for centuries in serious magic, seemed awed by what she had seen. At length she walked slowly forward and picked up the remains of the two pieces of roll that the magicians had dropped. She took the little flask from inside her robe and placed it upright on the turf, where the slab had been. As it touched the ground a second flask appeared beside it. She plucked a few stems of grass, rubbed them between finger and thumb, and placed them beside the flasks, where they became a woven grass platter. When she crumbled the two pieces of roll onto it the morsels reassembled themselves into a loaf.

She beckoned and Maja and the others moved to join her. She gave them each a goblet, and there, still in complete silence, they sat and ate and drank. The bread was the best Maja had ever eaten, and the water in one flask as delectable as the wine in the other. It was a simple meal, but richer and more satisfying than the grandest feast, because it was the final element in the ritual they had witnessed, an act of letting go, their share in the blessedness of the event.

Chapter 23

MAJA WOKE WITH an ache in her hip and a strange stiffness in all her muscles and joints. A few loose hairs were brushing against her mouth. Sleepily she raised her hand to push them away and found a whole mass of them covering the side of her face. Where had they come from? Her own hair wasn't long and silky soft like . . .

Yes, it was, now. Her last memory of the previous evening was sitting with the others in the moonlight, thinking about Zara and the Ropemaker, with never a thought in her head about what was coming in the morning. Now it all flooded back in.

Trying not to wake the others by groaning she pushed herself creakily up. It was a quiet clear morning, with the chill of the night still in the air. She never woke this early, even when sleeping on bare ground. She pushed a tress of her hair forward to where she could see it and combed her fingers out along it. It was a bit blurred –

she must be long-sighted – but she could see that it was silvery white, and feel its fineness. There was lots of it and it was long enough to reach well below her shoulders. There were several pretty rings on her fingers. She couldn't see them clearly enough to know what they looked like, but feeling them with her other hand she found that they'd be impossible to remove over the swollen knuckles. The fingers themselves must once have been long and elegant, but now wouldn't quite straighten properly.

She ran their tips over her face, feeling the creases and wrinkles. She seemed to have high cheekbones above slightly hollow cheeks, but her nose was firm and straight. Her mouth felt a bit too wide for such a face. There were smile-lines at the corners. No sign of sag beneath her chin.

She realized her bladder was urgently full. She was going to need to crawl to the rocks to help herself stand. No. What looked like some rather grand clothes had been neatly piled beside her bedding, with a silver-handled ebony cane propped across them. Using it she carefully eased herself up. Her bad hip shrieked at her as she rose from kneeling, but she forced herself through the pain and hobbled away.

Yesterday they had each found their own places for this sort of thing. Mercifully Maja had chosen one that didn't involve any scrambling among the rocks, a small grassy platform at the edge of the cliff, facing eastward across the ocean. The sun had started to rise by the time she reached it. When she had done what she had to she stood for a while staring out to sea and letting the faint warmth of those first rays seep into her chill-stiffened limbs.

Did Benayu really need to do this to me? she wondered. *Well, I suppose it means I'm not going to be a twelve-year-old girl trying to pretend to be an old woman. This creaking body will keep telling me that's what I am. I suppose it's a good idea.* And there was more to it than that. She *wasn't* a twelve-year-old girl. She was a strong, confident woman, used to being listened to and obeyed. She could be kindly enough to those who merited kindness, but very few people would be fools enough to offend her twice.

When she got back to the arena she found Benayu sitting cross-legged on his bedding, studying something in his lap. He wasn't wearing his normal clothes, but some kind of uniform, green with gold trimmings. She half remembered seeing uniforms like that somewhere before. In a dream, was it . . . ?

She peered at him, puzzled, and hobbled towards him, but her long-sightedness blurred him as she came nearer. He must have looked up and seen her.

'Good morning,' he said. 'I hope you got some sleep. I was a bit worried.'

'As you well might have been,' she answered snappishly, and was startled by the sound of her new voice. Even the words were different from the sort she was used to saying.

'Though I can see the reasons for it,' she went on. 'You have not yourself changed?'

'Easier for me if I don't,' he said. 'It'd be like doing everything through a screen. And we don't want them to

510

get it that most of the magical stuff is coming from me and Chanad. So I'm your servant-boy, carrying your stuff around, giving you a shoulder to lean on, that sort of thing. This is your household livery I'm wearing. Would you like me to help you dress?'

'I would prefer Saranja to assist me. But you may as well try to make me comfortable until she is ready to do so.'

She was pleased by how easy it seemed to play her new part, almost as if she'd done it all her life.

'Very well, Ma'am,' he answered, and rose. Close up, she couldn't make out his face, which was a blur, but she could tell from his tone that he was grinning.

'And you can take that smile off your face, young man,' she snapped. 'I would not be seen in public to allow myself to be so spoken to by a servant.'

'I'm sorry, my lady,' he said, actually sounding a bit chastened.

Maja leaned on his shoulder as she returned to where she had slept, and waited while he opened a folding canvas stool which she hadn't noticed before, padded it with some of her bedding and helped her to sit.

'I hope you don't think I overdid the aches and pains,' he said. 'I copied them from Lady Kzuva. She's actually the Lord of Kzuva in her own right.'

'There's a Lord Kzuva in the story we tell in the Valley. Zara used to be his household magician.'

'That's right. Lady Kzuva's his umpteen-greats-grand-daughter. She's a big northern landowner. Striclan told me about her. I'm sorry about your hip, but I was pretty tired and I'd got a lot to do. It's much easier for me to copy someone whole than start fiddling about with bits and pieces.'

'I will put up with it,' said Maja. 'You have in any case done more than simply copy her. I am, in some way, Lady Kzuva herself, with me, Maja, somewhere inside her.'

'Oh. I didn't expect . . . Oh, yes, of course – I should have thought of that.'

'Do not trouble yourself about it. You have done very well. After all, I am used to my aches and pains. I find my long-sightedness rather more of a trial.'

'There's a pair of spectacles in your reticule, along with other stuff you might need. Here.'

'Thank you. What is your name, young man?'

'I am Bennay, my lady.'

'Then thank you, Bennay. I think we may achieve a satisfactory relationship.'

'Very good, my lady.'

The spectacles ingeniously folded to fit into a narrow soft-leather bag. They sprang open at the touch of a button, and had a neat handle with a loop at the end. She slipped it over her wrist and used the handle to hold them in place. Immediately her vision cleared, so completely that she guessed that the lenses must be magical.

Angel Isle was at its most peaceful. The white seabirds were already at their business, calling and soaring. The lichen clothed the rocks. Ribek and Striclan were still asleep, both facing away from her so that she couldn't see whether Benayu had changed them too; but just beyond Striclan Saranja was sitting up, stretching and yawning. She didn't look any different from usual. A few years older, perhaps. Beyond her the horses were nuzzling into piles of fodder. Sponge lay beside Benayu with his head on his paws. There was no sign of Chanad.

Maja put the spectacles away, took a small brush and comb out of the reticule and started to tease the night tangles out of her hair while she waited for Saranja to dress. It was difficult to reach behind her head, but the hair was long enough for her to be able to drag it forward and comb the ends, which was where most of the knots were. The real Lady Kzuva would have had a servant to do this, of course, which was why her hands seemed clumsier than she'd have expected. It wasn't just the creakiness of her joints. They hadn't had any practice.

Saranja disappeared among the rocks and returned, dressed in her normal clothes. Instead of going back to where she'd slept she went and crouched beside Benayu to watch what he was doing. Maja could hear the quiet murmur of his voice as he explained something to her, and then hers, more briefly, asking a question. So it continued for some time, before Saranja came over to Maja.

'Good morning,' she said. 'I hope you managed to sleep a bit. You'd like me to help you dress?'

'If you would be so good.'

'Yes, of course. Benayu says you're playing the part to the hilt.'

'I am not playing the part,' Maja said sharply. 'I *am* the part. I could no more speak like the Maja you know than I could skip rope. I take it you do not propose to appear before the Syndics dressed as you are.'

'I'll change when I've done the horses.'

513

Dressing was a tedious process and painful at times, but the result was satisfactory – a splendid version of the women's attire standard throughout the Empire: a long-sleeved dress, dark brown velvet laced with silver, the hem of the skirt rustling at her ankles, the front lacing up to her neck and finishing in a flurry of fine lace; a triple necklace of pearls and rubies, with a matching brooch; and a long scarf wound twice round her head so that it framed her face and the ends hung down either side almost to her knees. The blue beads on the tassels – sapphires in her case – announced her rank and status. One of her rings bore a jade seal; the rest glittered with faceted jewels.

By the time they'd finished the others were up. Ribek and Striclan were wearing the normal outfit of most grown men in the Empire, but of finer quality than before and with more blue beads. Like Saranja, Ribek had changed little from what he'd been when Maja first saw him, apart from ageing ten years or so, with greying temples and a bonier nose. With the buried part of her mind she'd been vaguely wondering how she'd feel about him, now she herself was so altered. Suppose two old lovers who'd long ago separated without rancour were suddenly to meet again, they might feel like this, she decided. Peculiar business, this, both of them living their lives in the wrong order.

Striclan, on the other hand, was a stranger who happened to look a bit like Striclan but was clearly someone else. His hair was cut short and he had a neat little moustache and beard, wore spectacles and held himself with a scholarly stoop.

'All his own work,' said Saranja. 'He used his own hair for the whiskers. He had the gum and glasses in his wallet, but everything else he just changed somehow. He's full of tricks. Comes of being a spy, I suppose.'

'Where is Chanad?' said Maja. 'Is she all right?'

'She's a lot better. Apparently the Ropemaker passed on some of his powers to her, as well as his official ring, same as Zara did with Benayu, but she's still got to get used to them. She's gone ahead to deal with the Pirates' magicians. We're going to have something to eat, and then Benayu's going to make us invisible and take us to their control deck so that we can see what's going on before they know we're there. We'll just pop up when it suits us.'

Breakfast was a simple, homely meal: porridge, fruit, little cold sausages, bread and butter and cheese, warm milk, or water – all perfectly edible, but Maja felt oddly dissatisfied and crotchety. It must have showed, for Benayu rose and came across. (He knew better than to read her mind.)

'May I fetch you anything, my lady?' he said.

'Thank you, Bennay. I am accustomed to something particular at this hour. I cannot tell you what it is, but if you could arrange something . . . Perhaps you could see what my look-alike is having.'

'Very good, my lady.'

He stood for a moment in one of his trances. A salver appeared in his hands. On it were a pretty cup and saucer, a matching pot with a spout and a jar with a lid. Carefully he filled the cup from the pot, gave it to her, took the lid off the jar and offered it to her. She took out three small round biscuits, put them in the saucer and inhaled the rich, spicy steam that rose from the cup. The ache in her hip eased at the first sip. Magic, she guessed. No telling whether it was already present in the potion or he'd put it there himself.

'Thank you, Bennay. Just what I needed,' she said.

'Very good, my lady.'

Beyond him she saw Ribek's lips twitch. She produced what she was confident was a formidable glare.

'I see no cause for amusement in an old woman needing certain comforts after a night in the open,' she said. 'We would all do well to become the people we are supposed to be, as far as we can. A superficial resemblance is not enough. We cannot afford to appear before these barbarians as a troupe of actors, or they will sense the deception. I was already asleep when you made your decisions last evening, so would you be good enough to introduce yourselves to me now?'

It wasn't in Ribek's nature to quail before a glare, but he accepted her rebuke with a nod.

'Yes,' he said, 'you're quite right. The sooner we get used to it, the better. We are representatives of a coalition of different interests in the Empire who combined to destroy the Watchers. Saranja and I are using our own names. I'm a mill-owner, and I represent industrial interests, just as you represent the big landowners and agriculture in general.'

'And I'm going to be Captain Commander in the Women's Regiment of the Imperial army,' said Saranja. 'I can't be anyone grand, like you, because the Pirates probably know there aren't any women generals, but there's a lot of disaffection in the lower ranks of the army, Strick told us. I've seen a bit of fighting among the war-lords beyond the Eastern Desert. But I'd better go and get the horses done, so I can dress the part too.'

Striclan's thin lips moved into a smile as he watched her go.

'I'm looking forward to this,' he said. 'Well, I'm Alkip Ruddya. I represent the Imperial Administration. I was Under-secretary in the department dealing with the registration and control of supernatural affairs, Magdep for short. I assembled our coalition at the request of my own Permanent Secretary and several of his colleagues of equal rank.

'There is a further point about yourself that you should know. Chararghan society was originally matriarchal. The men went off to hunt or fight and the women controlled the homestead. The trait persists. Even powerful men such as those we will be meeting have an instinct to respect women such as yourself.'

'We sound a formidable enough group,' said Maja, 'few though we are. There are no professional magicians among us?'

'That is deliberate,' said Ribek. 'One of the things we want to persuade the Pirates about is that they won't be able to walk all over the Empire now that the Watchers are gone. So far they've just been nibbling away at the edges from the protection of the sea. They know almost nothing about the interior. So if they find that three of the four of us, who aren't professional magicians, seem to have considerable magical powers—'

517

'But none of us have them. I certainly have nothing of the sort. The opposite, if anything.'

'You will appear to have them. Look, the simplest thing would be if I tell you how we hope the show will go. We aren't in any hurry. It'll be much easier for Benayu and Chanad if they're close inland, where their powers are stronger. The Pirates are planning to anchor off Larg this evening and come ashore in the morning. All right?'

He was still talking when Saranja came back. The dress uniform of a female Captain Commander in the Imperial Army was a brass helmet with a purple plume worn over a shorter version of the standard head-scarf framing the face. Below that a dark olive jacket, tight-laced up to the collar, with gold epaulettes, belted in at the waist; a short, many-pleated skirt over close-fitting breeches; black boots, highly polished. A light curved sword hung from the black sword-belt.

They'd all been sitting while Ribek talked. Striclan rose and kissed Saranja's hand. She flushed, adding to the aura of romantic dash, but collected herself and turned to Maja, drew her sword and saluted her. The salute looked exactly right, long practised, though it can't have been anything she'd done before. As with Maja, she wasn't acting the part, but being it. Her body knew how to do that.

'Thank you, Captain,' said Maja. 'We are grateful that you were able to join us.'

They ate their midday meal off a table and sitting in chairs, while Benayu waited on them. He ate separately when they had finished. Maja's old body told her that it was used to a nap at that point, so she had one, sitting upright in her chair, and woke refreshed. Then Ribek asked her permission to join her and they talked for an hour or more about their imaginary lives. He was a self-made man, she learnt, having inherited a small watermill in a distant northern valley, done well by good luck and hard work, bought more mills and was now a wealthy industrialist with three children already in the business. To Maja, it all seemed perfectly real, as true as anything her buried self knew about him. And in another way he was still the same Ribek, himself through and through. He showed no sign at all of being overawed either by her high social standing or her formidable presence. As for herself, she had no need to invent. Every minute that passed, the real Lady Kzuva – more of her knowledge, her memories, her experience of the world – was there, present on Angel Isle. She told Ribek the name of the pet greyhound she had had when she was a child. She couldn't have done that when she'd woken.

Benayu had stood throughout a respectful distance away. At one point Maja had thought of beckoning him over to ask how long the effect of the potion he'd given her that morning would last, and whether it would be a good idea to renew it before they set off, but though his eyes had been looking towards where she sat he'd clearly been in one of his trances. Now, however, he came over with the salver already in his hands, and when she'd taken the cup and thanked him he turned to the others.

'Your pardon, ladies and gentlemen,' he said. 'I think

we should practise invisibility. It's not as easy as you'd think, because you won't be able to see each other. But if you all hold hands that'll stop you bumping into each other. It makes it simpler for me, anyway. You don't want to move around more than you can help, but if you have to you've got to remember where the others are and leave them room to get past things and so on. I may be too busy to put thoughts into your heads, so you'll have to pass messages along the line by squeezing or shaking the next person's hand. If you'll please hold hands you can sort that out between you now, and then I'll fetch the animals.'

Invisibility was, as he'd said, much harder than Maja would have thought. She was at the right end of the line so that she could use her cane, and she knew where her hands and feet were in relation to herself, but not in exact relation to the ground she was standing on except by looking down through her own feet and seeing where the grass was pressed flat. And she couldn't have told to within several inches where the end of her cane was. They practised getting out of Benayu's way without jostling each other when he walked towards them, and only got it right after several tries.

'I suppose that'll have to do,' said Benayu at last, and they returned to visibility. 'Here is your brooch, my lady. Shall I pin it on for you?'

'Please.'

The brooch was a plain silver bar, bearing three horses, their bodies overlapping, grazing beside a tree. Even at that scale, Maja could tell which horse was which. She nodded and he pinned it on to her dress. She

520

turned and saw that Rocky, Pogo and Levanter were no longer where they had been, though Sponge still lay there, drowsing untroubled.

'Well, there's clearly no question of our sneaking up behind some general and peering over his shoulder while he looks at a map,' said Ribek. 'Hello, old fellow. Coming along for the ride, then?'

The last few words were spoken to a golden squirrel that had come scampering up behind, climbed his body as easily as if it had been a tree-trunk, and was now perched on his shoulder. A small white owl floated soundlessly down and settled beside Saranja's left epaulette. A dark green snake slid to Striclan's feet. He picked it up and lifted it so that it could loop itself round his neck. Something brushed against Maja's cheek. When she reached to investigate it clambered on to her forefinger. She inspected it through her eyeglasses – a large, furry-bodied moth with rich brown wings that flickered with purple sheen where they caught the light. She lifted it so that it could settle onto her headscarf.

'It matches your eyes, my lady,' muttered Ribek.

She smiled, accepting the compliment.

'No doubt they have a purpose, but I think I must have dozed off.'

'We felt it might impress the Pirates if—'

But Ribek's explanation was interrupted by Benayu.

'All set, ladies and gentlemen? I'll be going ahead to choose a clear spot on the command deck for you. If you'd be so kind as to hold hands again . . .'

Chapter 24

THEY VANISHED, ANIMALS and all, and Angel Isle was empty apart from the calling seabirds. Now, suddenly, the inward Maja asserted itself and a wave of apprehension swept through her. They must all have been feeling a good bit of adult anxiety but been too proud to admit it, in the case of the Lady Kzuva perhaps even to herself. This was different. This was a child's terror of being set in front of an audience of important men and women and being expected to perform some feat that would be far beyond her, even if she'd had the slightest idea how to begin. Without thought she squeezed Ribek's hand for reassurance. He didn't return the gesture but started to shuffle to the right, then realized his mistake and laughed aloud.

'False alarm,' he called. 'Whoops!'

His grip on her hand tightened. Angel Isle vanished behind her. She felt a rushing motion, incredibly smooth, incredibly fast. She could see the glitter of ocean to her left, the glare of sky overhead, the mainland, but all hurtling away so fast behind her that even with her younger eyes all detail would have been lost. The movement ended as instantaneously as it had begun, without any jolt or forward lurch of her body, and she was in an enclosed space unlike anything she had ever seen before. She tucked her cane under her arm and used her free hand to put her eyeglasses to her face.

They were in a metal-and-glass room more than twice as big as the kitchen at Woodbourne, but with three curved, outward-bulging walls that consisted mainly of large clear windows. One of these was immediately behind her. Through the one opposite her Maja could see two airboats floating along, a small one fairly near and a larger one in the distance, with blue-and-white banners flying from their bows.

There were a couple of dozen people in the room, four of them soldiers guarding the two closed doors in the straight, windowless wall to her right. These wore baggy lime-green uniforms and carried things that must be weapons, though they didn't look as if they'd be much use for spearing or slashing or bashing anyone. Two more soldiers were sitting at a big table in the middle of the room, working at documents, another three were sitting at small fixed tables manipulating mysterious machines, and another was talking quietly into a shiny gadget he held in his hand. On her left, with their backs to the room, a dozen or more people were looking out through the single window that stretched almost the whole length of that wall. They were listening to a tall, pale, gaunt-faced man in a much smarter lime-green uniform as he explained to them something that was happening beyond the window. Looking at him, Maja saw at once why Saranja called the Pirates Sheep-faces. The language he was using was full of odd gargling sounds. Five of his audience were also in uniform, but the rest wore a variety of clothes, of a slightly odd style, neat but dull. Three of them were women.

She sensed a presence behind her shoulder.

'Chanad?'

'*I am here. I have their magicians. I am about to remove the guards.*'

A flicker of movement to her right caught her eye. She turned and saw that the armed men by the doors had vanished. She was certain that the doors themselves hadn't moved.

Ribek squeezed her hand twice in quick succession, waited and squeezed again – the signal for 'Ready?' She squeezed once – 'Yes.' He let go of her hand and they were visible. The man talking to the gadget broke off, stared and gave a shout. Everyone turned back to the room. There was a moment of astonished stillness. The men at the tables started to rise, somebody shouted an order, eyes turned towards the wall with the doors in it, expressions varied from baffled astonishment to equally baffled indignation, then several of the soldiers by the window made as if to rush at the intruders.

Maja gripped her cane at the centre and held it horizontally in front of her in a gesture that came suddenly into her head. A pulse of yellow light travelled rapidly along it, creating an invisible barrier across the room. Every movement beyond it froze.

'Forgive the intrusion,' said Ribek. 'Do any of you speak Imperial . . . ? Yes?'

A young man at one of the desks had thawed into movement. He didn't look like a Sheep-face. Perhaps, like Striclan, he was the child of parents who the Pirates had bought or snatched from the Empire.

'I speak both languages, er, sir,' he said, 'but I'm in Intelligence. There are professional interpreters aboard for the landings.'

'Please bring one of them to mind . . . Excellent.'

He clicked his fingers and a man appeared out of nowhere. His eyes were rheumy with sleep and he was wearing only his underclothes.

'Perhaps you'd better go and get dressed,' said Ribek, and clicked his fingers again. The man vanished. Ribek turned to the intelligence officer.

'While we are waiting,' he went on, 'would you apologize to the Syndics and officers for our intrusion and their temporary immobility, and tell them that Lady Kzuva will release them on condition that they will then listen to what we have to say.'

The man blinked and stared at Maja and spoke to the group by the big window. He was obviously saying a good bit more than Ribek had told him. Maja heard Lady Kzuva's name, and guessed he was explaining who she was, and adding that to judge by their dress the other intruders were also fairly important people.

'*You can lower the cane now,*' said Chanad's voice in her head.

Maja did so, and the magic-stilled movements completed themselves. The men who'd been rushing to confront the intruders pulled up short. A dozen voices spoke together. A man shouted an order and the voices were silent. He turned to the interpreter and spoke again in a steady, level voice full of controlled outrage.

He was short, stocky and muscular, bald, with a pale, square, flattish face and pale blue eyes. Another Sheep-face. The creases in his uniform trousers and the pleats on the pockets of his close-fitting jacket were as straight and sharp as ironing could make them. There were two broad gold bars on his epaulettes. He was a formidable presence. The inner Maja would have been terrified of him, but Lady Kzuva studied him with interest. She didn't like him much, but she recognized him as an equal.

'Supreme General Olbog asks who you are and why you are here,' said the intelligence officer. 'He would also like to know what has become of the men who were guarding the doors.'

'The guards are elsewhere and unharmed,' said Ribek, pausing between sentences for translation. 'We don't want anyone hurt. There has been more than enough of that around Tarshu. We will introduce ourselves individually later. For the moment I will say that we are a delegation from various major interests in the Empire, and we are here in the first place to persuade you to call off your assault on Larg, or failing that to prevent it; and in the second place to negotiate with the Syndics and your military command on a process leading up to

526

your complete withdrawal from the Empire. To clarify matters, I should add that the so-called Watchers have ceased to exist. The magicians you have aboard will probably have reported a major eruption of magical activity yesterday, some distance up the coast, off Barda. That was caused by our destruction of the Watchers.'

The final sentence was followed by a hush of astonishment. Several voices spoke together, all asking what sounded like much the same question. General Olbog remained expressionless, but turned to the intelligence officer and nodded to him to translate.

'The Watchers are destroyed? You did it?'

'We, at the instigation of the late President of the Grand Magical Council, recently returned from a long absence and on the verge of death. Please wait for me to finish before you ask more questions. The first magical outburst was our destruction of the Watchers, the second the passing away of both the Late President and the Guardian of Larg. Ah, your official interpreter is now dressed and ready. Shall we pause to allow him to collect his wits?'

General Olbog nodded and gestured. The soldiers moved smartly up to one end of the window and the Syndics drifted to the other. Maja's hip was starting to ache with standing, but as she was turning to beckon to Benayu, Ribek laid his hand on her arm.

'He's going to be busy,' he muttered. 'Chair? Right.'

The two groups by the window were keeping their voices down, but by the time Ribek had fetched a chair from the central table and helped her to sit snatches of what they were saying were whispering in Maja's mind.

'Now *we've* seen it all. I'd like to see bloody Olbog match that.'

'Think they're what they say they are?'

'The old lady's pretty impressive.'

'I really fancy the soldier lass.'

'Just conjuring tricks.'

'Have you still got a connection on that, Lieutenant?'

'Yessir.'

'Don't let on. I'll call you in a minute. Come over here with a couple of documents.'

'Will do, sir.'

'And find out what the hell's happening with our tame magicians. Supposed to have one here, weren't we?'

'Will do, sir.'

'What's with the menagerie? We're not children.'

'My Dad's a bug-hunter. He'd give his soul for that moth.'

'Prevent *the landing,* the fellow said. D'you think they could really do that?'

'One in the eye for bloody Olbog. Hope he tries it.'

'It'll take more than conjuring tricks.'

'Bring me the abort file, will you, Lieutenant?'

'Yessir.'

'Must say, I'd like to see our weapons in action after what we've paid for them.'

'I wouldn't mind seeing a couple of dragons – not too close, mind. Something to tell the kids.'

'Right, Lieutenant. Look over my shoulder. I'm showing you stuff in the file, right. You're through to Attack Comm?'

'Yessir.'

'Tell them Code Nine Jiddi Nine. Immediate action. Got it? Yes, Pashgahr?'

'We are still moving faster than the air cover is able to. Troops will be landing without air cover.'

'Weren't you listening? The Guardian of Larg has passed away. That means Larg must be without whatever defences it may have had. Check, Intelligence?'

'Nothing on a Guardian as such in the files, sir. Speculation by the agent reporting lack of magical activity within and around Larg that some powerful force must be maintaining the situation.'

'Hear that, Syndic? No magic in Larg? Wasn't in our briefing.'

'Fleet equipped to counter any magical activity they may meet, wasn't it? Covers the point, I suppose?'

'Right, Pashgahr. How long before the boats are off, as of now?'

'We got it down to seventeen minutes forty in drill practice, General.'

'You take over the operations side then. I'll spin things out here.'

'Very good, sir. I suggest, for the look of the thing, you get the Syndics to ask a question or two. Burdag is sound – he's got a big holding in Gas Avionics in his sister's name.'

'Good point. Time the bastards earned their keep instead of acting like we're laying on a firework display for their amusement. All set? Interpreter?'

'I am ready, sir. I must apologize . . .'

'You can cut that out. Ask these people to tell us more

529

about themselves and what proof they have of the authority they are claiming.'

'Everyone get all that?' muttered Ribek. 'They're playing into our hands. We've just got to get the timing right.'

'Find an excuse for Benayu to get me outside and disappear me,' said Saranja. 'I'll take Rocky, and if he keeps us invisible we can scout around and keep an eye on things.'

'We'll need you back here when the moment comes.'

'Bennay, my brooch, please,' said Maja.

'Very good, my lady.'

He unpinned the brooch, placed it briefly between his palms and showed it to her before he pinned it back on. There were only two horses on it now.

The interpreter, a lanky, anxious young man in an ill-fitting uniform, turned towards them. He too didn't look like a Sheep-face, but someone they might well have met at a way station on an Imperial Highway. Ribek nodded when he'd finished telling them some of what the general had said.

'As you wish,' he answered. 'Would you begin, Lady Kzuva?'

Maja rose stiffly, stood leaning with both hands on her cane, and spoke directly to the group of Syndics. There was a pale-faced middle-aged woman among them that she liked the look of.

'I am the hereditary Landholder of Kzuva,' she said, 'which is a large estate towards the north of the Empire and carries with it various offices and titles in the Imperial Household, and also considerable magical

530

powers. I use these only when I must, as just now. I am not, of course, a professional magician. I have better things to do with my time, so I employ a woman for that purpose. Some of the renegades you have on board should at least have heard of me.'

She sat down and waited while the others introduced themselves in the roles they had talked about on Angel Isle. Ribek claimed to have inherited one particular magical power, but had never used more than a small part of it to maintain a regular supply of water through his millwheels. Striclan said he didn't have any, as it was a condition of his job as Under-secretary in Magdep.

'I can do a bit of magic,' Saranja explained. 'Not just ordinary hedge magic – better than that. There's a lot of people like me in the Empire. Some of us could be serious professional magicians if we wanted, but we don't use it much. It isn't just that the Watchers cracked down on it, though there was that, of course, but even without them we don't. As Lady Kzuva says, it gets in the way. I'll show you.'

She drew her sabre and sliced the air in front of her. One of the empty chairs at the central table fell neatly in two.

'That sort of thing runs in a lot of old military families,' she added. 'Everyone in my regiment can do it, but we're a picked regiment. You probably came across a bit of it around Tarshu.'

Maja saw some of the soldiers glancing anxiously towards the Syndics. That must have been a good guess of Benayu's. Of course the Watchers would have given their troops magically enhanced weapons to fight the fantastical armoury of the Pirates, and of course (from what she now knew of them) the generals wouldn't have told the people back home about everything they were up against.

'And finally,' said Ribek, in exactly the same tone as he'd used to introduce everyone else, 'this is Sponge. He and the other creatures who have come with us represent the animals of the Empire. Sponge here will speak for them.'

'Speak?' queried the interpreter before translating.

'I speak for animals,' said Sponge. His voice wasn't the one Maja had forced into his throat in that other universe, but fully articulate, low in the register, each word separate from its neighbours with a slight snarl at the end. A couple of the Syndics clapped. Though others had frowned at them, Maja for the first time felt a little sympathy for General Olbog. The fate of the Empire might depend upon this meeting and here they were treating it as a show put on for their amusement.

'Animals do not want you in our places,' Sponge went on. 'You do not understand our places, our humans, our animals. Now I tell you this. We too have magic. I use magic to speak to you. Watchers sent dragon against us. I fought it. I became big. I grew wings. I flew. I fought dragon, killed it. It wounded me. See.'

He turned to display the new-healed scar in his flank.

'Now think,' he went on. 'You come to Empire. Humans use their magic. Fight you. We use our magic. Fight you. Not just big strong biters, tearers. One ant – little, little magic. How many ants in Empire? Millions and millions. Think. Ants, maggots, cockroaches, rats, mice in your foodstores, lice, bugs in your bedding, snakes in your path, mosquitoes, wasps, ticks on your flesh, birds, bats watching what you do, where you go, millions and millions of us, all fight you alongside humans. You fight us? How? Think.'

General Olbog spoke, his rage by now barely under control. His words had the shape of a question, followed by a brief order to the interpreter. Striclan's voice, distorted perhaps by its passage through Benayu, spoke in Maja's mind.

'Where are our bloody magicians? Why didn't they tell us any of this? Don't translate that.'

'May we please proceed?' said Striclan smoothly. 'I have not finished answering your questions. Let me do that, and then you can discuss what I've told you among yourselves before I try to answer any further questions that may arise. You asked for proof of the authority under which we claim to act. We have come in haste, in view of the imminent attack on Larg, and there hasn't been time to obtain writs with the Emperor's seal from Talagh – the Imperial bureaucracy is notoriously slow to move. However, the President Designate of the Grand Council has said that she will make herself available, if needed. She carries the Emperor's seal of office, in the form of a ring. To put your minds at rest, it is very powerfully protected from any form of magical tampering or duplication, as well as plain theft. Only the President or President Designate can wear it. Captain Saran will act as an escort. Ready, Captain?'

Saranja stretched her right arm out in front of her and opened her fist, palm down. For a fraction of an instant a small silver object started to fall, but in the rest of that instant it seemed to catch fire and explode, and in the next the blaze gathered itself into a great scarlet and golden shape, Rocky in all his splendour, winged and caparisoned, pawing gently at the deck with one front hoof as if eager for action. Effortlessly Saranja swung herself into the saddle, drew her sabre, saluted Maja, the Syndics and General Olbog in that order, and disappeared.

'The President Designate will be with us shortly,' said Ribek as easily as if they had just witnessed some everyday event. 'You will need your own magicians to authenticate the seal. You may have been wondering why they aren't present. The answer is that we took them into our temporary protection to avoid the possibility of a magical conflict, which would have been a very risky undertaking not only for the participants but also for anyone who happened to be present. Lady Kzuva, if you would be so kind.'

Maja beckoned. Benayu appeared at her shoulder, knelt, took three apples out of his wallet and placed them on the floor in front of her and stood back.

Maja touched each of the apples in turn with the tip of her cane. Instantly they shrivelled and vanished, leaving nothing but three small brown seeds on the floor. Rapidly these sprouted and became three slim stems, each with a single bud at the top. As they continued to grow, a pair of twigs appeared on either side of each stem a little below the bud. These lengthened into drooping branches with a few leaves sprouting from the ends.

When the saplings were about as tall as a man, Maja touched them again with her cane. They stopped growing and swelled. The buds became heads, the side branches arms and the leaves fingers, and three not-quite-human figures stood before them. One was naked to the waist, revealing a well-built muscular body with a tiger-skin draped across his shoulders. The head of the tiger was the living head of the man. The second was a woman robed from head to foot in shimmering black. Only her silver face and hands were visible. The third was a head taller than anyone in the room, but grotesquely thin. His eyes were three times the size of human eyes, vivid yellow, and had slits for pupils.

The Lady Kzuva part of Maja smiled at the sheer vulgarity of this attempt to impress the barbarians, then shook her head, still smiling, because it wasn't, after all, much different from what they themselves had been doing. The frivolous Syndics were right. It had been a show put on for their amusement. But still, the fate of the Empire depended on it. The shadow of a memory flickered in her mind. When she'd needed a new magician and interviewed applicants . . . Yes . . . The silver woman had looked almost human then, but that robe . . . she would be able to confirm that she was the real Lady Kzuva.

'Please give them a moment to recover,' said Ribek. 'It is an unnerving experience for any magician to be so mastered. And I should tell you that it would not have been done so easily if they had not been seriously weakened by being too long at sea, far from the sources of . . .'

He broke off abruptly and turned. Rocky had reappeared on their right and now stood waiting for his riders to dismount before he settled his wings. Saranja twisted down, neatly avoiding Chanad in the rear saddle, turned urgently to Maja, touched the hilt of her sabre by way of salute and said, 'My lady, the landing has started. We saw thirty or more boats laden with men, setting out for the shore.'

She turned to help Chanad dismount.

Maja swung round, ignoring the pang from her hip.

'Is this true, General Olbog?'

The General made a pacifying gesture with his hands and started to speak slowly and evenly, as if reasoning with a child. Striclan's voice spoke in Maja's mind.

'He is telling the interpreter to take it slowly. He is saying that it is an administrative error, and that the landing will now have to take place, but as soon as the soldiers are ashore they will be ordered to proceed no further.'

'Nonsense, General,' Maja snapped. 'We heard you give the order with your own lips. Do you think we would have been so stupid as to come here and rely solely on your own interpreter, without the means to understand directly what you were saying? With your permission, Madam President Designate?'

'Please do what you must, Lady Kzuva,' said Chanad shaking her head wearily, as if at the unplumbable stupidity of humankind. Maja turned back to General Olbog.

'Very well,' she said. 'Since you refuse to stop the landing, we are now forced to do so ourselves. Captain, Mr Ortahlson, please carry on. Bennay, your shoulder. Stand aside, please.'

Leaning on Benayu she hobbled up to the long window with the others following. The spectators already there made room for them. Now she was able to see what they'd been looking at. Ahead of them, still three or four miles off, lay the shoreline and hills around Larg, their colours already muted by the approach of dusk. She could see the undying flame crowning the rock pillar that imprisoned the demon Azarod, the waves breaking gently against the harbour bar, the mild swell on the last reaches of ocean glistening into bars of light under the westering sun. Black against that brightness, two medium-sized airboats floated shoreward ahead of the much larger one she was on. There were several more lined out to either side of her. Below them ships of the Pirate fleet advanced slowly on the city, first a screen of smaller vessels, then several larger ones, and then, almost beneath where she was standing, three big, broad-beamed vessels, obviously not warships but carriers. These had stopped moving and had lowered platforms something like the drawbridge of a moated town, leaving a wide opening in the bows out of which had emerged three lines of open barges, each carrying forty or more armed men. They were advancing on Larg far faster than the rest of the fleet. The leading barges were already almost level with the forward screen.

'Captain, Mr Ortahlson, you had better act at once.

Any nearer, and we shall discommode the good citizens of Larg.'

Saranja had Zald ready in her wallet. She drew the great jewel out and held it in her left hand, with the surface towards her. The fingers of her right hand moved in a careful, dance-like pattern over the jewels surrounding the central amber. That done, she spoke five resonant syllables, with deliberate pauses between them. Each seemed to linger in the air like a bell-note until she spoke the next. All were meaningless to Maja and probably to everyone else in the room except Benayu, who'd coached Saranja back on Angel Isle. As the last syllable faded away she lifted the amber jewel gently from its setting.

She cupped it in her right hand as if showing it to Ribek. He closed his own hand over hers and turned, not to the window, but to his right. North. *They have a different magic in the north.*

He started to sing, if you could call it singing. She remembered how oddly unable he'd been, on their journey through the desert, to carry the simplest tune, but this was different. Somehow she knew that he was singing it as it was meant to be sung, this steady, rippling drone, repetitive, endless but full of intricate little changes, like the surface of a flowing stream. In this hot country, far from the mountains of his home, he was singing, as his ancestors had done for generations before him, to the northern snows.

The sky darkened, and darkened further. The sea changed colour, from blue-green to a curious pale mottled grey. The advancing fleet seemed to have come

538

to a sudden halt. A snowflake drifted down past the window, and another, large as a child's hand. The sea changed colour again, as the sun, still reaching in from the west beneath the sudden astonishing darkness of the cloud-layer, dazzled back off the whiteness below. Then everything vanished, blotted out by the falling snow. The room was suddenly as cold as a midwinter morning in the Valley. The owl on Saranja's shoulder fluffed out its feathers and the squirrel on Ribek's was huddling against his neck for warmth. She felt a fidgeting on her head and knew that her moth must have been triggered into hibernation and was burrowing in under her head-scarf.

From behind the closed doors came the sound of alarm bells, urgent shouts of command. General Olbog was shouting too. Striclan's voice spoke in her head.

'*What the hell do you people think you are doing? You are endangering the ship!*'

Maja waited for the translator's more tactful version before she answered.

'Tell him that nobody will be hurt, unless they are stupid enough to harm each other. The ship is in no danger.'

Benayu's shoulder was trembling beneath her hand.

'Are you all right?' she murmured. 'You've done wonders.'

'I'm just about done for. I can't keep Maja's shield going much longer.'

'It is not needed. I am not sensitive, so the child is safe in my shelter. The sea is affecting you more strongly than you predicted?'

'It's just the last straw. I can manage the little stuff, talking in your heads, that sort of thing. But I'm not up to anything else big. Nor's Chanad. Ribek's in charge now. This had better work. Ugh – I didn't realize how cold it was going to be.'

He shuddered again. Maja turned from the window, looking for the three hired magicians. They were standing a little way back, their faces unreadable behind their chosen masks, but their postures tense and watchful. She beckoned them forward.

'I think I have met you before, haven't I?' she said to the silver woman. 'Your appearance was less, ah, striking then. You came for a post in my household, but I'd already chosen someone else. Your name begins with a Q, I think. Quirril?'

'Quiriul, my lady.'

'I'm sorry to find you here.'

'It was that or be conscripted by the Watchers, my lady. I chose what I thought was a lesser evil. The same with my colleagues here.'

'You must have had a hard time, so long out at sea.'

'Very hard, my lady. We became so feeble. It is like the weakness after a fever, and we dared not tell them.'

'Well, the Watchers are gone and that's over now, so you can return home. When you are recovered, you could perhaps offer your services to the President Designate. She is going to need a lot of help. Meanwhile, if you are up to it, you could provide us with some warmth in here.'

She turned back to the window. Still nothing to see but densely falling snow. The two generals seemed to be

540

engaged in a furious argument. Striclan came round to her other side. His snake had disappeared. Gone in under his shirt for warmth, presumably.

'Benayu is exhausted,' he said, 'and Saranja and Ribek are fully occupied. I may as well simply tell you what is going on. Pashgahr wants to abort the landing . . .'

'It is already aborted, is it not?'

'I would have said so. But Olbog is determined to go ahead, whatever it costs.'

'He probably thinks he has been made a fool of. It is the one thing that type of man cannot endure.'

'What I suggest would mean pretending we can do something I doubt we can in fact do, with Benayu and Chanad out of action—'

'I would advise against it,' Maja interrupted. 'The danger is that he might then attempt to destroy us before we can carry out our threat. Benayu is in no position to defend us. I have begun an attempt to suborn the hired magicians, but they too are greatly enfeebled. We are on a knife edge, Mr Ruddya. We must stake everything on what Ribek is doing. It seems to be as effective as we could wish. Ah, that's better.'

A faint draught had sprung up while she was speaking, warm, and smelling pleasantly of lowland pastures. Benayu stopped shivering.

'No doubt you are right,' said Striclan. 'Look, I think the snowfall is less than it was.'

She glanced at the window. The flakes were already smaller and fewer, and in two or three minutes had ceased completely. The late sun appeared over the western hills once more, shining in under the cloud-canopy on to a glittering island that reached almost into the shoreline of the bay and farther yet to north and south. It was far more than simply a rumpled surface of snow-covered ice, all at roughly the same level, every detail lost beneath the snow-cover. Cliffs and crags of ice rose directly from the sea, and then rose further into three jagged parallel ridges, culminating in a rough peak almost level with the window through which she was looking.

Scattered among the ledges and crannies of this forbidding surface lodged the snow-swathed ships of the Pirate fleet. Among them were two airboats, forced down by the mass of snow on their gas bags, which, relieved of the weight of the boats themselves, still floated buoyant above them. The remaining airboats were still aloft, but sinking steadily to join them. Maja realized that the *All-Conqueror* itself was far lower than it had been before the snowfall. What an end to a proud invasion! But she felt no triumph. Not yet. They were still on a knife edge.

Beyond the closed doors an alarm bell still sounded, but the cries of command had stopped. No doubt all orders had been given and the crew were readying themselves for the landing. There was silence too on the command deck, but not for long. Murmurs broke out and increased – astonishment, alarm, anger, apprehension. Ribek raised his voice above the incipient hubbub.

'Silence, please, ladies and gentlemen. I want to show you something more important than anything you have yet seen. Will you all come to the window and stand in a single line? . . . Thank you. Now, I want you to look through my eyes and see what I am seeing. I promise

542

you that I will not tamper with your inner selves in any way. You will remain exactly what you are, apart from having seen something that very few humans have seen before you, and perhaps having a greater knowledge and understanding than you have now. For that purpose, will you please hold hands all along the line?'

Maja felt him take her hand in his. She sensed a hesitation on her left and turned to see what was happening. General Pashgahr was already in the line, and two of the others had joined him, but the rest were waiting to follow General Olbog's lead, and he was still standing where he had been, a little back from the window, looking steadfastly at Ribek as if he could destroy him by glaring.

Even powerful men such as those we will be meeting have an instinct to respect women such as yourself. Maja moved a little back, interrupting his line of sight, held out her hand to him, and smiled her grandest, kindliest smile.

'General Olbog . . .' she murmured.

He came, a child at a party, who has arrived determined not to participate but then been overwhelmed by the greater moral force of the adult presence. Again he hesitated, but took her hand. His own was dry and muscular, the grip of a man who prides himself on a firm handshake.

'Be gentle with it,' she told him. 'Old bones, you know.'

He pursed his lips into the flicker of a smile and grabbed the hand of the man next in line. Together they turned to the window and saw what Ribek was seeing. She heard the gasps spreading along the line.

Nothing had changed, and everything. The impossible island was still there, not one snowflake, not one ice-splinter different. It was its nature that had changed. What had been a series of rugged infolded ridges was now the scaly loops and coils of an immense reptilian body. The dragon that had hunted them down the sunken lane above Larg would have seemed ant-sized beside it.

She had only a glimpse, and then it was gone, and the frozen island was there once more. Then, for a flicker, it was the incredible immense creature before the island returned. The flickering increased in speed until the dizzying double visions merged and she was staring more steadily at something that hung, poised, solid and real, between two possibilities, both equally impossible, the frozen island that in the space of a few minutes had emerged out of nowhere into these subtropic seas and showed no sign of melting, and the gigantic animal, far colder than any temperature at which life could exist, far larger than any size at which it could sustain itself.

Even in detail the uncertainty remained, as though every part of it refused to choose between One or Other, and insisted on its existence as both. The odd-shaped summit, with its swathes of snow lying between ice-green scars and outcrops, and pocked and pitted here and there as if some huge hand had thrown a fistful of boulders against it, was certainly an icy summit, but equally certainly it was the creature's head, resting on the curving outer fold of the body. The two largest holes were just empty pits, but gleamed with the liquid luminosity of deep-sunk eyes. Two apparently random mounds, marked by shallow pocks, also existed as a pair of scaly hummocks bearing the quadruple nostrils on the blunt snout, lidded with flaps of skin that stirred to the slow breathing of the cavernous lungs. Hollows and crevasses were folds and mouldings of the tough hide, as it followed the shape of the skull beneath. Beyond the central ridge was the vast reptilian body, curving round in the form of the northern ridge, and back again beneath the head to become the southern ridge as it dwindled into the tail. Every detail both This and That, occupying the same space at the same time. Things that could not either separately or simultaneously be true, but were.

Human eyes are not made for such seeing. Maja's fought for mastery, for the right to choose between This and That. Her mind resisted, fully certain of what it was seeing through those eyes, the absolute *thereness* of the creature, its presence, its power. All along the line she could hear murmurs of the same struggle.

She turned to see how General Olbog was taking it. He was also struggling, being forced to recognize the reality of the vision, and hating it. In the middle of your worst nightmare some part of you still knows it to be only a dream. What if you then wake to find that it's true? General Olbog didn't look like a man who paid much attention to whatever dreams he had, if he remembered them at all. As soon as he stopped gazing through the window he would try to treat the ice dragon like that – a trick of the light, another stupid bit of conjuring, pay no attention – but henceforth it would return to him in his dreams, and he would remember them on waking. For the moment, though, he couldn't tear his eyes away from it, but stood staring out of the window and shaking his head, like a drunk man trying to clear his mind.

'You are looking at the great ice dragon of the northern wastes,' said Ribek quietly. 'It and its partner to the south built and maintain the two realms of ice and snow on which the well-being of this world depends. We do not have the power to summon it, the Captain and I. Nobody has that, no magician or group of magicians, however powerful, has that. All that we two can do is ask it. Nothing that has happened since we came to the window was done by us – it is all the ice dragon. It came of its own will. It brought the ice and snow of its own will. If it had chosen it could have crushed every ship of your navy in the grip of its ice as easily as a cobnut is cracked open between two stones. Instead, of its own will it has chosen that you should see it. Though the power to call to it runs in my family, only once in several generations does one of us see it, and then never as clearly as you are now doing.

'Why you? you may ask. The task of the two ice dragons is to maintain the well-being of the world. More than once in the remote past, the earth has sickened and needed first cleansing, then renewal. The two ice dragons have extended their realms to cover the entire earth, frozen it for a long age, and then withdrawn to allow the life of the world to renew itself among the tiny, unnoticed creatures that survived below the ice.

'Now, once again, there were signs that such a time was coming. The so-called Watchers, with their insatiable lust for power, were one such sign. Their ultimate purpose was to incorporate all life on earth into themselves. In the eyes of the ice dragon they were the seeds of a disease that would in the end have sickened the whole earth. Fortunately we were able to act in time and destroy them before it needed to do so itself.

'I cannot expect you to see yourselves in a similar light, but I can assure you that the ice dragon does. It has not come here, as we have, to prevent you from committing a single great wrong. It has come as a warning to you of what will follow if you continue on the course that you seem to have set yourselves. The very name of the great vessel that carries us – the *All-Conqueror* – is a signpost on that course. I do not tell you this of my own knowledge. Like the vision of the ice dragon that you saw through my eyes, you are hearing through my mouth what it wishes you to be told.

'Now I think we have seen enough. It is dangerous to look too long on such a being. It can madden the strongest mind.'

He withdrew his hand from Maja's and the island was only a craggy patch of ice, littered with the ships of the Pirate navy. The tension broke like a wave breaking, into a hubbub of comments and questions. Maja turned to General Olbog.

'Thank you for joining us, General,' she said. 'It was interesting, was it not?'

There was nobody handy to interpret, but he caught her tone, favoured her with his mini-smile, grunted some guttural politeness, nodded by way of farewell and turned away.

'I've got to get us out of here,' muttered Benayu. 'Fading faster than I expected. Won't have anything left if I don't go soon. Need Chanad to help, as it is.'

'I will talk to Ribek. You go and sit down.'

A dozen people, Syndics and soldiers, were already crowded round Ribek, bombarding him with questions. Most were men, taller than she was. She rapped an officer on the shoulder with the handle of her cane. He turned his head, cut his protest short when he saw who it was and made a gap. The movement caught Ribek's eye. She beckoned, drew aside and waited for him to join her. Out of the corner of her eye she saw somebody sidling into earshot. The Pirates' translator.

'My boy Bennay's been taken ill, and I do not have the remedy with me,' she said. 'I must get him ashore.'

'It's time we went in any case, my lady,' he said. 'If you would be so good as to tell the others . . .'

He turned to his audience.

'Please,' he said. 'No more questions for the moment. We have to leave in a minute. We have done what we came to do by preventing your attack on Larg. This was an emergency action. We do not have the authority to act further on behalf of the Imperial Government. We will leave you to discuss what you have seen and heard, and we will be ready to meet you for a truce conference an hour before noon tomorrow morning on the headland you can see to the south of Larg. We will permit one airboat large enough to carry your delegation, but no larger, to be cleared of snow to bring them ashore under our safe conduct. This will be a sign that you accept our conditions. If we receive no such signal your fleet will be destroyed at sunset.

'So we bid you farewell, and hope to see you tomorrow on the headland. Madam President Designate, if you are ready.'

Chanad was talking to the three renegades. She turned and nodded. Maja and the others gathered around her. Saranja turned and saluted the room. Chanad made a gentle gesture of closure, and the space where they had been standing was empty.

Chapter 25

THE CITIZENS OF Larg had been watching from their walls in awe and fear as the Pirate fleet closed in on them, regardless of wind or tide – fear that changed to amazement as the ships and airboats were blotted out by a brief but intense snow-blizzard in the midst of the calm and sunlit bay, and then changed again to delighted relief when the blizzard cleared, revealing the impossible island of ice, with the ships stranded and helpless on it and the snow-burdened airboats drifting down to join them.

They saw three winged horses emerge from the largest of the airboats and some keen-eyed watchers recognized Saranja's streaming mane. So it was that when Saranja and Striclan, the only two of the travellers able to cross Zara's still-functioning ward, headed down the hill to tell the Proctors what was afoot, and what would now be needed, they found a welcoming party climbing to meet them.

Maja fell asleep under the stars once more, well fed and on comfortable bedding ferried up from the city. The needs of her Lady Kzuva self woke her in the small hours, and on her return she paused and stared out to sea. There, plain to her long-sightedness, stood the flame-crested pillar that imprisoned Azarod, black against the moonlit glitter of the island, both astonishing in themselves but still only rock and flame and ice, things of this world. The scene twitched, and now she was seeing them as they might have been seen in the worlds where they belonged, the raging demon and the immense unknowable dragon. She couldn't remember going back to her mattress, apart from a vague sense of having floated there, with all the quiet magic of the sleeping world vivid to her extra sense.

Nor could she remember waking and eating, though she must have done, because now she was standing leaning on her cane, fully dressed, with the taste of food in her mouth, while Chanad, Ribek and Saranja talked urgently together, and Benayu and Striclan stood and listened. Striclan had his arm round Benayu, supporting him. Benayu was looking really ill.

In that moment Maja understood what was happening to her.

'Listen,' she said urgently. 'Sometimes I don't know what Lady Kzuva's saying and doing. She's not protecting me from magic, either. I think I'm coming apart.'

'Indeed you are,' said Chanad. 'Benayu is exhausted. He cannot keep Lady Kzuva here much longer. I could do it, but it would take all my attention, and that is needed for the conference. If we don't send her back

551

where she belongs in the next two hours we shall lose you both. Do you understand?'

'Yes. I'm sorry. Even when we're together I – we – feel very odd. Dazed, dizzy. I don't think she knows what I'm saying now.'

'The trouble is we need Lady K for the conference,' said Saranja. 'She represents the Landholders, who've got a lot of say in the Empire, so she's got to set her seal on the final document.'

'Couldn't you send her home now, and just make me look like her? I think I could do that, now that I've been her for a bit. Act like her and talk like her, I mean, provided I don't have to say too much. I could tell them I'm tired after all that magic yesterday. I'm out of practice.'

'That is what we were talking about,' said Chanad. 'A *mugal* – a simulacrum controlled by a living spirit within it. Quiriul and her two colleagues could do it, I think. I've already arranged for them to transport themselves to us and tell us what has been happening aboard the *All-Conqueror*. I will ask them to come as soon as they can.'

'How long will the *mugal* thing take?' said Ribek. 'Will they be able to do it before the delegation gets here? The airboat will be ready to leave as soon as they've cleared the snow off its gasbag, and they're halfway through that already. It'd be nice to have Lady K in there to . . .'

Sudden and close, a jolt of magic. A glimpse of three figures just beyond Chanad's shoulder. Maja was back in her daze.

*

A hand gripping her elbow, shaking her arm. Ribek's urgent mutter in her ear.

'Wake up, Maja! Wake up if you can! We need you!'

With a willed effort she hauled her two halves into oneness and held them steady. She was standing beside him on the crown of the headland. All around them a gaudy encampment had arisen, pavilions, rest-tents and awnings, flags and pennons, and side by side in pride of place the green banner of Larg and the blue-and-white one of the Pirate fleet.

They were waiting on a level patch of turf that had been left clear beside the largest pavilion. The dignitaries of Larg were lined up to one side, with their President Proctor and the fake Imperial delegation in front of them. What seemed like half the citizens of Larg watched from the perimeter. In perfect silence the airboat descended into the centre. The gondola touched soundlessly on to the turf. Pumps pulsed briefly, then silence again, with the gasbag swaying in the light breeze. A section of the hull hinged downward and became a ramp and General Pashgahr appeared in the opening with a pale-faced dumpy woman beside him. Maja recognized her as the Syndic she'd particularly noticed yesterday.

They paused while a dozen trumpets sounded an elaborate fanfare. The President Proctor, with Chanad at his side, moved forward to meet them as they came down the ramp. The pealing of the bells of Larg sounded musically in the distance. Speeches began, but she barely heard them as the daze returned.

*

553

Another jolt of magic, this time as deliberate as Ribek's shaking her arm had been to force her to wakefulness. She was standing in one of the smaller tents, with both hands clutching the central pole. Just the other side of the pole stood a woman Maja had never seen before, with both arms outstretched, holding hands with two people out of sight behind Maja. She could sense that all three were magicians, and that she was standing near the apex of a triangle formed by their arms. Benayu was watching from behind the woman's shoulder. There were beads of sweat on his forehead. He was nibbling at his thumb-knuckle like a child, feverish with anxiety.

'I am Quiriul,' said the woman. 'We prefer our former employers not to recognize us. Now, if I may, my lady . . .'

She placed her own hands over Maja's.

'Brad is going to construct the simulacrum while Turbax prepares your shielding within it,' she said. 'Meanwhile I will separate your consciousness from that of Lady Kzuva and control your transference to the simulacrum. I have to warn you that you won't be shielded at all while that is happening, so you will have to prepare yourself for a brief period of considerable stress. And once the process has started it cannot be stopped without fatal results to at least one of you.'

Unwilled, a dreamy whisper issued from Maja's lips.

'Let it be me who dies, should that happen,' said Lady Kzuva. 'Maja has many more years to live.'

Quiriul hesitated, clearly taken aback. She sighed and shook her head.

'I can't choose,' she said. 'This is difficult enough as it

is. We must simply not let it happen. When the transfer is complete Brad will see Lady Kzuva safely back to her own place while Turbax and I coordinate the speech and movement of the simulacrum with Maja's intentions. Now, will you stand as still as you can and look into my eyes?'

Maja couldn't see them clearly without her spectacles, but they seemed to be just a pair of normal green eyes. Little happened for what seemed a long while. She could sense both Turbax and Brad busy behind her, sense too, beside the magic they were preparing, something amiss between them, Turbax's mild contempt for Brad, who was older but less accomplished, and Brad's resentment of it. She must warn Chanad about that, she thought . . .

'Now,' whispered Quiriul. 'Look, Lady Kzuva. Look, Maja.'

Maja concentrated. Quiriul's eyes were now clear to her. Green, yes, but flecked with brown. They grew larger, like two pools welling up in their hollows, joining together, covering lashes and lids, brows, nose and cheeks, the whole face. And at the same time the sphere of Maja's vision seemed to narrow until the pool was all that she could see, with the two black irises pulsing gently side by side while the brown flecks, glowing now with a smoky light, moved hypnotically around and between them. The eyes floated towards her, filled her vision, absorbed her. She felt dazed, drugged, only vaguely aware of her own body – whose body? Hers? Lady Kzuva's? She didn't know. Time passed, unmeasurable. All that changed was a faint, vague pressure against her shoulder blades, insubstantial as mist, but slowly becoming firmer.

Without warning the tent pole faded from her grasp. She heard Benayu's urgent mutter close in her ear. The shreds of her shielding vanished and she was naked to the triple whirlpool of magic swirling though the little tent. There was someone there with her, being whirled in the same tempest, inert, helpless – Benayu. Desperately, twisting to and fro, she flung her arm round him, clutched him against her, and with her other arm clung to the rock of her own selfhood, Maja, Maja, Maja . . . and then she was left gasping in a different kind of shelter, improvised and patchy, like a draughty shed that is still better than nothing in the blast of winter.

Shuddering with relief she looked around her. She was still in the tent, but with the entrance now in front of her. Her back was against the tent pole with some kind of sash holding her firmly in place there. She seemed to have no sense of balance and would have fallen without it. That must be Turbax to her left, but Brad was gone from her other side. Where was Benayu? She tried to turn her head. Pain lanced up her spine.

'Wait,' said Quiriul's voice behind her. 'You are not yet ready to move.'

Maja forced the unfamiliar mouth to cooperate.

'Benayu? What?' she croaked.

'I almost lost you. He came to help. It overstretched him. He is here, but unconscious. Wait. We must finish our work, or we will lose you again. Breathe deeply in, and out again.'

Maja realized now that she hadn't been breathing at

all. For a moment nothing happened. Then, with a rush, the air came. With a willed effort she forced it back out.

'Good,' said Quiriul. 'And again. And again.'

Maja obeyed. Her breath steadied and continued of its own accord. With a painful convulsion her heart began to beat. Saliva flowed, but she needed her conscious mind to decide to swallow it. Sometimes on her own, sometimes on Quiriul's instructions, she worked her way round all the normally unnoticed functions of her body. As each piece fitted itself into place others joined themselves to the growing wholeness. Her sense of balance returned.

'Well done,' said Quiriul. 'Now we will coordinate your movements . . .'

But turning her head Maja had seen from the corner of her eyes a green and gold hummock sprawled against the side of the tent.

'May I speak?'

'Try.'

Maja steadied herself, summoned the authority she had learnt as the real Lady Kzuva.

'Bennay. Benayu,' she said. 'He's more important than any of us. We can't just let him lie there. He came to the edge to find me and brought me back. We've got to do something.'

'I daren't interfere magically,' said Quiriul. 'He is far out of my reach. There is nothing any of us can do directly. He needs rest and quiet and peace of mind. He was desperately anxious for you. He knew we would be working at the limit of our powers. That was why he insisted on being present. So now the best we can do for

557

him is to finish our work. Even as he is he may be aware that you are out of danger.'

'All right.'

'Nod then . . . Exercise your neck . . . Now your right arm, starting at the shoulder, and down to the individual fingers . . .'

They worked systematically on. Impatiently Maja took her first pace.

'That will have to do,' she said, practising her Lady Kzuva manner. 'Thank you for your help. I know you are tired, but would you be kind enough to wait with my boy, Madam Quiriul, until I can send somebody to see him well looked after. And you, sir, you must be Master Turbax.'

He was the one who'd had the tiger's head. She could tell from the yellowish glow in his eyes.

'At your service, my lady,' he said smoothly, and managed a smile. But it was a smile that said, 'Why should I bother? You're only a child pretending to be a great lady. And who cares about Benayu? He's washed-up, done for. Better carry through with the charade. Important to ingratiate myself with the President Designate.' *Too late, Master Turbax. I'm going to warn her. You aren't as clever as you think you are.*

'And you are responsible for my shielding,' she said. 'I am most grateful. Now if you would be so kind as to see me to the conference tent . . .'

Several of the functionaries of the Provost's Court were waiting beside the entrance. Maja spotted the one who had come up from Larg with the old groom on the morning after the defeat of Azarod, to bring their breakfast and tell them to get ready for the visit from the Proctors themselves. She caught his eye and beckoned him over.

'My lady?' he said.

'My boy has been taken seriously ill. He is in that small tent with the yellow pennant. Please arrange to have him carried somewhere where he can rest and not be disturbed. The woman now with him will tell you what else is needed.'

'I will see to it myself,' said the functionary, as obsequious now as he had been haughty when Maja had first met him.

She thanked Turbax for his help at the entrance to the tent and went in alone. Striclan was speaking. He paused for the translation. By the time Maja was settled into her chair he was speaking again, about arranging for any citizens of the Empire aboard the fleet to be allowed to return home if they wished. Maja and Ribek muttered to each other during pauses for translation.

'How are you feeling?' he said.

'Tired, but I'll manage. Provided I don't have to talk much. What's happening? Where's General Olbog?'

'Under arrest. He wanted to load the airboat with armed men and make a surprise attack on Larg. The Syndics overruled him. Pashgahr supported them . . . Olbog must have guessed this would happen, and had given secret orders for his people to take over the command deck . . . The magicians were keeping an eye on things – Chanad had asked them to – and they told

Syndic – I still can't pronounce her name – begins with B – that one there . . .'

'Syndic Blrundahlrgh,' said Maja. The name seemed to be on her tongue. Syndic Blrundahlrgh was the dumpy woman who'd come down the ramp beside General Olbog. She was important because she represented the Homemakers' Interest.

'I can remember last night, not this morning,' she said as soon as the translator began again. 'Striclan coached us how to say it, didn't he?'

'She's on our side against the Olbog lot. When she heard about the mutiny she left the command deck and faced the mutineers down. Talk to her if you can. It shouldn't be that difficult. You'll have time to think what to say next while the last bit's being translated. Tell her you're not yourself. It'll be truer than she thinks.'

'All right. What's going on now?'

'We've almost finished. Pashgahr's desperate to get back to the fleet before Olbog's lot try anything. All we can do is agree a one-month ceasefire. Nobody's got any real authority for more . . . We release their fleet. They withdraw to Tarshu. Hostilities round Tarshu cease. Any troops still on shore re-embark in six days and withdraw to an offshore island called Anyan . . . There's just this last haggle and then we'll have a break for refreshments while the clerks draw up a document in both languages for us to sign and seal.'

It seemed to take forever. Maja barely listened, and spent the time rehearsing things to say to Syndic Blrundahlrgh. At last the President Proctor declared the proceedings closed and everybody rose, but Maja settled back into her chair and waited for the crowd at the entrance to clear. Quiriul appeared at her shoulder.

'Is Benayu all right?' said Maja.

'He is conscious, and whole, he says, but very feeble. He is being well looked after. He asked me to give you this. Lady Kzuva couldn't take anything home that hadn't come with her. You are wearing its simulacrum.'

It was a brooch. Very simple, just a silver bar patterned with ivy leaves with a single tree at one end. It had been prettier with the horses. Maja put it away in her reticule, making a mental note to take it out before the reticule disappeared along with the rest of the simulacrum.

'Thank you very much,' she added. 'I'll come and see Benayu as soon as I can. I've got to talk to Syndic Blrundahlrgh first. You've been wonderful. I'll tell Chanad.'

'Thank you, my lady.'

Maja watched her leave, but stand aside to let Syndic Blrundahlrgh pass between her and the table, coming in the opposite direction, followed by the young woman who was one of the Pirate translators.

Maja rose stiffly and switched her attention to the Syndic. Yesterday she had spoken little but watched even the most spectacular manifestations of magic with a sort of detached interest, but had otherwise seemed just a quiet, ordinary woman; and the same when she'd come down the ramp with General Pashgahr. It was hard to imagine her quelling an armed mutiny by sheer personal authority.

She blurred, of course, as she approached, and Maja raised her spectacles to her eyes.

'Syndic Blrundahlrgh,' she said.

'Lady Kzhuvargh,' answered the Syndic, and they both smiled, sharing their pleasure in the other's having made the attempt and their consciousness of their own failure. The Syndic, still smiling, spoke briefly.

'The Syndic says that we are all children at heart,' said the translator.

Maja blinked inwardly. Did she know? Surely not. She rescued herself with one of her rehearsed remarks.

'Forgive me,' she said, gesturing with her spectacles. 'I do not see very well close to.'

The Syndic waited for the translation, nodded and stood calmly while Maja looked her over. The impression she gave of being something of a dough-faced nonentity turned out to be entirely superficial, worn almost like a mask. The pale grey-blue eyes were bright with intelligence. The jowled chin merely distracted from the firm set of the mouth. The skin was smooth and clear, its pallor natural to it. She could once have been a peachily pretty young woman, Maja decided. The Syndic studied Maja in return and nodded again.

'Shall we sit?' she said, drawing out the chair beside Maja's, at the same time making a brief remark to the translator, who almost scurried to help Maja into her chair and then took up a post behind and between the two of them.

'I am sorry you are not well,' said the Syndic, as if deliberately giving Maja the cue for another rehearsed remark.

'Indeed I am not myself today,' she said. 'I am not pre-cisely ill, but it is many years since I needed to exert my powers to the extent that I did yesterday, and today I am paying the penalty. I shall be better as soon as I am free to return to my own place.'

'I'm hoping that one result of our work today is that one day I'll get the chance to visit the Empire in a spirit of friendship.'

(Not one of Maja's cues, but she mustn't hesitate. What would Lady Kzuva have said?)

'It is not all wonders and marvels, you know.'

(That was a start, but . . . oh, of course! She readied the phrases while the Syndic was speaking and waited for the translation.)

'I'm glad to hear it,' said the Syndic. 'Yesterday was enough to last me a lifetime. But even without that the Empire is so different from my own country. I would very much like to return in more peaceful times. I am sure our best hope for a lasting peace is to know each other better.'

'Indeed, yes. I live a long way north. But should your journeyings carry you that far, I should be glad to wel-come you under my roof.'

(A safe offer, surely. She wouldn't take it up. She must be a busy woman. And there was precious little chance of the Empire letting her in, even if she wanted to come. But no.)

'I shall make a point of seeing that they do. Tell me, my lady, how much do you know of the politics of my country? Our translator, incidentally, is my cousin's daughter-in-law and can be trusted.'

'I know a certain amount about your country,' Maja said, taking the chance to answer slowly, thoughtfully, as she tried to remember and repeat some of what Striclan had told them.

'But the invasion has turned out much more difficult than your pro-war party expected,' she concluded, 'and so opinion is swinging against them. We saw something of this aboard the *All-Conqueror* yesterday. I believe you yourself had a hand in suppressing an armed group of soldiers who wanted to reject our terms.'

The Syndic didn't actually blink, but paused and stared at her before she answered.

'You are very well informed, my lady,' she said.

'This is the Empire, Syndic. It is very hard to keep a secret without some form of magical protection.'

'Of course,' said the Syndic. 'Bluntly, I am asking for your help. General Pashgahr is a sensible man . . .'

Maja, tiring rapidly now, forced herself to listen as the Syndic explained how important it was to give General Pashgahr something worthwhile to take home, instead of an outright defeat of the invasion. Otherwise General Olbog, who still had plenty of allies there, would be able to present himself as the hero who had been betrayed by weak-kneed underlings. Maja decided what to say as she waited for her to finish.

'I don't think we can alter the document at this stage, Syndic,' she said.

'No, of course not. I think the most I can ask for is this. At present the Empire's borders are closed to all outsiders. If you were now to invite a delegation of politicians and business people, completely unmilitary in nature, to visit the country and explore the possibilities for mutually beneficial trade, this would be attractive to the business community, and help to get them on our side. I would hope to be one of the delegates, and that we would then be able to renew our acquaintance.'

'For myself I should welcome that, but I shall need to talk to my colleagues.'

'Of course. And there is a similar matter I'd like you to put to them. The ice dragon, or dragons – I understand there are two.'

'I know little more than you do about them. You will have to talk . . .'

'To Mr Ortahlson. Eventually. But this is urgent, and I have you alone, so I'm asking you to talk to him. This may surprise you, but I want you to persuade him not to insist too strongly on the physical reality of the creatures.'

Maja's turn not to blink. She tried to gather her wits, but the Syndic raised a hand to stop her before she could speak.

'I know my countrymen. I know the military mind, as perhaps you do not. Confronted with an overwhelming physical threat such as a real ice dragon would present – a threat that is not confined, as your magical powers are, within the borders of the Empire, but is potentially global in its effect – they will be determined either to take possession of it and control it, or to destroy it. They would be able to carry many of my countrymen with them in this.'

'That . . . that would be very foolish. An absolute disaster.'

'Exactly. But the ice dragon is not needed to justify our withdrawal. The stranding of the whole fleet on an island of ice magically appearing in a warm sea is more than enough, and that was manifestly not a hallucination. Put simply, my argument against the war party will be that we cannot attack the Empire because of its magical defences. Therefore we must make peace with it.

'I must repeat that the matter is urgent. Mr Ortahlson may already be responding to questions about the ice dragon. I'm not asking him suddenly to deny the creature's existence. Only to leave room for doubt.'

'Very well. Perhaps your cousin will be kind enough to lend me an arm.'

She found Ribek, Saranja and Striclan at a table in the refreshment pavilion. The men rose smiling as she approached. Ribek offered her a chair and they all sat.

'We weren't talking about anything serious,' he said. 'Just chit-chat. Staving off the Inquisitors.'

He nodded towards a group of the Pirate delegates hovering nearby, translator at the ready, waiting to pounce.

(How much could they hear?)

'This is serious,' Maja said clearly. 'I have word from Talakh . . .'

She lowered her voice.

'I've been talking to Syndic Blrundahlrgh,' she said and told them about it.

'Well, Striclan?' said Ribek, when she'd finished.

'They're both very good points. In fact I'd been thinking about them myself.'

'We haven't got the authority to commit the Empire to anything.'

'We'll have to talk to Chanad,' said Saranja.

'At least I can go and start doing something about the ice dragon,' said Ribek. 'Odd that that's the only thing about yesterday's performance that wasn't hocus pocus, and now you're asking me to say that it was.'

He rose and moved away, as if just easing his limbs. The inquisitors pounced. Maja watched him as he answered their questions. His body language was easy, nonchalant, almost amused. He was actually enjoying himself, she realized. Saranja was right. Impossible man!

'You know,' said Saranja. 'We're going to have to visit Lady Kzuva on the way home, and tell her.'

'Oh, can we? Please!' said Maja.

That had been the last vivid moment. Darkness swallowed her. The magical turmoil of becoming a *mugal* had already been almost too much for her, without the strain of trying to think and act and speak like Lady Kzuva, instead of letting her do it herself, as she'd done yesterday, while Maja had watched what happened from inside her, almost like a bystander.

She drifted up into consciousness. *Where . . . ? What . . . ?* She seemed to be lying on something soft, like a pile of cushions. Mutters from around and above her, anxious, vaguely impatient. Her whole body was full of aches and pains, but why didn't they really hurt any more?

567

'I think she's coming round. Lady Kzuva . . .'

Striclan. Oh yes, of course. The mugal. *The conference. The refreshment tent.*

'I'm all right,' she whispered. 'Help me up. I must set
my seal . . . Where's my cane?'

'Easy, easy . . .' (*Striclan again.*) 'Everything's ready.
There's no hurry.'

They must have carried her into the conference tent. She
could remember the sharp smell of the burning wax,
watching the purple drops dribble on to the parchment,
somebody holding her quivering hand steady and helping it press the seal-ring firmly down into the glistening
pool. Then darkness again.

She had woken in the evening – the next evening,
Saranja told her later – in her own body, lying in a warm
and comfortable bed. Her hand was clutching something under the pillow. She pulled it out, forced her eyes
open and looked at it blearily. It was the brooch with
the single tree.

PART FOUR

Kzuva

Chapter 26

DREAMILY, LULLED BY the hiss of the passing air and the rhythmic boom of the tireless wings, Maja watched the landscape stream away beneath them as the horses bore them north. She thought they'd seen a lot of the Empire on their long, slow journey south, but realized now that it had been almost nothing beside the things she would never now see.

Take that craggy range of hills, with a great gorge running through, almost every cliff-face festooned with the battlements and walls protecting what should have been a series of mighty citadels, but in fact looked like no more than a few stone cottages with steep red roofs, appearing to be piled almost on top of each other where they clung to the rock above the foaming water.

Benayu, after a week's rest at Larg, was stronger physically, but still seemed dazed and faraway, coming to terms with himself, perhaps, in the same way he had done on their first journey north from Larg. Maja, relishing her re-covery of her extra sense, hadn't asked him to renew her shielding. Now, for instance, she could tell that the costly-seeming fortifications had been built centuries ago by magic. But why here, and to what end? And how did the people who dwelt there now earn their living in such a seemingly barren place?

Or that yellow plain, featureless apart from one large dark patch like cloud-shadow. But the sky was cloudless, and above the patch, and nowhere else, forty or fifty huge birds circled. As the horses drew nearer Maja saw that the patch was an enormous herd of animals, several thousand of them. Antelopes? Wild cattle? And the birds vultures, hovering for prey? None of these, for as Maja watched, three of the creatures below detached themselves from the main body and she could see that they were also birds, each the size of a pony, but flightless. A moment later one of those circling overhead plummeted down and drove the strays back to join the main mass; then the rest of the winged ones seemed to notice the intruders' approach and flew shrieking towards them. Saranja, riding on that flank with Striclan pillion, shouted a warning and swung Rocky away. Benayu and Ribek followed. Sponge dropped back as rearguard, snarling over his shoulder. The birds, soon outpaced, turned back to their guardianship.

Then for a while they followed a river winding through a forest, fold after fold of tree-covered hills as far as the eye could see. Stretches of glassy-still water alternated with foaming rapids. Close above one of these, two massive chains had been stretched from bank to bank to hold two lines of rafts steady against the current. There were people on the rafts, wearing the normal dress of the Empire. Each of the women on the upstream line carried a large gourd, from which she was steadily sprinkling small handfuls of what looked like some kind of seed on to the water where it flowed between the rafts. The rafts immediately above the rapids were spaced further apart so that the men on them could thrash the surface into foam with implements like flails. The foam was brilliant orange, which persisted all the way down the rapids until it was lost in the stillness of the pool below.

In the middle of a clearing beside the pool a boy of about six years old, naked apart from a small gold crown, was sitting on an ornate throne watching the tumbling water. Either side of him a dozen yellow-robed men – priests, perhaps – stood with their spread hands raised in front of them as if they were causing the colour-change. None of the labourers above the rapids had even glanced up as the winged horses passed above them, so intent were they on their task. For a moment it looked as if the priests would also ignore the intrusion into their ritual, but then one of them shouted and pointed and they broke rank and rushed into the trees, stumbling over their robes as they ran. The boy remained, staring steadfastly at the sunset-coloured rapids.

'What on earth was happening there?' said Maja. 'It wasn't magic. At least, I couldn't feel any.'

'We'll never know now,' said Ribek cheerfully.

'No, we'll never know now. Never.'

'We could go back and ask, I suppose. Only I doubt they'd be friendly, judging by the way those fellows bolted into the trees.'

'We'd be doing it all the time. Going back and asking, I mean. There's so much. It was better on the road. There was time.'

'You want to get down and walk? You aren't in a hurry to get back to the Valley?'

'Not specially, not for me. I know you've got to, because the horsemen will be going back to their wives and families before the passes close, and then you can sing to the snows and stop them coming back next year.'

'Assuming it works again. Won't know till I've tried.'

'You've seen the ice dragon. And Saranja's got Zald. It'll be all right. This time, anyway. And Benayu wants to get back to his sheep, and Saranja's got to sort out about what happens to Woodbourne and see what everybody wants done about the forest . . .'

'And we won't know *that* for several years. Valley's never been quick to make up its mind . . .'

They had talked it over and over in the last few days since the Ropemaker's unsettling last words about the new times coming. It was both hardest and easiest for Ribek. Hardest because he would have been perfectly happy to go back to the old times, with the Valley closed off completely, and easiest because he still knew what he wanted and what he had to do – to live as a miller at Northbeck and to keep the passes closed if he could.

Saranja and Maja were different. They'd both hated their life in the Valley. Why should they care what happened to it? Saranja had already tried to leave it once,

574

and Maja might have done so too when she was older, supposing she'd had the nerve. But both of them, almost as soon as they were in the adventure, had assumed without thinking that the whole purpose of their lives, the one thing for which they'd been born, was to find the Ropemaker so that he could restore the Valley to what it had been for the past forty generations.

And now perhaps that wasn't true any more. The Ropemaker had said those times were over, and they themselves must sow the seed of change. This was what they had tried to do when they had met the Pirates on the hill above Larg, but it would take years – most of Maja's lifetime, perhaps – before she got to see what kind of a tree had grown from their sowing.

And if these were new times, did it even matter from now on if there wasn't anyone to sing to the unicorns, if no one ever again could hear what the cedars were sighing?

Anyway, how could the three of them decide something like that for themselves? The one thing that was clear to them was that somehow the whole Valley, everyone who lived there, had to choose. They had a few years more to make up their minds. Benayu had been firm about that. There was one important thing he had to do when he got home, he said, as soon as he'd recovered from his efforts at Barda and Larg, and then he was going back to simple shepherding until he'd grown to manhood and come fully into his powers. At that point he would help Saranja seal the forest if that was what the Valley wanted – she couldn't do it without him – and then he'd make up his mind about his own future.

So, a few more years. Call it six. Six years for the Valley to make up its mind. And Ribek his.

They fell silent, thinking their own thoughts.

'I know what I want for myself, of course,' said Ribek after a while. 'All the same, there's a funny sense of let-down. I mean, we've done so much against all the odds, gone so far, fought brigands and demons, ridden flying horses, visited another universe, found the Ropemaker, destroyed the Watchers, saved Larg twice over. But . . . I don't know . . . that last meeting . . . all right, we agreed a temporary truce – best we could hope for, best we could offer – but everything else is still up in the air. It was all too easy, though I suspect it might have been a great deal harder but for your friend with the unpronounceable name . . .'

'Syndic Blrundahlrgh,' said Maja. 'Anyway, none of them could manage Kzuva.'

'Not the only thing you had in common. Sisters under the skin, if ever I saw a pair. Anyway I found the whole thing very strange and unsettling. Not how I'd want it to end, if it was an ending. I'm like you, I suppose, except that it isn't the magic I'll miss. It'll be not knowing anything that's happening out here as a result of our efforts, not being part of it.'

'We haven't quite finished,' said Maja. 'We've still got to tell Lady Kzuva. I'm looking forward to seeing her house.'

They did that two mornings later, standing in the roadway, just as Tilja and her long-ago companions had done, and staring at the astonishing building. Maja had thought that she would know it already from that story, and yes, still the same river flowed calmly out of the wooded valley and under the massive bridges on which stood the same wonderful house, elegantly ornamented and pinnacled, more beautiful than any of the grand houses they had seen in all their journeyings. It was just what she'd expected, but yet she was not prepared for it. It was old, so full of its own placid magic, breathed into it through accumulated centuries.

Grand steps led up to a big double door. At Ribek's knock a wicket door opened and a footman in the green and gold livery of Kzuva came out. He looked them over briefly. Huh! Fifteenth graders, at best. Riff-raff.

'Your kind go round to the courtyard entrance,' he said. 'You can state your business there.'

'You mistake our kind,' said Ribek, speaking with all the authority of an ex-Imperial delegate. 'The brooch, Maja. Thank you. Now, sir, will you please take this directly to the Lady Kzuva? Put it into her own hands. She will know what it means. She will be exceedingly displeased if she learns that you have done otherwise than I ask.'

The footman stared at him, glanced at the others again, stared rather longer at the three horses, wingless but still magnificent, and retired, closing the wicket behind him. They waited. Footsteps – more than one set – on the paving within. Both the big doors creaked open. Four footmen this time. They lined up, two either side of the entrance, and bowed as Lady Kzuva hobbled out between them. She raised her spectacles but merely glanced at her visitors, then gestured to the footmen, who retired, closing the big doors behind them but leaving the wicket open.

Now Lady Kzuva studied the visitors one by one, starting with Maja. Maja gazed back. This was the meeting she had been both dreading and longing for. There had been no mirror on Angel Isle, no rock pool so far above the waves; all she knew of Lady Kzuva's appearance was what she had been able to see directly, arms and hands, the front of her body, her feet. Now she looked into deep brown eyes, enlarged by the spectacles, remarkably clear in one so old. She knew, from having seen through them, how they had given her a sense of needing to peer at the world, but there was no sign of that in Lady Kzuva's expression. No sign either of fret or temper in the set of the small mouth or the much-wrinkled, soft, leathery-brown complexion.

The nose was straight and well-formed, the stance erect, the whole effect proud without arrogance, dominant without contempt. No wonder the Pirates had been impressed.

'Maja,' she said.

Maja managed a curtsy of a sort.

Lady Kzuva smiled, amused.

'No need for that between us,' she said. 'We know each other too . . . intimately. Is it not strange that we have never seen each other? And the Captain.'

'Not really, I'm afraid,' said Saranja. 'I was a fake too, though at least I looked like me. But I'm really just a farmer's daughter. And I can't do much magic, either. My real name's Saranja Urlasdaughter.'

'You are welcome in any guise under my roof, Captain. And Mr . . . ? You have lost a few years, I think.'

'Ribek Ortahlson, at your service, my lady. I was something less of a pretender. I am indeed a mill-owner, though I own only one small mill. And the ability to call to the ice dragon does run in my family. I must explain, my lady, that we aren't here in the hope of exploiting your hospitality. We would have understood if you never wanted to see us again after our intrusion into your life. But events took place after you left us which you will need to know about.'

'There is a great deal that I shall want to know. It was certainly very frustrating to be whisked away so much in the middle of things.'

'It may take some time, my lady.'

'No matter. I hope you can spare me a few days, at least. And Mr Ruddya. You too have changed, but in some other fashion than the rest of you.'

'I was, but no longer am, a professional spy, my lady. I was reared from childhood by the people you call the Pirates to travel throughout the Empire and send my reports back to them. Part of my training taught me how to change my appearance.'

'Whoever would have thought that I should welcome an enemy spy through my door? But I do, and most gladly.

'And last but not least, my boy Bennay. I have been so worried for you. I am relieved and delighted to see you looking so well. And all those amusing wonders we appeared to accomplish flowed from you and Mistress

Chanad. There has always been a magician in my household, so I am well acquainted with your kind. Not one of them – and they were grown men and women – could have accomplished one twentieth of what you have done. How old are you? . . . Bennay is not your real name, I think.'

Benayu was looking a bit uncomfortable. He was usually a bit cocky about his abilities, but he wasn't used to this kind of praise from this kind of person.

'It doesn't matter,' he said. 'Benayu isn't my real name either, actually, but that's what I'm usually called. I'm fourteen.'

'Well, I hope you will not try anything of the kind again until you are at least five years older. I had a young cousin, not a magician, who . . . no, some other time. And here are Sponge and the horses. I am sorry to see them without their wings, but I suppose it was sensible. I will see that the horses are well stabled. There are hitching rings beside the stairs. I do not normally allow dogs in my house, but I will make an exception for Sponge.'

'Oh, he'll be all right,' said Benayu. 'Stay with the horses, boy. I won't be long.'

'Follow me, please,' said Lady Kzuva, and rapped on the door with her cane. Both leaves opened instantly. The four footmen bowed as she passed between them. Inside was a formal entrance hall with a grand flight of stairs. Lady Kzuva settled herself into a throne-like chair with carrying-poles either side. The footmen stood by the poles, ready to lift, but she raised her hand and turned to a worried-looking elderly man, wearing a rather grander version of the household livery, who had been hovering nearby.

'Rooms for my guests, Micha,' she told him. 'They may be staying several days and will need their own quarters. Show them for the time being into the little library and bring them light refreshments. There are three horses to be well stabled and a dog who will remain with the horses. We will have supper in the Orchard Room. Make my excuses to the company in the dinner hall.

'Now, my friends, I have business to complete. Beyond that I will clear my diary as far as I am able. And you must tell me your tale this evening. All I know is that I lay here in a coma for two nights and a day, and woke on the morning of the second day from the strangest, strongest dream I have ever known. And now you have brought this brooch to my door to tell me that it was no dream, but true.'

It was well towards midnight before they finished. Lady Kzuva asked a hundred questions along the way and remained alert to the end. When it was over she sat silent for a while, then smiled and shook her head.

'To my mind,' she said, 'the strangest part of it all is this. Here we were, all the so-called grand and powerful of this great Empire, living in constant dread under the rule of the Watchers, but not daring to band together to do anything about it, while you five, a simple miller, a farmer's daughter, a shepherd boy, a – shall we say wandering scholar? – and a child, accomplished the thing without any help from any of us. And then, almost as an afterthought, except that it was no afterthought but supremely important, though it was not in any way your responsibility, you brought about the possibility of peace with a powerful nation whose ships have harried our shores for centuries.'

They stayed five days at the House of Kzuva. Lady Kzuva spared them what time she could, cancelling any business that wasn't pressing. She spent one whole morning visiting some of her mills with Ribek and Maja, and talked earnestly with Striclan about the condition of the Empire and the mindset and culture of the Pirates. At one point she asked Maja to be with her as she sat in judgement on two disputes between her people, both involving accusations of witchcraft.

'My magician Stindul is well enough for most things, but at heart he is a scholar,' she said. 'He doesn't understand the peasant mind.'

One case was simple enough. The plaintiff was accusing his neighbour of causing his peach crop to fail.

'The trees belong to me,' explained Lady Kzuva, 'but I take only a third of the fruit. Still he needs to account for the failure to me, so he is trying to blame it on his neighbour rather than his own laziness in failing to keep the trees well watered. I would simply like to be sure before I pass judgement.'

Maja closed her other senses as far as she could and concentrated. No, there was no made magic there, only an ancient and obvious human magic.

'They just hate each other. That's all,' she said.

The other case was more interesting. A man's legs were infested with a horrible maggot which was eating him away from the inside. His wife was accusing another man of causing the affliction, because she had rejected his advances, saying that she would remain faithful to her husband. The husband had been carried into court so that Lady Kzuva could see for herself. The accused man said it had been the other way round, and the wife was taking advantage of the illness in vengeance for his having rejected her.

There was no spell, Maja could tell at once, and the accused man had no magical powers. But . . . but . . .

'Can we look at him close to?' she whispered.

She followed Lady Kzuva down to where the man was lying on his litter, sockless and shoeless, with his baggy trousers pulled above the knees to show the disgusting state of his legs. The woman knelt beside him.

'It's his left shoulder,' Maja whispered.

'And his upper body is unaffected?' said Lady Kzuva.

'There's nothing wrong with it,' said the wife.

'I would like to be able to compare clean flesh with the diseased part,' said Lady Kzuva.

'But it's his legs!' exclaimed the wife. 'There's nothing wrong—'

'Nevertheless, I wish to see for myself. Please do as I say.'

'But—'

'Justicer, will you remove the man's jacket and shirt, please.'

The wife rose and watched pale-faced while a court official knelt and bared the man's torso. As the wife had said, there seemed to be nothing wrong with it.

'On his back,' whispered Maja.

'Roll him over,' said Lady Kzuva.

'No!' screamed the wife.

High on the shoulder blade was a small crude tattoo – a snake, perhaps, but looking at it closely Maja saw it was meant to be some kind of worm. Whatever it was, it was nasty.

'That's what's doing it,' she muttered.

'A sigil of some kind,' said Lady Kzuva.

'That's right,' said the man. 'I'd a bit of an ache there, and Carna got this fellow . . . Carna . . . ? What . . . ?'

'You will need to explain yourself,' Lady Kzuva told the woman calmly.

The woman started screaming. The two justicers hurried her away. Servants carried the sick man off to the household magician to see what he could do for him.

When Lady Kzuva was busy, she arranged amusements for her visitors, riding or learning the elements of hawking in the woods, boating on the river and so on. Saranja and Striclan usually absented themselves for at least part of the day. Madly Ribek decided that when he was home he would have a hawk of his own, so he spent any time he could in the mews, watching the falconers train their young birds. It became obvious to Maja that she'd have to have one too when they were married, and then she got hooked herself.

Benayu spent most of his day in the library, working through shelf after shelf of old magical volumes, accumulated by generations of household magicians, and talking them over with Stindul. Strangely, the long hours of concentrated study of his craft seemed to have an almost medicinal effect on him, both in body and spirit. They saw this clearly on the fourth evening.

Lady Kzuva was listening to Saranja talking about her time among the war-lords, and at the same time, as she often did, casually fingering the brooch on her head-scarf. She must have noticed Maja watching her, because she smiled and said, 'I think I shall wear it for the rest of my days.'

'I'm afraid it was much prettier with the horses,' said Maja.

'Yes, but that makes very little difference to me. It is not why I wear it. I can always put them there in my mind.'

'Do you want me to do something about that?' said Benayu.

They stared at him. Not once on the journey north had he shown the slightest interest in practising his art, either for pleasure or purpose. He grinned.

'Got to start somewhere,' he said. 'Touch it again, my lady. Now do what you said – put them there in your mind. Ready, Maja?'

One brief, easily endurable pulse, a twitch of Lady Kzuva's arm, and the silver horses were back in their place beside the tree.

Benayu looked thoughtful for a moment, nodded as if confirming a decision, then yawned and stretched, as if waking from a long, soul-restoring sleep.

'Next stop, the mountains,' he said.

It was their last evening in the House of Kzuva. They had decided so after breakfast that morning. As far as

Maja was concerned, she didn't mind how long she stayed. She was already fond of Lady Kzuva. She felt a bond with her, like the family bonds she should have had, but never did. But Ribek had to get back to Northbeck. Though it would be a month or more before the time came to sing to the snows and close the passes, what harvest there was after the ravages of the horse people would be in by now and it was high time that the mill became busy again.

So far, Maja had assumed that she would go back with him, but the next few years, until she could marry him, were something of a blank for her. All her imaginings and longings had been focused on what came after that, and even the thought of that long wait, so close to him all the time, was beginning to make her vaguely uncomfortable.

But Saranja too wanted to get back to the Valley. She wanted to get the whole business of Woodbourne over and done with, so that she and Striclan could settle into their life together. And Benayu needed to get home in time for the great autumn sheep markets. So the time had come to move on.

Lady Kzuva had given them no hint of her own feelings, no sign either that she was wearying of their presence or that she wanted them to stay longer. Only, when they told her about their decision later that morning she sighed and said, 'Well, I suppose you are right. And I too have business to catch up with. We will talk about it at supper this evening.'

*

The Orchard Room was Maja's favourite among all the wonderful rooms in the house. It was medium sized, pretty rather than grand, with carved panels on three walls. The fourth consisted entirely of windows that could be folded all the way back, opening on to a pillared veranda and beyond that the so-called orchard, which was really a flower garden with lawns running along the river. There were just enough fruit trees to justify the name. That evening the servants had hung hundreds of little lanterns among their branches.

'I cannot give you oyster-and-bacon pie so far from the sea,' said Lady Kzuva. 'But my cooks have done the best they can. Nothing too rich, I told them, just before a journey. This wine, on the other hand, is the oldest I have. The grapes were harvested in the year I was born. I must warn you that it is very strong, which is why it has kept so well, so drink it sparingly, and take plenty of water.'

Maja had never tasted wine before the journey began, and then hadn't cared for it much apart from the wine that Chanad had given them, that evening on Angel Isle. They drank this one out of little silver goblets, only half filled. It was a deep greenish yellow. Intense odours fumed off it. She had no need to taste it before its inward magic exploded in her mind, so vividly that she seemed to be somewhere else, a landscape that she could feel almost as if she could see it, a steep, scree-strewn slope so barren-seeming that she would not have thought that anything could grow there. But there were the rows of vines, only shoulder-high to her, but heavy with fruit. The harvesters were working among them, singing. The river glistened below, with a little town on its further bank . . .

'Maja, come back,' said Ribek's voice. 'You haven't even tasted it yet. It's astonishing.'

Maja blinked and returned to the Orchard Room.

'I was there. Where the grapes were grown,' she said, and described the scene.

'Yes, you were there,' said Lady Kzuva. 'What is more, you were there then, in the year of my birth. The next year those vines were stricken with a disease and had to be grubbed up and burned before they infected the rest of the vineyards. They were very old, and all attempts to grow them elsewhere had failed. This wine will never be made again.'

Their chairs (which Lady Kzuva preferred because the piles of cushions that were the custom in most of the Empire were too low for her comfort) were arranged along one side of the table so that they could all see out. They ate and drank for the most part in silence, watching the stars come out and the lamps mimicking them more and more strongly below as dusk deepened into night. It isn't only the wine, thought Maja. There will never be another evening like this. She sighed.

'You echo my thought,' said Lady Kzuva. 'I rue your going, but I understand you must go. Before that, I have a proposal to put to you. Tell me, each of you, how you see your own immediate futures. Let us start with Saranja and Striclan – forgive me for assuming from what I have seen of you that you propose to share whatever future that is.'

Maja couldn't see them from where she sat, but there

was a pause – while they looked at each other, she guessed. Striclan must have nodded or something, because it was Saranja who answered.

'I don't know. It depends what's happened at Woodbourne. Presumably everybody thinks I'm dead. My brothers can't inherit it, if either of them's still alive, because it descends in the female line, so it would go to the nearest female cousin who can hear the cedars. I suppose one of my brothers might marry her. I just don't feel I can leave it all up in the air. Striclan can do anything, so I suppose he could be a farmer, but I'm not so sure about me. I don't have patience.

'I've been thinking about this. One of the reasons why my father was always so angry was because the farm didn't actually belong to him. I'm his daughter. I could easily have gone the same way for the opposite reason. I wanted to do something else with my life and not spend it stuck at Woodbourne because I was who I was. But now, together, we've done that something, enough to last me a lifetime, and perhaps I could settle down at Woodbourne and be happy there. I can stop being angry now.

'We've talked about it a lot, Striclan and I, but we haven't got anywhere, except that if we can find someone to take over Woodbourne we'll probably come back to the Empire. I don't know what we'll do.'

'A good spy can always find employment,' said Lady Kzuva. 'Now Bennay – Benayu.'

'There's one more thing I've got to do,' said Benayu. 'I've been saving up for it. Resting. Getting ready. After that I'm going back to shepherding – a bit of hedge magic, perhaps – charms for sheep-scab – that sort of thing. One day, perhaps, but nothing much bigger, not for a long while.'

'I think that is very wise,' said Lady Kzuva. 'This is not good sheep country, and I know you would prefer to be among the mountains, but you will always be welcome under my roof. Perhaps you can use your lesser powers from time to time to bring yourself here for a short visit, and read in the library and talk to Stindul.

'Now, I have kept Ribek and Maja for the last. I am not going to pretend that I do not know – that all of us do not know – that Maja has strong feelings for Ribek, which perhaps when she is older Ribek will be able to return. And you in your turn may have detected that there is a special bond between Maja and myself. When you came to my door I used the word "intimate" to describe it. I chose the word casually, but I was right. For a little over two days we were one person, distinct still in our oneness, but one despite that. The experience has left us with a tie that is stronger then that between twin sisters, closer than that between passionate lovers. It will last until I die . . .'

'Not even then,' said Maja. 'Not till I die too. Even then . . .'

'That is my hope,' said Lady Kzuva. 'Now I am telling you this because when you hear my proposal you might very reasonably guess that it arises from a desire to keep Maja to myself. Not so. I rejoice at your affection for each other. I should rejoice if it were to ripen into adult love. I hope to rejoice at your wedding, though I have to be carried there on a stretcher. If I were to die on that very day I should die happy.

'But meanwhile, what is to become of Maja? Where is she to live? I would very strongly suggest that it should not be at Ribek's mill. The balance you presently maintain on the border between strong affection on Ribek's part and what I know to be genuine love on Maja's will become increasingly precarious as Maja grows towards womanhood . . .'

Normally none of them interrupted Lady Kzuva. Ribek did now.

'I've been thinking a lot about that too,' he said. 'It's not going to be easy. And anyway, it's far too soon for her to make up her mind the way she has. Striclan and I are almost the only men she's ever got to know. She needs to meet boys her own age – Benayu doesn't count. She needs girlfriends to talk to about them. Experience of the world too. Again, what we've been doing doesn't count – ordinary life isn't like that. You're suggesting she comes back here? It's up to her, but I'm all for it.'

'Wait,' said Lady Kzuva. 'There is more to my proposal than Maja simply coming back here. You tell me there is going to be a peace conference. I have every intention of participating. I shall renew Maja's acquaintance with Syndic Blrundahlrgh – I of course did not experience it directly – and accompany her on part of her travels. With the disappearance of the Watchers there will be intense power struggles in Talakh. I shall throw my support behind Chanad and persuade my fellow Landholders to do the same, and so on.

'Where do you three, Saranja, Striclan and Maja, fit

in? The case of Striclan is obvious. I doubt if there is anyone living who has his experience and knowledge both of the Empire and the Pirates' culture and politics. Simply to have him there as my adviser would be invaluable. Saranja, as a member of our truce delegation . . .'

'But I was a complete fake!' said Saranja. 'Everybody will know that I wasn't ever a captain in the Imperial army, and then they'll realize that the whole delegation was fake.'

'You are mistaken. Maja, if you would be kind enough to look in the top right-hand drawer of the bureau there . . . There is a sheet of parchment, with wax and seal beside it . . .'

The parchment was thick and creamy. Elaborately penned writing filled one side.

'Now that little silver dish. Thank you. Take one of the candles from the table and tip it a little sideways over the parchment and hold the dish in your other hand to catch any drips from the candle . . . A bit lower . . . that's right.'

Wide awake this time, Maja watched the scarlet pool of wax forming, and then Lady Kzuva's many-ringed fingers pressing the seal firmly into the wax. *Much better than I managed*, she thought. *I wonder what the penalty is for forging a Landholder's seal. Death, at least, I should think.*

'Among the less absurd privileges that Landholders possess,' said Lady Kzuva, 'is that of appointing an officer to a regiment in the Imperial army. All Landholders travel with an armed escort, which will be much more effective if one of them can act with the full authority of an Imperial commission. Congratulations on your appointment, Captain Saranja, of the Women's Regiment of the Imperial Guard. You will see that the commission predates our conference at Larg.'

Ribek laughed aloud, and Striclan too. Saranja stared at the parchment. Maja had never seen her so put out. She turned white, then red. Her mouth opened and shut several times before she could speak.

'Oh,' she said at last. 'Oh . . . Thank you. Thank you very much. I don't know what to say.'

'You have already said it, my dear. I should add that I do not expect you to be a mere ornament in my train, though you will certainly be that. But you are manifestly a woman of action, full of fire and purpose, a born soldier, one whom others will follow. We may well have need for that. And your horses – they are now wingless?'

'I can give Rocky his wings again if I want to.'

'And the other two,' said Benayu. 'I can fix that for you.'

'Again, an obvious asset. Finally, Maja. You shall come as my ward, my dear, so it is natural that you should accompany me. But in many circumstances in which we may find ourselves, with unchecked magic now loose in the Empire, your special talent may prove invaluable, as you have already shown me in my little courtroom. And more important to me than any of your separate gifts is that I can be confident, both from the story you have told me and from what I have seen of you, that I can trust you completely.

'Now, unless you have any questions, I suggest that I should leave you to talk my proposal over among yourselves, and you can tell me in the morning what you have decided.'

She unhooked her cane from the arm of her chair and waited for one of them to help her to her feet. Nobody moved. Maja looked at Ribek, who had already turned to her. He raised his eyebrows. She nodded. He pointed at her. Surprised, she turned to Lady Kzuva.

'Yes, please,' she said. 'Thank you very much.'

'I was about to say the same thing, rather more elaborately,' said Striclan from the other side.

'Me too,' said Benayu.

'Excellent,' said Lady Kzuva. 'Nothing moves quickly in the Empire. I shall need to send to Talakh at once, to prepare the ground, but I should like to be on the road as soon as the snows are gone. If you can be here by then, well and good. Otherwise you will need to find me on the road somehow. With wings on your horses you will travel far faster than I.'

Chapter 27

AGAIN THE EMPIRE reeled itself away beneath them as they flew on, still passing none of the country they had traversed so slowly on their journey to Tarshu. The detour to Kzuva had taken them well west of that, and now they were heading back towards the sheep pastures north of Mord. There seemed to be an unspoken joint desire that they should stay together as long as possible, and this was the simplest way. They would say goodbye to Benayu and Sponge at the pastures, cross the mountains by the way they had come when they'd been escaping from the Pirates, and after a couple of days at Northbeck leave Ribek and Maja there. Saranja and Striclan would fly on with all three horses to see what was happening at Woodbourne. When the time came for them to leave the Valley, they would return by way of Northbeck, pick Maja up, take her to Lady Kzuva and all travel south together when the snows were gone.

Now, far ahead, they could see the glitter of the snow-peaks. Farms and woodlands flowed beneath them, and there was the river, skirting the plain of Mord, and Mord itself, smug and snug behind its walls. The Watchers' Eye was gone from its southern gate. More and steeper woodland, and then . . .

Then, where the pasture should have been, utter desolation. A dismal black slope of scree and tumbled rock. A crater at the centre. Not a blade growing on the slope itself apart from one or two strips of turf running down from where the whispering cedar had stood. Not a tree standing within several hundred paces of it. Benayu shouted, pointed and wheeled to the left, up the slope. The great wings pounded the thinning air, spiralling up beside a cliff-face to a wide ledge, clothed in scanty grass. They landed there and slid or swung themselves down from the horses.

'What on earth happened?' said Saranja.

'I told you,' said Benayu. 'Fodaro got it wrong. I was pretty sure we'd find something like this, and I've been getting ready for it. Ever since we left Larg, pretty well. Tell you later.

'You stay here and hang on to the horses. You'd better take their wings away, Saranja. We don't want them bolting. This is going to be fairly big, Maja, and I won't have much to spare, so I can't afford to shield you. I could put you to sleep for a bit, if you like.'

'No. I want to see. I'm a lot tougher than I was when we started.'

'All right. It shouldn't be too bad – you'll be in the lee

of the cliff. Only don't get too close to the edge. Well, here goes. No, boy. You stay here.'

He vanished.

Maja moved towards the drop, and found she couldn't see much of the slope below without going right up to the edge. She looked around. On either side of the ledge the rock-face ran sheer up and down, and the ledge itself was the bottom of a wide cleft in the upper half of the cliff. The others had led the horses to the back of it and turned them to face the cliff. Ribek and Saranja were blindfolding Levanter and Pogo. Pogo didn't like it. Saranja had already done that for Rocky and was starting to remove his wings. These days Maja barely had to brace herself for stuff like that.

She scrambled up over the boulders that had fallen against the side of the indent in the explosion of magic, found a viewpoint and stared at the bleak, black wound that had once been sheep pasture, and the tumbled woods around it.

She had seen nothing quite like it before, and yet a familiar unsettling throb pulsed steadily from it, the background magic of that other universe, beyond the touching point on Angel Isle. This was where Fodaro had discovered Jex, where he had studied the stars in the pool Benayu had made for him – still there now, gleaming untroubled amid the ruin around it – and where he had worked out his equations, and with Benayu's help had begun to experiment on how to use them to destroy the Watchers.

This had once been a touching point too.

Benayu was there now, a tiny figure standing close by

the central crater. He raised an arm and waved towards her.

'Ready?' she called. 'He's starting.'

The blast of magic came not from him, but inward, to him, invisible at first, but then a vortex formed, a thickening of the air that could be seen only because it rumpled itself as it gathered, like something seen through an uneven pane of glass, or heat waves rising from a furnace. When it reached its centre over the crater it spiralled upward, denser and denser. And at the same time, far overhead, invisible dust particles gathered out of the clear, pale sky and hurtled inward – pale racing specks at first that joined and became flakes, puffballs, clumps, cloud-streamers, darkening all the time as they crammed themselves tighter and tighter over the vortex below until they formed a single, roughly circular, mile-wide mass, darker than the darkest thundercloud.

Maja's whole being shuddered, reverberated like a bell, to the steady drum roll of the forces pent there. She cried aloud at the sudden clapper-stroke of their release, not into any outward explosion, but into a single aimed downward stroke from the centre to the centre of the vortex below. The two joined, and for a while she was looking at a thing like one of the flat-topped desert trees she had seen at the start of the journey north from Larg, a sky-high tree of darkness, a tree that was growing backwards in time, its whole top shrinking inward and down through the trunk until there was only the pillar of the trunk itself plummeting down . . .

And then the light.

She had an instant of warning in which to close her eyes as the flash of the original explosion gathered in from its furthest reaches. The world turned white and eyelids were not enough. Hands across her face were not enough. For a moment she could see her finger bones black against the impossible whiteness. All vanished in thunder. Then nothing at all. She could neither hear nor see. Not even the dark of not seeing.

She opened her eyes and still she could not see. Nor hear. There should have been the screams of the panicking horses, the shouts and grunts of the others trying to calm them, Saranja's voice, perhaps, grimly calm, 'I think I've gone blind . . .'

Nothing. Not a whisper. Not the rustle of movement. No movement at all, even when Maja tried to move. She wasn't breathing. Her heart seemed to have stopped between beat and beat. No sense of any of the marvellous magic of the world.

It's all over, she thought. *I'm dead. How disappointing. Ribek . . .*

She would have wept with frustration, but even a tear must move.

Benayu's voice in her head.

'*I'm sorry about that. I should have realized . . .*'

Sorry! When I'm dead!

'*Hang on. I'll sort it all out in a moment. I'd better deal with the horses first.*'

Yes, being dead must be like this. One everlasting wait in utter silence, total non-seeing.

Benayu again.

'*Ready, Maja?*'

The pulse of his presence. A gentle puff into her nostrils. The touch of fingers on eyes and ears.

She was alive, herself, breathing and feeling and hearing, not on that mountain ledge but the long slope of green cropped turf below. The others were beside her, the horses still in their blindfolds, the people, even Striclan, looking as dazed as she felt. The peaceful woods stood round, their leaves already colouring as the world turned towards winter. Only the central crater remained, unhealed.

'Look,' said Saranja in a voice of wonder. 'There's an ant! It's just as if all that had never happened.'

'Yes,' said Benayu. 'That's why it was easier than I thought it would be, except for the last part. Sorry about that. But it was all still there, waiting to come back into balance, all but the touching point itself. That's gone.

'It's all over now. Fodaro won in the end. We'd never have done it without him. I've left the crater like that for him. No one but us will ever know what it means, but that's enough.'

They stood in silence for a while, gazing at the strange memorial to a brave and lonely genius.

'I'm hungry,' said Benayu. 'Let's have something to eat. Oyster-and-bacon pie, anyone?'

'Really?' said Maja. 'I didn't get any first time because I was a rag doll, and second time Ribek wouldn't let me have more than a mouthful.'

'In that case I'll have some too. Shall I make it oyster-and-bacon pie all round? Fine. That's for the Empire. And rhubarb-and-ginger crumble for the Valley. And

600

mountain cider for me and Fodaro. He adored the stuff. It'll take a few minutes.'

'You're not too tired?' said Saranja.

'I've got a bit left. Lucky I did it at the end, mind you. But like I said, the rest of it went a lot better than I'd budgeted for. Get your saliva working.'

He was off somewhere else in his head for less than a minute, then settled down and sat staring gazing out eastward. The sun was halfway down the sky. It wouldn't be long before the pasture was in the shadow of the mountain behind him. The same thought must have struck him.

'It'll be cold up here in the hills, this far north,' he said. 'Sleep out here all the same, I think. The cottage is still there, and there'd be room for all of us, but it'll reek of Watcher-work, and I don't want to waste our evening together sorting it out. I'll get it done tomorrow, and then you'll be welcome to stay as long as you want.'

'Nice of you, but I must get back,' said Ribek. 'Harvest's later up here, of course, but they'll already be behind with the milling.'

'Us too,' said Saranja. 'We don't feel right, taking all that money off Lady K and then swanning off to deal with our own affairs. We want to get it all settled.'

(Lady Kzuva had characteristically insisted on paying Saranja her salary from the date of her commission, and Striclan for a year in advance. Ribek got a lump sum to compensate for his loss of earnings in the service of the Empire – as much, he said, as he'd have earned in ten years' milling. Imperial coin wasn't any use in the Valley, so he got gold. There was a leaving-bonus for her boy

Bennay, as large as if he'd held that post for sixty years, and for Maja what seemed to her a monstrous amount of plain spending money.)

'Ah, food,' exclaimed Ribek. 'Nothing like mountain air for a healthy appetite.'

The dishes assembled themselves neatly on the turf. They sat in a circle and passed them round.

'I got second helpings for all of us,' said Benayu.

The silence of contentment fell, until Ribek broke it with a sigh.

'You know,' he said. 'I think there's only one thing I regret in all our journeyings. I feel we didn't do right by the Magister at Barda. All right, he was – is, I hope – a pompous ass, but that doesn't alter the fact that he was a good man who did his best for us. And the Watchers came, and we ran away and left him in deep trouble. I hope he came out all right.'

'Want me to look?' said Benayu. '. . . No, he isn't at Barda – they've got a new Magister. Wait . . . Ah . . . He's still alive . . . He's been in prison in Talakh, but they've let them all out now that the Watchers are gone. He's lost about half his weight. He's trying to get back to Barda but he hasn't got any money. Shall we just send him some? He'll wake up and find it in his pocket.'

'He was sad that he'd never seen the mountains,' said Maja.

'And here we are eating bacon-and-oyster pie,' said Saranja. '*His* bacon-and-oyster pie, good as.'

'All right,' said Benayu. 'And Ribek can say sorry to him for all of us.'

Again that momentary absence, the blip of made

magic, and a ragged, unrecognizable figure stood beside them, staring bewildered at the snow-capped mountain range running away north and the immense landscape below it. He seemed not even to have noticed their presence on the turf beside him.

Another blip, and his tatters became clean, well-fitting clothes. He must have felt the change for he looked down at himself and ran his spread hands over his body, feeling the quality of the cloth. His right hand bumped against something in a pocket. He felt and pulled out a purse and weighed it in his hand. It was clearly heavy.

Suddenly he raised his head and sniffed. A dribble of saliva ran from the corner of his mouth.

'Oyster-and-bacon pie, Magister?' said Ribek. 'We're delighted to see you again, after all the troubles we brought upon you.'

The Magister started at the voice, looked at Ribek and stared at them each in turn.

'Dreaming?' he whispered. 'Dead? Heaven? Oyster-and-bacon pie?'

'No, you're in the real world, Magister. Please sit down and taste some pie to prove it. Oysters from Barda, and there's nothing else like them, not even in heaven. I'm sure you remember us, if not necessarily with pleasure. Saranja, Maja, Benayu and me, Ribek Ortahlsohn. You haven't met Striclan, though.'

'My dear sirs! My dear ladies! Barda oysters! I thought I should never taste them again. And the mountains, which I was never destined to see!'

Trembling, he sat. Benayu heaped his plate, filled his goblet and gave them to him. He ate slowly, in silence,

603

savouring every mouthful, while they told him their story and why they had treated him as they did.

'The mountains of the north,' he whispered as he put his plate down. 'The heroes who saved the Empire! With my help! With my help! And the oysters of Barda!'

Gentle magic flowed and he fell asleep. It flowed again, and he vanished from the hillside.

'His heirs are squabbling over his estate,' said Benayu. 'So his house is still empty. He'll wake in his own bed.'

Maja woke somewhere in the depths of the night and lay gazing at the friendly stars of the North. There was the old Fisherman, with his rod bending under the weight of the Fish, so that its tip pointed directly at the Axle-tree. At Barda they had all been out of sight. At Larg he had been half hidden, and the Axle-tree barely clear of the horizon, with the Fish still below it. Now, at last, here they all were, shining above the glistening snow-peaks.

The others seemed to be asleep. Ribek was only a couple of paces away. Striclan and Saranja lay further off, snug in their shared bedding; Benayu was even further away, so that the persistent buzz of his powers didn't disturb Maja's dreams.

She and Ribek could have been alone together on the hillside. He was a heavy sleeper. If she were to slip out of her own bedding and ease herself in beside him, he probably wouldn't even notice. It was only a whimsy, a fancy, but unwilled it bred the longing. A desire. A physical ache. *What was the harm in that?* whispered her body.

She wasn't going to do it, of course. It wouldn't be fair on him. But she couldn't stop thinking about it. She was astonished, frightened, by the sudden power of the demand. Night after night they had slept almost within reach of each other. Night after night she had dozed off during another episode of her fantasy life at Northbeck. Naturally, being husband and wife in the fantasy, they slept in the same bed, but she had spent no time imagining the experience. It was just a detail, a way of making the fantasy as real as possible, like the stuffed owl on the kitchen shelf.

Now, without warning, it was central to the fantasy. Nothing could have any reality without it. And it still wouldn't work unless Ribek felt the same about her. She had no doubt at all that he would one day. But when? They'd talked about it a bit in his dream when she'd been a rag doll in that other universe. When she was six years older, she'd suggested. He'd said eight, but that had just been haggling. Now, lying under the stars on the mountainside, feeling what she was feeling, even six years seemed a wilderness of waiting. Surely four would be enough. Or three, if she coaxed Benayu into giving her a love-charm.

And then, what would he feel after . . . ? There'd been a farmer who'd liked girls Maja's age. He'd done something with one of them, because Ribek thought he would have been better dead and had told him to take his wheat elsewhere for grinding. For a vivid moment she seemed to see the shadowy cavern of the wheel-room at Northbeck mill, the great wheel slowly churning round, the white water tumbling over the scoops, and dark against that the shape of a man dangling by his neck from a rope tied round one of the beams.

In that moment she made up her mind. She wasn't going back to Northbeck with him. Even one night there would make it harder to leave him, and harder and harder every night that passed. Benayu had had powers enough to fetch the Magister from Talakh and send him south to Barda. He would find it a simple matter, surely, to send Maja back to Lady Kzuva.

Tomorrow she would start her new life.

Life without Ribek.

The words whispered in her mind, desolate, the sigh of a wandering spirit lost in a wilderness. Silently she breathed them between her lips, and again, and yet again, over and over, like a charm to help her get used to the idea. Gradually her whole mood changed. For a while she simply lay there feeling more and more deeply at peace. Then she found herself beginning to imagine what her new life would be like, in a great house full of people, or on the road with Lady Kzuva's entourage, speeding along the sections of the Highways set aside for grandees, or in the mighty and mysterious city of Talakh.

She wasn't scared, hardly even nervous. In fact she was looking forward to the adventure. What had become of the terrified, tongue-tied child cowering in her lair under the barn at Woodbourne? Gone, gone, vanished like a dream, vanished like the old nightmares of pursuit. When had she last had one? Not once in the whole journey. In the moment she had made up her mind and rushed out from her hiding place crying, 'Take me too!' she must have left them behind. And even when the pursuing monster had at last caught up with her on Angel Isle and shown her its true, terrible reality, she hadn't tried to hide or run away but had fought back with all her small strength beside her friends, and between them they had given Benayu time to destroy the demon.

How much she had changed since Woodbourne! From time to time on the journey she had considered the way her extra sense was growing and strengthening. But the changes in herself had passed unnoticed. Where had her self-confidence come from, her readiness to speak and act? From her friends, of course. They had needed her for her gift – they couldn't have found the Ropemaker without her – but they had valued her for what she was, encouraged her, trusted her, worried desperately for her when she had driven herself to the edge of darkness, so much so that both Ribek and Benayu had almost died to save her . . .

All right, so they had needed her for her gift, but how much she had needed them for everything else! Always on the move, they couldn't give her a place to belong, like Northbeck in her fantasy – and Northbeck in her real future, if all went well – but they were people to belong with, sharing trust and purpose in the same spirit as they shared their evening meals. Ribek most of all. She had loved him, she now discovered, not for his sake but because she needed somebody to love. Now, of course, it was impossible to imagine that anyone else might have done, but still, there had been a sort of selfishness in her love. She had attached herself to him like a mistletoe to a tree, feeding her need. It wasn't enough. She guessed he knew that too.

Now they were going to spend six years apart, and that was all right. It was fine, in fact, better like this, and she could do it because she didn't need him any more. Not in the way she had done so far. But there was another kind of need, the need that Saranja and Striclan had for each other. She had felt an inkling of it only a little while ago, waking on the hillside under the stars. In six years' time, if she and Ribek both felt like that, perhaps . . .

If. Perhaps.

Mentally she released herself from her unspoken vows, and felt a sudden, marvellous lightness of heart. She had trapped them both somehow in a room, locking the door and dropping the key out of the window, and now, by pure luck she had found a spare key and unlocked the door and set them free. Free to choose when the time came.

As soon as he woke, here on the neutral hillside, she would tell Ribek she was going back to Lady Kzuva and tell him why.

As it turned out, she slept longer than he did.

The sun was just beginning to slide above the far horizon when she heaved herself into a sitting position and looked around. His bedding was empty. Saranja and Striclan were already up. She was oiling his back for him, ready for the exercises he did, and she did too now, every morning. Benayu seemed to be fast asleep. He'd be tired after yesterday, of course. If they had to wait for him it might be a long time till breakfast, but Striclan kept the saddlebags well stocked. No Ribek. Probably in the woods somewhere, easing his bowels, which was just as regular a need for him as Striclan's exercises.

No, there he was, further up the slope by the whispering cedar, staring at something in the sky above the forest on their left. She followed his gaze. The landscape below the pasture was scarfed with early mist, but the sky was a clear pale blue. Only one thing marked it, a single bird, circling slowly on motionless wings. With nothing at all to judge its distance by it was hard to tell how large it might be. Big, she guessed. She wriggled the rest of her body out of her bedding and climbed barefoot towards him.

'Is it an eagle?' she said.

'That's right. A blue-shank, by the look at it. Marvellous great birds. They nest in the cliffs above Northbeck, you know. I'll show you.'

'I'm not coming to Northbeck with you. I'm going to ask Benayu to send me straight back to Lady Kzuva.'

'Ah,' he said slowly, still watching the eagle.

'Do you want to know why?'

'I think I know . . .'

'Not all of it, you don't.'

'All right. Tell me.'

She did so, all of it, feelings and thoughts, without shame or shyness. He listened gravely and nodded when she'd finished.

'Thank you,' he said. 'I'm afraid I have to tell you that I still think it will be an impossibility. Even supposing both of us are till unattached at that point. Perhaps you'll meet some courtier . . .'

'You might fall for one of those farmers' daughters you told us about.'

(She didn't mention the jewel-dealer at Mord. That would have been mean.)

'True,' he said. 'But even supposing we both escape those fates, and I'm not already in my dotage . . .'

'I don't want to hear any of that nonsense. The Ropemaker gave you ten years more than he borrowed from you. Interest, he called it. You actually said you felt ten years younger. And you told me when I was a rag doll that that'd be enough.'

His laughter cracked the morning stillness. Pogo stopped grazing, raised his head and whickered, evidently thinking there might be horses who made a noise like that.

'So that's it,' he said. 'I knew something had happened, but hadn't realized you were such a scheming, colluding minx. You're going to be in your element in the middle of court intrigues.'

'It was his idea. Promise. But in six years' time . . .'

'I thought we agreed eight.'

'We didn't finish bargaining. Anyway, that was in another universe. Time's different there. It's six here. Five-and-a-half, actually.'

'All right, clever clogs, we'll see what we both think.'

'Feel, you mean. That's what matters. We don't owe each other anything. We haven't promised anything. If we don't both really feel we want to more than anything in the world, then we'll each marry someone else.'

'And we won't even see each other till then?'

'If Lady K's at Kzuva, Saranja can fly two of the horses over and bring you back for my birthdays. And you can read all about hawking in the library. And if you've got married you'll have to bring her too.'

He stopped watching the eagle, turned to her and grinned. She flung her arms around him and laid her head against his chest. He rumpled her hair, a carefully adult gesture, made to maintain the tricky balance to the end.

'Breakfast,' called Saranja from below.

They walked down the slope together, not even holding hands.

Appendix

According to Big Bang theory, in the very early stages of the formation of our universe there were more than the four dimensions we are familiar with. String theory, for instance, involves tiny strings of energy vibrating in ten dimensions of space time. Thirteen also seems to be a popular number. Anyway, once the first few micro-seconds of the explosion were over, the unwanted dimensions were 'folded up and tucked away', whatever that may mean.

These conclusions were arrived at by applying complex mathematical processes to the observed behaviour of subatomic particles – quarks and so on – in gigantic particle colliders – and of light arriving from the most distant reaches of the universe.

Fodaro came to his rather different conclusions by very similar means. He was able to observe such things as the formation of stars and the outermost limits of the universe through a very powerful telescope –

Benayu's pool – and the behaviour of subatomic particles in the form of magical impulses. He was also a mathematical genius. He wasn't, incidentally, an untaught genius. Before he abandoned his career and took up shepherding he was Imperial Professor of Applied Mathematics at the University of Balin-Balan – the youngest ever to hold that prestigious post.* He continued his work in his spare time after his retirement and made his breakthrough when his observations of certain magical anomalies led him to the discovery of a place where our four-dimensional universe comes almost, but not quite, into contact with Jex's seven-dimensional one. He called such places 'touching points'.

It is impossible for our four-dimensional minds to imagine what such a universe might be like. We can to some extent describe it with mathematical equations, but we can't envisage it, can't form any kind of mind-picture of it.†

The dimensions of any universe must compose a perfect whole. This means a five-dimensional universe, say, cannot simply have our four plus an extra one, because our four are already a whole and the extra one has nowhere to fit in. This makes it impossible for

---

* The prestige, of course, derives from the fact that the field to which the mathematics is applied is magic.

† We are more familiar with this sort of thing than we realize. It is impossible to imagine the square root of minus one, but formulae that involve it can have important practical results, such as the atom bomb.

even one atom of four-dimensional matter to be transferred to a five-dimensional universe, and vice versa. The consequent destruction of matter would involve the creation of energy, as in an atomic explosion.

Subatomic particles are another matter. We are already familiar with these in our own universe, in the form, for instance, of the aurora borealis, which is caused by streams of charged particles arriving from the sun and being trapped by the earth's magnetic field in the ionosphere. Rather more mysterious are the bursts of gamma rays that appear to emanate from the central bulge of our universe, and arrive in our atmosphere carrying the extraordinary charge of 511 kiloelectronvolts.

Particles of antimatter are created in the big particle colliders, but survive only an instant before they collide with particles of matter, wiping each other out and releasing a burst of energy in the process. Fodaro knew nothing of particle colliders, but was able to use the touching point he found in a very similar fashion, observing the steady leakage of particles from Jex's universe into ours and measuring the bursts of energy released when they collided with their four-dimensional counterparts and were mutually destroyed. Owing to the inherent weirdness, to our minds, of a seven-dimensional universe,* this energy took the form of what was known to pre-Fodaran thaumatology as

---

* It is perhaps worth noting that we have intuitively designated seven as *the* magical number.

'wild magic'.* Without understanding its source and nature, over the centuries the magicians of the Empire learnt by trial and error to exploit and shape it into a powerful set of tools, usually described as 'made magic'.

Pre-Fodaran theory evolved a complex system of 'levels' to account for the observed phenomena. Like pre-Copernican astronomy, this worked well enough for most practical purposes, but at the cost of ignoring an increasing number of anomalies and unexplained phenomena, such as the acknowledged difficulty experienced by almost all magicians in progressing from third- to fourth-level magic. In Fodaran thaumatology this is accounted for as a result of the different degrees of complexity between universes with numbers of dimensions other than our own. First-level magic, 'hedge' magic, uses only the impulses from the stray particles inherent in our own universe; second- and third-level magic those from the simpler two- and three-dimensional universes; fourth-level, confusingly, those with five, six and seven dimensions, and sixth-level any beyond that.

Certain people are born with innate magical power. This is something like a magnetic field, in that it can capture the magical impulses from other universes. The

* In *The Ropemaker* wild magic is said to be released whenever someone dies. This is only partly true. It can come from other sources, including touching points, but the death of any living creature involves the departure of the individual anima into hyperspace, with a compensating flow of energy in the reverse direction.

615

stronger the field, the greater the number and variety of the impulses it can capture. But a magician cannot use it until he or she has learnt to control and shape the flow of impulses within the field. What in pre-Fodaran thaumatology was called wild magic was the result of random and transient combinations of impulses; made magic was produced by magicians using their craft; while natural magic arose from certain combinations in wild magic that turned out to have survival value and evolved of their own accord into more and more complex forms, such as dragons and unicorns.

Demons are another matter. Most of them arise from attempts by ambitious magicians to shape and control some phenomenon of natural magic for their own purposes. This then proves to be beyond their powers, and they themselves are absorbed into the result. Since their original motive for making the attempt was almost invariably bad, the resulting monster is more or less powerfully malign. Angels arise from well-intentioned but failed attempts to do the same thing. Hence their rarity.

Further information can be found on the website of the Thaumatological Department at the University of Balin-Balan.